To Nikki:

Derail This Train Wreck

Daniel Forbes

Great to have you in my corner!

Cheers,

Dan Forbes

Fomite

Burlington, Vermont

Second Edition
ISBN-13: 978-1-937677-84-8
Library of Congress Control Number: 2014945829

Fomite
58 Peru Street
Burlington, VT 05401
www.fomitepress.com

Cover design: J. Forbes

For Herself, a True Gift Beyond all Others

Every apathetic citizen is a silent enlistee in the cause of inverted totalitarianism. — Sheldon S. Wolin

Philosophy should always know that indifference is a militant thing. It batters down the walls of cities and murders the women and children amid the flames and the purloining of altar vessels. When it goes away it leaves smoking ruins, where lie citizens bayoneted through the throat. It is not a children's pastime like mere highway robbery. — Stephen Crane

Contents

PART ONE

Chapter One

The Telltale Bulge

My backpack adding bulk to heft, I breasted the waves of commuters spilling from Penn Station, important people breaking on the prow of a heavily laden ship. Aghast at the impertinence of this slack vessel plowing doggedly forward, some sleek, overpowered types barely veered clear. Why, it carved entire seconds from the start of their Thursday.

Crossing Seventh at 34th Street, I saw it was pushing 9:00 a.m. Almost Leslie time, when the well-mannered pit bull graced hundreds of little radio and TV stations around the country with more real news in her introductory headlines than you'd get from hours of the mewling accommodationists on Narcissists' Permission Radio, never mind the shouting elsewhere on the dial. Leslie's assessment of another loathsome day, her measured jeremiad, brought to mind Brando's *Wild One*. Asked what he was rebelling against, Brando's biker replied: "What've you got?"

I dug my little silver transistor radio out of my pack, stone-age technology fine by me. But I didn't walk along holding it cocked to an ear – a tad too doofy. So there was the occasional odd stare at the curious bulge resting on my shoulder under my shirt. My yap closed, despite looking like a mouth-breather, the yakking wasn't coming from the fillings in my teeth. Hell with 'em, cause the last several blackouts, people crowded around to hear the news, no one snickering then.

So as not to drown out my imminent pronouncement, I'd silence Leslie (fervently wished in many a quarter) once she finished her initial take on the world. Given the tenor of the times, I certainly wasn't messing with cops while carrying a bulky backpack *and* having some weird bulge tucked under my shirt. Weren't bulges one of the lies the London bobbies hurled at that Brazilian – plumber? electrician? – shot in the head way back when? Anyhow, should fortune smile, and my pack and I get plucked for a search, my statement would be short:

Officers, I hereby assert both my right not to be searched and to continue my journey. As you know, having sworn an oath to uphold the Constitution, the Fourth Amendment prohibits "unreasonable searches and seizures." The simple act of carrying a backpack by no means a reasonable cause for suspicion, I now require a statement from you that I am free to leave.

If the cops stood there scratching, I'd take it from the top until sheer, ready fury prompted the type of police action I'd already seen way too much of that week. Focusing on the three key elements: Fourth Amendment; no reasonable cause; and their acknowledgment I could go; I could fumble my way through it easy enough.

Leslie caressing me under my shirt with the day's news, I headed for the main entrance to Penn Station, the execrable rabbit warren tucked under a mid-Manhattan office tower and the dreary round hatbox of Madison Square Garden. To the degree her professional persona ever cracked (just an occasional *hunh* muttered under her breath before her next question), Leslie sounded quite exercised

2

about a D.C. circuit court ruling permitting a U.S. "administrative annexation" of a vast swath of Venezuela for the latter's own defense. The court leaned heavily on HeadMan's recent "manifest rights" decree during the Current Permanent Crisis.

The crowd a thicket still a block from Penn, I saw six cops on horseback hanging out a little ways down a cross-street. Cops my meat that Thursday morning, they merited a detour from my usual, Seventh Avenue entrance. I walked up all but whistling, I was such a happy-go-lucky fellow. The equally sanguine cops sat way up high chatting amongst themselves. Seeing them in their black leather boots and shiny helmets towering overhead on their choice NYPD horses, no wonder the Aztecs believed the Spanish horsemen were gods.

Cops on the clock doing their usual in a vastly over-policed New York, no grist for my mill. But lookey-there: an official station entrance tucked away on this side street. Never a reason to skip the main entrance before, it was new to me; it just might let me scout out any bag-search operation down below. Spy one, and I could retreat back to the main entrance to stage a calm, full-frontal approach for a safe encounter with some undoubtedly twitchy police. Busy pawing through citizens' stuff at their rickety table, like Chilean Cassandra had said the day before, they knew damn well they couldn't safeguard even themselves let alone the rest of us.

An escalator spat me out up at the Jersey Transit level. But loyal to the land of my birth, I wound down and around a stairway to a narrow public corridor, signs pointing the way to the Long Island Rail Road. Despite my bum ankle and a pack full of books, I motored along at a good clip. Otherwise, that part of midtown, you're left for the crows to peck. Plus, having passed through this dump all my life, I was curious where this unknown corridor led. The wall on my right stretched unbroken; on the left a big opening lay just ahead, perhaps the main LIRR hangout where folks lingered to be shot from a cannon once their track was announced.

And Leslie started declaiming about the Disaffected Exonerated. Not nearly as amorphous as they liked to seem, the group of bike riders was suing the NYPD over undercover surveillance of the heinous crime of riding en masse through city streets. Such is the physics of a fluid mass – blow on a dandelion and try to corral the puffs – the last Friday of the month their sheer wheeled numbers allowed several hundred of them to thumb their noses at the cops. Doing so, the group became a wildly disproportionate obsession of NYPD Commissioner Walk-on-Water Ted.

Month after month, expensive phalanxes of menacing police lined the cyclists' presumed route, then scrambled to their vehicles to catch up when the procession took an unexpected turn. Undercovers with cameras peeking through holes in their shirts, open whole-vid operators capturing the biometrics of every face, helicopters thundering overhead to promote hysteria, mass arrests, Boostings, the whole nine yards – playground-bully Ted achieved little beyond looking foolish.

Enjoying Leslie's account, I careened round the corner on my left and about knocked over the shorter of two Metropolitan Transportation Authority cops accompanied by a National Guard soldier as they came racing around from the other side. We collided but then were propelled back and apart like two magnets of the same pole, as much from the force of my and the lead cop's involuntary "Yahs!" as from the jarring collision itself.

My chest still aching from a recent police encounter, he'd clocked me with his nose in nearly the same damn spot, the lead cop maybe only 5'8" as sense memory had it. I stood there panting, having stumbled back several yards into my corridor. Also propelled back around their side of the corner, they'd yet to reappear.

Granting three armed men the initiative, I froze, my hands well away from my body and Leslie blaring away from my shoulder. Let her talk. I sure wasn't touching any hidden piece of shiny silver metal until they reappeared. Damn, oughta make 'em wear bells, like cats in a bird-filled backyard. Double-damn, did I scare them or what? How long was I supposed to stand there? Didn't these guys know this was *my* day, one intrepid soul about to hold the forces of state control to account?

And then the three of them came around the corner, the short guy in the middle with, yup! some blood bright on his upper lip, less so where he'd smeared it wiping off his chin. None looked any too happy. Fuck a duck! Just putting one foot in front of the other, I'd gone and bloodied a cop, broken his nose probably.

The bloodied one was maybe thirty, good looking with a shock of dark hair and wearing his uniform just so. The other cop was older, taller, bulkier and with the sort of '70s aviator glasses that did his face no favors. Crouching with his feet spread, the soldier kept his hands poised to snatch any West-Nile virus mosquitoes flying by.

Adrenaline shooting between us, no one but Leslie said a word. Amazingly, an NYPD honcho had agreed to grace her airwaves. She launched one of her usual, low-keyed, take-no-prisoners questions and said, "Deputy Commissioner Morris, your response please."

Morris replied in New Yawk cop-tawk about squashing groups with criminal intent. "And make no mistake about it," he warned. "I've seen the T in the eyes of these filthy young Subversives running roughshod on bicycles. The Disaffected Exonerated just don't get it that when the Commissioner *himself* says enough, you damn well better stop already."

A don't-mess terrier even – especially – with blood on his face, the short cop erupted. "How's he got a NYPD white-shirt coming off a speaker? Who the fuck are you? Get your hands away from your body!"

Assuredly, they were.

The tall cop said, "Frankie, what's he got in that backpack? And what's that on his shoulder? You see that boxy thing under his shirt there!"

Frankie said, "Yeah, and look at that cord going down the strap." Indeed, my swank, army-surplus pack featured a number of accoutrements and attachments, clips for water bottles and whatnot. Stepping back, Frankie barked into his radio: "Homeless Disgorgement Team requesting a sergeant immediately! Corridor B-7!"

And the soldier said nothing, his eyes boring into me as all they retreated a couple of steps, their hands on holstered guns. Then Frankie's nose started trickling blood again, undoubtedly rendering him harder to control. I took a step forward. "Hey, man, I'm sorry about your nose. I didn't see you coming around that corner. I mean, it's not like you saw me either, right? Look, I got a paper towel with my lunch in my pack – it's clean."

I started to reach, but first to silence Leslie talking quite unhelpfully about a subpoena for records of police undercover activity. And Frankie said, "He's doing some kind of Demo with a tape about the cops or what? Who is this guy?"

"Officers, no. This is a radio playing a regular station. Actually, pretty darn unusual, but still right in the middle of the FM dial, as long as HeadFu – you know – lets it last. Let me just get at it so I can deal with you gentlemen properly."

I reached up across my body to my shoulder, my hand (shaking a little and, damn, I didn't like giving them that satisfaction) trying to push past the heavy pack's strap and under my shirt.

And one cop yelled "Hey!" and the other yelled "Watch it!" They all backed up another step, and Frankie stashed his radio back on his belt. Behind me came the determined clack-clack-clack of a pair of darting high heels, a sound that might normally turn my head. I said, "No, man, come on. Let me just show you what the deal with this is – that it works."

And I pulled out my little shiny silver radio. Smiling at my lonely, ridiculous dependence on such a simple thing, I saw the younger cop draw his gun. "Hey, guys, come on! Maybe I should just shut it off. Or let me tune in something you officers'll like on AM. Just about any station, right? You'll see."

Trying to position my hand to flick the little switch from FM to AM, I stretched it out to show them. And the bloodied, good looking cop with the crease in his pants and the shine on his shoes put one hand under the other and pointed that thing at my face. Our eyes locked, him looking all twisted and tragic and – Christ! sighting through one eye. It all too quick for me to get hysterical, I stood rooted as his face scrunched up like a five-year-old trying not to cry after his big sister walloped him. Then the gun exploded, the noise beyond measure in the metallic corridor.

The older cop screamed, "Frankie, what the hell are you doing? What the hell did you just do! Damn it, I told them you haven't been right since you got back." Frankie not answering, the other cop took out his own gun, aimed carefully at the floor behind me and fired.

Sounding like she was underwater, but all the louder for it somehow, Leslie cut deep through the roaring in my ears. Before anything else, that pain had to stop. A tree hit by a car, not knowing if I was yelling or whispering, I said, "What's your problem? Wait! Can you please just let me take care of this so I can deal with you."

And then this man standing fifteen feet away put his hand under his wrist again and again fired as the soldier leaped to knock the gun upwards.

After a bit, I realized part of the throbbing in my head was a woman behind me screaming her own fool head off, and who could blame her, shots flying all over. I felt the blood coming down the side of my face and swooned to the floor.

It's true what they say: your life *does* pass before your eyes. I'd experienced it as a teenager lying near the bumper of a car that'd just screeched to a halt, your story in a fleeting whirl you never quite forget. Lying crumpled on my side, my dumb pack full of books half-humped on top of me, I looked up at the two guns dangling from two hands and was glad that no panorama-of-me flashed by. But my relief was tempered by the fear I might've wet myself when I felt blood on my face. I didn't dare move my hand down to check.

The blood dripping off my head to the floor, so much for any exalted martyrdom to the Fourth Amendment. So much for emulating Bartleby taking a stand at Lincoln Center two nights back. So much for the master of disaster always thinking he could control any situation no matter how slippery. Amateur semiotician and first-rate fool, I kept telling them, just let me *deal* with you, a charged, murky phrase. Forget my dumb mouth, maybe a shiny silver radio was simply no longer safe in a micro-zap world.

Shot in the head. Not good. It's one thing to get rubbed out in some grand, Give Me Liberty or Give Me Death moment refusing a search. Me and the self-immolating Vietnamese Buddhist monks – right on, right on! A pretty fraught combo: a jumpy, dopey cop and a careless dope whose tongue flapped wrong. Heaven knows how long-gone Moondog would've fared these days, the peaceful New York poet and composer who dressed like a Viking and carried a spear.

The soldier bolted towards me lying defenseless on the floor. Rather than finishing the job with his big black boots, he ran on past. I turned and was confronted by baby-blue panties on a serious blonde sprawled on the floor, keening and clutching her stomach with both hands trying to staunch the blood seeping through her short, tight green dress. Had the first shot hit her too, or the second ricocheting off the floor that his partner had fired for cop-cover-up solidarity? Or was it the third, bouncing off the ceiling when the soldier hit the bloodied cop's wrist? She was entitled to scream.

The soldier bent to the Blonde. Less than a minute since the third shot, maybe fifty people had come racing around that idiot corner. Luckily, seeing two folks bleeding on the floor and two cops with their guns out, the stampeders shimmied to a halt, more and more newcomers jostling up behind to crane their necks. I slumped down further to rest my head on my arm on the floor. From this odd angle everyone led with their knees, their faces swimming awfully high up.

A skinny yammerer in a sleeveless shirt and a bald guy with a gut in a pricey sports coat started shouting questions and suppositions. I tried to sit up, but couldn't shrug my way out of my rhinoceros of a pack.

The older cop got out his radio and said, "Dispatch, we got a 10-13, repeat, 10-13, officer needs assistance, in LIRR corridor B-7. Repeat, LIRR corridor B-7!"

Great. Now every cop within a square mile would rush up with his gun out, looking to protect his brother officers. Hey man, it wasn't the cops, but the civilians that needed assistance, our life's-blood dripping on a grimy floor.

The short cop – Frankie, *that* was his name – stood there mooning, his gun loose and disowned in his hand. Maybe he'd drop it to go off again to finish the job. He suddenly started kicking the wall's metal baseboard over and over, the booms in my head worse than the shots, Frankie squalling deep in his throat about how his wife was gonna kill him. That she was gonna be really pissed. That this'd probably be the last straw for the two of them, if he got kicked off the force and lost their health insurance.

A jellyfish tossed up on a crowded beach, I lay in the middle of the floor with the crowd edging ever closer now that it looked like the shooting was over. I managed to haul myself to my elbow and then scooch back to lean the pack I couldn't unharness against the wall, some thick hardback, probably the damn Solzhenitsyn, assaulting my kidneys. The effort costing, my head lolled on my neck like a newborn's. The world twirled, then wavered. I got ahold of my hair on the side away from the blood and pulled my head upright. The corridor swam until it slowed and eventually righted itself. I found I could maintain.

Bending over the Blonde, the soldier yanked something out of that pouch they wear strapped to their leg and pressed it to her stomach. Man, look at her! No matter what, she was gonna steal my thunder on protesting the searches. Not that I'd get to make any. With a beautiful girl gut-shot by one of our Heroes patrolling the perilous front lines at Penn Station, big-galoot me was damn sure getting cast as the villain of the piece once everyone started pointing fingers.

My ears roaring and my breath somehow rasping *inside* my skull, I tried to keep my head still. The soldier rose from the Blonde, muttering and grabbing for his radio. He talked into it, then reached out and banged its base against the wall I was leaning against. Another bomb in my head. Striding back, he stepped over my legs and took Frankie's radio off his belt, the cop not noticing. Yelling with his arms outstretched, the other cop tried to stem the crowd. And the soldier, praise be, got through on Frankie's radio and started hustling up medical assistance. Realizing I'd soon be passing through others' hands, I confirmed my drawers were dry.

A lady in a LIRR shirt elbowed her way through the crowd towards Frankie, demanding the who/what/why.

That snapped him out of it. Ignoring her, he came over to me and bent quick for the radio. My hearing screwed, I'd spaced on it blaring there in my hand. Frankie refocusing my attention, I heard Leslie revisiting the Venezuela story, something about a proposed bombing campaign designed to spark a national uprising, though, improbably enough, by the people getting bombed *against* their own government.

If Frankie had bent for the radio nice and slow, I might not have reacted. But he darted too quickly, and I got a good grip on it. He started prying my fingers open, then picked up the whole limp noodle – to bite me? If he disappeared it, whatever I'd pointed at them could be said to have gone lost in the general confusion of the growing crowd, it then soon morphing to some kind of pistol. Poor procedure to lose it, but both cops had done their best.

"Hey, Frankie," I wheezed. "Haven't you done enough for one day? It's a radio, like I told you. It's always gonna be a radio, and it's mine!"

Saying nothing, he started digging his nails into the sides of my fingers. Lucky for me, intelligence from the far reaches of my empire wasn't transmitting all that well back to headquarters. But this little struggle obviously wasn't lasting long. I took a deep breath and remembered to generate volume from my diaphragm. "Help! Somebody help me! This cop shot me, and now he's trying to steal my radio so he can say it was a gun. Folks, this ain't right!"

My feedback loop rampaging since the first shot, I didn't know whether I was shouting or squeaking. But right on cue this big Asian dude with magenta hair and a slinky white girl dressed in a heat-wave smile and a sneeze, both about nineteen, pushed their way out of the crowd, the guy lugging a clunky, presumably licensed, old-school whole-vid camera. Not looking like one of the few, HeadMan-approved visual media, he was probably one of the rare film students grandfathered into a whole-vid.

The girl bent down to see Frankie's badge and called out, "Marko, this guy said the cop's name is Frankie. He's MTA and his badge number is 5-9-4-7. Get both their faces, including their ears if you can. And get his head wound too, though it doesn't look too bad."

Some highly starched dude started yelling at them to just let the Protectors do their job, but these kids, bless 'em, ignored the swelling pro-cop chorus. Frankie said a whole lot of bad words jumbled all together, put one hand up by Marko's lens and the other painfully on my knee to push himself up, and vanished through the crowd that parted for his uniform and his gun. I clicked the damn radio off, then six or seven soldiers came rushing up, two with big guns they used like halberds to push the crowd back. Finally a use for those things in a crowded train station.

The gutsy young girl was obviously a precocious med student who knew all about entirely superficial head wounds. Illustrating why HeadMan had banned them for almost everyone, Marko's whole-vid became an instant press pass. He went over to film the Blonde who'd slumped to the floor, her head cradled by a female cop. And two paramedics came rushing up with enough equipment to invade Normandy, took one look at me and headed straight for her. Two more then barged through the crowd, and one put ammonia painfully under my nose, cut my sleeve off and got some goop flowing into my arm.

The lifesavers didn't tarry. As the crowd grew and pressed against the soldiers and then a swarm of cops, they wheeled the Blonde past, the same lady cop running along besides her stretching a fluid bag awkwardly over her head. The crowd melted for them and then flowed back like wet sand at the water's edge where some kid has dug.

My two guys, the chunky one with the big stud in his ear stood up and stared down at me, while the skinny, hawk-nosed one tipped me forward and with some difficulty wrestled me out of my pack. He applied a heavy-duty band-aid of sorts, then wrapped some gauze around my head and taped it down on the good side. He asked if I had any kind of weird taste in my mouth, and when I said no, Skinny said, "You know what – relax, cause it just grazed you. Didn't even penetrate your skull. You're either lucky or the most hardheaded bastard I've ever seen."

Chunky detached a portable wheelchair from the back of his largest case. I told them I could get up myself, but they each got under an armpit and hoisted me into the chair. The walls going wavy again, I managed to pop the radio, hopefully unseen, under my ruined shirt.

A dough-faced cop in a white shirt showed up bellowing for everyone to move back, that he was the "Incident Commander." Maybe four bystanders retreated a step. He then yelled for someone named Frost, and Frankie's partner came up with a crisp salute. "Thought I told you to keep Reisner out of trouble," white shirt said. "Where the hell is he?"

"Captain, he's here. He must be gathering evidence."

"I see. You fired your gun too, Frost – that new, well, not Reg but …?"

"Captain, I – "

"Right, Frost. Say nothing till the Response debriefing. I think Nembach's running it today, a Calfer, thank God." Pointing down at me, "This the perp?"

"I guess so. I mean –"

"That's an affirmative regarding this Suspect. You have two daughters, don't you, Frost? I don't imagine you're going to try to swing college – not for both, post-Plunge – but still."

Rocking back and forth on the balls of his feet, almost strutting in place, the captain stared at his subordinate. Finally Frost saluted and took two steps back, almost tripping over a weasely guy crowding in, his stained tie a bad match for his stained polo shirt. He'd already caught my eye by continually blowing little saliva bubbles.

The captain turned to Chunky and said, "This Perpetrator's, uh, *cut* is not life-threatening, correct? As the Incident Commander, I will rule on the timing of his release to medical authorities. If he cooperates, we can arrange a visit to a city clinic soon enough. But right now he has several statements to sign."

Chunky smiled to himself, shrugged and half-turned away. The captain sputtered and almost reached out to grab the big EMT by the sleeve. Thinking better of it, he turned to his uniform and said, "Frost, you and –"

"Captain, not even close," Skinny intruded. "This man is our patient, so forget that 'incident commander' stuff. We don't recognize it – certainly not from the MTA. This man's health is my responsibility, and he's leaving for Bellevue immediately. He's at risk for swelling, intracranial hemorrhaging or maybe a stroke. I'd think you'd want him to get the quickest treatment possible. But either way – let's go!"

This last was directed at Chunky, as Skinny pushed him around to the back of my chair and picked up my knapsack and deposited it – umph! – in my lap, his hands soon full with his and most of Chunky's gear.

The captain darted in front of us, my toes up against his shins, his hand on his gun. He said, "Frost, write down this man's badge number." Skinny turned to Frost and plucked his medical-service badge away from his chest for easy reading. "All right big-shot band-aid man, you can take this Suspect to Bellevue for short-term medical clearance. After that, he's mine, B.E.I. And believe me, we're going to find out who's behind him and his T. I am not having Everidge's plans for all of us loused up by a no-account Subversive. You got that, Frost? You play your cards right, and we can find a cush spot for you too. Though you should probably wait two more years till you get your twenty in."

"Captain, I'm going to ask you to get out of our way. Now!"

"Sure. Sure thing, Mister MD. But one more thing: whose pack is that you gave him? That's not yours?"

"That's his property," Skinny said.

"That means it's mine. This is a crime scene and that's evidence. Have you even bothered to check its incident significance? It looks awfully bulky to me, not exactly his laundry home to momma."

I gaped up at them, curious whether Skinny would defend my property rights. The captain bent to the pack. I put one hand on my shirt so the radio wouldn't fall out, and the other weakly gripped a strap. Suddenly a bunch of bright dots flared up all around. "Hey, this is my stuff – my books – so keep your hands off and let me get to the hospital. Listen, I don't feel so good right now."

"So go to the hospital, Subversive. We'll be there waiting for you." And he knocked my listless hand away, but failed to scoop up my brand new pack with one hand. Getting a better grip, he handed it to Frost. Chunky then wheeled me down the corridor to an escalator and spun me around none too gently to tip my chair and ride me up backwards. I peered down through my feet at a couple of hundred people milling around, the crowd densest over by where the Blonde had been. They started peeling off around the edges to start their day, their murmur fading as I rose.

A cop outside helped hoist my chair up to bang painfully into the back of an ambulance. Chunky driving, Skinny got in the back, whipped out a blood pressure cuff, but then started listening to my heart. I asked what the matter was, but he ignored me. One of the back doors opened, and an older guy with colorless, greased-back hair and a shabby, metallic green suit clambered aboard with surprising deftness.

Skinny bending over me with his back to the doors, I said, "Hey, is he coming with us?"

Skinny turned and, crouching low, advanced on the man. "You've gone too far. This is my bus – *mine*, inside and out! I don't care if you're deputy chief of the whole damn department, this is my ambulance and my patient. And you're getting out."

"Steady there, sonny. Just making sure a crucial piece of evidence doesn't leave the crime scene. Now if you don't mind, I – "

And Skinny put his head down and charged forward and basically forced the cop back out. The cop grabbed a handle going down as his other hand scuffled under his armpit for the cops' usual helpmate. Skinny engaged a latch on the doors and banged hard on the wall – man, that went right through me – yelling to his driver, "Move! Let's go!"

Chunky made the siren scream, wheeled into a U-turn and full-tilt-boogied the wrong way up Seventh Avenue two long blocks to 34th Street judging from the hard right turn he wrestled us through. The guts of my brain wobbled horribly as we beat our way to Bellevue, still the best gunshot ER in the City.

The way everything felt loose and goosey upstairs and with all the dots flashing up and winking out, maybe that slinky girl who'd rescued me from Frankie wasn't such a great diagnostician after all.

Chapter Two

Behind the Mesh

Man, if I'd have known getting shot was on tap that Thursday morning, I would have let it alone, probably, nothing to be done in HeadMan's America aside from a Demo over by the highway with the same three-dozen weirdos you marched with the month before. They gave you that pebble down a deep, dank well, less trouble to ignore than put the crunch on. After all, should HeadFuck try to control all aspects of our former lives, then *everything* became a potential avenue of protest. So he didn't. In fact, simulacra of news, communications, politics, social intercourse – of life – all remained. Just don't peer too close.

Post-Nicki bereft, I didn't get out much right after she and I went to hash. Then I woke up and the hell with moping; I'd been set free, damn it. Sprung. And so out I went into the world at large and all its women to witness bim, bam, boom – Saturday, Sunday, Tuesday – the MoFos going ape apparently just because they could. Yeah, one heck of a week, the week Frankie shot me.

The whole mess started the prior Saturday on the train out to Long Island, followed by Sunday at Coney Island and, worst of all, Tuesday at Lincoln Center, two nights before I got shot, when my man Bartleby had dared say no – plain old Nope, not now, MoFos – and he and his wife made it stick for most of one amazing hour. Then they paid a heavy price, a broken wrist probably the least of it. Bad things coming in threes, making my way home Tuesday from witnessing the Lincoln Center atrocity was when I decided to stuff books in a backpack. Decided, a bad train coming, somebody needed to steal some spikes to loosen the tracks. And so I ended up Thursday in an ambulance to Bellevue. If you had to point to one single thing, you could say that Tuesday night at Lincoln Center sparked the whole megillah.

That said, it started the weekend before I got shot. (No. It actually *started*, of course, way back, years before HeadFuck.) But proximately, the whole shebang started on the LIRR the Saturday before Frankie unloaded, when I decided to foist myself on my parents' fridge out on Long Island.

The early evening journey from Manhattan began promisingly enough, me on time to grab the seat with extra legroom by the door, the only one where I wasn't scrunched knees by ears. And lo and behold, look who chose the seat across the aisle, though she wasted the bounty of legroom. Pretty, sure, and mid-thirties, she was the right age. Propinquity offering hope, I snuck another peek to see – darn! – with her Sally Striver haircut and high-heeled sandals she couldn't walk six blocks in, she was regrettably not my cup of tea. Not the type to go tramping by the water in some far corner of Brooklyn or the Bronx just for the hell of it as Nicki and I oft did in happier days.

Aside from the priss and podiatric aspects, she also looked a little shaky, with her lipstick fudged, a far-off stare and a cut-up white sock secured with red duct tape bandaging the back of her hand. Right: never date anyone with more problems than you. She had a cat along, so that was something. Though she never tried to comfort it imprisoned in a mesh-walled little rolling suitcase and moaning deep in its throat.

We got moving, and a conductor came flapping in from the short end of the car, chirping about tickets, all tickets, please. The LIRR's among the world's least flattering uniforms, he was styling nonetheless with a shiny pompadour and big-frame Vegas glasses on a gold chain resting just above his little belly roll.

He turned to the woman, and the cat – who'd momentarily stifled his steady complaint – launched himself at the thin mesh right by the conductor's leg, yowling and hissing like some sort of woozle getting skinned alive. The conductor dropped his ticket punch, loosed an oath and stepped back, breathing heavily.

To recapture the dignity that accrued to his station in life, one way or another, cat and owner would pay. Drawing himself up, he demanded she put the permeable, wheeled case up on the luggage rack where it belonged; she mildly replied that she had to keep an eye on the cat. The conductor persisted, and she finally agreed. But she couldn't lift it, not without grabbing it in a bear hug and thus exposing herself to his claws through the mesh. If he wanted to put it up there….

No, that wasn't part of his job, he said.

Technically not, but he was at least equally afraid of the spitting monster. She offered to move the case to the other side of her legs, where it'd be up against the bulkhead and no trouble to anyone. This a summer weekend train, there were quite a few backpacks and suitcases scattered about, and she wondered why hers was being singled out.

"Not that it's any concern of yours, but I may well get to those other bags. They *are* a passenger hazard in case of T. Things have gotten a little slipshod. But that's going to change, starting now with your bag, Miss, a bag with a vicious animal in it. I'm warning you, I have issued a Direct Request."

"Oh, come on. Look, this is my sister's cat and, you're right, he probably is vicious. But he's secure in his case, and I've been working to calm him down. If you'd just let us be, I'm sure he won't be any more trouble."

"It's already been far too much trouble, and you have a lot of nerve bringing an animal you can't control onto public transportation. Considering your attitude, I'm tempted to have you charged with assault-by-proxy once we reach Jamaica. No, don't laugh, Miss. Assault-by-proxy is a federal crime, a *Homeland Control* crime. Assaulting a conductor in uniform – or a ferry crewman or tow truck operator or any transport official – would, I imagine, lead to a Boosting."

The cat didn't buy it either, launching loud into his full repertoire. Jesus, a Boosting over this nonsense. Things had spun out of control awfully quickly, even by the hair-trigger standards of the day.

I clutched for some way to derail this train wreck, loath though I was to step in it yet again.

She gave a tense little laugh, then smiled up at him, trying to slow things down. With one of those quirky ferret faces, she did have a fetching smile despite the bollixed lipstick. "Let me ask you, do you really think a pussycat constitutes a proxy? That hissing at you is an assault? Come on, you deal with the public every day. Stop for just a minute, Big Boy, and ask yourself. And what does that mean, anyway, 'assault-by-proxy'? Every time you turn around, there's some new way to get in trouble – or get 'Boosted,' whatever that might mean. All the homeless since the Plunge, give one a quarter and you risk a ticket. Now, Ted so pissed, you can't even ride a bicycle with a few friends without getting some sort of ridiculous permit."

"Hey, don't forget all the biometric scans everywhere."

They ignored my little contribution. The tin-pot conductor stepped back and put his glasses on to study her properly. He got out a pad, wrote a moment and made a big production of checking his watch and jotting down the car's serial number. Jesus, here it came, a whole fine mess from a popinjay's pique.

"Miss, you have refused my Direct Request regarding passenger safety in a time of T. Therefore, you will have to bear the consequences. And believe me, consequences there will be. Now I have tickets to punch." He dismissed her to a rattling good hiss from her ten-foot python. Aside from naturally opposing this martinet, that was the other reason I didn't just put the case up on the rack myself.

He turned for my ticket with a tremulous hand. I said, "Feeling all better now, Big Boy?"

"Sir, your comment is not helpful. Please do not interfere in a private matter."

Yeah, private, with him a government employee talking right out loud of a Boosting. My echoing her tag for him earned a smile as he moved on down the car. So, "I don't trust that guy talking about consequences. Not these days, MoFos lurking under every rock. How far you going? … Huntington, huh. Too bad you're not changing trains at Jamaica, cause he sounded serious." Not able to see through the dark mesh, I asked if it was a Siamese. She said yes, and how did I know?

"No other kind of cat makes a noise quite like that, moaning and gurgling like some soldier shot through the throat, trapped in a World War One no-man's land bleeding to death." Stolen from something I'd read the day before, I was pleased to echo it right on cue. She, however, was almost as cute looking horrified as when smiling up at Big Boy before that all went south. Since she wasn't, I laughed for us both and asked why a Siamese.

"Ask my sister. I'm just taking him cause our mother's sick, and she's staying with Mom out in Huntington a few days. I thought this type of cat was supposed to be refined – my sister wouldn't have it any other way. But he fought like a tiger getting put in his case. Just look at my hand." She held it up, the red duct tape over the sock the same as was wrapped crazily all around the top flap of the case.

"Homemade bandage, huh?"

"My sister'll be furious I cut up one of her socks, but I don't care. Eating out and taking taxis everywhere she goes, I don't think she ever cuts herself, so the sock is all I could find. I wonder how much blood I lost, cause I really don't feel well."

"Eat some cookies when you get to Huntington. That's what they always gave us donating blood at school." Boy, a regular Florence Nightingale was I. At least we were talking, but – years of rust or no – that was lame. Walking the mile from the subway to my hovel in her idiot sandals would prove a challenge, but maybe that's why God invented her place.

A pale soul, she studied her hand, then admitted, "I guess it wasn't right sliding those books at him under the bed. But what could I do after he scratched my hand so bad when I reached under there? I'll probably get reported to some *new* authority."

"Minders Turn Elsewhere!" I intoned by rote just to be polite.

She looked up surprised. "You don't really believe all that crap about Data Minders and Boostings, do you? I mean, no offense, but a guy like you."

Aside from the baggy cutoffs, work boots and a *newer* tee shirt on yet another in a long string of sulfurous, woolly-headed, heat-stroke days, whatever could she mean? "You mean, is the Data more than just rhetorical underbrush to trip us up? I don't know and don't want to find out."

"I try to ignore it. Just another one of HeadFuck's idiocies." She shot a sidelong, little glance to check that I was onboard with *that*, a risky sobriquet out in public with someone you don't know.

I gave the standard nod of concurrence with HeadMan's vulgate name, as she mused about a tetanus shot, cause her hand sure hurt. I said only if the cat's claws were rusty. And despite that tripe earning her first real laugh, there things stalled. She soon closed her eyes, so I fished an old *Book Review* out of my back pocket to sneer at anyone with the gall to get published.

****

The train slowed approaching Jamaica, the big station in Queens where the LIRR sorts out who's going where. Then, for some reason over the public intercom, someone who sounded suspiciously like Big Boy told the engineer to radio for an emergency police response to the third car.

"What are you talking about? You sure a *4-7G* is necessary? And why are you on the public channel?"

Offended, the first guy's voice rose. "Forget the channel. It's all there: failure to comply, threat undetermined, outcome unknown. I'm not taking it from these people anymore."

"Come on, James. You sure you want to do this, or is this just another one of your little scrapes? You even know they have plat-form-ready cops at Jamaica on a Saturday night?"

"They got cops, MTA or state troopers, at Jamaica 24/7. So just radio them to the third car. It's on me."

"Roger, James. But after what happened last month, this is definitely on you."

"I'm authorized, B.E.I., and I'm doing it."

Threat undetermined, outcome unknown. Hell, just more of the standard daily static since HeadFuck burrowed his way to the top. No big deal, I told myself.

Soon enough, a woman conductor treated us to the usual ver-biage about Track 7 for the train to Hempstead, etc., followed by the pro forma, oft-ignored instructions not to bellow into your micro-zap, keep your feet off the seats, and take your trash. Plus, "Ladies and gentlemen, please be advised that backpacks and other large containers are subject to random – repeat, random – search by police." That seemed a bit much pulling *into* a station, but....

The warning that you might get searched was just more of the background noise of travel, like the drone about emergency exits by the wings. Never mind that in a less timorous age, it might've led to marching in the streets.

The mob switching trains pushed on and off at Jamaica, one guy dropping a big suitcase by the door to join the monstrous one left there unsupervised since Manhattan. The train jerked to a start, and again the announcement: hush with the micro-zap, feet, trash, and kiss your rights good-bye, tough luck locked on a moving train, this last particularly asserted.

Once underway, a large state trooper came striding through the short end of the car looking neither left nor right. In his early forties, tall, dark and handsome, he moved stiffly and held his head like it'd been removed for servicing and just recently stuck back on his neck. Yup, he stopped and looked down at my snoozing new friend, her bandaged hand clenching the handle of the cat's odd case.

"Miss, Miss! You're capable of waking? I need you to open that bag. Now! There's been an official report of a concealed threat – type, outcome unknown – capable of impacting the riding public. As a designated first-tier responder, I need to clear that bag."

On thin ice already, she cracked quick. "I can't. It's just a cat, but he'll escape – I can't control it. And then he'll run away somewhere and my sister will kill me."

The cop started to say something, but she plunged on. "You don't understand. My mother's sick, and I have to take this stupid cat out to Huntington. Why do you have to look in my bag anyway, all these suitcases and stuff all around? We're not bothering anyone, the cat was finally quiet."

Not anymore. Apparently finding pants of State Police gray no more appealing than he'd previously found Big Boy's LIRR blue, the cat again launched himself at the black mesh with a cry from deep in the jungle. I couldn't decide which turned my blood to water more, the moan or the hiss from what I clocked as a 19-pounder. Not flinching a whit, the cop said, "Miss – shut it. You say it's a cat? Procedurally, that's of no significance." He'd looked bored approaching us, but now confronting someone, however slight, with the temerity to refuse, he kicked into full stentorian gear.

"There's been an incident response request over official channel 12-41, a transmission logged by state, local and federal dispatchers at Jamaica, Albany and at Fort Meade, Maryland. Whether it rises to the Data Minders' concern is up to you, but I cannot dismiss it without issuing a ruling. Now, do I delay this train, and all the hundreds of Homelanders *and* others traveling properly, to have a Crisis Disposal Team equipped with a mechanized arm meet us at the next station? Or will you submit to lawful authority?"

"Maryland? What are you talking about? It's a *pussycat*! But it's not mine, and I can't control it. And neither can you or your stupid team, I don't care what kind of arm it has."

Furtive whispering wafted up the car, and I peered back to see folks standing and staring, some grinning, most appalled. Grab 'em and pound 'em the norm since HeadMan's installation, everyone was riveted by her hen's-tooth refusal. I'd done all of nothing a half-hour back to help my comely new friend with that clown conductor. So I decided to toss a little pacifying fat on the fire.

Painful personal experience having taught it's best to approach crazed authority types man-to-man, I hauled myself up and ended up standing closer to a cop than I should, especially being as big myself as one this big. A gun accessible on their hip, cops are skittish, like horses. It went with being hated and feared these days. My mollifying tone was meant for a cranky six-year-old. "Officer, perhaps I can be of assistance. She and I were just talking and, well, that's a Siamese cat. I happen to know a little about cats, and the Siamese is a particularly temperamental breed. Just look at her hand. You see – "

Without word or warning, he stepped back, drew his nightstick from his belt and jabbed me hard in the collarbone, knocking me back down in my seat. I yelped, and was almost as pissed at myself for giving him that small victory as I was at a MoFo going ape for no reason. Somebody back there yelled, "Hey, watch it!" But that was the extent of all those folks' outrage – well, that and more yowling and spitting at our feet.

The trooper stared down and said, "Maintain a seated position at all times, mister. Or you'll be taken in for interfering with government administration, obstructing a T investigation, assaulting a sworn Protector and resisting arrest. I'll let you think about that last one, B.E.I."

B.E.I. my fat red ass. As when lecturing Cat Wrangler, he puffed up for these pronouncements plucked from air. Stepping back, he almost tripped over one of the big suitcases by the door. He kicked it aside, put his nightstick under his arm and struggled into the too-tight, black leather gloves that cops favor. Thus fortified, he launched in again.

"Now, Miss. According to the new Regs, during the Current Permanent Crisis, any hand wound requires a formal case ruling. Your wound was possibly caused by something sharp. In fact, Homeland Control refers to a machined edge. Be aware that I will examine your person shortly, focusing on coagulation. The bandage, which looks to be an improvised field dressing, will be removed to rule out concealed weapons, explosives or toxins."

She and I turned to each other, torn between horror and protest. Great. I'd managed to work my usual turd-touch magic pointing out her cat scratch.

"Now, the statements regarding a cat have not been proven. Irregardless, your baggage is strange, Miss. All these little holes in its sides, are they possibly a bio/chem passive-delivery device?"

She jumped up and turned to face the longer portion of the car. "People, do you hear that? He's trying to turn a cat case into a weapon. I'm starting to think I really need to document all this because" – her voice broke – "I don't, I don't know where it's headed. Is there anyone here with a licensed whole-vid who's willing to film this? Or maybe even someone good at old-fashioned taking notes?" No reply from the mostly bent heads to a very dicey request, she wavered to a stop, barely as tall as the fourth button on the cop's shirt. "People – nobody?" She turned and crumpled back into her seat.

Taking notes, un-huh. A resurrected art since HeadMan banned whole-vid-capable micro-zaps once it became apparent some few folks would risk lengthy jail time to whole-vid police acting ugly on the street. Savvy observers might whisper to very close friends that the official pretext that cops – that MoFos of all stripes – were 'endangered' by people recording their brutalities was nonsense. Such observers branded the edict as a boon to an over-saturated, decidedly mature, micro-zap industry, its sales blistered by the Plunge. Boon or not, all but a few, onerously licensed individuals were forced en masse to buy retro micro-zaps incapable of producing whole-vids. Ever since, simply jotting down notes branded you worthy of MoFo attention. Might as well have print-outs from the wrong website littering your coffee table when the cable guy showed.

Feeling left out, but butt parked firmly in seat, I ventured to inquire, "Hey, pal, what is this 'ruling' you keep talking about – that you're going to *rule* on things? Is that some kind of special state-cop thing?"

Was his talk more than mere blowhardism run wild? They promulgated anew on a monthly basis, so who knew. He turned, and I steeled myself not to flinch. But he just curled his lip like a dog you're foolishly trying to pet tied up outside a store. "You're asking for a Boosting with that kind of talk, mister, the Data Minders with a spot for you right up top."

Damn right I shut up at that, but he had more intriguing prey. "Now, Miss, you've yet to prove that your portable storage device's noise, which is loud enough to act as a diversion, comes from a live animal."

Never mind that the cat at that moment was bashing its brains out against the mesh, mere facts didn't deflect him from his appointed path. Six-foot-four, broad of beam and in his prime, he was rarely interrupted once he got it in gear. But she made him pause by *laughing*, then saying, "You don't have a leg to stand on, do you? And you know it. That's why all you guys yell and bully and manufacture all this empty authority so no one will look behind the curtain. B.E.I. and everything, it's all crap, isn't it?"

That elicited a gasp from some lady as the trooper plowed on. "If all you have is a cat as you claim, I have the training, experience and equipment on my person to handle such a threat. You, Miss, need to produce this alleged cat's license. Therefore, you will open this bag or – "

"Go ahead, you big jerk. You open it! I hope you have a net or something on your 'person.' And this guy is right: since when do cops make 'rulings?'" Both of them taken aback by her outburst, she finally said, "I hope he bites your fucking head off!"

The earth not parting at her feet, swearing at a cop who richly deserves it can be massively liberating. Short hair just so and wearing those horrible Capri pants, I'd pretty much written her off. But talking like that to a sworn MoFo – hotdiggity!

A well appointed old dame not far behind us started in about being good with cats and maybe she could help. The trooper said, "Button your mouth, Ma'am. Not a word during this T investigation. This operation is being monitored by Homeland Control. Do I make myself clear?"

The old lady's mild offer cracking the dam, some guy called out, "Yo, that cat's from Asia. That's what we got coming up next, invading them countries after we finish off all the Sands. All them people – watch out!"

The trooper put up his nightstick and leered down at my new hero. "Now, Miss. You're already in enough trouble as it is without directing a foul tongue at a duly sworn Protector. If you are transporting an uncontrollable animal, I cannot be held responsible liability-wise. Any resulting damages and/or injuries are the responsibility of you, your guardian or your heirs."

"What makes you think a woman my age has a guardian? Forget that – what's your name? And how come you're not wearing a badge? What the hell kind of cop are you anyway in that gray uniform?"

"My name, Miss, is Officer Schiakoczyk of the New York State

Police. As to my badge, know that my Commander cleared me for patrol at roll call today."

"Schia – what? How the devil do you spell that?"

"Treat my parents' name properly, Miss, or HateCime defamation of a sworn Protector will be added to your charges."

Marveling at the practiced nonsense he spun so as not to spell his name, I told her I thought I had it pretty close written on my hand.

Given the general pusillanimity, the cop had probably just met with more resistance than he'd faced in weeks or months. He worked his jaw, adjusted his gloves and bent to the cat. Out of nowhere, a conductor almost as tall and a lot heavier than the cop rushed up the aisle from behind. "Hey, Statie! I'm still running this train, no matter what you guys think. So let's talk about this a minute, cause I am not having a *cat* loose on my train!"

And moving quicker than he had a right to, the tall, barrel-chested conductor, pushing sixty and with a full shock of white hair, bodied the cop away from the bag. Caught by surprise and off-balance from bending over, the cop fell back into the vestibule, stumbled on that same giant suitcase, righted himself and half-drew his nightstick. Obeying the brown-out Regs on saving power during the weekend, the train crawled through eastern Queens as dusk fell on a Saturday.

Chapter Three

You'll Stop Twitching Soon Enough

The cop kicked the entangling suitcase aside and put his stick back. Hands locked on the bars that edged the walls framing the aisle, the ample conductor trapped the trooper by the doors. Both men in uniform were unaccustomed to challenge in their domain, the conductor's being the train and the cop's wherever he found himself.

Bags everywhere, the conductor asked why he had to search this particular one. The trooper said he'd gotten a Homeland Control 4-7G Emergency Response Order at Jamaica initiated by conductor badge number 37-946, who then directed him to this specific bag. "So, Conductor, with only four years until my earned retirement, I'm making no negative career decision here tonight. As God made me, Conductor, I will not still be clocking in at your age, B.E.I."

Somebody, a black guy by the sound of him, started bellowing in a voice that'd shake a brick from a wall. "Leave her alone, you turkeys. This is bullshit and you know it, picking on that lady cause she's small. Why don't you pick on someone your own damn size?"

A chorus of boos failed to shut him up. "I'm a sergeant major in the United States Army with twenty-four years in, Fomenting Democracy all over the map. And I got the medals to prove it. I don't take no guff from anybody under a major, so I sure ain't taking any from some lame-ass state cop. You heard me, a damn police worrying about a cat on a train, ain't got nothing better to do. Is that the deal under HeadFuck now? Cause all you people but Jack and Jill up there are sitting here taking it."

A woman from somewhere back there – ah, democracy in our rolling town square, one of its few remaining venues – objected to the sergeant major's outburst, each plummy word pried from very tight lips. "Young man, that's a Protector standing there, one of the true-blue heroes putting his life on the line *daily* to keep us safe during the Current Permanent Crisis. As to your despicable term for your commander-in-chief: *Bold. Extolled. Impregnable!*"

Several dudes chanted "B.E.I., B.E.I.!" till they were drowned out again.

"I didn't fight all them warlords and maniacs – seven tours in four different countries – to come back to this shit here at home. And now I'm hearing rumors about going to a whole new place for tour number *eight*! Me just trying to go visit my kid cause his fool mother thinks it's better to raise him out here with you knuckleheads. Try this mess in Brooklyn, it'd be another story."

Amidst the loud, ugly hubbub, the trooper got his radio out, then put it back and, slapping one fist, leather on leather, into the palm of his other hand, tried to push past Boss Conductor. Re-anchoring his hold on the walls separating the vestibule from the aisle, the conductor snarled, "Look, Statie! We are not having a riot over a cat on my train! This is *my* train, Goddamn it, and you're the one talking about a career decision here. You never had anyone swear at you before, you with sixteen years in?"

"Get out of my way, Conductor – now! That's a lawful ruling."

"That's right. Get out of that big bastard's way. I'd like to see if he really does come back here. Probably have to call his momma on that radio first." This from a soldier with way too many Sands under his belt.

Dropping his hands but standing there, the conductor said, "Look, *Officer*, you want me out of your way, just say the word."

The cop said nothing. Eight tortuously long, silent beats later, Boss Conductor laughed. "I didn't think so. It's always the same when somebody calls your bluff, guys like you."

I grinned over at Cat Wrangler, incredulous that our tormentor had been exposed as such a paper tiger by a smart old man and a voice of doom from in back. The conductor now made some pronouncements of his own. "Statie – it's a cat. You got that? We've already determined that radioing you here was bogus, and my conductor is in more trouble than he'll know what to do with. Cause this lady is no more a T-Fiend than I am."

The cop started sputtering, but the trainman continued, reaching for the hole card he'd been fingering all along. "Mister, I don't want to hear it. Not with you assaulting this passenger here for nothing. That's right, I saw it. Now we both know, even these days, he could make your vacation go up in smoke."

"Conductor, that was clearly self-defense. Everyone saw that man charge me."

"Charge you! I just stood up right here in my seat, and you went bat-shit cause someone had the nerve to try to talk to you." But he shouted me down.

"Only concern for passenger safety kept me from drawing my service weapon in self-defense in response to this Suspect's assault. I will affirm that with all the power of the uniform I wear."

Their uniforms had special powers now?

"I will also run the Perpetrator's ID through several national T Sets, and unless he's adopted an uncommon alias, a match will be found, B.E.I. The same goes for the female Suspect. The Data Minders will be notified, of course. In fact, Conductor, iris profiles, along with facial-recognition templates, will be obtained on both Subversives. Finally" – and here his voice grew tight – "the female's fresh wound will be examined by the senior first-tier responder present here tonight before she can cauterize it, negating key evidence along its ... *unstable* edges."

I tried to figure how to get the hell off the train without this guy scratching me to capture some skin under his nails. Boss Conductor's voice rose above the clamor. "You can 'affirm' from here to next week if you want to, Statie, but I know what I saw. Meanwhile, and this isn't even your fault I'm sorry to say, I got a 4-7G to make disappear. Now – no, mister, it's my turn to talk – we write it up so that we just throw her off at the next stop. But the Regs are mandatory that it has to be the next stop. 'Exigent circumstances: refusal to comply with search' it's called. We determine she's not an imminent threat – in her case, that'll last a couple of decades – throw her off the train and everything's fine. You got that?"

The trooper nodded.

"You write it up exactly like I say, and you're covered too. But I am not having a *cat* loose on my train! The last time was four years ago, and I am not over it yet."

The cop crossed his arms and looked at us all in turn – conductor, Cat Wrangler, feline, then me – leveling his harsh gaze on me the longest. "Conductor, this field operation does contain exigentness. I will now determine the origin of the female's wound before the next stop, which is what?"

"New Hyde Park. But wait a – "

"Now, Miss!" the cop barked as he tried to edge past the conductor. "Home Front defense requires you to present any and all wounds undressed for inspection to determine if they were caused by a sharp edge. Or duly sworn authority will remove the bandage."

The conductor remained a wall as she rocketed back up. "You're deranged if you think I'm letting you touch me. You don't even have a badge on. All you have is a gun and a twisted little mind."

She leaped and tried to claw his face over the conductor's shoulder, and for a moment, he shielded cop from citizen. The trooper stepped back and rested his hand on the butt of his gun.

A woman started chanting, "Shame! Shame! Shame!" Another

woman weakly joined in before they were hollered down by a bunch of guys bellowing "USA! USA! USA!" I loved when they did that, lowering their voices by two octaves. The Lake Placid hockey team that beat the Russians must've gotten on at Jamaica without me noticing.

The conductor told the cop they were getting her off the train momentarily, so he could forget about examining anyone's hand. Then Cat Wrangler seized on a good point. "Conductor, maybe you didn't hear this. But I already gave him permission to search my bag. So this is all nonsense. Go ahead, look in the cat's carrier if it gets you off *and* you think you can control him. I don't care anymore. Believe it or not, people have problems and lives and stuff that have nothing to do with the Long Island Rail Road!"

Everyone forgot she'd told the cop to go ahead and fool with the cat if he dared. Sparking the cat's paroxysms by grabbing the case's long handle, the conductor said rules are rules. She had, for reasons of her own, delayed a *timely* search, and – passenger safety his ultimate responsibility – really, his hands were tied. What's more, she certainly didn't want her cat getting loose, now did she? No, no, that wouldn't do. Another train would be along in an hour, he said and, pulling a voucher from his shirt pocket, he told her to just give it to the conductor on the next train for a free ride.

He was about to grab her by the arm and tug her up when the old lady, who I wanted by my side my next back-alley brawl, piped up. "Just a minute, Conductor. If she and her kitty are such a danger they have to be removed from this train, what about the passengers on the next train? How can you put them at risk?"

This bull's-eye roused some scattered applause as the cop drew his stick and pointed it over the conductor's shoulder at the old lady. "Ma'am, I have previously warned you about interfering in this federally mandated T-Operation. Data Minders are available for notification 24/7. I will not warn you again."

Boss Conductor bent and grabbed her by the arm and tugged her up. Cat Wrangler snarled and hopelessly tried to wrench her arm free. She started swinging with her free hand, but he easily held her at arm's length. An enormous guy, quite a specimen remained beneath the fat and the years. As the train pulled to a stop and the doors opened, a chorus of boos and leave-her-alone and throw-her-off underlay a rich stream of invective from the foghorn of a sergeant major and a veritable catophony from the enmeshed.

Again moving quicker than you'd think, he lifted the hissing, spitting case, dragged the girl by her arm, bodied them past the trooper and flung her, who he outweighed by 170 pounds, onto the platform and out of my life. Scratching and cursing, she had about as much effect as did the cat.

I sprang for the door, but the cop blindsided me and pushed me back down in my seat. "Not you! We're not finished with you yet."

Yelling at his minion at the far end of the car to close the doors, Boss Conductor got out his flashlight, pushed the frantic girl back and signaled the engineer to go.

Three guys who'd been watching in back started yelling, hey wait, this was their stop too, but that was lost in the general uproar. Some said it wasn't right putting her off at a lonely stop like that near dark. Others argued that she should have just let them look in her case, mangling that she'd given her permission long before. As in any shout-fest, the facts quickly grew obscure. But the talk leaned heavily against her, people on the train having been inculcated over the fractious months and years like everyone else, the flame under our kettle ever higher. What was she trying to hide, and what exactly was that vicious cat guarding in that weird case?

Damn, never came close to even her name. So, Comrade, with your spunk, I don't care what kind of shoes you wear. Let fortune smile and throw us together again someday.

I shrank in my seat as the cop approached, my broad LIRR shield no longer between us. His interest in the girl, if he'd ever had any aside from subjecting her wound to his lawful scrutiny, vanished with her off the train. He now focused on the mope posing a threat to his vacation, not that little old me had made a peep about it.

"Alright, Subversive. Produce your ID for determination of your record and outstanding warrants. Now!"

"You know, Officer, I don't think I will. Cause legally I've done nothing to require I show you ID." Quite a stretch, that, but I was pissed about Cat Wrangler's exit. "But how 'bout some spit? I thought all you needed was DNA." This last didn't cut much ice, me cowering in my seat.

He reached down – to turn me upside down and shake my wallet out? – but then straightened and got out his radio. He didn't care if Joe was in the john, he told whoever was on the other end, "Get him *now*!" Nice to know he used his favorite word with his fellow officers too.

His combat-ready black gloves as daunting as intended, I needled him while he waited. "Hey man, why don't you take those gloves off? That mean old pussycat is off the train."

"That's right," boomed the sergeant major. "Take the damn gloves off. Skin on skin, baby!"

Ms. Locust Valley Lockjaw, who'd plummily instructed us to shut up and support the cops, protested. "You say you're a soldier, but I'm sure they didn't teach you to disrespect sworn Protectors like that in the military that serves *my* United States. Now, if you can't conduct yourself properly in public, I suggest you return to wherever it is you said you're from. Furthermore – "

"What do you mean, get back to Brooklyn with the rest of my kind? You better hope Chicken-Shit's shoes ain't glued to the floor up there by the doors, cause you notice he ain't come nowhere near back here."

The cop sneered down at me. "You hear all the trouble you and your little girlfriend have caused? Well, don't you worry, punk. None of it's going to stop our little tango. The gloves mean: no marks – no marks on me. Sitting on a beach on my vacation, I wouldn't want my hands scratched up by you clawing like a girl, now would I?"

Wow, he could talk like a real person when he wanted. Somebody squawked on his radio, and he stepped back and said, "Joe, that you? This the private channel? Now listen, Joe. I need two troopers for a job. Call it a W-17, eastbound at Mineola."

Joe squawked, and he said, "Damn right with a tazer, and I need them now. Mineola's my next stop, an ETA of about five minutes. But Joe, two *good* cops, B.E.I. And do *not* radio anything about an officer needing assistance. I don't need any Mineola cops getting pushy on their home turf…. Yeah, a real wiseass. No – he's poor. Right. Nothing a little juice won't fix. What? … Shit no, no National Guard! You out of your mind after what happened in Hempstead? Those soldiers are not – negatory – not team players. That nigger soldier may still drag me before the D-Board unless somebody wakes him up."

Drooling at the thought of kicking my ass, the bastard didn't care who heard what. But this second time confirmed that he talked like any other jerk at the end of the bar when he wasn't blowing smoke. I had to escape and quick, cause I sure didn't like his talk of tazers. That's how folks end up dead at the feet of cops zapping them with 50,000 volts. Several cops typically present, they couldn't just sit on some guy like in the old days. They don't like getting their hands dirty anymore, so old ladies and guys already cuffed or in wheelchairs get the juice.

Mineola wasn't actually the next stop, but we'd hit it in a few minutes. My only hope was to raise a ruckus there on the snow-ball chance that, rather than scurrying from the train, folks might throw off their blinders and rise to my defense against three cops in uniform. Un-huh. Why the hell had Cat Wrangler have to freaking sit across from the one seat I fit? I made to get up, but he moved quick to stand painfully on my foot, pin me with his shin on my knee and keep talking.

"Joe, listen. You work this out quick and quiet, it clears that marker you owe me. And you know that's no small deal. All right. Affirmative, the next stop – Mineola."

He then addressed the car at large. "Suspect, you will be charged with obstructing a T Investigation, assault on a sworn Protector, disorderly conduct and resisting arrest. Your refusal to supply identification also rules you an imminent T Threat. You will be taken off this train at Mineola for a full and immediate search of your person for any papers, marks or wounds."

"All right, cop. That's enough of you spewing your shit. I hear you had a problem with a 'nigger soldier' in Hempstead. Well, you got a problem with a natural-born, one-hundred-percent, nigger soldier in your face right here, right now."

Indeed, the sergeant major was standing in the aisle about six feet behind us.

"I ain't seen twenty-three of my own over the years – that's right, twenty-three *nigger soldiers*! – blown up or shot by them maniacs in all them Sands to hear talk like that of any kind from a man in uniform and on-duty! No sir. A man ain't fit to shine them boys' boots. They're not here anymore, but this white boy here is, and both of us know damn well you're planning on jacking the shit out of him you get him off this train."

The cop worked his mouth but was too slow.

"Come on, coward. I ain't slammed anybody in the whole two months I been home. You like messing with civilians never been in a real fight their whole lives. Well you're about to commence a real fight now – no tazer, just skin on skin – with a fighting machine from the Third ID!"

"Soldier, back up and produce identification now! Your interference in my lawful detention of this T-Threat will not prevent your redeployment to Mesopotamia, the Central Front, Operation Enduring Struggle or any future Sands. Your incarceration stateside is merely delayed for the duration of the Current Permanent Crisis."

"Come on, man. Make the first move, cause then it's self-defense from the jump. Come on, ofay-man, I'm calling you a coward in front of all these rich white people paying you to keep people like me down. Ain't no backup on this train – just you and me. So what you gonna do about it? And I do hope you make a move for that little cap gun you're wearing. Nothing'd give me more pleasure than you try to shoot me for calling you a name – pussy!"

The ensuing pandemonium washed over me as things both sped up and slowed way down. The sergeant major wasn't terribly tall, but he stretched his tight green shirt everywhere you looked, and his flat boulder of a head rested on a girder of a neck. The venom pouring off him, sheer mass was the least of it.

The cop stood dumbfounded as the train started slowing. I had eyes for nothing but his hand by his gun. Crouched down in a fighting stance, the sergeant major had moved back a couple of steps to, what, commence festivities with a flying kick? A couple of women were screaming, and some louts were again bellowing in that exaggerated bass, "Yo, break his face!" and "Kick his ass!" A white man in uniform versus a menacing black man, little mystery whose face these Long Islanders wanted broken, whose ass kicked.

The cop drew his club. "All right, Bosco! I've given you too much rope already, let's see how you swing." His baton sniffing the air between them, he moved slowly forward, finally freeing my path to the door. I darted up and turned to watch. Further back, a young black guy was struggling to break free of the woman begging him to sit down. Ms. Lockjaw started in on "God Bless America" in her shrillest Ethel Merman, interrupting herself to demand that those physically able should support the Hero manning the front lines of Homeland defense, with the elderly and infirm joining her in song.

The train shuddered to a stop at Merillon Avenue, a little jerk-water station in ritzy Garden City before you hit Mineola, a stop unknown to the cop, who probably patrolled all over Long Island. Shit, what about the conductor? There'd be no clean getaway with him throwing his 290 pounds my way. But he leaned on the partition studying his nails. I thought it, but he said it, great minds thinking alike as I bolted for the doors and out to the platform: "Happy now, asshole?"

People piling out of our car's doors, I ran back up the platform, bent and saw through a window the cop raise his club and pose nicely for a righteous blow as the soldier lashed out and hit him hard in the throat. Down went the cop and up came the soldier's foot for the first stomp. Four or five people scuffled in the aisle, including the young black guy who'd escaped his woman and a hefty broad in a pink polo shirt wildly swinging her purse. The soldier's piston of a leg drove down again, then he turned and nodded straight at me before grinning and raising it again. Not knowing I could still do such a thing, I grabbed the rail at the platform's edge and vaulted up and over, down a lot further below than it looked.

Chapter Four

Tighter Still to Cut the Pain

Christ, I could only hope that soldier was wearing sneakers rather than his no doubt highly polished Army boots. I pulled myself up to make tracks, just gone, a cop looking to arrest me getting stomped. I could almost feel the damn do-gooder throwing himself at my heels, but all the high-testosterone types were fighting in the aisle.

The doors whooshed shut, and the train took off faster than I knew an LIRR could go, its horn blaring as the engineer raced for help at the big Mineola station, the passengers abandoned on the platform yelling all the louder.

Thrilled to escape a Data Boosting (I'd recently learned my Tier was already way too high) and too freaked to attend to the ankle sprained by my leap over the railing, I ran … where? OK, my folks' place in Mineola, that being the quickest route off the streets. Yup, this whole grim farce, my part in it anyway, arose from being so newly, miserably alone that my Saturday-night plan was to seek succor from those that bred me rather than moping around the Hovel or out lurking and staring at women who stared vacantly back somewhere over my right shoulder.

Garden City nice and dark – such a rich, lily-white town didn't worry about lighting its streets – I jogged the long way less traveled, scurried across the couple of busier streets only when the coast was clear, and tried to remember if LIRR trains had surveillance cameras. My throbbing ankle finally forced a halt to tie my boot tighter to cut the swelling and pain.

Crouching there proved all the excuse a dog needed to steal up and leap, his jaws snapping shut a couple of feet from my head, the shock wave bowling me over. Awash in his foul, kibbly breath, I scuttled away on all fours like a beached crab, mangling the ankle more. But rather than advancing the few feet to finish the job, he snapped and slavered and growled, hopping up and down right at the edge of his lawn, a brute with a remarkably well defined sense of territory. I braced to fend off a Doberman with my bare hands.

Ah-ha, a buried canine electronic fence. Can't Touch Me! The dog twitched and growled as I tugged the boot's laces from the bottom up. Suddenly the house and lawn were flooded in light, and I forced a gimpy trot. Intent on never acknowledging the whole painful episode to my parents, I braved a gas station to call and cancel, hunched over at the exposed phone booth. I'd deliberately left my micro-zap home, the better not to hear it silent on a Saturday night, no one caring to inform me they'd just arrived at the corner of 22nd Street, having stopped for a slice on 19th. Pop answered and affirmed that he'd cope with my absence. "I didn't get why somebody newly single was wasting a Saturday night coming out here anyway. But no big deal either way." Great, Pop.

I gimped along familiar blocks and eventually snuck into my parents' garage and collapsed on some tarps in the back around ten. Scared and depleted, I fell into a fitful swoon, but kept jerking awake jarring my ankle. Once I woke and saw the name, Schiakoczyk, scribbled on my palm and scrubbed furiously with spit to erase the incriminating mark. Amidst dreams of car headlights shining on me and sketchy people flitting dubiously about, I later woke without a clue where I was or what I was lying on. It was a bad moment until I pieced it all together, my rising panic made worse by apprehending that I hadn't been drinking, and so how in blazes had I ended up sleeping rough in some musty little building?

I got up sometime after five, judging by the murk overhead,

my chest aching where that bastard clubbed me and starving from having squirreled myself away the night before, not willing to risk a bite somewhere public. As the night dragged, I'd had to stifle the urge to raid my own damn parents' own damn fridge. Not that my folks would ever turn me in – Pop would rather take a dump on the Mineola cop-shop's lawn. But, consumed by the rigors of age, they just didn't need another worry heaped on their own growing pile. From vague ribbing from his two older brothers, I was dimly aware that Pop had had his own dealings with the boys in blue. Not that he'd shared with his only kid any tales of his days as a youthful reprobate and then a union man out at the airport.

Turn me in for what, damn it? But such was the calculus in HeadFuck's America. After all, I'd been declared a Prosecutorial Prospect or whatever the day's verbiage hiding the truncheon. Another man fighting in my stead, shame dripped from my heels as I fell to sneaking through town and a night of nightmares on a cement floor, unwilling to ask my own mother for a crust or enjoy the sleep of innocents in my teen-age bed.

It didn't feel like anything was broken. But man, I saw in a coffee-shop bathroom mirror, the bruise on my chest had spread. The bull's-eye still an angry red, a lot of purple and blue had splotched all around. Fearful of breakfasting cops, I grabbed coffee and an egg sandwich to go. But as the first food in many an hour kicked in, I almost convinced myself there was no way to trace me from the train.

I decided I'd read somewhere that the train itself had no cameras. Nothing to be done about the ambient taping galore at Penn Station where I'd started my trip, but with a ticket already stashed in my wallet, nothing linked me specifically to that particular train. Having leapt from the middle of the platform, hopefully the Merillon Avenue platform cameras by the stairs hadn't captured me. So the cops couldn't database my eyes, ears, and full, sensitive lips, nor deputize the entire city by splashing a Merillon Ave. image all over the front page. If my luck held and I didn't venture to Long Island any time soon, maybe I wouldn't get nailed. Yup, rather than standing up on my hind feet, filing assault charges, and suing Statie for a cool quarter-mil, off I skulked down a dark back alley.

Stopping to loosen my boot on a swollen foot, then stopping a block on to tie it just a bit tighter, I stewed about not throwing my shoulder to the wheel. No, I wasn't just turning and leaping on Statie's back. I wasn't the sort to do that to unarmed civilians let alone MoFos with guns. But I could've vaulted some seats, gotten, yeah, behind the sergeant major and ... yelled at that cop. Called him a liar, that impermissible word.

Yeah, and how long had I known that vicious, deranged soldier anyway? A stranger, huh? Then why did he risk getting shot to protect me? And why did we arrange to travel together but sit apart? What's more, what was my relationship with the woman who'd disappeared so precipitously into the night? The woman whose criminal recalcitrance triggered the whole spate of anti-state violence. Exactly how many thousands of dollars did I have spirited away for a good defense lawyer for the T they'd conjure with a snap? Nope, just suck this one up.

Such was snuffling victimhood during the Current P. Crisis. No spine, no resistance – and no potentially fatal tazer. I tempered my shame with the thought that I was better suited to assist damsels in distress with logic, my winning personality and little knowledge of cats beyond which end to pet. Battle-shaky Sands vets looking for any excuse to slam somebody – well thanks, Sergeant Major, but I'll offer my encouragement while tumbling far over an LIRR railing.

I limped down my old hometown's quiet, Sunday-morning streets, pushing through gauze already hot and thick at dawn to pay cash for a bus to Queens and then the subway home. The set of my jaw indicating I wasn't a bum though I was walking on Long Island, men my age up early with their dogs failed to meet my nod. Guys with wives along with dogs, and houses and kids and a spewer or two, giant vehicles crowding driveways built for cars. And the thought flickered yet again that maybe Nicki was right.

Chapter Five

Scrambling Rats, Shrinking Cheese

I reached Queens without incident and plodded home to the Hovel from the subway, swimming against the tide streaming early to lousy jobs they were glad of in the City. The occasional odd bright flash darting across my field of vision was normally a sure sign of getting toasted. But it only felt like I'd been through the late-night wringer since I'd actually crawled onto that tarp far too sober, early and alone.

Eight on a Sunday morning and no one with a badge or a licensed whole-vid banging on my door, nothing for it but to get horizontal again, wiped as I was. But of course I couldn't shut it down. No, not about the riot on the train, so new it wasn't implanted in my brain quite that way yet. Instead, there I lay fending off thoughts of the Wife, who, pending the arrival of Monday's mail, I was still *legally* entitled to call Nicki.

I only called her a hack maybe twice, both times when she was hassling about money. Besides, I never said she couldn't write, even if she sometimes spent a week on a few lines of copy. Her ad agency, Fornix & Foyst, paid her by the week – not my by-the-word freelance servitude – so who cared.

"Let Others Worry," the brand line for the giant SUV from India that won such applause for raw honesty was Nicki's, though, truth be told, at least half the ad's impact came from the unaccustomed shots of the monster bullying its way through dense city traffic rather than the usual bounding unfettered by some waterfall.

Also Nicki's, for the woman raising the bushel on her dimming light, the $399 do-me shoe, "Enervation: The Heels for a Taut Calf." People loved the obscure name with its possibly louche undercurrent. Then came the golden PR of some feminist website stringing up a baby cow (taut indeed) in homage to the crippling four-inch heels.

And my favorite, her tag for CheeseSpray, the genetically modified goop that came in a can but didn't clog you up: "Deracinated. So It Binds to Your Taste Buds, Not Your Bowels." Again, the odd word no one knew to rarify the brand. Her bosses always freaked, but after the focus groups endorsed it, they'd go with Nicki's gut. That it made no sense became something of her trademark.

Still, I'd like to get my hands on a little of whatever the client was on when they approved mention of bound bowels. At the CheeseSpray launch party high atop some garish Midtown hotel, not a soul – not even some client-services lackey instructed to throw his stomach on a sword – touched a single can of the stuff so lovingly arrayed on silver platters around the room. Except me, who discovered that one reason no one sprayed 'cheese' was the cans were glued to the platters.

A tall slinkster in an orange cashmere dress sidled by just then, every sculpted inch of her shrieking Client Manager for Morons. That being appropriately dazzled me, I picked up the can with the platter still attached and *sotte voce* (sure) asked her what the deal was. Nicki flew across the room before the woman could say a word, draped herself smotheringly on me like she hadn't done in public in ages and said, "Melanie, I see you've chanced upon my husband. Mitchell, you must remember meeting Melanie Artenunotte of *The New York Dispatch*. She's one of their main advertising writers now, a real up-and-comer."

"Oh, a gentlelady of the *Dispatch*. Nicki, you've been derelict in not introducing us sooner. As colleagues, I'm sure we have much to speak of." That nonsense at least turned us from the canned cheese whose purveyors had bought the drinks in our hands not to mention, ultimately, Nicki's own tight dress, new for the occasion. I had no particular desire to mess with her job.

46

How so, Artenunotte barely managed to inquire. She stopped listening to my not brief enough reply long before she fled. But I spread the butter with a generous enough knife that Nicki was merely miffed, not furious. I hid behind how was I supposed to know Artenunotte until Nicki reminded me I'd met her in that very room six months back. Like I was supposed to remember every *gosh*-but-ain't-getting-slippery-with-her-either encounter at one of these things.

Nonetheless, the room's general acclaim for "Deracinated," etc. left Nick in a sterling mood. Verbally mauling her from the podium, a client top-dog left so many paw prints, if I was any kind of man at all I'd have socked him one mid-slobber. So sterling and giddy, we actually fell into it when, deliberately snooping stumbling out of the hotel two hours later, we ended up in a deserted banquet room with a nifty little outdoor balcony. Much of Manhattan sparkling before us, Central Park dense and dark at our entangled feet, the hem of her fabulous dress shimmied up her back as I pulled Nicki hard by the shoulders for some ooh-baby right *there*!

There were beaucoup giant shrimp at these affairs up amidst the Midtown rooftops, always a new one more gaudily bathed in light to try to penetrate the murk. (Do the math.) I've had worse than fifteen-year-old whiskey pleasantly redolent of coal with a touch of freeze-dried cat urine thrown in for nose, each snoggerful on someone else's dime a bit smoother than the one before.

At least at Nicki's advertising parties a good portion of the room grabbed at a good time. Sometimes there was music, however techno-disco lousy, and dancing. But at the journalism snoot-fests I wrangled my way into for about five minutes – my dollop of Warhol's standard fifteen – guests fled from fun. All the rats in attendance were too busy clawing and scrambling for an ever-shrinking chunk of cheese. Deciding whether to come along, Nicki would ask whether it was just another "boring, rat-chasing-cheese party." Particularly scrawny, yet thinking *I* was the one with the squirrel's transformatively bushy tail, I'd gesture around the lush, dark or maybe bright, shiny room, everyone clutching and gabbing, and lob my standard, droll proffer over the net: "So, whadiya think of all this wretched excess?"

And the dude's incomprehension as he looked around and saw nothing excessive and certainly nothing wretched, everyone glossed and starched and sheened, would turn to disgust at my stab at fun. Humor? When I'd presumed to a precious moment of his time, he with not another invite in hand till the following week? Humor, when there'd been a momentary gap in the fierce scrum round the Chief Assistant to the Assistant Chief of Deluge & Devour hobnobbing with the Senior Enervationist at Crutchem and Baggit – a gap he'd foolishly failed to exploit thinking I might actually be somebody?

That morsel of cheddar always just beyond reach, my five minutes were up soon enough. Far better to be a mere spouse at Nicki's shin-digs, my heavy but sole obligation not to embarrass her. A minor guest, I was free for leering conversation with all sexes. Nine years together, and I kept rolling the conviction uphill that Nicki didn't take her ad-drivel seriously despite the increasing pay and recognition. That everything was and would forever remain jake between us as long as we went dancing once in a while and wandered around Throgs Neck, Bay Ridge or Jamaica Bay for kicks, the sun setting over some body of water. We had mediocre pizza over the years, or spicy shredded meat, in every part of the City even remotely near the water. Then, as my freelance work dried up (ill-suited to the times), she got the big promotion to VP that sparked her move to Manhattan by herself.

Though we'd been dating only a year way back when, we were both old enough for me to have dropped to one knee, ring in hand, when that kid unexpectedly elbowed his or her way on stage. Sure, we got married three years later – malingering on my part for at least half of that – but, despite lots of fine, fun times traipsing all over creation, we never quite recaptured our full groove. There's a well-worn path for a couple to maybe recover. But despite always saying sure, she'd think about it next month, she never mustered the faith to deliberately harbor my seed.

Chapter Six

Nipped

Propping up my bum ankle (nothing to be done with my sore chest), sleep finally came that Sunday morning in the midst of recalling our oddball outing to Bayonne some years back to gaze at big ships and their attendant big cranes before plopping down in a park, a pair of decaying bridges soaring off over to the right. Nick and I sat and sipped and watched the planes land at Freedom International across the big bay, the interminable trek home to Queens still in the offing.

I felt better after a couple of hours sleep – that is, rested and in pain. Neither the two "all-tripe, all-the-time" radio stations nor any local news sites had anything on any LIRR fracas. Cops doing the boogaloo on folks tired old ground, I was more freaked by the fight on the train, its outcome unknown, than by getting assaulted. Monday would be the test, whether any grainy photo of me surfaced under the headline, "Protectors Ask Help Finding this Prosecutorial Prospect."

Mooning around that afternoon, I risked pacing, sweating and swearing, followed by beering and staring – a sure route to waking up feeling lousy Monday morning. Lousy knowing I probably wasn't storming the barricades alongside whoever was standing up to a goon with a gun. Far better to stick to the weeks-old plan for that Sunday: Shenanigans by the Sea, the free, two-stage throw-down they had every summer out at Coney Island. The Furred Tongues, of all people, were promised on the second stage, a *current* band whose music I actually owned. Presumably a couple of the other bands, nothing more than names on a list to me, also funneled a groove.

Bathing suit under my shorts, I grabbed a book, underwear, towel and my standard PBJ club sandwich, the third slice for extra heft – then and later. Still with Nicki, I probably would've skipped the swim and just gone to the music. But then, still with her, I wouldn't be spending Saturday night with the parents and so wouldn't be wincing every time I forgot and took a deep breath. As it was, along with the bands and the prowl's scintillating disappointments, Mother Ocean's soothing embrace also beckoned, a reliable Rita Moreno to Jack Nicholson's diminished scoundrel at the end of *Carnal Knowledge*.

I got off the train with a bunch of kids – Don't Trust Anyone Under Thirty! – looking to get sloppy in the heat. We trooped through a spruced up station, meant to spark redevelopment amidst the general squalor. With its soaring glass walls and huge glass roof, it looked like some crystal-palace European train shed. Gazillions for glitz, part of the campaign to get Hiltons and Hyatts lining the boardwalk. Though the surrounding environs were little changed, should Coney Island ever shake off the Plunge, bye-bye old and in the way – two-legged included. One of New York's last down-at-heels good times slated for the heap.

The throng shuffled down a long ramp, pushed through the turnstiles and swung left around a wall. Ambushed, we fell into the clutches of a mess of cops not just standing around as usual, but steering people one way or the other. They looked to be plucking out some of the freakier dudes and sending them over to a rinky-dink table with two cops behind it.

Godfreakingdamn it, there was no escape even way out here by the sea, even having *left* the subway though still on City property. I'd apparently been moping round my little corner of stumblebum Queens too much to know what the heck was going on. None of the kids transporting a Siamese cat, those chosen plunked down their stuff for the paw-through. Some looked pissed, but most had these idiot grins pasted on like they were glad of the chance or would at least get in less trouble the less trouble they made. Pretty disconcerting to see some macho psuedo-punks holding their bags out eagerly as if for scoops of ice cream. Maybe they had something problematical secreted away somewhere and were hoping for a pass.

Not carrying (more's the pity) and old by this crowd's standards, they weren't gonna mess with someone limping along staring at the heels of the guy in front. *Take him, not me!* Could they possibly pop me for the underwear in my bag for conspiracy to disrobe on the beach? Nah, I'd paid my hassled-by-cops dues for some considerable time. So good luck, guys (oddly, not a single girl), but get me out of this sweaty crowd and into that salt water.

I made it past the cops but against my better judgment stopped to watch. I heard not a peep of protest as they chose a steady stream of the more outré males for the privilege. Were they just punishing the types they didn't like? In any event, so much for a *random* search cause, with a dozen bands on two stages, there was enough music to appeal to almost any taste or type. Yet the cops chose not a single one of the clean-cut prepsters in polo shirts and the flip-flops that made no sense heading to a scrum before the stage.

(How you gonna cope with a zombie crisis in flip-flops? Fleeing down an alley in shower slippers, how kick down a side door to escape come the next robot uprising? How fall over an LIRR railing and then tie it tight for a gimpy forced march?)

At the table, a kid in a wispy beard and old-time, flower-power shirt lost it. "What – you're gonna arrest me for an open nip bottle? You gotta be kidding me. There's exactly two swallows in that thing. You going nuts or what?" He was heading for a fall with that kind of talk.

Looking like a circus strong man with his big pink slabs of arm disappearing into the same too-small black gloves that Statie favored, the cop doing the honors was beefy, buzz-cut and wired way too tight. The sergeant on the scene advanced to state primly that an open container, no matter the size, was in violation of this, that and the other, including the rank nonsense of endangering the welfare of any minors on the train.

Make a bad left turn, you get drug-tested, and your biometrics are harvested on the spot. Everyone knew that. But now you had to be like new-blown snow *exiting* the train? They brought up the hand-held to iris-scan the kid for any priors or warrants – yeah, and arrange for a Boosting, he made any more cracks about "going nuts."

Buzz-cut asked his sergeant, "So you want him with the potheads we got waiting for the van?"

I hadn't noticed the five guys off in a corner being watched by yet another cop costing a whopping $120K a year, maybe, you throw in pension and benefits, plus all the T-overtime. The downtrodden mix of hippies and punks wore those mass-arrest plastic cuffs around their wrists. Imagine: a joint at a big outdoor concert. Not worth a Boosting, it'd just screw up finding a job or an apartment. And holding on to their driver's license (if they had the wherewithal to get one) might end up costing thousands for months of coerced 'treatment,' not to mention years of vastly inflated car insurance. The cops knew giving the clean-cut preps a pass side-stepped a lot of reefer, so were they just afraid of popping some rich kid whose dad might make a stink?

Possessed of a weary grandeur, the sergeant weighed Buzz-cut's question on adding the nip offender. Not caring who heard, he said, "Callaghan, we're already pushing it. Some captain starts running stats and sees a cop got OT processing a nip-bottle arrest along with all the marijuana, we're screwed – and that means me."

"Come on, Sarge, what's the odds on that? Besides, this fruit really needs to learn some manners, know what I mean?"

"He does. But we still can't get greedy. If the lieutenant takes that guy with the roach – and the van shows up late like I told them – we only need one more doper for everybody here to get OT. So focus on the golden goose however long it keeps laying. And hope for another, you know ... *incident* down the road, as long as it's not in New York. Just give him an open-container ticket, but make it seventy-five, not fifty. Maybe that'll teach him some manners."

Sarge went back to gleaning hopheads from the invading hoards seeking a beachhead at Coney Island. Processing the arrests, his men would get maybe $175 each in piece-of-pie OT, more if they had some years under their belt.

I'd never been angry immersed in Mother Ocean before, the salt's sting on my roughed-up chest not helping.

****

I threw my sweaty sheet off and barked my sore ankle. And it welled up from somewhere the next day's blue Monday mourn that I'd messed up worse than a night's foolishness that left me with gravel in my mouth and wet wool in my head. Finding myself in the Hovel's vertical coffin of a bedroom rather than a cell and only my chest and foot sore, there'd apparently been no new insult visited upon me. Despite that accomplishment, disgust at some unspecified pigheadedness gripped me, and the aspirin and water were five long steps away.

Emily! was her name it came to me as I gulped, she of the delectable cutoff shorts. My glasses, I'd noticed, were lying unbroken on the bathroom floor for some reason, so I held my palm close to search for some remnant of the phone number I knew wasn't there. She'd been shucking and jiving by herself by the second stage, old enough – mostly – tall and with the requisite long dark hair, though she didn't look *too* much like Nicki. (A carbon copy just made your friends snicker and you crazy with unwarranted hopes of duplicating the memories plaguing you.)

Emily laughed at my japes, and we even danced when the Furred Tongues kicked it their last couple of songs – face-to-face and responding to the other person's moves, an ancient courtship ritual otherwise unseen among the day's thousands of music lovers. Blasé youth apparently falling into bed with no preliminaries, we looked to be among the very few flirting at all.

No guarantee, even (especially) with someone so appealing, I had to get greedy and write her number on a piece of paper rather than on my hand when she had to leave early for a family dinner. (Hanging with her family, a good sign that.) Unforgivable but understandable, that paper, since I hadn't been at such a munificent scene in years. Not single, anyway. Ever the strategist, I figured a number smeared on my hand would only complicate getting a second one. Safety in numbers, diversifying one's assets – all clown-talk.

I guarded the paper fine until the unsurprising tussle a couple of sodden hours later with some overly entitled big meathead in flip-flops and a rugby shirt trying to cut in line at the bodega. Boxing him out to keep him behind me, I fumbled in my pocket for change and *half*-sensed the paper falling to the floor. He even more soused and aggressive, in the midst of fending him off, I certainly couldn't let my guard down by bending to the floor as I paid quick for that crucial, that necessary, last beer. Heading out, I silently dared him into throwing the first punch cause then it was self-defense from the get-go, right Sergeant Major? And nary a thought for that shot at happiness lying trampled on the floor.

I should have written Emily's number on my forehead to see it come Monday morning, cause her laughing eyes as we gyrated to the Tongues promised a generous soul in a fabulous package. There improbably alone, she was no doubt newly unencumbered like myself. Remembering her 718 area code, I needed to start dialing till I found her. Fingers don't fail me, cause women like her un-unencumber quick.

Chapter Seven

At the Behemoth's Beck and Call

By my rough calculation, I quit dialing 0.0000079% of the way towards finding Emily. That left a ways to go, but I abandoned my quest when some little girl sounding maybe age seven got all excited when I asked to speak to Emily, and she said her name was Emily! Pleasantly surprised myself, I goofed with her a moment until she said something about us two having to meet. Then her dad got on real quick and said he had my number and so would the cops before he took another breath.

Nah. Despite Emily's perfectly toned arms, arms that spoke volumes, and all that dark luster that whipped deliciously round our faces as we danced, I wasn't quite desperate enough – yet – to start dialing at random. Emily the *first* damn woman I'd met in years tossed aside like a greasy paper plate, the pizza gone, nothing for it but hoist myself back in the saddle. So, a concert that might've ordinarily seemed a bit old-fogeyish, especially since he probably wouldn't sing "Alice's Restaurant." But my blood was up and, besides, it was free.

And so was I – thank you, Nicki, very much – and time to prowl off the beaten track on a Tuesday. I managed to iron-horse it to Lincoln Center with nary a MoFo encounter, and early enough to grab a seat near the front, but way towards the far aisle. Cause Damrosch Park was packed, the big plaza – technically a City of New York park, I saw on a sign – abutting the Metropolitan Opera filling up with folkies and lefties and graybeards (many embodying all three) along with a bunch like me just along for the ride. I'd prefer some dark joint where you could shake it a little, but this lonely boy could tolerate a talented, free tune-slinger well enough.

A cheery crowd though we soon aped sardines, the loose and goosey hoot-and-holler was happily (and rarely) redolent of the days when HeadFuck was still an obscure back-bencher from the Midwestern berg that vomited him forth. Folks letting their hair down, four or maybe five-thousand drawn to a city park still a haven amidst the overarching glass towers. As the sky darkened, people bored with playing with their pencils on the Group W bench called Arlo to the stage. And eventually the old pro and his band settled in and channeled mellifluousness right enough.

That there were no NYPDs was compensated for by all the Lincoln Center MoFos parading around in the aisles with nothing much to do but model their ugly brown uniforms. Whether it was the unaccustomed absence of men with guns or just the nature of an audience come to hear Woody's son, folks called out all sorts of stuff in between songs. One die-hard crazy started up bizarrely enough with Lets-Go-Mets, which quickly went nowhere. Innocuous stuff sure, but still a welcome change these days to let loose out loud about anything. Some shrill dame kept yelling for "Alison's Restaurant," and everyone was in such a good mood, no one corrected her.

Then it happened, after maybe the fifth song, the likes of which I hadn't heard – not all naked and unabashed – since the Disruption following HeadFuck's installation. But hear it I did from the well assembled guy sitting a row ahead and a little closer to the left aisle, sitting with his girlfriend, probably, since they looked young to be married.

A lifeguard, maybe, cause he had quite a pair of lungs. The band waiting on a tuning bass player, this guy cupped his hands and bellowed to the sky: "People, listen! Why do we sit here and take it, not allowed to whole-vid a good performance like this? To maybe watch this again at home? There's no police action here tonight, there's not even any police here. So why can't the MoFos figure out a way to give us whole-vid back for non-political stuff? I mean, what the hell – right?"

Wow, a direct verbal assault on HeadFuck himself, as loud as this guy could make it in as public a setting as possible. Cause the ban on whole-vids came early, back when a puissant HeadFuck strode the stage triumphant, and he made damn clear the ban was his decision "to keep our Heroes from besmirchment." He said it more than once. Wow, indeed! Calling HeadMan out like that all out loud just wasn't done. A regular New Yorker the guy looked, mid-twenties, clean in jeans and a sports shirt, well suited to the pretty girl with the long red hair in a summer frock.

The band started up abruptly, then stopped, the musicians not all on the same page. The silence was broken by the buzz of many, many shocked people whispering. Maybe the far reaches of the crowd hadn't heard, but hundreds of people turned to gaze upon this wonder. Most looked alarmed, some were grinning, a few even nodded in agreement.

Arlo filled the moment by relaying a yarn about a pizza delivery gone bad. But no one was listening, so he banged out the intro to a raucous Chuck Berry number on his piano and the band chimed in.

Mid-song, a Lincoln Center guard leaned into the aisle and pointed at the guy. "Another outburst like that, mister, and you're in big trouble. Lincoln Center, like nowhere else, isn't the place for that kind of talk. So listen up! Cause all these Homelanders here are here to behave themselves and have a good time."

"Oh, come on, listen to yourself. Did I really impact anyone enjoying the concert – I mean, really? Cause otherwise, you're talking silly."

The guard pondered that a moment, then walked away. Soon a bigger, don't-mess guard came over and gestured for the guy to come speak in the aisle six or eight seats away from where he and the redhead were sitting. The rows tight, he got up and nudged his way past, only one person not shrinking back to make way. But he stopped short of the aisle. This was getting good. Curious to hear, I moved a seat, up next to a woman whose eye I'd so far failed to catch.

Finally accepting that the guy wasn't offering himself up in the aisle alone, the guard said what he'd come to say. "Look, mister. That's sedition what you just said, and my audience members did not come here to hear that. We all know who issued the Reg banning whole-vids, so that's close to T right there. And what's this about recording concerts? That violates copyright. But mostly, just who exactly are these 'MoFos' you're talking about. You care to identify them for me?"

I could only see the back of the guy's head, but it sounded like a smirk graced its front. "You know, buddy: if the shoe fits. Now you're messing with me why? You just don't like the cut of my jib?"

"I'm not interested in any of that. I do know you can applaud – clap your hands – at the end of the songs. But if you yell again, you'll be removed."

"You're joking, right? Or do you have a decibel meter on you to see if I'm 'yelling?' "

"Is that woman there with you?"

"Leave her out of this."

"You've been warned. Got it?"

"You know what, people still – that's right, *still* – have the right to free speech in this country. Despite everything. There's no Reg specifically prohibiting it. That's one bridge they haven't crossed yet. So that means you can all go take a hike!"

Technically, he was correct, maybe. Though ask any ten folks on the street, I doubted more than one would agree in any practical sense. He returned to his seat, having to push roughly past the deliberately obstructive knees of some blocky guy in a white shirt who didn't exactly look like Arlo was his cup of tea. Girlfriend rubbed his back once he scooted past her to his seat on her right. The guard glared, started to say something, then turned on his heel. Did anyone within ten rows, front or back, think that the last of it?

Arlo was two songs along by the time nine guards (I counted) gathered in the left aisle a few rows back. Ah, something to amuse themselves with, cause it wasn't like this decidedly mature crowd was hunched over rolling up the reefer or anything. And a man in civilian clothes stepped forward and demanded the guy come speak with him in the aisle. "To talk about what? Anything beyond you giving me the bum's rush out? So how about I just sit here so we don't disrupt one of your biggest concerts of the summer?"

"Mister, I'm serious."

"So am I. Look, I can hear you perfectly, just like you can hear me. And we all know what'll happen if I come to the aisle. Because you sure don't need all those men there just to talk. So let's 'talk' about how big of a ruckus do you want. Before answering, think about how tight you got these rows of seats crammed together. And then think of how loud you already know I can get. Who knows, I might even get some help, this particular audience." He turned and looked around at us all as White Shirt snorted.

The man in mufti again demanded that he come to the aisle where it was indeed all too apparent what would happen. And redheaded girlfriend piped up, "And who exactly are you, sir? Do you work for Lincoln Center, because the sign back there says this is a City park."

"I'm the head of Lincoln Center security tonight and, according to our contract with the City, you fall under my jurisdiction."

"So you say," said the guy. "You got any identification, or even a name, and maybe a copy of this contract?"

"None of that is necessary. I'm telling you for the last time – *both* of you, now that the lady has involved herself – to come to the aisle. Now! To talk."

His crew, ten of them by that point, large and less so, white, black and brown, were all on the balls of their feet ready to spring.

"Actually, I would prefer not to. We're obviously having no problem hearing each other. Or what about this empty seat right here next to me? The seats are free, my man." He patted the chair on his right, his girlfriend beckoning from her seat closer to the aisle. Man, with a bulwark like her, I might mount some active resistance myself.

"That's not convenient for me. Or for the members of my audience who are here to act properly," Head Security said. He walked back to his muttering crew.

"Let 'em look, freaking Napoleonic-Complex rent-a-cops," the girl whispered to that lucky dog. Could they possibly pay attention, because they held hands and turned back to the stage.

Stalemate overlaid three ballads, then a muted hubbub stirred the folks further back. I turned to see four NYPD cops and their sergeant march up to talk to Head Security. Jesus H.! Refusing to acknowledge the guards' existence, never mind their potential impact on their lives, Bartleby and his Girlfriend attended solely to the stage. I whispered, "Hey, you guys, the guards got company. Look!"

They turned and peered over their shoulders. Bartleby thanked me as Girlfriend said, "Who cares? The more the merrier." And they turned back to the stage, Arlo in the midst of a particularly convoluted tale with just a hint of refusal, the first he'd ventured all night.

Head Security finished his briefing, pointed at the pair, and the sergeant came up. He leaned into their aisle where they sat just out of reach eight or nine seats in, most still occupied. "OK, you two. Play time's over. Get to the aisle. Now! I need to talk to you."

And Bartleby said, "You know, Sergeant, this is now the third invitation to conversation I've had tonight, always for some reason in that one special place. So can someone please tell me why everyone, including now a squad of cops, is so interested in what I have to say!"

"I'll tell you – I mean Lincoln Center will tell you. But first you need to get over here. That's where we need to talk. Now these

Homelanders and others have paid a lot of good money to sit here and listen without being disturbed by some Subversive. So let's go!"

"You know this is getting old, don't you? I'll repeat what I told the guards before five men with guns showed up: I can hear you fine. Now what do you want to talk about?"

The sergeant caught on quick. They again each uselessly importuned the other. The cop cursed under his breath, spat for good measure and then retreated to his public/private platoon. No fan of empty threats, he issued no *you better or else!* And so, the sheer physical layout of all those tight rows of seats, combined with a recalcitrant duo and Lincoln Center's abhorrence of a mid-concert scene, stymied the MoFos for maybe the first time in a long time. Telling the cops – the *NYPD* – get-out-of-my-face no *and* making it stick just wasn't done, not under HeadFuck and certainly not under Walk-on-Water Ted. It wouldn't fly out on the street somewhere, that's for damn sure. But Bartleby and Girlfriend pulled up their drawbridge and enjoyed the show. Whether they really were such cool cucumbers or their insides churned, I couldn't say.

Fifteen uniformed MoFos stood there, glaring, impotent, stuck to their flypaper. I laughed way down deep as the murmur all around us rose to a buzz. A point for our team – who'd a thunk it? Arlo's rhythm guitarist came to the far edge of the stage and stopped playing to shield his eyes from the stage lights with both hands to try to see what the hell was going on. At some point a large bottle shattered on the pavement over to the right, and a tipsy woman started in swearing and complaining. But such was the dire threat close at hand, not a single guard moved that way.

Wearing their favorite, tight black leather gloves, three cops came up and evicted everyone sitting between the deadly duo and the aisle, White Shirt moving with, "But of course, officers, B.E.I.!" The chairs welded together at their feet in sets of five for easy handling, they removed one set, but three empty chairs remained as buffer. Quite a mismatched little Mexican standoff, just a few steps of concrete and some empty chairs their shallow moat. Yet the MoFos remained rooted, pawing the ground in frustration.

Our whole part of the crowd joined the group sing-along to "This Land Is Your Land" with particular gusto; normally thinking it lame, I belted it out without irony. Then another crowd-rouser, something about a train, and suddenly the lights came up and the concert was over. No sheltering encore.

And everyone but the foci of all the attention stared in wonder. No mention of come with us, no you're not free to go – certainly no whisper of any arrests – they acted accordingly. The lights up, though the crowd still clapped for more (it had been quite a show), they stood and turned to their right, headed towards the center aisle, Bartleby first.

Holy mackerel, were they getting away with it? But no, they must've been a flight risk, shuffling along like that in the crowd. Because, in a cowardly, blindside sneak attack, one cop (who'd shed his gloves) grabbed Girlfriend way too familiarly, and another two launched themselves in a flying tackle, leaping almost horizontally, whomp! into Bartleby from behind, slamming him hard to the pavement, some bony part of him walloping a metal seat on the way down. Chairs all ass-over-tea-kettle, people were yelling, and already a thin, pellucid chant of "Shame! Shame! Shame!" arose. Then a lady yelled, "Randall, stop saying that. You'll get us both a Boosting!" White Shirt came flying past me, frothing to get at it, and then an eager guard slammed one of the five-chair units into my knee and down I went. I found myself near Girlfriend, who was hunched over on the ground trying to shield her chest in her heat-wave dress, a cop and a guard at her, she screaming, "Get off me you bastards! Keep your filthy hands off me!" I looked over at Bartleby, what I could see of him anyway, two cops and a guard rolling around – pulling this, tugging that – getting comfortable on top of him. All that weight, his shallow breaths ran a race with his need for air. I scrambled up not sure of my intent and took a few steps forward till a cop snarled and cocked a gloved fist at me. Bartleby started gasping out, "What's the charge? What's the charge, Goddamn it?" So the sergeant raised his boot to slowly force his head down to the pavement, and there he remained, boot on check. Bartleby mouthed at me, "Is Jennifer OK?" I looked over and, aside from the assault on her dignity, she looked unhurt. "She's OK," I mouthed back. And at that, he closed his eyes. Despite the bleeding, my knee felt structurally intact. So that was something. Most of the crowd was pushing pell-mell for the far aisle and away – a damn good way to get trampled. But thirty or forty people encircled us and chanted "The Whole World is Watching" and "Shame! Shame!" Such an old-fashioned notion, shaming someone, yet its cloth cut to the times more than ever. These folks were the portion of the crowd sporting longish, grayish hair and practical clothes. And Jennifer managed to struggle to her feet and force her way over to scream at the sergeant to get his foot off Dexter's head and his men off Dexter's back. That he couldn't breathe like that. And one guy did get off him to protect his sergeant from a woman so enraged, so that was also something. An older guy with a ponytail called out, "You know what – hey, people, listen up! This guy was right. We did need a whole-vid here tonight. It's the only way to stop the MoFos from brutalizing us." And White Shirt stormed up and punched Ponytail in the gut and then turned and ran through the group of five or six Lincoln Center guards standing there and out the other side of them and gone, the guards ignoring an assault to let him go. Half-doubled over, Ponytail gave chase till a guard grabbed him. And the sergeant lifted his foot, thank God, and said, "OK, that's enough. Get this Subversive out of here, B.E.I., before he really pisses me off." They hauled a dazed Dexter up to stand there gulping air and, surrounded by those half-dozen Lincoln Center

Guards, marched him limply out to the cop car they'd pulled up to the last row of seats. His hand dangled so oddly, his wrist looked broken. Towards the back, I could hear him again yelling, "What's the charge? What's the Goddamn charge?" And Jennifer started screaming, "That's my husband! Where are you taking him? Wait, you need to tell me where he's going. I don't even know what precinct you're from. How will I find my husband? How many days? You have to at least let me say good-bye!"

Husband, huh. They must've had quite the groove-thang going to get married so young. The sergeant said, "Pipe down, Missy. Don't worry, you're going the same place, at least to start." Then, "Take her to my car, Jensen. I'll transport her myself personally." And a mature, professional looking woman started up with, "I need someone to take my card. I saw everything and I don't care anymore. You hear me: I'm sick, and I don't care, and I need to testify! Now who's taking my card and coming with me?" And a guard grabbed her and hustled her off as sirens rent the air. I saw Head Security looking at me and willed myself invisible.

Then a fight broke out on the other side of the center aisle, and a woman screamed, "Watch it, he's got a broken bottle!" And I made for the back exit onto 9th Avenue, not out onto Broadway by Lincoln Center's famous fountain. I snuck all the way down to 14th Street to connect with the G train that left me in Queens still a couple of miles from the Hovel. But it didn't journey back up through midtown, and thus didn't bring me anywhere back near the night's disaster.

So I walked and stewed, dried blood down my leg from my knee – the knee opposite Saturday night's Merillon Ave. sore ankle, they kinda cancelled each other out. Yup, a huge, rich institution snapped its fingers for some muscle, and the NYPD sent five forelock-tuggers on the double. Somebody should do something. Draw a line, maybe, or at least sue the bastards. Back at the Hovel that Tuesday night, I fumed by my one window, cursing and nursing a forty.

PART TWO

Chapter Eight

Inching Ahead Bowed and Barefoot

"Get up! Move! You think this is a game? You think this is funny?" Trying to get away, I rolled over on my bad side Wednesday morning, and the residual pain from Statie's club woke me up and away from the oversized brute in a weird, shimmering uniform. I was in someone else's seat, my ticket apparently good for the night before, and I wasn't moving fast enough. It took a moment to grasp who was what, and that my heart was racing from a dream. My sore chest waking me throughout the night, I slept on my back as if pregnant, my dreams lousy with menace.

And the prior evening's scene at Lincoln Center swam into view. Damn, that guy had guts, telling the cops to stuff it. Just plain, *Nope, not right now, cop.* So it was indeed possible to say no. For a little while, anyway, provided you're willing to pay the price. Had they gotten him to a hospital for his wrist, given him anything for his pain? Or was Dexter locked away somewhere, uncertain of when he'd surface and in what shape? There were all kinds of rumors about all kinds of places. One thing certain: he was getting a Boosting, Jennifer probably too. Man, they were magnificent, the two of them turning their backs on those fifteen cowards, holding hands and tapping their feet to the music. Nicki would have done the same, maybe, our first six or seven years together, anyway, back before she grew so fabulous.

The first several weeks post-Nick, I'd licked my wounds solely locally, up one long, deserted residential block and down Bumfuckville's even more boring next, sneering at the people gathered companionably behind their lit windows, a cold tallboy of Ballantine surreptitiously in hand, the Entertainment System (as I laughingly called the transistor radio perched on my shoulder) and its baseball cloaking the break-up pain more than anything else I could grab. Damn dreary, but that's what I wanted. Didn't want to venture out by the pretty people – *shallow*, pretty people having fun and soon to have a whole lot more once they got behind closed doors.

Near two months of that, and I found myself trotting out to Long Island the prior Saturday, even if just to see my parents. Then came Coney Island's targeted searches/arrests on Sunday, followed by Lincoln Center on Tuesday. Three bouts of bad in four days – and Monday I'd stayed home.

I got up, and damn! my knee. Not particularly big, the gouge was deep enough. Fluids out, fluids in, I retreated back to bed. Soldiers littered the streets, snoops were everywhere, the Data Minders remained amorphous, their capabilities veiled, and on increasingly rare occasions, HeadMan hurled odd, stunted bolts from on high. And, no longer content with their dogs molesting you on the train, the cops were going nuts with the searches. Too damn bad I couldn't fall back asleep, more sleep shortening another stifling day before I could thankfully strike it from my allotment.

I deserved a snooze. Monday and Tuesday had been pretty frantic churning out a two-day article for a (very) eventual two-hundred bucks on the mass disinterment, cremation and co-mingled re-burial of many hundreds of skeletons to clear land for the New Jersey Devils hockey arena in Newark several years back. The dead, including forty-seven veterans of the American Revolution, were accorded little of the ceremony or – my article argued – respect normally accompanying the disposition of human remains.

Given the skeletons' surprise discovery and overwhelming number, haste decreed they end up as co-mingled ashes, an outrage driven by the time-value of the $310-million (in pre-Plunge dollars) that particular hockey palace cost. The indignity heaped upon them contrasts poorly with the fate of 3,500 human remains found in a potter's field during construction of a nearby N.J. Turnpike exit in Secaucus. Those folks – "the poor, the insane and criminals" a plaque read – were afforded the costly and time-consuming dignity of individual reburial that was denied Newark's high and mighty.

The cemetery's owners, Newark's First Presbyterian Church, which dates to the theocratic founding of Newark in 1666 and whose pastors helped found both Princeton and Yale, were adding insult to injury. They had originally paved over a big section of their cemetery for a 400-space parking lot in the 1950s. They removed a number of bodies then and perhaps considered the issue resolved. But laying asphalt for a parking lot and digging an arena's deep foundation are endeavors of a different stripe. When the backhoes started digging, hundreds and hundreds of skeletons were discovered. And so a small army of archaeologists was eventually deployed, working seven-day weeks and sworn to secrecy. As it was, each body was dug up following proper archaeological procedure before being shipped to the ovens.

As Prime Minister William Gladstone observed, "Show me the manner in which a nation cares for its dead, and I will measure with mathematical exactness the tender mercies of its people, their loyalty to high ideals, and their regard for the laws of the land." Or, as one of the participants I interviewed told me somewhat less grandly, "These people were people at one point in their lives."

Staring out my one window and pondering another hopefully two-day article, the radio caught my ear. "And the news overnight from the Central Front, Bob?"

"There is no Affiliation news from that particular Sands, Phil. Well, actually just this: Endorsed Proscription News has learned of a previously unseen combination of T-Fiends – comprised of ethnic groups traditionally hostile to each other – confronting Affiliation Heroes on the main road just a quarter-mile south of the Exclusion Zone. Surrounded, our Boots tried heroically to – "

"Bob, I think EPN has made it clear what's suited for the breakfast hour. In other news, Jacquine stated that her missing dress – "

Yikes! I silenced the claptrap to carve some space to think. Snarling cretins haunting my dreams, I had to do something. Something more than fiddling and piddling, clicking and calling, searching for a story idea not already done to death till a couple of tallboys lubricated the evening's baseball unaccountably on real TV. And thus another day done, praise be.

Heck, like all but a few in a nation unspooling a string of wars, I'd leaned on a soldier whose name I didn't know. Then I fled that LIRR car, taking up arms with the throngs fighting over the biggest piece of crumb cake. And the night before, I'd watched a proud woman get abused and her husband brutalized, though not a blessed thing I could've done for Jennifer and Dexter but offer up my own back for a pounding too.

Had I slip-slid my way into Auden's vast kennel "where the dogs go on with their doggy life"? Nicki pulling the plug on the two of us, had I joined the ranks clutching at booze, sugar, pills, Enhancements, digital pacifiers, borrowed money or oversized/miniaturized screens – whatever combo it took to tolerate outrage with a shrug?

Outrageous: "going beyond all standards of what is right or decent." Your license plate Data-enshrined just for driving into Manhattan – no problem. Snatching folks off the sidewalk? Wasn't happening to anyone you knew, except for maybe that dude down the hall with the stringy hair who always wore boots and those baggy, disgusting shorts. He fell off the ferry, or a woozle got him, no one knew. Acquitted but still imprisoned? What the times demanded. Arrested, or maybe just foolish enough to travel abroad – cough up your micro-zap for *copying*. Write the wrong letter to the editor and join the millions (tens of thousands more each month) on the proctological flying list. Encounter a cop in almost any circumstance, whoof! there went your DNA and other biometrics into their files, lurking for when they needed to make a match.

Sure, you can show up at some caged, 'free-speech' zone and march in all the damn circles you want under a bridge at the edge of town, hemmed in by hundreds in helmets glad of the easy OT. Just make sure to smile for their biometric cameras. Ignored by every TV station in town, such *permitted* (in both senses), official marching was a wisp in the willows an hour after completion. The press, from the little scratch-and-claw news sites my byline graced on up, was also showered with malign neglect. HeadMan found it easier to ignore its pillowy output than to shut down the dwarfed, dispirited and depoliticized fourth estate, especially since the new Reg that outlawed anonymous content. Enforcement was somewhat slipshod on the more self-infatuated margins of the Net. But any text and certainly any whole-vid that resembled 'news' demanded a supposedly real name up top.

I probably lacked the guts for Dexter's direct refusal. Still, cops indulging a whim to rifle through your stuff cried out for a stick in the spokes. That might be something I could manage. Time to stop huddling behind the wall with the other mice bemoaning the existence of cats. A fool's errand, probably, a dumb, quixotic line in the sand in a fearful nation groped by strangers. Laden with false bravado and enslaving labor-saving devices (how did they ever build the Empire State Building in just over a year without them?) knuckles rapped, without compass, glad to be permitted a magazine on board, we inched ahead bowed and barefoot.

Reproductively stymied, my lonely struggle against undue semen buildup proceeding entirely unaided, who better to check the Hammer raining down on short and tall alike? Anyone call for a fool?

****

Unsurprisingly, it was Police Commissioner Walk-on-Water Ted who issued the edict that the cops could randomly search anyone who dared venture onto public transportation. His dictate applied, apparently, to any cop in any jurisdiction within range of his well-broadcast voice, never mind that their ostensible civilian overseers in their little berg didn't answer to Ted. He pronounced and everyone fell in line.

Ted's astonishing admission that he'd wanted to do this for years and had just been waiting for the right moment got no play beyond a single story deep in the paper. This one guy, however square-jawed, rectitudinous and all that piffle he might be, burned the aged parchment in full view of the cameras, the mayor shouting muffled encouragement from his locked trunk. Where were the screaming headlines, *Top Cop Proclaims: Leave Your Rights at Home*?

Instead, cable news, shout radio and the macro-transmitters all buffaloed us along for the ride. Cause there was *chatter* out there, chatter galore – shake it on your cereal for regularity. Rather than nipping at anyone's heels, the media preferred social engineering like the Mercedes radio ad – no joke – that "Homeland Security" will immediately taze any dumb bunny who raises the slightest objection to them looking in his car's trunk. A twofer: model acquiescence to getting searched and normalize tazers as punishment for noncompliance.

The apparent indifference was fueled in part by the notion that you could feel free to refuse a search and turn on your heel – forget getting to work on time, the next station ten blocks away. Of course that threw any results-based rationale out the window, anyone with ill intent just going to another station. Also, what was the point of doing bags unless they actually frisked the tens of thousands of subway-riding homies of any race in clothes four sizes too big? Mere security theater to cow folks into accepting the next outrage on tap. Not for nothing had the civ-lib trampling Brits rejected the scheme as useless.

The cops always looked a little chagrined searching citizens. They preferred to amuse themselves racing around the city in caravans of fifty, lights flashing and sirens blaring, supposedly causing nearby Bad Guys to melt, overawed, onto the sidewalk, but merely proving that's the only way to cut through Manhattan traffic. (*Bad Guy*: like T, a term justifying any excess, reminiscent of a little kid's cry chasing playmates around the backyard, his finger a pistol.)

Thus did the searches blossom on any vehicle that took a ticket, all on some uber-cop's decree. And then they spread nationwide, including Boston, Los Angeles and DC. Not from any particular threat, the LA cops actually said, but just to keep pace with New York, all that T money at stake. On the PATH trains (the subways from Manhattan to New Jersey) regular announcements "strongly encouraged" passengers not to carry anything they couldn't fit in their pockets. Or they'd face a search.

And I'd heard of not a single teeny-tiny arrest over the principle of the thing, no one gripped by sufficient umbrage to risk a Boosting.

So, high time to take a Goddamn stand, block that kick, an army of one, sis boom bah and Fourth Amendment fame. A nice, neat civ-lib arrest if I dared, a Boosting likely – screw it – but hopefully not the pounding Dexter got. A grandiose comparison, sure, but why not sit down at the local Woolworth's lunch counter and demand service? Some old-fashioned, one-man street theater, a bit of agitprop, a *contribution*. You have to draw the line somewhere, otherwise it ain't worth chewing through the leather straps to start your day. Like the Mahatma said, "Whatever you do will be insignificant, but you gotta do something." Or, as somebody put it, "Don't burn the flag, wash it."

Seeing the cops in place, what might happen if I didn't offer my knapsack for the paw-through or flee to another station? Simply refused, started proclaiming loudly about the Constitution and continued towards the turnstile brandishing my Metrocard? Hard to predict the outcome messing with jittery cops who saw obeisance as their due.

Hard, indeed. But bereft, bothered and bedraggled, cast adrift by the Wife and responsible to no one, maybe I plain didn't care. Plain didn't give two shits. Should something, like, *tragic* ensue, the parents would assimilate their grief somehow – buoyed by a healthy dose of I-told-you-so, Pop probably not long after they finished shoveling dirt. And Nicki? Let her feel real bad real long.

Christ, was *that*, that dirt-shoveling solution to all my problems, what lay behind this oh-so-principled plan? Nicki had kicked me out and then immediately joined the flies buzzing round that gilded pile across the East River. (Melt glaciers, melt!) I didn't even know her new address in one of those anthill-stirred-by-a-stick towers in Manhattan's soulless East 80s. Why the secrecy, Nicki? Ain't no stalker. Got a little more self-respect than that.

I'd washed up on the decidedly less gilded opposite bank of that same river in Bumfuckville, Queens, at a crumbling, carved-up old mansion that stank of frying onions. Kids from the projects a block away brought their dogs to crap on the sidewalk out front, none of the rabble of single men from all over the world who occupied the many cells inside caring to echo the crabby old landlord's objections.

I paced the Hovel's kitchen one-and-a-half strides in each direction (hell to pay some day, all those footprints on the wall). Would refusing a search be just another dumb tree falling in the forest on deaf ears, or does he howl most poignantly who howls alone? Shoot, somebody had to do it, write about it, then put his freaking name on top to satisfy the new, no-anonymous publishing Reg. Weren't no spineless politicians or media big-foots objecting.

Chapter Nine

HeadMan

Statement. Yeah, me, cause what did I care? Damn few of them since HeadMan's ascendency. The last presidential election had featured the usual prolonged and excessive vitriol – only more. Much, much more given all the unleashed 'citizens.' Benefiting from a splintered opposition (the delusional versus the merely rapacious), the incumbent squeaked out a narrow victory. But, though he'd already served four years, three weeks after the election a lower federal court declared him "illegitimate."

The capper: upholding empty principle all the way to the grave, the two self-righteous mooncalves he'd appointed to the Supreme Court in his first term recused themselves when it hit their desks, something inconceivable to the other side's judges. So, in an entirely unsurprising four-to-three verdict, the president's 'illegitimacy' – and therefore his running mate's as well – was upheld. He slunk away as, shockingly, did the vice president, amidst fervid whispers of threat and inducement.

Then the real shocker: though he'd run a racist, fire-in-the-belly campaign, the challenger refused to serve under such tainted circumstances. Was he plain bought off, or had Gov. Mel Marlmon been threatened with exposure? Were there indeed some very dicey old whole-vids lurking about of him … *performing*? Nonsense. Marlmon asserted he just had too much respect for the country to be rammed into office in such partisan judicial fashion. By his side's judges. Astoundingly, he made that weak cheese stick. Despite the uproar, despite the growing tumult in the streets, neither plea nor threat could force him to stand on the Capitol steps and solemnly swear.

So…. Third in line to the presidency, the Speaker of the House was a back-bench thug whose election to that august office following the previous Speaker's sudden demise was the year's prior political shock. His elevation to the Speakership apparently had something to do with a zealous, eschatological claque rumored to be sweeping Capitol Hill. Something about *constructing* the proper catalyst to usher in End Times.

In any event, after a confused and sporadically violent interregnum following Gov. Marlmon's refusal – the whole country up in arms except, mystifyingly, the two parties' two standard-bearers with greatest claim to the presidency – the buffoonish Speaker was invested as a caretaker of sorts. The Plunge still plummeting, many millions of folks were distracted by the little matter of getting food in their kids' bellies. Besides, though nary a Brooks-Brothers 'rioter' in sight, it wasn't much more of a coup than the last one.

Half-pregnant politesse, the Speaker wasn't immediately given the title of president, so his street-name, HeadMan, stuck – reinforced by his own loopy, third-person usage pounding the podium. Giddy after years of deserved obscurity in the House, the snarling bastard probably even liked the HeadFuck it soon morphed to in many (most?) circles.

Soon the Disruption broke out – was engineered, *happened*, at any rate – and HeadMan revealed our future. The economy Plunging for years by then, everything crabbed and cramped, the first food riot broke out in Chevy Chase, Maryland, of all places, its hazy spark much debated. The governor of Virginia in his pocket, HeadMan precipitously deployed the Virginia National Guard across state lines against the vocal opposition of the governor of Maryland. A youngish distance swimmer, Maryland's governor suffered a bizarre 'stroke' at a raucous states' rights rally. Railing at the podium against troops crossing state borders unbidden, parts of him crumpled and parts went ramrod stiff as he struggled to denounce HeadMan with only half his face working. For twenty months he lay in a coma doctors couldn't explain before his wife finally won the right to pull the plug.

All the instantly viral whole-vids of folks getting run over or shot while Disrupting led to the removal of whole-vid devices from private hands. Things fracturing badly as the Disruption gained steam, that brave, emulating fool in Pittsburgh should've known an *American* tank wouldn't stop. The remarkably *non*-spontaneous smashing of supermarket windows spread to a dozen states in ever hazier fashion. (Bricks for the purpose trucked in on pallets were discovered in Hartford and Cincinnati). And increasingly lethal Guardsmen ranged far from their home states.

Sure there were voices in the wilderness – many at first. But the 'illegitimate' incumbent's party had already SOP-folded like a cardboard suitcase. Most Americans were struck dumb in fear and amazement at pictures of tanks ringing the Capitol building and rolling through Times Square. Sixteen soldiers, 357 cops and 11,912 civilians, an unknown number of whom were just caught in the cross-fire, lost their lives the fearsome ten days it took the clamp-down to fully clamp down. After two scary forays to Manhattan to sidle wide-eyed along the edge of protest, following the bloody Battle of 45th Street, Nicki and I joined the majority in hiding under our bed.

Some media reported courageously during the Disruption's worst days, but the loudest and slickest outlets pretty quickly went along for the ride once it became clear where things were headed. And why not, HeadFuck not messing with *them*. Blaring from every screen, he was initially hard to escape. Unlike most politicians, he didn't mind being hated – seemed to relish it, actually – which really freed his hand. But it went to his shaved head and, proving too hot for TV, he was eventually dialed way back. He still speechified on occasion, but like some of his predecessors, only in strictly managed, limited doses. No more thrusting that giant turtle head at roaring crowds. Of late, he'd just *appear*, seated stiffly behind his Oval Office desk or, once in a great while, behind a freakishly large podium addressing a select military or defense company audience in stilted fashion. No rope line handshakes, the audience was always ushered out first beneath his vacant gaze.

More and more of the government's authority seemed to rest on HeadMan's personal motto: *Bold. Extolled. Impregnable!* Usually shortened to a muttered B.E.I. – each letter enunciated – it became a conversational touchstone, at least for the burgeoning numbers professionally or emotionally nourished by T real or imagined.

Yup, HeadFucked. All the forms and much of the rhetoric, the empty observances and staunch words, the enabling courts, impotent press and institutional shells – heck, government's grand marble buildings and the Easter Bunny – all remained in place. Some dereliction or abuse would occasionally rear its head, soon to fade from view; revealed again, it would fade anew. Peering through a telescope from Mars, much would look the same. The simulacra remained in place. There was nothing so head-scratchingly extreme as – and this an admittedly minor Nazi atrocity – the Nazis' 1936 ban on art criticism, Goebbels having mistakenly determined that the evil Jewish press was pumping degenerate modern art to enrich Jewish gallery owners. Still, with elections bought and sold in newly naked fashion, the centuries-old Great Experiment fizzled out, and the Hammer commenced to clubbing. To think that a great many Americans initially embraced HeadMan as a needed strong hand.

****

Whether HeadMan personally orchestrated the Data or just acquiesced to the Data Minders' brute, surveillant inevitability was kicked around some back when such was still discussed.

Americans' heads-down response to this whole new infringement helped speed our political demobilization as a furtive populace – cut-throat conservatives and laptop liberals alike – largely disassociated itself from much beyond gossip and scandal. Tough enough steering the wolf to someone else's door, just recite: Minders Turn Elsewhere! as we learned to do, and time for a snack and a screen. Had the latest Beach Blanket Smackdown streamed yet?

The Data assigned all Americans to one of four inelegantly named Levels. Those few at the top, in the Mirror, suffered the most intense scrutiny. Next came RoundUp. The third Level had the ham-handed name of Middling Severity. And the largely ignored mass at the bottom comprised the Null Set. The middle two Levels – RoundUp and Middling Severity – were further sliced into eleven Tiers. Neither the sparsely populated Mirror at the top nor the vast Null Set at the bottom were split into Tiers. Finally, getting kicked up a Tier for some transgression was referred to as a Boosting; scrutiny was said to increase incrementally as you rose from Tier to Tier.

So, from the top: the Mirror, RoundUp (11 Tiers), Middling Severity (11 Tiers), and the Null Set.

The taxonomy, clunky names and all, soon became second nature. Late of an evening in a bar, you might silently wonder your new friend's Tier, all the flirting leading you to assume she was in Middling Severity like you and everyone you knew. Poor form to ask too quick, like asking about HIV, it was best done delicately. Also like HIV status, by no means did everyone know.

In descending order: the Mirror, RoundUp (11 Tiers), Middling Severity (11 Tiers), and the Null Set.

The highest Level was called the Mirror because basically any endeavor was mirrored in the Data *in real time*. Rather than a passive recording mechanism, someone with eyeballs – a human – was into your shit. The Mirror was almost a status crime in and of itself: you were headed for trouble, it just remained to be seen for what. Not that anyone knew anyone in the Mirror.

The Mirror's intense, present-tense shadowing of every jot and tickle (electronic, commercial, romantic or political) was reserved for roughly half-a-million Americans. That was the estimate you'd find online – should you dare a search for such problematical information. None but the adept knew for certain, and no one knew any of them to ask. Tiers weren't necessary in the Mirror, for how fine could you slice a walking colonoscopy?

The second Level, RoundUp, captured some five percent of us, or 17 million Americans, in its eleven Tiers; the lower the Tier, the less intrusion. Though with far less intensity than in the Mirror, actual human beings also poured over RoundUps' Data in real time. (For the 95 percent of us below the top two Levels, the surveillance was almost entirely automated.)

Which of the eleven Tiers RoundUps found themselves in determined how global and draconian the real-time human monitoring of their phone and Net use, their micro-zapping and e-mail, their health care, love lives, friendships, consumer purchases, vices, charitable contributions, travel and porn. At RoundUp's bottom, some semblance of a normal life was thought possible.

Also eleven Tiers, Middling Severity was a stupendous maw of automated Data unseen by human eye unless the subject did something dumb. There was always the hope that this third Level was just a big, impenetrable jumble of 120-million people. Self-censorship became a way of life for this thirty-five percent of the country, people instinctively knowing what malodorous phrases shouldn't slip from fingers or lip. It was like back when the simple term, *liar*, a powerful judgment on any playground, became verboten in regard to our leaders.

The fourth Level, the vast Null Set, anchored the bottom. The Minders hadn't bothered to slice this apolitical sixty-odd percent of us into Tiers. No need to mess with subsets for the over 200-million who did the cleaning, the picking and packing, the heaving and hoeing, the post-Plunge begging and staring and – along with all the foreign Boots seeking Homelander status – the fighting and dying. The roofers, the loafers, the shop-girls and the clerks, the security guards that covered the land like dandelions, the pothole fillers and the bus drivers, all had to throw a bomb (of some sort) to attract real notice.

Of course, the Data did track the Nulls with a basic, passively collected file: over the course of time it would presumably come to note that he or she lived here, worked there, stole that content online, moved, married her or him, had that one DWI along with the two kids, one foreclosure and three bouts of illness. Divorced him or her, had this, that and the other micro-zap, messed up on his or her taxes those two years, moved and remarried and then moved again. The Data's automatic overlay of a Null's passage through life would accumulate as the years fell one upon another.

But otherwise the Minders weren't that interested in the back-bowed souls who propped things up for the rest of us. By definition, the Nulls didn't participate much in politics, or they'd be Middling Severity or higher. They typically needed three or more jobs per couple – and damn lucky to get 'em – to survive. They'd totter home at an odd hour from some grueling job and collapse in front of a screen, hoping the kids were asleep or, better yet, out playing in traffic.

Finally, speaking of kids, came the Newbies, sort of a place-holder Level for children under ten, also with no Tiers as far as anyone knew. It got them registered in the Data and helped grout their minds right. Kids would get properly assigned once they started generating their own Data, especially once the ongoing mental health tests to mandate appropriate pharmaceutical correction kicked in in fourth grade.

Since the bleak day HeadMan announced the Data, no one actually knew where it was 'located,' who ran it, the untold scores of billions it cost, or how many multitudes toiled away in its bowels. Forget that no one knew anyone who had ever met a Minder, no one had encountered anyone who even emptied their trash. The Data was just there, like gravity to someone walking atop a cliff.

But one thing was firmly established, one of Congress's last gasps before it turned fully Potemkin. In its third and last concrete response to one of HeadMan's state-security edicts, Congress required the Minders to make formal notification, in person, of Elevation (as it was called) from the Null Set to Middling Severity, from MS to RoundUp, and from there to the Mirror. You wouldn't hear of getting Boosted up a Tier. But get kicked up a Level – that is, suffer an Elevation – and the Minders had to tell you face-to-face the very next day, Christmas included. The rise from Middling Severity on up to RoundUp (from passive digital harvest to peeled, human eyeballs) was the crucial step to be avoided by the ninety-five percent of us below RoundUp.

The stark, single-sheet Elevation notice was hand-delivered in a pale blue envelope, the Minders employing their own squads – armed, silent, implacable. The operative phrase: Getting a Blue. Traveling in teams of three, the standard-issue goons didn't argue or explain. Everything about the Data was arbitrary and capricious. No transparency, no recourse. They just hammered it to your forehead with a rusty nail, leaving you to wonder which of your many sins theoretically ended life as you knew it. *Theoretically.*

Not that I knew anyone who'd gotten a Blue. My Middling Severity tier indicating a margin for error horribly thin, could I head out with a backpack to refuse a search and hope to maintain my ignorance?

****

Amazing really, looking back over HeadFuck's three years so far, that the Data's inner architecture had been exposed at all. But the zipper wasn't quite to its chin in the Data's earliest days, Congress still with a breath of life back then. Most of what we know slipped out at an aborted hearing convened by Rep. Webb Hendon (I-OR), the rogue chairman of the since defunct Subcommittee Overseeing Scrutiny. (Disgusted by HeadMan's rise from his party's ranks, Hendon had turned Independent but retained his chairmanship of this particular subcommittee since no one else had the guts for the job.)

Doing nothing with the high-flown evasions that passed for answers, Congress gave up on anything but show hearings. What was the point, the executive so … unitary? What's more, an early HeadMan decree abolished congressional subpoenas, so *invited* witnesses rarely appeared. Before they retired or were otherwise ushered off-stage – damn those unreliable little campaign jets – a few stubborn subcommittee chairmen would invite twenty or more officials, delving deep into the bureaucracy in the hope that a stout-hearted, mid-level somebody might appear to spill some beans.

A sore thumb who wielded his backwater subcommittee with aplomb, the wily Webb Hendon managed to insert his swollen digit in several deserving eyes before he died. The nine subcommittees that theoretically authorized and funded Homefront T initiatives held not a single hearing on the Data (or much of anything else) during those whirlwind days of HeadMan's first efflorescence. Hendon's the only hearing, he was also the only member of his subcommittee with the gumption to sit and hear the sole witness who showed of the twenty-eight he invited.

And so the brave, doomed Data private-sector subcontractor spilled, making a big mess all over Hendon's hearing as the chairman intended. Testifying behind a screen, he emptied one can of beans. Then his distorted voice indicated he was opening his second can just as an unseen but nonetheless imminent tornado interrupted the proceedings. Previously uncommon in Washington, vague but none-theless treacherous tornadoes often forced the Sergeant at Arms, that newly engorged *manager* of democracy, to interrupt the rare hearing of substance. The weather so unsettled, any but ceremonial hearings soon faded away.

This a Friday, Hendon doggedly scheduled an immediate resumption for Monday. But fate deemed otherwise as he, his wife and his mystery witness all died in a horrific fireball of a wreck that night following a late supper at an obscure cafe way up in Northeast DC. Hendon was safeguarding his own witness for the weekend, for he had no staff he trusted beyond the one old lady who, having nothing else to live for, declared she didn't give a hoot about the threats that'd stampeded everyone else. Officially the subcommittee's librarian, the chairman couldn't even give Edith Chestnut a raise when she became his strong right hand.

Though Hendon had been avowedly sober for years, an empty pint bottle of Everclear – pure rocket fuel – was found in his car. As if any driver wouldn't toss such an incriminating empty. It and a blood alcohol level 4.6 times the legal limit 'proved' he'd marked the day's partial triumph falling far too far off the wagon at dinner. The staunch librarian insisted at her one press conference that Hendon was sober dropping her off at her apartment before the short drive to his Maryland home. The foursome's only member to survive the night, Mrs. Chestnut vanished three days later. Said by HeadMan's tut-tutting henchmen to have fled for absolutely no reason, she was assumed to be as cold and stiff as the others.

She was roundly contradicted by one of the restaurant's waiters (soon become assistant catering manager at a certain lofty think tank) who said he encountered a very jovial Hendon in the john who offered him a belt of some weird clear liquor that knocked him on his ass.

The accounts of the affair focused on Hendon's alleged boozing. Little was said of the hearing's witness beyond that he carried no ID, his facial markers had been destroyed beyond reading in the fiery crash and – common among security MoFos – his fingerprints had been chemically erased years before. His charred remains were buried in Oregon besides the crusading Congressman and his wife, their mourners serving for his.

And thus the Subcommittee Overseeing Scrutiny died also, neither Tweedledum nor Tweedledee willing to don Hendon's fatally independent mantle. Digging and scratching on some short-lived, pirate Dutch server, folks willing to brave the search online were *sometimes* able to locate the testimony of Hendon's final witness, by far our best description of the workings of the Data. Should a (small) glass of Everclear ever accost me, I'll raise it high for the courageous subcontractor, old-lady librarian, a wife doomed by loyalty and the bull-headed subcommittee chairman.

****

For most Americans, their progress up the Data's perilous ladder was a question that loomed unanswered. In polite society, it was thought best to avoid Middling Severity Tiers One and Two. Rather than resting thus too close to the déclassé Null Set, better to be an unobjectionable MS Three or Four, though some thought MS Three lacked ambition.

Both Nicki and I learned our Tiers when her sniggling little ad agency somehow won a huge Army 'minority' recruitment account. The home team faring so poorly, the prior agency had tripped badly over the hurdles to rustling up black and brown Boots. Fornix & Foyst's win pushed Nicki, who'd been churning it out to sell fake cheese and the like, into the realm of T-tinged commerce. And that was fairly astounding, her own boots having long joined mine on the ground at many an anti-war Demo before those faded and died.

Winning his first T account, F&F's owner, Ernesto Padwick, was thus informed of his employees and their spouses' Data status, and he was required to disseminate this information himself in a personal 'counseling' session. Damn embarrassing, said the office wags, Ernesto trying to keep his mail clerks straight.

Like all our ilk, Nicki and I had assumed we were Middling Severity. She used to worry about my getting Boosted when I occasionally published something with teeth, then stopped. Was she already halfway out the door, and so didn't care? It turned out our Tiers weren't close and, yes, that dangerous disparity didn't help. All the coupling since Adam and Eve, all the accommodation forged between Man and Woman, and suddenly a whole new thing to mesh. As the Chinese proverb does *not* have it: May you find a woman whose Tier fits. Nicki landed in coveted Middling Severity Four and, like most at that relatively benign level of surveillance, could hope to stay there unless some harsh light shone upon her. I perched uncomfortably high on MS Nine, only two thin Tiers below Roundup.

Had Nicki joined me up on MS Nine, Padwick told her she'd have been fired on the spot despite the fact that her bizarre verbal contrivances on his behalf helped lead a desperate Pentagon to F&F in the first place. As it was, he made cold inquiry about the health of her marriage.

Challenging the cops' train searches would probably Boost me on up to Middling Severity Ten. Hell, insulting, really, that all my rabble-rousing articles hadn't already landed me in RoundUp. Insulting that all my pissing up thin, obscure ropes left me still shy of the 95th percentile of the nation's dissidents.

The Data Minders be damned, this citizen retained the right to lay siege and catapult a suppurating, dead cow over the wall. Forget strategizing with some earnest, civ-lib legal beagles (bless 'em) round a battered table littered with mis-matched coffee cups. Forget lining up behind a rumpled know-it-all at the conclusion of some righteous panel for the question period's open mic. This galoot prowled alone, even if in that forest full of trees that fell with no noise.

You supposedly had to work it to hit RoundUp. RoundUp involved human monitoring and therefore cost HeadFuck money. I could hope my useless little one-man Demo wouldn't Elevate me there. Not, post-Nick, that I gave much of a flying fuck. And, you come right down to it, maybe that was why contumacy fell to me.

Chapter Ten

Chilean Cassandra

I sat and scratched and pictured Dexter getting slammed. Finally I hacked a path to a decision on challenging the searches: let someone else deal my hand. Wednesday it was, and if there was no news about Sarge and Statie throwing down, I'd count myself in the clear on that and time to head to Manhattan (though nowhere near Lincoln Center) for my next bout of trouble. If I found no news, make some my own damn self.

And … and … nothing I could find about any fight on the LIRR. The prior Saturday's hysteria was stillborn. What, the sergeant major and the trooper picked themselves up, agreed it had been one doozy of a dustup and went their separate ways into the night? Capping a career of artful fiction, Boss Conductor wrote a report that made it all melt away? And the passengers were all too embarrassed as Americans – no, as Long Islanders – by this wrinkle in the fabric of their social comity to make a fuss?

Maybe the overarching sway of HeadFuck's Army led the LIRR and even the State Police to hush it all up. Or maybe a cop and a soldier sparking a minor race riot on a train was just so much dog-bites-man during our induced national nervous breakdown. Forget Statie. He was laid up in a hospital somewhere, his neck in a brace, an IV in his arm, a balloon on his willie and absolutely no memory of what landed him there. Forget living in fear.

Hell, turn the page, not that I was justified in closing the book on Statie, his and my pages still all gummed up who knew how.

Nor could I find a word about any incident at Lincoln Center. And why, amidst all the fearful whispering, should there be official notice of something as pedestrian as a man getting slammed and his wife groped, two fool troublemakers in a city of millions? Happened all the time, probably. So, another of the quirky little participant/observer stories I'd chased of late. Why not me, all my milk gone sour.

Despite my aching chest, I needed something large enough to attract the cops' attention to prompt my high-minded hissy fit. Therefore, my brand new, decades-old, bona fide East German Army backpack. Hot and murky on this the forty-seventh day of August, I debated stuffing the green canvas pack with wadded-up newspaper so it would be light but not flaccid. (Ah, and weren't them the days!) Nah. Books were the obvious choice, and not no Dick and Jane. Subtlety, after all, wasn't the key the MoFos sang in.

I hunted down the right few manifestos from boxes untouched since my move to the Hovel. Why bother unpacking, not knowing how much longer my scrambling would generate the scratch for even the Hovel. Anyway, good old Tom Paine; *The Gulag Archipelago*; *1984* (duh!); Upton Sinclair's *It Can't Happen Here*; Roth's Lindberg as a Nazi; *Fahrenheit 451*; Madeleine L'Engle's marvelous fable about fighting group-think, *A Wrinkle in Time*; *Darkness at Noon, Catch-22* and *The Handmaid's Tale*; old-chestnut *Brave New World* and a couple of Philip K. Dick. And, to pound home the point from the flip side, *Mein Kampf*. I paused a moment before tossing in this last, but weighing it in combination with all the others, the hell with anyone who didn't get the point.

HeadMan banning whole-vids expressly to keep folks from immortalizing the cops' antics, a simple open notebook would attract their attention. And then just freaking approach them with both hands well away from my body and the right puppy-dog ingratiation in a voice leavened by jock jocularity. Oh, and bow before them with frequent use of the word, *Officer*. The NYPDs typically professional enough to offer everyone (pale) a way out, they weren't gonna shoot me at some mobbed Midtown location. Not with me getting all high and mighty on them, thrusting out my wrists for the cuffs.

****

I slogged my way to the train through a mile (how else could I afford the Hovel?) of the sweltering gray gauze we called air, on the verge of a major political statement. Heck, talk is cheap: about to launch a Goddamn army of fellow refusniks. The article couldn't focus too too much on the swell ballsiness of it all before my clarion call for throngs to follow suit. And since I'd packed a couple of three-slice PBJs for my big field trip to the City, I could blow the nine bucks in my pocket any way I liked.

I'd hit Times Square, Grand Central, 34th Street's Herald Square and then the belly of the beast, Penn Station, home to the LIRR, Amtrak, a slew of Jersey trains beyond any sane person's care or understanding, a bunch of subways and more searches than any-where else. Proud of my chic, new backpack, one of my few recent luxury items, I risked a ticket propping it on the seat next to me, the floor sticky with goo. The crowd from the 7 train piled on at Queensboro Plaza, and a trim, well-dressed, older woman carrying a thick hardback planted herself in front of my pack, and I reluctantly plopped it in the *goop* (technically, not goo). Up in years, she sported thick, jet-black hair and chunky-chic glasses resting on an alarmingly long, elegant nose. Not pretty, per se, but you sure grabbed a second look. She wore a vintage pale blue dress with bright, multicolored threads shot all through and stockings! – the only pair on six trains in the heat.

She settled herself, opened her book, but turned to me. "I'm glad the satchel is yours, and I wasn't forced to delay any number of trains contacting a policeman. There's one of the posters there." She pointed to one reading, *Be Embarrassed or Be Dead.* "According to my companion, a man of some experience, yours is just the sort of bag – large and new in appearance – that is of particular concern." She spoke with a cultured, old-world precision, her Spanish accent strong.

"No, it's mine. But that's interesting: new, like it was bought for something specific."

"What would you do, I wonder, if you found yourself sitting next to such a pack accompanied by such a man? Judging by your looks, not that looks alone signify, perhaps one of the 'lone wolfs' the news-readers like to talk about?"

I figured street-hexer me could orchestrate this little escapade, but I hadn't even made it out of Queens. Folks were awfully twitchy – and why not with the T Index given along with the radio's traffic and weather. So helpful in deciding whether to grab your potassium iodide, the numerical scale would shoot alarmingly from 88 up to 92 and then drop reassuringly to 86 two days later. 100 indicating a current attack, the last time it fell below 85 was HeadMan's birthday. It hit 95 a month back, following the hijacking in Abu Dhabi of a sheik's jet carrying two prize stallions bound for Kentucky – like that had anything to do with riding the subway. Yup, cower and marvel and thank our Wisers and Betters when the number magically declines, thank the gods when the volcano doesn't blow. But best throw another virgin on the fire just in case.

"Oh, come on, lady, you're making awfully free with some pretty inflammatory talk. I know they're discussing it, but they haven't outlawed packages yet. Besides, look, it's just books. Here – books." I flipped the flap. "I'm returning them to a friend so I can borrow some more."

"A generous friend, a regular Carnegie of books. Such friends, real or pretend, are not to be sneezed at."

That her dismissal, she turned to her own book. "OK. There is one thing, though. These really are my books. I just picked them out, these particular titles, Tom Paine and all, to make a statement."

"Of course they are your books. No person with any sense returns a dozen books at once, carrying a bag like that in heat such as today's. So, teach me: what 'statement' do you make transporting books in a closed satchel?"

What was the harm in telling her, maybe the first in my throng? She certainly was no MoFo – I didn't think. "Well, I'm actually doing a little test, or more of a civil-liberties type exercise, finding where the cops are doing their stupid subway searches and hoping they'll pick me. Then I'm gonna just say no and see what happens. See what the cops do. Because someone's gotta make – "

"Are you sure you have thought this through, or do you just not care? Maybe you think this is all a type of game – another American expecting flowers at his feet no matter his actions. Despite my years here, the sincerity of American ignorance never fails to impress. Do you not read your own newspapers or have any sense of HeadFuck's America?"

Head*Fuck*, OK. "What do you mean, 'thought this through?' The worst they can do is arrest me, right? And as for the news, isn't it mostly pretty darn sanitized? I get the real deal online some weird little places."

"Certainly on the most important avenue, television, despite the hundreds of stations, one is hard-pressed to know this is a country sunk in war. But I am talking about developments here in Manhattan." She paused as the train brown-out slogged through the tunnel under the East River, a stretch of time between stops. "You say you do not fear arrest. If true, you have led an inconsequential life. But then that is the culture in your country: banality mixed with aggression."

"What?"

"Not a single policeman is happy conducting these searches, exposed behind their worthless tables. Why not just detonate there, a man in uniform always the richer target? Plus they have no defense against the youth with their silly loose clothing that hides everything. All this they know but do not say, and they are tense. At least you benefit from being white and clean shaven, not brown with a beard. With those glasses, your longish hair – why do you not grow up? – and a face relatively unlined, you have something of the over-ripe graduate student about you. This may work in your favor."

"My hair isn't so long anymore. I just got it cut – well, cut it myself, it's so damn hot."

"Listen, please! Now, if you are going to make a speech at the police, which I do *not* recommend, think more of your body language than of what you say. Your political content will mean much to you, but little to them unless they think it might add to your charges given the new HateCrime Reg."

"That HateCrime thing, I need to find out – "

"Please! With that pack – do you not have a smaller one, an *older* one? – if you challenge them as you intend, they will be all eyes, not ears."

"Right. But not *challenging*. A principled refusal on the searches is all. Plus I have to make a declaration so it means something. And the books I have, let me show you."

"I can imagine what books: *1984* et cetera, given Americans' tendency for the obvious. Personally, I would carry Zamyatin's *We*. Though it is good that Mr. Paine is again receiving some small portion of the attention he deserves. But I'm getting off here, a stop early, because I must say I am not entirely sure if you are simply foolish, or if this is all, what is the word, *artimana* – a ruse. Might it be that you feel compelled to make a confession of sorts, a boast, maybe, to one of your intended victims and are now just waiting until the train is more crowded in Manhattan?"

"Lady, you're talking crazy!"

"Crazy, or blunt, as my age permits. Given where I have come from and what I witnessed there – Chile, if that means anything to you – I banish uncertainty from my life as I am able. So I will indeed get off a stop early."

"Of course I know about Chile. Chile was the straw that broke the camel's back changing my life. You see, one afternoon, three different bankers – "

"I can imagine. Do you think you are the only person who has challenged an unjust regime? Who has taken a stand with far more than the carrying of books?"

She hid her face on her shoulder a moment, then turned back, her eyes glistening. "Nonetheless, I applaud you and hope you get to make your 'statement.' It takes a brave or foolish person, or perhaps just an uncaring one, to make statements in such a country."

"You don't like us much, do you?"

"It is not my preference to be away from what family I have left. Some of my colleagues, people known still in my country, argue differently, but it is not for me to return. My heart would break to walk the streets of Santiago." She indicated a ten-year-old with his father across the car. "Depending on your skill, on luck, on many things – who knows, you may fan a flame to help brighten that boy's way."

"A flame. Yeah, maybe."

"Be aware of your body language, specifically your hands. Trying to get through their day like anyone else, the police are not as sure of themselves as they like to pretend."

The train slowing, I groped for what to say. Thanks, probably, but also that I knew what I was doing for Chrissake.

Her coda was worst of all: "Consider most your mother, if she's alive. Think as a man younger than you, more's the pity, should have thought of his mother. Carrying books – might that have saved my son, I wonder."

And with that she jumped up, darted around some big lunk and out the door.

A dame with a past, that's for sure, if a bit opinionated. Too bad I didn't get the chance to tell my story about Chile, the one that ended my long stint as an informational handmaiden to Wall Street. To think that I got a buck a word and more in *pre*-Plunge dollars churning out oligarchic pap way back when. Reward for producing such dry stuff, sure, but mostly for being on the wrong side of the barricades. After years of misgivings, plus a few good years sneaking *slightly* progressive views into a thoughtful monthly review, I found myself with a steady freelance gig writing on global stock markets.

Never mind that I knew nothing of such, I'd mastered the fairly easy lingo and had a smattering of world politics. More to the point, I knew how to work the phone, top dogs with jeweled collars delighted to lead me by the hand in exchange for a quote. I coughed it up for years back when Nick and I first met until the afternoon that would've doomed me to a scraggily beard if I hadn't quit because I'd be unable to look myself in the mirror to shave. Three different global portfolio managers (not bankers, actually) echoed each other almost to the syllable: "That Pinochet," they blared into my phone admiringly, "perhaps he was a little rough around the edges. But, boy, did he whip that Chilean economy into shape."

If I had any spine at all, I would have hung up on the third one and gone off beating my breast in search of some blind old duffer to usher across the street. Not sure of my conversion, though, I finished the article, for I'd had many a moment over my informational-hand-maiden years recoiling from what I'd massaged into print. In fact, I gave this, what was indeed the last of my many enabling-the-De-spoilers articles, a fine polish.

Chilean Cassandra's words shimmering ominously before me, I shouldered my pack.

Chapter Eleven

Moo!

And got out that Wednesday at the crossroads of the world to find rivers of people but no searches at any of the six entrances to the giant Times Square station. By my rough count, 227 folks entered in five minutes at one entrance west of Seventh Avenue. I figured that made the article's point well enough about sheer numbers overwhelming any search. I grooved a moment to the busker pounding away on the plastic buckets and tin pots that made such fine drums in the booming, hard-surfaced space, and only then saw two cops standing way over to the side, one staring vacantly, one writing in his memo book. I walked over and planted myself fifteen yards away, turning to profile my bulging pack. But they looked right through me.

Strolling over to Grand Central Station further east on 42nd Street, I walked by a presumably huge hole in the ground where, amazingly, a post-Plunge behemoth was rising. Would have liked to play 'sidewalk superintendent' as little boys of all ages and sexes used to do in New York from time immemorial, helping supervise the initial stages of the city's skyscrapers through the holes conveniently cut in the plywood fence. But, as usual, there was nary a chink in this one's armor. Another decades-old pleasure punted, no one knew why.

No NYPDs at either the Sixth or Fifth Avenue subway stations along 42nd Street, I hoped that Grand Central, with all those rich Westchester and Connecticut commuters, wouldn't be naked to the world, the suburban trains having their own Metropolitan Transportation Authority police force. And indeed it wasn't, one small part of Grand Central's huge main hall quite safe, with three cops (one cradling a stubby auto-matic), two dogs and a sergeant standing around chewing the fat or lying chin on paws. My pack and I stood well within sight, planted near the famous circular information booth, watching for ten minutes as a sea of humanity broke around us. But, two cops with their backs to the crowd in the noisy station, none seemed particularly interested in their surroundings. A ways off, a pair of National Guard soldiers stood aloof, actually scanning the crowd.

My ankle and I limped down to the huge subway station at 34th and Sixth, Herald Square. No cops graced that entrance, so I tooled down an underground corridor and hit pay dirt a little after five o'clock. A couple of stairways descending from 32nd Street were roped off, and three NYPDs shuffled people into a cattle chute of the familiar blue wooden police saw horses. Denied their usual quick jostle at the turnstile, a long, sweaty line of New Yorkers disappeared on up to the street at the sole open stair. Down at the business end of the line where I'd popped out of the corridor, the remarkably patient herd passed one or two at a time through the chute and then by a fourth cop, the Decider. About one in five were sent over to place their bag on a table for the blind laying on of hands by two more cops, the rest were supposed to head for the turnstiles.

HeadMan and the vast swath of the populace he'd turned into security MoFos of one sort or another had things locked down so tight, it wasn't like there was much actual *crime* for the police to contend with. So, all in all, a nifty little cop-full-employment scheme. Six cops at the same hundred-grand-plus their Coney Island brethren earned, you include OT and 'fringes' to die for.

Though the Decider kept repeating loud and clear, "Unless I stop you, keep going," many commuters directed to continue their journey still bovined up to have their stuff 'examined.' Knowing darn well they carried no bomb, it somehow reassured to have some cop uselessly rifle their stuff for five seconds. Cops with X-ray fingers, for just patting the outside of the bag allowed the officer to magically divine its contents and declare them safe. A purifying act granting dispensation to the citizen who surrendered her or his rights. An empty exercise all around for a guileless, gullible public quite deliberately frightened. Scared and thus compliant, unquestioning of HeadFuck's many resource wars. *Take him – no her! – not me.* Empty indeed, since anyone could still just turn and walk to any of this *same* station's half-dozen other entrances, all of them unguarded.

A large man loitering with a big, bulging pack in a cramped, harried spot where no one lingers; a guy openly taking notes on the whole operation for crying out loud; then just standing there; then strolling around to observe it from all sides – I must've drunk my invisibility potion at lunch. Begging for attention so I could tell 'em to bugger off, I planted myself within ten yards of the gauntlet's lead cop. But the threat had been declared to the trains. Any accelerated rush of enclosed matter seemed immaterial this side of the turnstiles.

Humping it a lot harder than the MTA cops at Grand Central chatting with their backs to the crowd, none of these NYPDs looked any too thrilled. It wasn't what they'd signed up for, this overly tactile 'stickiness' with an ever-swarming public. It wasn't easy their: 'No, not you, *you*, sir – over to the table. And you, you, and *all* of you keep moving.' Too many sacks of meat incapable of following the simplest instructions. Oh for sitting stuck in traffic in the cocoon of a patrol car, white-cop lite-rock on the FM – cops play the radio like anyone else marooned in traffic – Esposito in the passenger seat blathering on about sports, food, family or, the one constant, precinct politics.

The rush hour crush in full bloom, the trains' screech filling the narrow stairwell from below, the numb line stretched out of sight who knew how far. Was it simple lack of gumption that kept folks from walking to a different entrance, or merely the commuter's comforting habit? *I always enter here and go stand by* that *pole on the platform to ride in the* third *car.* So much for the practiced New Yorker slipping past mothers with lagging children.

If I tried to make a statement here, would anyone notice in such a fractious scene, or even hear me in the shriek of rusty brakes from below? Nothing to see but the endless pas de deux of the Decider steering folks left or right, I wearied of the cops' indifference and left to confirm the other station entrances were unguarded beyond a woman with a cup belting out "Midnight Train to Georgia."

So the far too curious dude with the big pack hanging close for many minutes but no obvious purpose was allowed to leave. Other subway stations, or maybe the mess of tourists queuing for the top of the Empire State Building, were a block away. What, some sort of anti-T triumph if the tourists got exploded rather than the same number of people traveling underground?

＊＊＊＊＊＊＊＊＊＊＊＊＊＊＊

I navigated the long block to Pennsylvania Station to push through the six o'clock madhouse and peer down at the LIRR level from the top of a long escalator. And, yup, there were two MTA cops very occasionally funneling someone over to a table off to the side.

Going the long way around to another way down, bulging-pack-dude then lingered a few yards from cops for the fourth time that afternoon. People dashed or trudged through the chaotic swirl, others met and hugged by the little waiting area, one couple loudly admiring how big a friend's kids had got. My pack and I galumphed around big as life, one of us taking notes, but earned not a nibble from cops focused solely on the relentless swarm off the escalators. Anyone of ill intent could approach them unmolested from the throng coming up behind. As Cassandra said, it'd be a tense cop who allowed himself to think about it.

And lookey-there: every time they sent some eager-beaver over to the table, one cop jotted something down. That meant they were being held to a standard of some kind, their efforts statistically evaluated. Despite the media's steady drum-beat about the *random* nature of the searches – everyone's equal when no one has any rights – I just hoped these cops drowning in a rush-hour Niagara afforded the melanin-deprived our just props in the T Hall of Fame. (Though, following their attacks, white men were invariably described as merely deranged – not as T-Fiends – including the anti-government Texan who crashed his plane into an IRS building.)

Still, reporters need to confirm the obvious. After, perforce, disappearing into the men's room, I approached the two officers with a big chamber-of-commerce smile plastered on, all but wagging my tail.

"Jeeze, you guys are working hard today, huh?"

The cop affirmed that such was their lot. His sergeant edging closer, I got to the point.

"So, uhm, I'm kind of a curious guy, and I've always liked watching how police work. You know, this deal with these searches is really something."

Oops. However aw-shucks amorphous, that cut a bit close to the bone. His whole body stiffened as he glanced at Sarge but said nothing.

"I mean, with all you gotta do here, keeping all these hundreds of people walking by every second safe, it seems like they're dumping a whole extra chore on you guys." Nobody likes the boss, right?

"Sir – you're right. We are busy here. What do you want?"

"Well, I couldn't help but notice that every time you send someone over for a search, you make a little note. So I was just wondering if you were jotting down what type of person you picked. You know, their age or sex or whatever?"

"You're right again. We're keeping statistics on who we choose – on their approximate age, their race, their class, their sex – like that. They give us our targets, and then they add up all the information from all the MTA cops doing this today to see how we're meeting our goals. That way we get a truly random search."

Class? Offering his professionally blank stare, he added, "Anything else?"

"No. Thank you, officer. That sums it up pretty good: a targeted, random search. I appreciate it, and I appreciate the work you do."

"During the Current Continuing Crisis, that's how we keep everyone safe. Now, you get home safe yourself, sir."

He stayed glued on me as I nodded and drifted off, our little exchange – Travis Bickle talking to the Secret Service agent about his gun – immortalized by any number of Penn Station cameras. So much for the PC shibboleth we all bowed before, the oft-repeated contention that the searches were random. Random – like train tracks across the prairie.

On the big LIRR board listing departures, it read at the bottom: "IF YOU SEE SOMETHING, SAY SOMETHING. CALL MTA.PD." Now, a child counting on her fingers might figure that wasn't quite enough numbers. The nearest phone booth confirmed that turning those five letters to numbers yielded the bum-number recording. *Citizens! Remain vigilant, ready to report! Such misdirection is merely a test of your capacity to participate in your own defense.*

Two National Guard soldiers were stationed by the stairs, one with an M-36, the other a sidearm, both vigilantly up against a wall at sort of right angles to each other, doing their best to watch each other's back. Their posture a far remove from the several willfully oblivious cops I'd seen, it meshed with the seriousness of the soldiers at Grand Central.

There were no searches at the Jersey Transit/Amtrak operation one level up, but the portentous Brit-chick train announcer with the Oxbridge upper-crust grated like hell. It was worse than all the TV and radio ads, including amazingly enough one for the Mets' farm team, the *Brooklyn* Cyclones, that featured her honeyed murmurings or those of her even more supercilious boyfriend.

Feeling craven about not joining the half-hour line at the subway search back at Herald Square, I made my way back to the escalator feeding people down to the MTA 'search' at the LIRR level. Unsure how testicular my intent, I stepped off into muddy water. Giving my pack and me a hard stare, the cop I'd interviewed (whether he knew it or not) moved his hand quick to his gun. Leaving it there, he merely shot the slightest of nods as I met his gaze invitingly. Ah, the dreaded experimenter effect.

Falling to entice at Penn, I headed back to Herald Square, thinking it would be less frantic there an hour past rush hour's worst, and I could nail my protest to the cathedral door with good, or at least audible, effect. But the cops had pulled up stakes and, my ankle barking to beat the band humping the damn books, so did I.

Chapter Twelve

The Wife Replies

I lay in a sweaty bed early Thursday trying to convince myself my fumbling the day before was for the best, that it enabled me to mine atmospherics. The few soldiers I'd seen were seemingly more on-point than the cops, for instance. Plus the scrappy New Yorkers at Herald Square submitted as meekly – no, eagerly – as did the generally snazzier Long Islanders a block away. Best, of course, was the decent little nugget that at least one police department, the MTA, organized its searches along demographic lines. For them, random was a lie.

It was all shouting into a can on a string, perhaps, depending on any impending melodrama and the status (speaking loosely) of my eventual publisher. But I couldn't think of a better route to some brief, mild satisfaction than to flee the Hovel for a second day in a row and tell the men with guns I wasn't moving to the back of the bus, que sera what may. Assuming I got a nibble, home to phone a few of the usual, increasingly marginalized (though HeadFuck didn't bother to actually swat the fly), civ-lib types for a quote or three underlining the swell chutzpah – I mean, necessity – of it all. Then write it up on spec like usual and force some news site to take it out of sheer marvelousness.

But first, I needed to write the Wife to declare my serious intent to someone. It'd been a week since I'd e-mailed her (five whole days, but who's counting), so I felt entitled to seize the excuse for contact, even if only via the screen she'd made clear she preferred. Work e-mail was pretty much all she read ... so. I doubted her bosses were snooping on a top-gun creative like Nicki, even with that huge new Army minority-recruitment account. No one in F&F would care that her estranged (at best) husband was showing a little spine with a puny, one-man civ-lib Demo, Boosting be damned.

At least I'd stopped fabricating absurd excuses to call on a Sunday morning, like the bleak embarrassment a scant *four* days after I got tossed when I'd phoned, entire minutes after nine, to oh so sweetly ask if she'd kept all three of our little can openers in the bitter flurry of my leaving. Wobbly from my obligatory post-breakup *Saturday* night, I'd been up for hours already that morning and by nine o'clock really needed that tuna fish omelet – all I had on hand to throw on top of some eggs. There'd been no labeling of cartons, 'Kitchen Stuff,' etc. during my grab-it-and-gone. Just some: "No, no – that's mine, damn it. You never even heard of Savoy Brown before you freaking met me." She hadn't yet filed for divorce and maybe never would if Fortune – Deep Throat, Jr., say – somehow tripped me and beat me to the floor.

So:

Thurs. Mourning

Dear Nicki:

A little something going on that I thought I should tell someone about. Mostly just an excuse to talk with you – my quotidian temptation. And, yeah, I still remember you laughing when I used that word on our first date.

Hope the Big Town's treating you well, though not too damn well. I doubt you've found a fruit/veggie joint as cheap as out here. And I hope Charley at work isn't making you any crazier than usual – and that he doesn't freak if somehow this note to your work address sees the light of day during the, you know, Current P. Crisis. It's just I know you delete scores of personal/home e-mail without a glance, and I want you to make sure this note gets some play on the infinitesimal chance it proves necessary. It's not like either one of us is in RoundUp, thank God, so it'll presumably just go down the Middling Severity Memory Hole a month from now (assuming that's what happens).

Anyhow, I've gotten awfully pissed about this lousy submit-to-a-search regime. I encountered it in spades last Sunday at the Coney Island music blowout we always went to. Looking to get some OT on stupid reefer busts, the cops were going nuts with targeted, not random, searches LEAVING the train. Worse than that money-grubbing was a disturbing incident Saturday, the day before, involving a trumped-up search on the LIRR of all places, me out to visit the Aged Ps.

(Not to mention the pure random police violence I saw Tuesday, two nights ago, at a concert at Lincoln Center. That's got me more pissed than anything, but since it didn't involve searching anyone's bag, let it rest.)

It all adds up to another of my little participatory/ observer deals to hold their damn feet IN the fire and get rich and famous all at the same time. Like Arthur Miller said, that play we saw in Brooklyn – *that* night, remember when we got home? Anyway: "There's a universe of people outside that you're responsible to."

I'm surprised the hullabaloo on the LIRR last Saturday didn't make the papers, it got so ugly. And, no, I'm not being my usual self-aggrandizing self. It all started when someone had good reason – an uncontrollable cat in a carrying case – to actually refuse a search and, shocko, shock, I got sucked in trying to help. Then this butthead psycho-cop poured a whole lot of gasoline on the fire, leaving me rather bruised and breathless. And, no, that's not a metaphor as I'll explain someday if your glamour-puss new life ever allows for an audience.

Which ain't to say, Baby, that I don't shoulder some of the fault myself for what happened to us. Problem is, as the weeks keep rolling on, our groove-thang fading quick and relentless, that's just brackish water under a rusty bridge.

As to the point for now: Gonna venture out today (Thursday) for the second day in a row with my luxurious new East German backpack (and you say I'm in a rut) filled with some deliberately chosen books and hope to galoot around enough to spark a search and then draw myself up in high dudgeon for a principled refusal. Then I'll have a big boffo piece on it for the big bucks. A stunt, yeah, but drawing the line, damn it, with the sort of participatory/ observer stuff that's seemingly gone out of style.

So, a real martyr to the Fourth Amendment, maybe. No,

I'm not gonna do anything stupid – I know how to mess with cops. Still, I feel so damn obvious with *1984, It Can't Happen Here, A Wrinkle in Time* and *Mein Kampf*, etc. But they underscore the point I'm trying to make. (Remember your brother freaking when he saw me reading *Mein Kampf*, and I said, however evil, it was a 'necessary' document? I knew you were the one when you understood.)

Nicki, you should've seen it yesterday at 34th and Sixth: people were just delighted to trot up to have the cops trod all over the Constitution and *pretend* to paw through their stuff. One cop kept telling a majority of the people to just move on, but maybe a third of those folks – dumb bunnies who'd already been dismissed! – lined up anyway.

Yeah, just a metaphor, I imagine, about being a martyr to the Fourth Amendment. Not that I give a flying fuck, I miss you, Baby, oh so much. Anything happens, you'll know what to do.

Warm, deep, personal regards,
Mitch

Lo and behold, Nick replied in the time it took to make a couple of PBJ club sandwiches, her at work before eight in the morning. God knew F&F was paying her enough to churn out the suet, though it was a proper indication of where things stood that I hadn't a clue the precise number of $Ks. I forced respiration and opened it.

Hey:
I don't know what to make of your rambling note, though the emotional blackmail at the end is as clear as it is unwelcome. Just more of that rampant narcissism of yours from being an only child. Being a martyr is "just a metaphor," though you don't give a flying fuck – oh?? Well isn't that too, too clever and convoluted. As you never tired of telling me, even the day before we split, you're the real writer in the family, crafting your lofty shit.
Sounds to me like you need a job, but I'm tired being blue in the face on that one. So who are you writing this for, or is it another one of your 'adventures' you're going to end up publishing somewhere for fifty bucks? (See re job, ad nauseam.)

Still, be careful. There's probably better ways to become famous. I am pretty surprised no one has tried to challenge Walk-on-Water Ted about his useless searches. Millions of riders a day and not one stoned hippie chick, drunk model, coked-up Wall Streeter, righteous Hip-Hop Nationer, civil-liberties lesbian soccer mom or mush-mouthed Unitarian has irredeemably lost it in a sweat-bath of a station and just said no – plain old get the fuck out of my face, *No!* Sad to say, it just might fall on your beefy shoulders – *if* you can get anyone to pay attention. Though it'll be tough in this ONE instance, writing it up, focus on the story, not yourself.
Anyway, wasted too much time on all this – what, like nine years?
Actually, your dumb conundrums are more interesting than what I'm trying to nail down for this 'edgy' new client. Maybe I should just quit this nonsense and sign on as some Mormon's fourth wife to keep his young slut-puppies in line. I guess not all of those nine years were wasted. We had us some good times, especially those fool expeditions of ours all over creation. Don't know how many guys there are out there willing to take a subway and then a bus just to go walk along some shoreline and then a bus and subway home, getting wiggy with a five-dollar half-pint of Clan MacGregor on the way back. I'm too old for that swill now, but still. So, chum, you never know. The cat is way out ahead of me on this, but I do miss you.
Be careful. Is there any point in asking you to stop and think about this? You say you're not in RoundUp *yet*. But at Middling Severity 9, you're a hell of a lot closer than me. And remember about watching your hands with the coppers like we talked about once. You catch them standing around, tell them to go grab a broom. That's rhetoric or something, you big dope.
Nicki

I was spinning in my chair at this first positive indication of any sort. *Chum*! Of course my e-mail's talk of martyrdom was metaphorical. Something to catch her attention. Exit stage-left via cop? It wouldn't be remotely fair to the cop just trying to make his way uneventfully through his shift. Just my luck, he might skip the usual overkill, and I'd end up rolling around in a chair, a bag of piss by my feet.

Besides, *misses me*, she'd written right out loud!

I re-read her e-mail a third time and floated out the door. Her biological clock winding down, had she decided she'd run out of time to cast about for the four guys needed to replace me? Would she stoop to dragging in our cat, Otis, if her little tease held no water?

On a roll, surely my bait of a pack would lead some carp of a cop to strike, and I'd get to deliver my denunciation. Right, just have to make sure to watch my hands. (I'd probably been a little cavalier dealing with the cops the day before.) Should the resulting article get some play, it might even turn Nicki's head a notch or two. Humping it to the subway still early on a Thursday, I decided that heading straight to Penn Station offered the best odds on a search.

PART THREE

Chapter Thirteen

The Crimson Colleen

Yeah, I watched my hands right damn smart in that LIRR corridor. Though Cassandra had warned me the day before – echoed by Nicki in an e-mail *less* than an hour before Frankie shot me – I watched them hold something silver and shiny and then point it at a cop whose nose I'd just bloodied, me idiot-talking all the while.

After all the whiz-bang getting to Bellevue, I fell off the ER's radar once I got up on a bed, and Skinny and Chunky started gabbing at someone in the middle of the room. With Skinny's help, I'd shuffled from my chair, each foot a slab of brittle concrete to be arduously lifted, swung slowly through a brief arc and then placed gently down lest it shatter. My ears remained full of gunfire and siren, two aural assaults I'd never encountered at such close range before, such had been my innocent shamble through life.

It felt like I'd just run a long way, and moving my head meant the contents took a moment to catch up to their container. I eventually managed to slow my shallow, quick breathing and fight off a patch of nausea, only to have a sandbag of exhaustion fall from on high. The ER a swirl of controlled chaos, the nurses' station featured a gathering of nations in a rainbow of scrubs writing, or peering at computers or murmuring urgently. The people crisscrossing before me moved with the sort of weary haste immune to a simple day off.

My bed near a corner, I noticed a great bustle of activity catty-corner across from me. The curtains closed, that stall's occupant was confirmed when a peppery little South Asian doc with dried blood flecked on his green pants came rushing up asking, "Is this the Penn Station shooting victim? Her pressure's stabilized? Good. Let's get her upstairs, stat." They wheeled the Blonde out and away, amidst a swarm of people and two tall poles. I said my first real prayer in a long time for her.

What was my culpability for walking around with a backpack full of admonitory books that HeadFuck and crew would consider *unhelpful* and Leslie nestled under my shirt providing the day's news? For the pursuit of principle despite the warning from that prescient Chilean ghoul? For putting one foot in front of another in a corridor in Penn Station armed with a photo ID, nine dollars, a couple of sandwiches and a memorized statement?

Frankie's face kept intruding as I lay back and drifted off, all tragic like he was the one getting shot. Had the bullet that got the Blonde ricocheted off my head, I wondered – touched me last and so, like 'electricity' in a kids' game of tag, was my responsibility?

I was jarred awake by the grease-bag in the green suit who'd invaded the ambulance rifling through my jeans, grabbing them off the little metal table by my head. I snarled to leave my wallet alone and was about to muster as much noise as I could when a guy I hadn't noticed wearing a top-cop's white shirt told me from the foot of the bed to shut up, that they were MTA police. He was Captain Mumble and that was Detective Mangle.

"I don't care if he's Winnie the Pooh. Tell him to get his hands out of my pants and leave my wallet alone! That's your guys' favorite trick, isn't it? Lift someone's wallet, then they have no ID so you can force a match with some Fiend's biometrics and poof! – gone who knows where. Well, you're too late. Bellevue's already got my info."

He threw my pants on the floor and wrestled the metal table's one drawer open, as the white shirt clucked at me from the foot of the bed about proper police procedure accompanying a "weapons discharge."

"Then go back to Penn Station where the shooter is. That's where your investigation is. You got nothing on me, cop. Get the hell out of here before I start making some real noise, Goddamn it! This is still a hospital, despite everything. Hey! Yo. Help!"

"Shut up, schmuck," said the detective. "Here's your wallet. It's so heavy, I can hardly lift it. You think with the nine bucks you got in it you got enough for the lawyer you're gonna need?"

He flung the wallet at my chest, then turned to the captain and said, "Let's go, it's not here. Leave this wannabe to this nurse I know. I'll tell her on the way out about the air bubble in his IV."

The captain said, "You sure it's not there? The one thing both of 'em said, the only thing they agreed on, was that it was silver. Frost said it was a radio, that he had some kinda pinko news on."

"Imagine that," said the detective. "Alright, let's scram before some jerk shows up with a press pass that makes him think he shits lilacs."

They left before I thought to check my wallet for the license that was still there. A more thorough rousting would've found the radio wedged painfully between the hard plastic mattress and my lower back. I consoled myself musing about the supporters soon to amass behind my gurney leading the Demo, strong lads competing to push it, everyone waving little transistors over their heads instead of the wallets used to protest a cop-killing long past.

A doctor came in as I was drifting off again, shined a light in my eyes and did some weird little hand-dance darting his fingers past my face. I half-yelped the first time he did it, but he told me to relax, that I was in a hospital, so everything was OK. They eventually moved me upstairs to meet my roommate, Luis, an older Puerto Rican gentleman who lay on top of his blanket in slacks and shoes along with his hospital gown.

Then a nurse dropped by, tossed me my own backless gown that turned you into a three-year-old, did temperature and blood pressure and departed without a word. Some Asian kid came in and introduced himself with an embarrassed smile as Dr. Hwang, though he didn't look old enough to drive. He unrolled the gauze from my head and spent a long time snipping the giant band-aid off in pieces to minimize the pain. Cutting off more hair than seemed necessary, he then scrubbed what he called a scalp abrasion none too gently, making things all wobbly again, and slapped on a truly giant band-aid. Again the little hand-dance and shining a light in my eyes which allowed him to conclude I'd had a concussion. He couldn't say how severe with these crude tests. But from talking to me, he thought it mild, and I'd probably be better in a couple of days.

Days? That ushered a whole new worry screaming on to my radar: who was paying for this little sojourn? The MTA, right, which had landed me in Bellevue. And try telling that to the guy eventually calling me about some overdue nineteen grand.

A headache was inevitable, but I was to call a nurse quick if I got any sharp pains or numbness in my hands or feet, or if my vision deteriorated, Dr. Hwang told me. And, such are the joys of post-Plunge municipal medicine, he burrowed in his lab coat pocket for a couple of white pills complete with pocket-fuzz that I should take when the headache kicked in. Then he wished me luck, telling me I was going to need it, "politics-wise." Great.

Feeling quite breezy in a gown meant for a much smaller person – humiliation: hospitals' route to compliance – I despaired of hiding the radio in my bed. Scanning the room's few options, I realized that Luis watched me more closely than hospital etiquette normally allows, lying there on top of his ratty blanket. He said he'd gotten to the room with "pains in the stomach" shortly before me. Rather than ask what happened to my head, he rattled off a string of questions about where I'd gone to high school and college, what my father did for a living and did I belong to any political "groupings." I stared and grunted and ducked his questions. He then asked, "What's your favorite Internet pages, besides the porno, of course?"

Having to say something, I said I was mostly interested in baseball and tried to fend him off with sports talk, neither of us much interested in our rote assessments of the local nines. Then I told him, bright-eyed, curious bastard that he was, that I was feeling sleepy and so would pull the curtain closed round my bed. Back in bed, my head swimming from that tiny effort, I clutched the radio in my hand under the covers, determined to stay awake until I could hide it who knew where when my entirely too nosey roomie went to the john we shared by the door.

I jerked awake knowing I sure didn't like the guy talking low in a Spanish accent out in the hall and tottered out of bed to explore the valance attaching the curtains to the wall. A lousy hiding place, but better than the rolling nightstand or wedged in any of the boxy, metal equipment all around my bed that I thankfully didn't seem to need. Any port in a storm, I stashed my exculpation up on the valance, up at least out of anyone's line of sight. Luis raising his voice in farewell, I slipped hustling back to bed, unleashing the sharpest pain yet right under my bandage. The rest of my head felt full of the stuffing you see leaking from the sodden stomach of a teddy bear washed up by a trash-strewn creek.

Damn, with the Entertainment System now officially hidden, I couldn't get any news. I had to get ahold of someone, find out what the cops were saying about the shooting and whether reporters were buying it. And I had to get someone there to spirit the radio away.

The Blonde checked out, God forbid, I hated to think how important it might become. So that meant my erstwhile in all but name wife. The two of us having endured a number of encounters with them over the years, Nicki plain did not like cops. Plus, our morning e-mail exchange meant this wouldn't come as a total shock. Probably, maybe, I still had a couple of chips left to cash in with her.

There was always Ralph, though we hadn't talked in weeks, not since that scrappy night he dropped by the Hovel. My only visitor so far, and boy was he impressed. Through thick and thin way back to college, Ralph had proved himself, provided not much was required. Some fancy-pants twit got uppity at a party and needed a little verbal flaying, Ralph'd be right there to double-team his ass. But with something huge like this shooting, if a cop or reporter somehow found his way to leaning on Ralph, that might spark his tendency to drop the ball in big games. Our king-of-the-hill routine meant he took nothing I did seriously.

Hey, Ralph, guess what. I discovered a cure for cancer this morning. Yup. Found it festering on a ham sandwich I got bored with late one night about a month ago and shoved under my bed so I wouldn't step on it getting up in the night to empty out the beer.

Cancer? Cool. No, seriously man, that's good. So – what are we getting, pizza or Chinese?

Call the parents? Nah. Pop was getting frayed around the edges, and Mom had never been cut out for this kind of stuff. Best not to drag them into this disaster until I got a better handle on it. And I had no siblings that Pop had ever owned up to, thank God.

There were Rob and Owen, boulevardiers and friends, but steadfast circumspection didn't exactly spring to mind with that flighty pair. What about Millie, the local librarian Nick and I had hung with some – could I hope she might overlook working for the City in such a Minder-sensitive job?

Pretty slim pickings. Face it, with Nicki's far greater flair for friendship than sourpuss me could ever hope for, I'd been a tail to her kite for years. Better make it the Wife. I'd get to see her for the first time since getting the boot, see how the big town was treating her – hopefully like heck. Maybe she'd put on weight, missing me so, though that'd be a first.

Then I remembered: heading for a station house lockup, maybe, if I'd actually gotten to refuse a search, I'd left my micro-zap safe at home. There were a couple of anonymous sources squirreled away in the damn thing who'd just as soon stay that way, including a couple on that new Newark cemetery story. Guess I'd have to sweet-talk someone at the nurses' station in to letting me use their phone. Or maybe grab someone walking by in the hall, offer them a dollar. Reach Nick at work, tell her Fate decreed a second lunch-hour this Thursday, and please hustle on over to Bellevue cause I needed her to hold on to something real important real tight.

****

Done with brooding, I sat up too quickly, and the room started to twirl, so I fell back. Damn, the spins, which I hadn't had since college, and not a drop to drink. As I tensed for another attempt, a celestial vision in a bright red V-neck sweater with a crucifix dangling just so loomed over me, a raven-tressed Grace Kelly the audience's first glimpse of her in *Rear Window* bending deliciously to a laid-up Jimmy Stewart.

"So you're the mad bomber all of Bellevue has been warned against? You look like more of a milk-lapper to me." Her smile coated the goofy insult with sugar, and her accent confirmed her a black Irish beauty, my nurse for the next however many radiant hours, fittingly enough named Maureen. "Walking with a backpack full of books were you? Well, that'll teach you. Now hold still while I make sure your heart is still pumping after the morning's glorious engagement."

115

And she leaned in close and started pumping that little bulb.

"So – 'glorious engagement.' What are they saying about the MTA's Mutt and Jeff?"

"There's talk of a few of the titles you were carrying, so I surmised you're a bloody fool. Actually, we don't know what to make of you despite what the cops are saying. Now quiet while I take this. Your pressure is much higher than it was an hour ago, and I'm daft if I can figure why."

And she popped a thermometer in my mouth so quick I was saved from any dumb reply. She actually met my gaze until I looked away, fighting a toddler's impulse to pull the covers up over my head. Nurses – Irish nurses. Holy mackerel!

She retrieved the thermometer and went to the foot of the bed to write in my chart. Then she smiled again and said she'd be back soon for another try at my blood pressure. "Or, should I send Miss Tubbins in to do it properly? She's rather up in years, I'm afraid."

"You, please. But, Maureen, wait. I need a phone – no one knows I'm here."

"Just you wait, sonny boy. They will. One reporter has already snuck in up here, along with the two who made it upstairs to hound Ms. Fiore, and the score and more downstairs."

"Ms. Fiore – is that the girl from Penn Station? How is she?"

"I was wondering if you'd be thinking to ask of her. You don't know her, a man like you? She's still in surgery, but there's a rumor it's going well. It's still true: if you have to get shot, even in the stomach – especially in the stomach – then make it near Bellevue. My girlfriend downstairs says the way the railroad cops are sweating and pacing, you must be innocent."

"I had books, and I was just walking. That's it. Oh, and a – " I almost mentioned my radio.

A pause, then, "And a what?"

"Nothing. Just books. Just putting one foot in front of the other in Penn Station."

"OK, books it was then. Let's leave it at that."

"But I still need a phone," I whispered. "So how about borrowing one at the nurses' station?"

"You don't know, do you, boyo? You have no idea about the shite piling up around you, men in boots with calloused hands and stout shovels. And no, I'm not talking about the fool Minders everyone's shaking over but no one knows why."

I assumed the cops'd play their usual games, perhaps unearthing certain past minor indiscretions. Nothing heavy, just the hardscrabble transaction costs of moving about the city of an evening manufacturing a certain hackneyed *joie de vivre*. "And who are these shovelers?"

"The main one is some old warhorse NYPD detective they like to send cause he's friendly with the Commandant. That's what we call the nursing supervisor for this entire floor. A battle-ax, she's been here forever. She and the detective supposedly had the wee romance donkey years ago, though personally I think she's a virgin. Anyway, he's been up here before when the police blanket someone, this being the high-security ward that keeps out the weirdoes and death-freaks, but especially the press."

"What do you mean high-security? I'm on some kind of locked ward? They got no right – I didn't do anything."

"Not locked, the doors open out. But they're locked coming in, and there's usually a Bellevue cop nearby. They have *two* of our cops on the door now, which I can't remember seeing before."

She went and sat on the window sill and stared at her feet. I was happy to watch this man-slayer who looked to be in her early thirties. A smart man knowing his limitations, I'd certainly never chased anyone remotely in her league, even back when I was her age. "That detective yanked her string, and the Commandant decreed: no phone calls for you. But anyway, gobshite, the bullet bounced, and you had the audacity to live. You're a walking rebuke who just might, you have that cussed air about you, make some noise. Throw some marbles at their feet. My family back in Belfast, our politics tend towards the … *preemptive*. You? You're locked in a box that's only going to shrink. Men close to me have languished in that box with nary a smile, so just think of me as the USO from the other side."

"You're talking about the New Troubles."

"If that's what you want to call them. We're mostly killing each other over jobs now, all the rest just a gloss of old habits. Given our neighborhood, for my Da and my brothers, it's mostly self-defense – except for Donald, our redhead, when he's had a drop."

She stared off, sighed, then said quite aloud, "As far as Bellevue Hospital is concerned, there are public pay phones at the far ends of each corridor. But you'll fall flat on your face you try to make it that distance under your own power. I'll speak to Dr. Hwang about ordering you a wheelchair."

And leaving me jonesing for another of those smiles, she walked out.

It was still only mid-afternoon. Or so it felt, cause there were no clocks anywhere, I noticed. Man, even the lower right corner where the time would normally be displayed on the screen of the chest dilapidator was blocked by a dark stain etched into the glass. Nothing for it but wait and see if the doc would authorize a wheelchair, though I didn't see that giggly kid overruling anyone named the Commandant.

Chapter Fourteen

Bedlam on First Avenue

I wriggled my way up from a deep dark pool towards the twilight at the room's window. Taking inventory, it felt like the Stuffing had fluffed some to press against my skull, and I wondered what it meant that I wasn't remotely hungry. I saw no wheelchair to go call Nicki, and it sure didn't feel like I was taking any long walks.

Nothing to do but lie back and ponder the cheeky enigma of my nurse. But worry over the Blonde – Ms. Something or Other Fiore – soon elbowed Maureen aside. Normally disdaining such competition, Maureen was thrown off-stride by a rare encounter with someone equally captivating though more of a juke-joint slap-and-tickle than her smoky jazz. Thankfully Ms. Fiore was a young … athlete was she? – God, my head – with presumably well-toned powers of recuperation. Imagining what the papers were going to make of such a glamorous, innocent victim, it dawned on me: I was an innocent victim too, Goddamn it.

Why would the MTA send two guys to try to steal the radio if they didn't think they were to blame? I was peering through the wrong end of the telescope. Befogged, damaged to a degree unknown, flat on my back with my butt hanging out, time to stand up on my hind legs and rage to the heavens about some MoFo trying to kill me – and Carole! – that was her name, both of us innocently going about our business.

Or maybe Plan B: the acknowledged civ-lib freak on a patriotic mission slugging it out with the cops in the ring of public opinion over the next few days – provided I wrangled access to a decent megaphone. Somebody with little to lose drawing a big fat line in the sand and sparking a groundswell of resistance. Wasn't that the point of this whole search-refusnik deal? Right on, right on. Time to call the National Lawyers Guild and the *Northwest Queens Disgrace* to demand next week's cover to trumpet my intent.

I could already hear it: *What the devil did he mean, setting out to challenge the Protectors in a time of T?*

Far better, maybe, to maintain I was just listening to the Entertainment System and taking some books out to me sainted mum, soon to enrich her old age with a course of study of some of the more trenchant dystopian novels of the past century. What man born of woman could say otherwise?

Nick for one, it hit with a big, bright flash. Cause I'd sure spilled the beans in the morning's e-mail. Alright, time to tell her to keep my note under wraps and get her sweet ass to Bellevue to secure the radio. Let Louie try to stop me. Old-man shuffling round my curtain, my head was pulsing already like the forest inhaling and exhaling late at night if you lay in your sleeping bag and allowed the ebb and flow to wash over you. But, his mouth gaping, Luis was hard at it sawing wood.

Out in the hall, up came my man, a porter with a huge, multi-shelved food cart, a tall, skinny older beatnik dude pushing fifty with a gray soul patch, thinning black hair back in a ponytail and no chin whatsoever. And a micro-zap right on his belt. I edged round his cart the long way so it sheltered me from the nurse's station thirty yards down the hall. "Hey buddy, what's doing? Got that primo food we've all been waiting for?"

"Man, you get two if you want 'em, as much money as the cafeteria's been making with all them reporters and cops downstairs cause of you."

"Thank God the fuzz aimed for my head instead of something important. So let me ask you, brother –"

"I didn't know we were related."

"Right – sorry. Anyway, I really gotta call my old lady. I'm not even sure she knows I'm here. The phone in my room ain't working, and I'd probably fall down I try to walk to them pay phones at the end of the corridor."

"You are looking a little green around the gills."

"So, whadiya say. Could I borrow your micro-zap a minute?"

"Call your girlfriend in Hong Kong if you want. Like I said, you got butter."

OK. Almost seven I saw on a clock on the wall, Nicki wouldn't still be at work on a Thursday, not my newly unencumbered wife. Suddenly, Luis called out from behind, "Henderson, you still on the clock? You still work for this department?"

I peered around the cart to see some young Joe Friday with jug ears standing slack-jawed at the nurse's station, bewitched by Maureen. Hands on her hips and her posture a marvel, she was smiling one of her smiles, tommyrot spilling from cherry lips, Henderson floating out by Jupiter's ninth moon. Having orbited there myself, I laughed for real for the first time since getting shot and said, "What's the matter, Louie? Your tummy hurts?"

Zeke stood up holding a tray and the cop yelled, "Henderson, you got five seconds to keep your fucking job!"

Henderson ran up blowing smoke out his ears and startling Luis with his salute. An unruffled Maureen sauntered up behind; designed for it so well, maybe she just liked torturing men. Henderson said, "Sir, I need you to give me that micro-zap and return to your bed. You're a sick man."

"What? I gotta do what you say cause you're wearing a suit?"

"Sir, I'm not going to tell you again. I need that device now. You're in enough trouble as it is. I mean – you're injured. For your own security, you need to remain in bed."

"I'm not *injured*." Echoing something someone said to me some weeks back, "An injury's something you get playing basketball. I'm *wounded*. You got some kind of ID on you, Officer Henderson? Some indication of your command for when I sue your ass if you touch me? Some kind of, I don't know – *writ* preventing me making a phone call? You clowns shoot me, and *I'm* the one in trouble?" I would've felt better saying all this if I wasn't barefoot with my drawers hanging out the back of my smock.

And Zeke came to stand by my side. "You on staff here, mister, or can I just ignore you too? Cause I've been handing out slops and picking up the leavings here for seventeen years, and I've never seen you before."

Henderson turned plaintively to Luis. "Sir?"

An ally, no a Gibraltar, like Zeke at my side, I grinned over at Maureen, who just imperceptibly shook her head at me. I retreated a few steps, and Luis yelled "Henderson!" as I dialed. And Zeke – heck, what was his real name, my hero? – swung the enormous food cart at a perfect angle to block Henderson and throw Luis hard up against the wall. Henderson started to come around the other side, so Zeke swung his cart again, this time with a great clatter of trays and plates onto the floor, its long side pretty much sealing off the hall. Luis slumped against the wall, looking vacant and holding his left side with both hands. "I can hold 'em for about fifteen seconds!" Zeke yelled.

"Nicki, I'm stuck in – "

And a clever hand darted over my shoulder and snatched the micro-zap from behind.

"Hey – what the hell!" I yelled, forgetting my head and turning quick. The Stuffing doing leaps and bounds, I staggered and reached out blindly and pulled another tray onto the floor for luck.

When things stopped spinning, I saw a tall, busty broad in her sixties in a traditional nurse's uniform of starched white skirt and blouse and white stockings and shoes. Some stray wisps of steel poked out from under a nurse's cap that would have done a WWII home-front movie proud. I'd seen nothing remotely like this getup all day. She handed the micro-zap to Zeke, saying, "Alfred, I believe this phone is yours. I suggest you store it in your locker while on duty as regulations require. Now please attend to this mess you've made while I inform dietary that we will need – I count eight trays on the floor – eight additional meals. At this time of night we will have to take what they can give us. So much for our patients' individual needs. I just hope, Alfred, that no patient's health is impacted as a result."

Zeke/Alfred had just assaulted two cops with a heavy, hard-edged metal cart. Luis was leaning against the wall holding on to himself, breathing heavily and trying to gauge the damage. Henderson was standing there bedecked with cling peaches acting eponymous, his gun out – of freaking course. Yet man of action Alfred cringed before this pillar of authority.

Ladling honey, Maureen drew close and said, "Officer Henderson, we don't need that here. Put your gun away, baby."

Two big Bellevue cops came rushing up from the door down the hall, but the boss nurse said, "Gentlemen, thank you for your assistance. But I believe I am going to ask you to wait on the other side of the door. We have matters entirely in hand here. Don't we people?"

She looked at each of us in turn. I felt so infantilized I was torn between saying yes, ma'am, and sticking out my tongue.

Ratcheted down, Alfred spoke barely above a whisper. "Commandant, I can explain. You see this patient here was shot this morning, and I couldn't see why he shouldn't be able to tell his family. I know – *absolutely* know – there's nothing worse than being stuck away inside somewhere, and your people don't know where you are."

"Alfred, seeing the obvious strain you are under, I'll overlook just this once the name you just uttered. Now, there are patients to feed."

He nodded mournfully and bent to a tray on the floor as I stumbled two steps to the wall, anchored my back to it and slid down, glad of my drawers. I heard the Commandant say, "Well that was not unexpected. Maureen, please get Richard and get this patient back to bed." And she turned to the cop. "Luis, your charade is over, so let me state categorically you know how I feel about guns on my ward. This man Henderson, who I am surprised was considered equal to this assignment, will leave Bellevue immediately, never to return. Is that clear? And I need to speak with you in my office. Little as it pleases me, I'm afraid Dr. Ralston must now be apprised of the course of treatment we have planned for this patient – under Dr. Hwang's signature, obviously."

And I heard no more.

****

Someone was digging her fingernails hard into my forearm. Really hard. Then a hand went over my mouth, a hand attached to a crimson-clad arm that disappeared down over the edge of the bed. The hand released me, held up a shush! index finger, and I propped myself up to see the lustrous black hair crowning the rest of Maureen. She whispered shush! though I'd said nothing.

"Is it near morning? It feels like I've been sleeping forever."

"Not nearly long enough with that head. In fact I hated to wake you cause it's just past nine."

"At night?" Sending the Stuffing spinning, I foolishly jerked my head towards the window to confirm the darkness behind the light thrown by the hospital and the FDR Drive down below.

"Not too many oats in the barn on your best days, I suppose you did have a fifty-fifty chance of being right."

I scanned the patch of wall I could see and, as I stretched to look up past the unused machines to the wall behind me, she lay a hand on my arm. "Don't trouble yourself. No clock, and tomorrow you'll find Bellevue entirely uninterested in your twelve dollars for a television. The faster you're disoriented by a little isolation, the better they like it."

Tired of crouching, she risked leaning against the window sill. "I must say they've got a heavier thumb on you than any I've seen.

124

Something involving the MTA brass *personally* somehow." She added that Luis – changed to a jacket and tie – plus the warhorse NYPD detective, the Commandant and her supposed boss, a Dr. Ralston, had all been closeted away arguing in the Commandant's office. Plus Carole was out of surgery and said to be doing well. Then, "I have a phone for you, that's why I woke you up, though it only accepts calls since you haven't officially rented it. Now let me leave before your Da calls. A little scattered, but still forceful, your father – the apple didn't fall far."

"They're starting to really piss me off. What is this with the phone calls? I'm calling Uzbekistan to report on my progress? I just want to let my wife – well, my about-to-be ex-wife – know where I am and that I need her help."

" 'About-to-be ex-wife.' That's nice. You know, I heard you altering your speech, you cute whore you, talking to Alfred. Though God knows any kind of operational spontaneity is at a premium these days, everyone led by the nose by their micro-zaps."

She ran her fingers through her hair – ah, do that again, please, nurse – and grinned down at me. "God knows it's going to get worse after Alfred's antics with his food cart. Word is the cops aren't going to charge him because otherwise it *might* come out they're up here spying on patients. Still, that was a proper assault, cracking two of Luis's ribs. I've never seen Alfred poke his head up out of the gopher hole like that before."

"People of all stripes are getting tired of getting pushed around."

"The bully-boys are mostly worried you're going to call a reporter. With Fiore out of danger, my girlfriend downstairs says the reporters are pacing around with nothing to do but get steamed there's so little out on you. They're all wondering what it is you were carrying in that big pack of yours. There's all kinds of crazy talk."

"It was books."

"OK. But what kind of books? *Unhealthy* books? Taking them to who and why so many, carrying them around in the heat, a big lug like you?"

"You say the nicest things, nurse."

She waited for more, then said, "Christ, I wish I could move back home! Just leave this Godforsaken country and its petty cruelties, every day a new thug with a gun on his hip…. So how is your mushy head? You didn't need that spot of excitement out in the hall."

"It's full of Stuffing."

"I'm not happy with how long it took you to respond to pain. Did you not feel me clawing your arm off?"

"It takes me a long time to wake up, that's all."

"Well, I'll see to it that Dr. Hwang orders you a CT scan first thing in the morning. Now let me go before your Da rings on that phone, and half the bully-boys in Manhattan come running. Tell him not to come in the morning, you'll be upstairs getting scanned."

She stood looking down at me a moment. I asked if she'd be working the next day, and she said she was on-duty until noon and then off for two days. Then with a lilt that flirted with song, she said, "Don't worry, gobshite, I'll be charting your progress from afar. You're a funny one, and I may hear of you again. But, believe it or not, I do have other patients. So here's your nurse's instructions: talk to you poor Da, eat this delicious Salisbury Mistake Alfred left you an extra large portion of, and then to bed with you."

And again she walked out without a look. Maybe having to do it too permanently too often, she had issues with leave-taking.

How many years would have to pile on Maureen before I'd have a ghost of a prayer? A decade, assuming I didn't age a day? The alabaster face framed by luminous hair, the cherry lips, big coal eyes, cheekbones marvelously mammary – wrap her up with a big red bow.

Saved by the bell. "This is your father," my father said, grave like I hadn't heard in years. "Schulman down the block called and said you're all over the news. But there's nothing on cable that makes any sense, and the crappy radio stations aren't much help either. Are you all right?"

"I'm OK, Pop."

"The radio said the girl, the innocent bystander, was out of surgery and expected to make a full recovery. But all they said about you was you'd been shot in the head. And nobody would tell me anything at that stupid city hospital except you couldn't take any calls. They wouldn't even say what ward you were on."

"Yeah, well things are pretty weird here at Bellevue. It's like – "

"It's strange the way the radio made a point of saying there was no information on your condition. Usually they say critical or stable or something. Makes you wonder why they're leaving things so open-ended. Like anything might happen."

"Pop, I said I'm fine. It just grazed me, and I have a minor concussion and I'm kinda foggy, which will hopefully go away in a day or two."

"Nothing like what those poor soldiers get when something explodes near their head, huh?"

"Right. But things are creepy here. They had a cop in a hospital gown in the next bed, but now he's stopped even pretending he's not a cop. And they won't let me make any phone calls. They're actually physically stopping me."

"You need a lawyer, somebody who still practices law like from before. Not like everybody afraid now to defend a cow for kicking over a pail of milk."

"Pop, I'm as much an innocent bystander as that Fiore woman. I was – "

"You don't know her, a broad like her, do you?"

"What? No. Listen! I was heading through Penn Station when this stupid-ass cop ran into me, I mean right into my chest with his face. He's short, and I guess the cops are used to everyone getting the hell out of their way."

"So why didn't you get out of his way?"

"He came round a blind corner, and we collided. And he got all pissed off cause his nose got bloody, and so he ended up shooting me."

"The radio didn't say anything about any of that. No bloody nose or nothing. It did say the cops said you had some kind of silver device, some little square thing that hasn't been recovered. A micro-zap, or maybe some kind of gun or even a *detonator*. That's the word they used, can you believe it?"

"Pop, it was that little transistor radio of mine. You've seen it a million times."

"They said it got lost in the confusion after the 'weapons discharge' – another of their cute words, like the guns shot themselves. Plus you had 'an unusual number of books' – underground books or something."

"Yeah, books. So what."

"One of your stunts, right, more of this crap you write about for next to nothing? Look, you need a lawyer. Maybe I can still find a real one, I make some calls in the morning before your mother and I come in to see you. Parking's gonna cost me a fortune."

"Pop, I'm shuffling around like an old man. I – "

"Look, don't say nothing to nobody. No cops, no foxy nurses – they do that with dames, you know – nobody. And don't sign anything."

"Pop, don't come till the afternoon. I'm having a CT scan in the morning. Just a precaution."

"The afternoon, great. Just in time to hit rush hour coming home. So that girl who got shot, she's gonna live?"

"That's what I hear, thank God."

"The papers are gonna fall all over themselves over her, plus they're gonna back the cops. Hero this, Protector that bullshit cause they put their pants on without falling down in the morning. So listen to me – don't say nothing to nobody. We'll see you tomorrow afternoon. And, hey, I love you."

"Uh, me too."

Of all the shocks of an astounding day, that grabbed the biggest piece of pie by far. Even contemplating my father getting mushy made my head hurt in all the places it didn't already. Damn! My mind so blowed, I forgot to tell him to call Nicki about doing nothing with that stupid e-mail until she heard from me. The Stuffing was messing me up cause, if that got out, I'm down twenty points starting the fourth quarter. Get her to bury the e-mail and hope against hope it stays buried. Then cling to the story that my new 'apartment' was so small, I was taking some books out to my folks' basement in Mineola. Yeah, the sort of books such a happy, commodious fellow certainly had no need of during the Current P. Crisis.

As Maureen promised, the phone wouldn't call out. So, time to march out there quarters in hand and *persevere*, damn it, until I found myself in front of a pay phone. I wasn't under arrest until somebody said so. Standing up, the walls still met at right angles. I yanked the cord out and put the phone on the night table by Luis's empty bed and shuffled out of my room to find they had indeed taken the gloves off.

A cop in uniform ran up and basically got in front of me as I turned towards the doors at the end of the hall away from the nurses' station. The Commandant appeared and told him "to keep that patient in place, he's unwell." It wasn't hard, groggy me, barefoot and nearly naked against this buff, motivated kid. Then Luis showed, and the kid spread his arms wide. Though I didn't like turning my naked back to him, I tried a laughably slow spin move that sent the Stuffing whirling.

The Commandant came back, not that I'd seen her leave, dragging Dr. Hwang by the ear and saying that obviously I was delusional. Since they couldn't restrain me – I might do some real damage straining against the straps, or so she said – he needed to sedate me ASAP. He balked about sedating a concussed patient and then asked for Dr. Ralston's OK. But Ralston was off the ward, and there was no time to wait. I was in real danger as anyone could see.

I pushed against the kid, cursing and clutching my quarters tight in my little fist, all but expecting my mom to come and spit on a tissue to scour my five-year-old face clean as we headed up the walk to visit some smelly dowager aunts, having to sit still for way too long till they brought out the cake. "I have a right to make a phone call – this is still New York, no matter what you MoFos say. I'm getting all your names and suing the piss out of all of you, personally and institutionally. And what the hell is your real name, anyway, Commandant?"

Though he hobbled himself with one hand on his gun, I kept pushing against the cop to no effect until two burly men in scrubs came up and held me against the wall and pinned my arms. I squirmed and twisted until the Commandant yelled at her gorillas to keep me still so the needle wouldn't break off in my arm, and the bigger one's grip turned from a vise of iron to the jaws of death. Hwang hit it home, and I turned to rubber before the needle was out. As they none too gently marched me the few steps back to my room, I saw a blurry, crimson figure with her hand to her mouth shaking her head slowly back and forth, back and forth.

Chapter Fifteen

Lurch

Like surfacing that morning in my folks' garage – ah, the carefree days of Statie's assault and the riot on the train – I came to with little notion as to where or why. Again, it didn't feel like I'd been drinking, but I'd sure been doing something. Or, piecing it together, had something *done* to me, a doctor pouring sludge from a needle. Gingerly rising and turning, I saw that the curtain, his bed and Luis himself were all gone.

He'd been replaced by yet another large cop in uniform, this one sitting in a metal folding chair. He was an intense, misbegotten enormity, from his hooded brow, awkward nose and horse-teeth, to his cantaloupe shoulders and huge mitts, on down to the tug boats berthed in shoes way too fancy for his ill-fitting uniform. He micro-zapped someone to report that I was awake.

Still needing to pee, I continued towards the john. He got up to block the open door to the hall. "No phones for you," he said. "They still have lots of needles right outside."

So I was indeed a prisoner, held incommunicado and without charge. Pecking and scratching ever closer, the chickens had finally come home to roost. "This is for your own security," the cop continued. "It ever occur to you that a certain blonde's family, a bunch of them right downstairs, is looking to put some serious hurt on you."

"So you're gonna dope me up again – for my own protection now – if I try to use the phone? Well screw you with an eggbeater." Hopefully Nicki had been out all night working a truck stop, with no time to forward that incriminating e-mail I'd sent her. Soon enough, the cop banged on the door to the john and yelled it was time I was done.

A Brave Sour World indeed. I took my time and flushed twice to throw them off my DNA since I couldn't recall them taking any blood yet. Having been knocked out, I should check I still had both my kidneys. The cop blocking the door to the hall like it was the portal to another dimension, I pretended to study the view out the window and peeked up to see the Entertainment System by the valance bracket.

"All right. Enough of that – get back in bed."

"Do I move my left foot first or my right foot?"

"What? No. Just get in bed. You'll be getting breakfast in a moment."

"All the narcotics I can stand, huh?"

"This is a city hospital. The City has agreed to work with us – with my employer – as to your level of care. Shut up and get in bed."

I lay down. His *employer*? They'd call it the department, but no real cop would say that. I filed that away and tried to keep the conversation going in my usual cheery fashion. "Level of care, my ass, cause I haven't gotten any damn care at all. In fact, I'm leaving."

"You're not going anywhere until you're medically released."

"So now I'm supposed to believe you got two doctors to sign the papers overnight that I'm a danger to myself or others?"

Were they ever going to formally arrest me or, Lurch here barring the door, was all that moot? Did they even bother to arrest folks anymore, or just lay hands on you where and when they wanted? Should I be grateful not to be a Null, given the rumors about them disappearing? "I asked you a question, cop. On what basis are you keeping me here?" I was just about screaming, my head paying the price, but maybe Maureen would hear me if she wasn't already tied up somewhere. Or was she one of them too, the strawberries and cream version of this guy?

A plump, black orderly bustled in with a tray for me and a glare for the cop. "Miss, can I ask you what time it is, please?"

"Why sure, Sugar. It's – "

"No talking to the Suspect!"

"Like I was saying, it's just after nine o'clock in the morning."

"Friday morning?"

"That's right. Now, I'm afraid this oatmeal has gotten cold and lumpy. The head nurse herself wouldn't let me bring it earlier. But there's juice and I got fresh coffee. Oh, and an apple I wouldn't feed my dog. For some reason the Commandant – you've had the pleasure? – wouldn't let me give you the pineapple that everybody likes."

"Miss – shut it!"

"But I'll make sure you get your lunch early. Your stomach's probably a little iffy right now anyway from that medicine they gave you for your seizure last night."

"Miss, that's enough! Or do I need to take your name?"

"My name's Aretha Franklin. What's yours, Bull Connor?" Turning back to me, she said, "Now, you need anything, you call me."

"Miss, wait! What seizure?"

"There's talk of you having had a seizure, so they had to inject you with diazepam. And if you've had one seizure, that means you might have another and need another shot – you hear what I'm saying?"

The cop moved on her and barked, "Miss. Out. Now!"

She took her sweet time sashaying out, staring at a spot on the wall over his head – yeah, a clean, round spot where a clock once was. Gulping the coffee, I decided the Stuffing was a little more cohesive this morning. The truly ugly cop sat down, then stood right back up and made a big show of pulling a copy of the *New York Node* out of his back pocket. He held it high to peruse its innards like a kid hiding behind a book to eat candy in study hall. As intended, I scanned its front and back pages.

The back-page, second-day story on those two Yankees' marital dustup almost certainly would have been the front page except for the classic, Weegee-esque photo they'd found for page one. Since, aside from Carole at the beach in a yellow polka dot bikini stretching high to catch a frisbee, it would be hard to imagine a saucier photo.

Under the banner headline: "*Backpack Bungler, Beauty Shot; Startled Cops Forced to Fire*" vast real estate was devoted to an apparently candid shot of a very healthy Ms. Fiore in a low-cut, shimmery, midnight-blue spaghetti-strap number, leaning forward at a party or something and laughing fetchingly, all them pearly whites exposed, charm spilling all over the page. Below the photo it got worse the only way it could: "*Fireman's Fiancée Fighting for Life*". How long before phalanxes of uniformed smoke-eaters lined First Avenue to waft their loud encouragement to Carole somewhere up above?

There it was, the whole story, no need to turn the page. The sex kitten (cat in her case), a wounded innocent hanging by a thread; the poor, frazzled cops, no doubt the victims of a sneak attack, who were passive-voice *forced* to unload; and the "Bungler" who laid them all low, no mention of his medical status. Man, I had to escape Bellevue and get my story out under my own damn byline, no matter how much any lawyer shepherding my eventual lawsuit might squawk. This shit had to be answered and quick, cause once the Swift-Boat sailed, you had about a day-and-a-half, tops, till you sank.

"I gotta hand it to you," Lurch said, "you raised the T Index to 94. That's the highest it's been since the Danube Six and that fire-hose fungus of theirs."

"You sure you're holding that high enough? I don't know if they can read it out the window over in Queens."

"Queens is that way, huh? Anyway, they got a little side article here quoting some big-shot ex-prosecutors as to the right charges to ice you down good and long." He lowered the paper to – apparently – grin at me, a botched job I did not want to witness again. "Let's see, they're talking about: resisting proper authority, and refusing a lawful order. They'd work, but they don't give much time. There's always interfering with government administration, but that's too weak for a double shooting. So is attempted disorderly conduct. Resisting arrest is out just this one time, but attempted planting of a false bomb ain't bad. That's actually more time than a real bomb. And here's one with some weight that sounds like I should have heard of it before: that you manifested a clear and present danger."

A clear and present danger – if that don't beat all.

Waiting me out, he finally said, "Actually most of them have decent time once they're T-enhanced. It's getting tough to remember all the different kind of Fiends, but … an Anarchist, maybe? Or a Black Separatist – you wish. Homegrown Islamo? Possible. Ah, the Lone Wolf – a sicko like you, my money's on that. Militia? I doubt you got the balls. Special Interest? I always forget – what is that, for fags? – so maybe. Or White Nationalist? Again, a balls issue."

"I guess alphabetically is easiest to remember."

"Of course there's all the charges you get for assaulting Protector Reisner. First they have to enhance the Penn Station whole-vid, see what a skilled technician can cough up. Maybe I can loan them one of ours." I liked this, me saying nothing, him spilling, cause what is his outfit if he's loaning the MTA a skilled fabricator? If he's some kind of supposedly local cop who doesn't know where Queens is? He shook the paper at me and said, "Cute chick, huh."

"Puppies are cute. I don't think cute is the first word that comes to mind with Ms. Fiore."

"So what's the deal – you were carrying what the paper says were peanut butter and jelly sandwiches made with three slices of bread. It says, 'The purpose of this extensive supply of food remains unknown. It is unclear whether he expected some sort of siege.' "

Them clutching this straw, I laughed out loud. "Dude, look at the heft on this bed over here. I had errands to run. You have any idea how much it costs someone like me eating out running around Manhattan all day?"

Shit. Bad mistake. I wasn't running around the City. As I'd more or less decided, I was taking those books out to Long Island. But man, that's why they get you talking – just like on the idiot cop TV shows – get you trying to prove how clever you are.

On cue, he said, "And what about all those books? They don't list any titles in the paper so as not to give people – you know, Homelanders – any ideas. But an MTA buddy of mine says you had Hitler's book and also *1984*, which everyone knows is Red. And, wait a minute." He unfolded a piece of paper from his shirt pocket. "OK. A book by a guy named Roth that's got a swastika on the cover. A Jew book – Roth, right? – with a Swastika? And something by some Russian guy, obviously another Red. You were humping a lot of weird, thick books around, the mercury up in the high nineties. So you into all that Nazi and Commie shit? That's what this is all about?"

Again I had to laugh at his disingenuous throwing bread on my pond to see what rose to the surface. "Man, if you're calling *1984* Red, then I don't know if I can properly discuss literature with you. Not to mention Solzhenitsyn's slice and dice on the USSR and Roth's *anti*-Nazi novel. American Nazis – you'd like 'em."

"You know, I've been looking to meet some American Nazis – off duty of course." Then, casual as popping the evening's eighth beer, "You know any?"

I smirked rather than strike at such a soggy morsel.

"You were also carrying *Catch-22*. That's against the Army, isn't it."

"Well, a satire."

"And what's this, porn? *The Handmaid's Tale*?"

"She's French, obviously."

"*A Wrinkle in Time* – that sounds suspicious right off."

"Way too many dimensions, dude. Plus, it's aimed at kids."

He stared right through me. "Targeting innocents. That's gotta add some major time. So what about this *Darkness at Noon* my guy said you had. What is that, Goth?"

"It's mostly updated vampire stuff. There's an eclipse, but it gets stuck, so the vampires can operate in the middle of the day. It's a whole new take on vampires you gotta check out."

"Maybe I will." Again the pause and, "So you know any – vampires, I mean?" And he started snorting through his honker, apparently how he laughed.

"Tell me, Lurch, someone teach you this nifty, hey-we-can-talk-here style of interrogation, all demotic and shit? 'A guy named Roth' – oh what a sly spider to the fly art thou."

"You lost me there, Einstein. But let me ask you this: it says here – "

"Tell you what. How 'bout I buy my own damn newspapers when I leave here in an hour or two and read them for myself."

"How about you just tell us what you were up to, Suspect, and I'll let you know when you can start thinking about leaving!"

"Screw you! And what's your name and your Goddamn command? Now that I look, you don't have any insignia on that uniform you're trying to fit into, do you?" He had a big Glock or some such on his hip along with some cuffs and his micro-zap, but no name tag or bars on his collar indicating his outfit. His badge was kind of a blur, like the Oscar statuette's crotch. He and Statie, badgeless birds of a feather, unfettered, amok.

"Officer Krupke, Police Department, New York City."

"How about I just call you spook?" Some discombobulationist up from Fort Meade? Cause he was so proud of his *West Side Story* taunt, he flubbed the line. The formulation is, 'NYPD' or if you want to get fancy, 'Police Department, City of New York.' No one who's spent any time within fifty miles of the place would say what he'd said.

Where the heck was Maureen? Unless the Commandant had her transferred to the TB ward, the longer my sainted Mata Nightingale stayed away, the more she seemed the catch-more-flies-with-honey version of this brute. How come no one came to even take my temperature? Just sassy Aretha with her demoralizing pothole quick-fix in a bowl. I found the buzzer and pressed and pressed again, no idea if anyone heard, cared or was allowed to respond. Done trying to draw me out via the newspaper, Lurch flipped to the sports pages and settled more comfortably in his chair.

Came a knock at the door, someone no doubt coming to spray me with eau de wet dog. And Lurch asked *me* who it was. The ghost of William Kunstler, I said, as he admitted a muscular young guy in scrubs pushing a wheelchair. He had a shaved head and Japanese(?) letters disappearing around the back of his neck. The orderly said it was time for my CT scan, the one Dr. Hwang ordered back before I'd morphed entirely from patient to Suspect.

Lurch studied the paperwork and finally said it was OK as long as he accompanied me upstairs. The orderly said he could fly to the moon for all he cared, his job was to wheel me upstairs. Neither sought any input from the slab of brisket they were fussing over. I consigned the Entertainment System to its fate and settled into the chair.

Lurch held us back with one hand as he peered out in the hall to see that no one was lurking, no Ed Murrow or hordes of Fiores with baseball bats. As we left, he nodded curtly at an older man in a fancy suit sprawled in a comfy leather desk chair across from my door, a big briefcase at his feet. He scrambled to his feet with a questioning look. Lurch ostensibly just a pot-scrubber in uniform, it was easy to see who was calling the shots the way the suit leaped up and that Lurch alone approved my leaving to get scanned.

The dash of scarlet hunched over a computer down at the nurses' station was Maureen, who didn't look up. Were her hands tied or had she cut me loose? The orderly scooted down the hall and then abruptly one-eightied so he could bang out the door with his butt. The Stuffing got shaken *and* stirred, but my plea that he slow down went nowhere. The spook, or haint or general purpose scumbag playing dress-up in his vague uniform strode along unhurriedly in his seven-league loafers and, when it opened, ordered some frightened little Latina in scrubs out of the elevator.

Off the Restricted Ward and out in 'public', it dawned that I could shout an appeal to anyone I met. How much of a commotion could I make and, more importantly, to whom? I'd need some big-balled doc or administrator to have any prayer at all of Lurch – armed and 'in uniform' – not just blowing them off, my plea falling unheard to the faded linoleum as I was whisked away.

We got off on a lonely hall, and pusher-man barreled up to a door and wheeled around backwards again to bang through, Lurch right behind. But he stopped the spook in his tracks. "No, man, you can't come in. There's way too many *distributed* gamma rays loose in this room for anyone to enter without first getting weeks of the antidote. I had to work in the kitchen for a month before they'd let me do the job I was hired for."

"Don't be stupid. I go where the Suspect goes."

"You married? I mean, like, actively? Planning on having any kids?"

I'd like, I *think*, to see the woman who'd walk down the aisle with him. Lurch not answering, it's the sort of question that gives anyone pause.

"OK then. I couldn't live with myself if I let you in here. You'd be lucky if the kid looked like a frog or something you could actually recognize rather than just a blob. Worse than Uncle Sam's depleted uranium. You wait there in the hall while I take him inside."

What about me I wondered as, Lurch stymied, we banged inside. I planned on getting active again someday, if not necessarily reproductively. Like next week, damn it, with someone with a ghoulish taste for cop-shot civ-libbers. The orderly turned me around to face the usual big metal donut with a bed threading the hole, then rushed to the back of the room, pushed through a door and disappeared without a word. An energetic young man.

Chapter Sixteen

Fleeing Lurch and All His Works

I sat for a minute waiting for the scan technician to appear. But where did that door lead, and how far could I get barefoot, in a smock and without a dime? Could I make it downstairs to nab a reporter to smuggle me out for an exclusive limited to the tale of ferrying me home? Have her or him let me out five blocks from my door, promising not to follow? Cause what began as the significant, yet simple tale of refusing a search had grown monstrously. Call it "The True Tale of the Penn Station Shootings," it just might get my foot in a slightly more ornate door than usual.

More to the point, did I need Pop to show up to secure *me*, never mind the radio? Lurch had made it clear I was caught in their net, nothing remotely legal about it. So what came next, a ride in a small plane out over the Atlantic? The shootings splashed all over the news, how far could they take this here in the middle of New York freaking City? By locking me down, some might say they'd taken it pretty damn far already.

The door in back opened and in strolled Maureen cool as can be. She held a bag, hopefully a PBJ club sandwich, cause I suddenly realized I was famished. "Maureen, where the hell you been, leaving me alone with that brute?"

"Shush, eejit. They let none of us in to see you, not even Dr. Ralston, who surprised me allowing himself to be kept from a patient. They've got you locked down like I've never seen. And it was a ton of favors I used to get you up here and to have the CT technician disappear. So that cop, or whatever he is, bought Jimmy's story about how dangerous this room is?"

"Gamma rays. But why are they acting so crazy? They're just delaying my leaving, cause I feel a lot better already."

"A lot of people have made fools of themselves predicting how far they'll go since long before HeadFuck. Anyway, the papers are trashing you pretty good, that shite-storm I was telling you about just beginning."

"I figure it's a fair fight."

"The last thing you need is to be fighting fair. They won't. How's your head, lad?"

"Pretty good today, till Jimmy started playing ping-pong with it."

"That was a disgrace, a concussion patient getting injected with diazepam last night. But the papers aren't your biggest worry. Some big-shot MTA cop was in the Commandant's office bellowing about your 'treatment.' He kept yelling that she didn't know how much was at stake. And that it should be easy, you already shot in the head.

"What kind of treatment?"

"Not to scare the bejesus out of you, but I moved heaven and earth to get you out of Bellevue *now* – not later, not even this afternoon. Cause they've got 'tests' planned for you that make getting shot in the head a walk in the park."

"What Goddamn tests?"

"Head injuries let them pick what they like, but they're all intrusive. And then things slip – *instruments*. And you're not the same afterwards."

"Jesus, Maureen."

"They've had some bloke hidden away for the last six months up on the seventh floor somewhere. And he didn't even stop one of their bullets or make it into the papers. Just came in from a holding cell spitting up blood and with an attitude like yours only worse – a *genuine* hard case. He pissed the wrong people off, got the 'tests,' and now he pretty much doesn't remember who he is."

"Who was this guy in the Commandant's office?"

"Some MTA white-shirt. He was yelling about how a lot of people were hoping that ogre in your room this morning – who the cops all seem a little afraid of – could squeeze you. But tell me, boyo, you beat up an officer of the law?"

"Don't be ridiculous. I slay with words. He ran into me around a blind corner. Bloodied his nose on my chest and started this whole freaking misery. By the way, how's Carole?"

"She's fine, at least for a few years until gravity does its job on her. Just an accident it was then? So I'm risking … repercussions for a civilian? And, no, I'm not talking about the Commandant, feck her very much. You're iffy, lad. Still, the *Node* says you assaulted a cop. That probably covers things with the lads on my end – technically. Let's go with that. That and I like your guts tangoing with them not once but twice yesterday out in the hall like a drunken bear. So here I am on my white charger."

"That picture of Fiore the *Node* got. She – "

"*Node, The Daily Chirp* and the *Dispatch* – above the fold – all three front pages."

"Jesus, a fireman's fiancée. You sure she's OK?"

"She's already asking to get out of bed."

"If only she'd rounded that corner first, she probably wouldn't have bloodied his nose."

"Smothered him, maybe."

Damn, Maureen was fine, even giving her bitter little laugh. Five-foot-nine she looked, the perfect height, not that I'd ever actually stood up next to her. A smooth throw through the gears from the moment she handed you the keys – and leagues beyond me (an intrepid carrier of books!) in the Troubles she's seen, the hard-boys she's known. What tempest had tossed her up at Bellevue, rather than ending up a craps dealer or weather girl or just some Despoiler's trophy vixen? She caught me looking and briefly flashed the sort of smile that'll curl your straight ones and straighten your curlies.

"Well this is a grand reunion. But how about you throw your clothes on and get out of here."

"No CT scan then?"

"You're fine. I can tell by the way you're talking."

"I'm sorry, Maureen, but I can't go. There's something in my room I need to establish my innocence."

"Your radio is gone. I was meaning to tell you, but as soon as Jimmy wheeled you out, that old spear-carrier outside your door went in and came out a minute later crowing and holding it in his hand. He ran to the Commandant's office and then came out with a grin that split his face like your ass. That's the only reason I was able to get your clothes. And it won't happen again, so get on with ya."

"I am royally screwed," I said, taking off my gown and standing up extra straight.

"Before it ends up on the bottom of the East River, that radio'll become a gun or worse – which they're already talking. You did have some pretty explosive books from what I've heard."

"That's right, *books*. Godfreakingdamn it! They shoot you, then they rob you, and then they frame you."

My poor ruined shirt already on, she handed me my jeans. The Stuffing kiboshing me putting on the second leg, my hand darted out to grab her shoulder. She steadied me, then bent down and – Jesus! – got close to reach around to pull up my pants. She rose and we were more or less dazzlingly eye to eye for the first time. I quit staring at the sun and reached for her again, this time for real. But she stopped me cold. "So what were you about, carrying all those type of books then?"

"What – oh, nothing. Just taking them out to my mother on Long Island."

And she laughed like maybe she hadn't in a while. "That's good, boyo. Maybe I'm finally teaching you to keep your big trap shut. Now your smelly shoes. Quick!"

She led me out the back door and down a short hallway to a flight of stairs. Walking in the hall was OK, but it got fuzzy negotiating the stairs, my feet too far down. Afraid the several flights down were too much, she said we'd go to Plan B after I rested a moment.

The fuzzies reminded me. "What the hell is this the breakfast lady said – and put her on the same team as you and Alfred – that I'd had a seizure?"

"You'll probably be schizophrenic as well as epileptic before they're done. Never mind that the fake epilepsy diagnosis itself – with all these new mental-health Regs forcing meds on you for the safety of the Realm – lets them inject you any time they want. 'Oh, your man's looking cross-eyed, give him a shot!' That was another thing I was meaning to tell you."

"You were meaning to tell me a bunch of stuff, apparently."

She barred her teeth. "If you think this was fecking easy, arranging your escape from tests you don't recover from, then stealing your clothes, getting my girlfriend in cardiology – who I now owe feck-all, though she'll probably end up sweet on him, the ninny – to occupy the CT tech, then you can bloody well think again."

"Maureen, look – "

"And if it ever came out I lost a job on the Restricted Ward, which wasn't easy for a foreigner to get, for a mere *civilian* … well, paying my rent is the least of my worries."

"Maureen, I'm sorry. I owe you an awful lot. It's just this is all starting to fall into place way too easy. That bizarre, giant cop buying Jimmy's gamma-ray nonsense, and you being able to get my clothes *just* as they find the radio."

"Well aren't you a piece of work, actually using your head for something besides catching lead."

"You come right down to it, I'm not doing them any real good hidden away in Bellevue. But if I 'escape,' the MoFos can see where I go and who I contact. See if my flailing about to keep my head above water leads them anywhere." I stopped and stared at the sun again, which smiled right back but said nothing. "You know, Maureen, I gotta thank you properly someday."

"Don't bother. I – "

Her voice suddenly breaking as she stood a step above me, her face went tragic.

"What?"

"I guess it all comes down to what they did to my brother. Michael, not Donald. A heroic man, a rock others once built on, he's not been capable of leaving our parents' house alone going on four years now. And if Donald was hard to control before that…."

"I'm sorry."

"So you'll understand why I need to get you out of here. And why I don't get too concerned over what fecking Data Tier I may or may not be in. Me and mine have been on the wrong end of too many men – very *tangible* men to worry about any of that."

She slipped her stern mask back on, led me out of the stairwell into a hall and then straight into a staff bathroom she unlocked. I willed the room to steady itself. "Maureen, I've never been held prisoner in a hospital before. So if I said some dumb things…."

"Don't worry, gobshite. It was worth it to see the look on her face when you demanded the Commandant's real name last night."

"So, you meant that about a one-way trip to the rubber room?"

"You'd end up worse than Michael. I've never seen them jump on anyone like they have you. It's like you challenge them in some fundamental way. Or maybe it's cause of all the front pages with the girl with the garbanzos and a headline about the mystery man with the metal head – who's about to get a whole lot more mysterious by disappearing."

"Damn. Carole couldn't be some big, goobery-ass dude or immigrant or something?"

"Are you sure you want to go home? I have somewhere safe you could hole up till you decide what you're doing. Talk to a lawyer, one of the few who isn't in their pocket."

"Your place?" She just laughed. "Look, I did nothing wrong, so I'm going home, marching up my front steps and answering the phone when it rings."

"Maybe so. The old ways, taking to ground, don't work so well anymore, not with all their new tracking gizmos, not to mention the damn drones. OK, lad. Roll up your other sleeve to match the cut off one. Then turn left out the door here and you'll find an elevator straight down to the middle of the ER. Press G. It's the busiest spot in Bellevue, so hopefully you won't be noticed. Paste a smile on your face, do *not* meet anyone's gaze, and walk straight across to the far side and out that entrance by the ambulances. And then – you have money? – get in a cab and go."

"Maureen, I don't even know your last name."

"You're catching on." With another knee-wobbling smile, she added, "If you get dizzy going home, take this. A pinch of dexedrine – all the interns are on it. But try not to. Either way, sleep as much as you want, not that you'll have much choice. And by tomorrow you should be better. If not – if your head is squirrelly in any major way come Sunday – go to a private doctor out in Queens, some Jew or Muslim who's open Sundays. But not a hospital, especially not a City –"

I leaned down to her. She kissed me back without hesitation, heaven on earth for days on end until I turned to get a better angle of attack and she pulled away.

"You have my number in my chart. Call me."

"So you're not such a goofus after all. But no calls. Let's try this: first Tuesday of every month, for a couple of months, anyway, I'll be having a bowl of soup in the coffee shop on the corner of Third and 34th at noon. The soup's good, and that's far enough away from the hospital. You got that, Writer-Man? Did you not think I'd google you? Though I must be starkers to be even thinking of another writer.

Now get on with you!"

"Do I need to wipe any lipstick off?"

"Why? I don't wear any."

"You're kidding. First Tuesday, Third and 34th, noon."

"You can remove that bandage Monday. Till then, try to stay quiet. And no boozing, you, for a couple of days anyway."

And with that she reached around me. I puckered up for another kiss as she leaned in, opened the door just enough and pushed me out.

I melted into the ER's frantic swirl, the standard United Nations of scrubs, white coats and patients' families, plus a worrisome couple of cops sprinkled about. The giant band-aid on my head clamored and throbbed as I pasted on the sales clerk's vapid half-smile, stared off over everyone's head and shuffled forward, my invisibility ring slipped on for the bored hospital cop by the door.

Then I was free, outdoors if not off the Bellevue campus, out in a tangle of ambulances, a couple of EMTs leaning on them smoking, one reading a paper festooned with Carole in all her cheesecake glory. If I ran into my ambulance crew from the day before, Chunky wouldn't care, but would Skinny just assume I'd been discharged?

I strolled out the old, ornate front gate, misjudged the distance to my feet and staggered, the ground rising up at me. Waves pooling gently around my ankles, I waded across First Avenue and raised my arm for the cab I couldn't afford.

PART FOUR

Chapter Seventeen

The Morning After Nick's Big Night

But of course I could, I had nine bucks.

No lipstick! Was I really to believe such a professional man-slayer was set to purring all on her lonesome by the sight of me in a pale blue gown? Might Maureen someday come to think of me, if not a rock like her brother, as particularly cohesive landfill?

Who was I kidding? Awfully convenient, her being able to grab my clothes like that. And what about all those *pertinent* questions, like about my books and how Frankie had bloodied his nose? Formerly hot grease when they toss in the fries, Lurch had been stymied awfully easily by gamma rays, as Maureen killed time with tales of ice-pick lobotomies. Holed up in Bellevue I wasn't exactly helping them figure out what I was about, so why not arrange my daring, slow-mo escape – right past the hospital cops in the ER?

Regardless of Maureen's true loyalties, there was no doubt I'd been held prisoner, denied even a phone call, doped when I'd tried to make one, and warned that more needles plus tests to permanently scramble my eggs were in the offing. All a strong case for leaping in a taxi and gone, my first cab without Nicki in years. But first, make sure the Wife sat on my idiot e-mail – Minders Turn Elsewhere! Just pray she hadn't already sent it to some obscure haven of digital discontent to then blossom far and wide, because I was still unsure about disclosing my true intent at Penn Station.

I stumbled on the curb and paid the price between the ears. OK, barely out from under Bellevue's roof, so much for holding off on the intern's-little-helper Maureen slipped me. At the phone booth that hopefully shielded me from prying eyes in the hospital across the street, the Wife started hyperventilating from hello.

"Nicki, wait, let me ask you. That – "

"I didn't know what to think. I mean, last night I get this message, you sounding all breathless, that you're "stuck" somewhere, and then you never called back."

"Believe me I would've called back if I could. Wait till I tell you. But first – "

"Then this morning I hear you've been shot! So I called Bellevue, and they were a total joke. One guy mumbled in a silly accent he totally put on cause I heard him ask someone about you, and his English was fine. Somebody else hung up on me, and then this lady said the computer had no patient by your name."

I'd shunned the ballooning implications of no one coming even to take my temperature when I woke up. Were they really thinking of turning all my verbs to the past tense, simple as that? It happened to perceived irritants – reporters who knew of the wrong politician's drug history, say. But it was usually in roadside motel bathtubs out in Indiana somewhere, the lonely truth-seeker just happening to succumb to a final bout of depression despite being on the verge of an enormous scoop. Hell, concussions like mine cause blood clots often enough, and once they start migrating around.... I could only hope the Wife would fight to keep my perfect body safe from autopsy.

"Nicki! Did you send out that e-mail?"

"Yes, of course. But don't worry, I edited it like you told me to. I took out all that self-serving crap of yours."

So much for deciding what to say about my intent at Penn Station. "Christ, who'd you send it to?"

"Wait, forget the e-mail. You have to hear what happened to me coming to work. First, how are you? Are you OK?"

"I'm fine. A little woozy. And I literally had to flee Bellevue. So who did you freaking send it to?"

"You know, I told you all your wise-guy snarking around at my advertising parties was going to come back to haunt us, but I thought it'd be me at work. So, Mister Big Stuff in all the papers, do you remember the CheeseSpray party?"

"CheeseSpray – Nicki, what the hell are you talking about? *Who* did you send it to?"

"Well, someone remembered you from the CheeseSpray launch party. Melanie Artenunotte of *The New York Dispatch* remembered you waving that tray around. And some *Dispatch* police reporter knew the name Fremson that, for some bizarre reason, I happen to share with you. He remembered me getting some award – he started out as a clerk on the business desk – and asked Melanie if I was connected to you."

"Some Goddamn reporter from the *Dispatch*?"

"This police-beat twerp, Eric Benson. He ambushed me outside my office before eight this morning. I thought he was joking about you getting shot, and he thought it was weird I heard it from him. Like we're all supposed to remain glued to the horrible news the world churns out."

"Well, we are theoretically married."

"Yeah, anyway. So I told Benson about your theory that participant/observer journalism is one of the last best avenues open to a freelancer."

"*Nicki*. What else? Wait. First, Goddamn it, who did you send the e-mail to? And why did you hit send without checking with me first?"

"Screw you! I have your stupid e-mail printed out and hidden right here in my drawer, and – wait – here. You end it with, 'Anything happens, you'll know what to do.' Well, something sure as fuck did happen."

"That was in case I got killed."

"Sounds to me like you came awfully close."

"But I hadn't done anything yet. That's important. I was just minding my own business walking through Penn Station. Which is true. But with that e-mail out, now I'll get painted as some kind of freak challenging the cops –a T-symp or maybe even a Fiend myself! Plus Carole getting shot is gonna be all my fault too."

"*Carole* – you know a girl like her?"

"I'm supposed to call her Ms. Fiore cause we've never been formally introduced?"

"You better hope you don't get Boosted *two* Tiers for this, not one. Which I do not want to talk about on the phone here at work. And what's all this about a detonator?"

"See what I'm saying? It was my stupid radio – you know, the 'Entertainment System' – which they stole from my hospital room. They freaking had cops in my room the whole time, first one acting like a patient and then one in uniform, if he even was a cop. And when I tried to bull my way out of my room last night to call you, they shot me up with dope and I was out for hours. And now this nurse – well, I just kinda escaped."

"They made you a prisoner, and then they drugged you?"

"Yup. And they're trying to say I have epilepsy. I'll have horns and a tail next."

"What a minute: you had to *flee* Bellevue? But this is still New

York for Christ's sake, not Washington with that storm-trooper cop they got running things down there."

"Flee, as in down the back stairs and out. So, Nicki, who did you send it to?"

"I couldn't think after that *Dispatch* guy got me so twisted. He was practically skipping down the sidewalk he was so thrilled with interviewing – well, your wife, I called myself. He said you were the huge black hole at the center of the story, and he had an exclusive with me."

"Who, Nicki!"

"*Naked Opposition.* You know, you seemed to like them, the couple of articles they published of yours."

"You sent it to Stanley?"

"I didn't know anyone's name. I just sent it to their general mailbox."

"Jesus. Maybe I can sweet-talk him, or threaten him somehow, not to run it. You sent it from work?"

"Not my official work e-mail. People all over the office have already been giving me the hairy eyeball, and God only knows about Charley, who's still closeted away upstairs."

"I'll call you later. Don't do anything until you hear from me, OK? But wait, you got 'twisted' with the *Dispatch* – what the hell does that mean?"

"Nothing. I mean, he loomed up and caught me right at our door when I'm just trying to make it to my desk to suck down a Dr. Pepper. He said he recognized me from pictures from awards dinners, probably that horrible, goof-ball shot of me laughing with my mouth open. And I'd had nothing to eat."

"What do you mean, Dr. Pepper and nothing to eat? You out all night or what?"

"All I knew was that blonde bombshell was on all the front pages cause, for once, everybody on the train had a newspaper. *Everyone*, it was amazing. But I was reading my book and figured I'd catch it when I got to work."

"You didn't answer me."

"You want to hear or what? So this puppy in a brown velvet jacket – something weird in this heat – jumps me by F&F's door and asks if I know you. And, I don't know, it was something about the ritzy jacket and he was cute and all. So just goofing around, I said, 'Why, does he owe you money?' And he fucking wrote that down, can you believe it. I mean that's a joke, that's a line, everyone knows that. But he kept pushing that there was some money angle, like you set out to get shot so you could sue the City."

"Shot in my metal head."

"So I just blurted out that well, of course there was a money angle. That you're a writer, that's what you do."

"Nicki, for Pete's sake!"

"Listen, or I'm hanging up. I mean I didn't even know you'd been shot. Plus no one knew anything about your condition. Even the *Dispatch* had been trying to pry it out of Bellevue all night, he said. So of course I was bothered by that."

"Perturbed, verily."

"But I did *not* say anything about protesting the searches or anything. I figured you'd want to tell that in your own words, in that e-mail. So then he went back to the money angle. At that, I just said I was late for work and had to go."

"Money angle. Maybe I should just go find another shaky cop with a gun. This guy was real young?"

"Yeah. Why?"

"He's gonna make it as sensational as possible to make his bones on my ass. What else?"

"I don't know."

"What else did you freaking tell him, Nicki? Come on, I gotta go reach Stanley before it gets ruined even worse."

"I didn't *ruin* anything. I'm not made for all this, some twerp bushwhacking me first thing in the morning about somebody I know getting shot. I'm just an advertising hack, remember?"

"I said before *it* gets ruined – I didn't say *you* ruined it. Now, come on. Stop getting hysterical and tell me what else you told the Goddamn *New York Dispatch*."

"I don't know. Mostly that you were kind of a nut – you know, in a good way – about the Constitution. Like that means anything now. And that you'd been kind of floundering lately, having trouble getting published, but that now, after getting shot, maybe you had a big score. Something to get you back on your feet."

"You told him that? Do you ever listen to yourself, how that sounds with Carole having to get her guts stitched up?" The Wife: at her absolute best in an early-morning twerp crisis.

"Look, no one told me to get up early and have a big breakfast because some reporter was gonna leap out of the bushes at me cause my chump-change husband is in all the papers for all the wrong reasons. I mean, it was kind of a big night last night if you really must know, and I might even have still been a little drunk to tell you the truth, nothing in my stomach to soak up the alcohol."

"Spare me the details. So: 'somebody you know,' huh?"

"What?"

"That's how you referred to me before. Pretty much says it all, doesn't it?"

"Go reach Stanley. Tell him I made a mistake sending the e-mail, and he'll just have to understand, that's all."

"Sure. He'll be delighted to punt the biggest story he's ever gonna see – dropped out of the sky into his lap."

"Appeal to his better nature. You're sure your head's OK?"

"Yeah, I think so. See you later, alright?"

"I guess."

The silence dragging, hard to say who hung up first.

Time to appeal to some scrambling web-dude's better nature and tell him to forego a sketchy and premature disclosure regarding that little Penn Station imbroglio. Right. The Stuffing fluttering, I stood in the street waving for a cab, nothing but trouble beckoning back, the sun emanating like all get-out from wherever it had gone. Bleating horns the only sign of life from the stalled traffic three long blocks from the rent-a-computer joint, I got out to beat the meter turning over again. My feet in better focus thanks to Maureen's pill, I motivated a block, feebly swinging my arms to grab some momentum, then stopped to call Pop. He was glad I'd felt well enough to get discharged because Bellevue sure acted weird when he called earlier – full of no information. He wanted to drive in with Mom, but I said I was probably sleeping most of the day. Saturday, Mom had something she plain couldn't miss, so we agreed they'd visit on Sunday, high time they found out why I called home the Hovel.

So Nick had had a "big night." Hotdiggity, raise the curtain on a standing-room-only engorgement. Hard to say which was worse, that she'd felt the need to tell me, or felt that she could. Hell with it – all of it, including her lousy sacral dimples. I woofed down a corn muffin from one of the carts the City amazingly hadn't shut down in favor of stores that sell worse for twice and wondered the number of eventual morning-after Dr. Peppers it was going to take to get over the Wife.

Chapter Eighteen

Stanley the Obdurate

Rolling up my one long sleeve, I crept into the shop feeling odd among people safely ignoring the cops, the Constitution and even their own plummeting reputations to find *Naked Opposition* happily commentating on some same-old same-old.

Stanley had previously published some of my unadulterated musings, two tasty morsels, plus a hasty story to prevent getting scooped. Yet I'd never spoken to one-man-band Stan to gauge his age or anything else. I didn't even know what state he lived in, though his rants under his own byline hinted rust-belt. Whoever he was, he ran a good site – a bit raw, sure, though fundamentally legitimate, a good daily clearinghouse of raked muck, a veritable lake of dug truth and punchy alternatives.

At least Stanley never had me sign the damn release that pervaded freelance work, the one that stated that if the subject of any story so much as says boo, never mind how airtight the article, the publication washes its hands of the writer, with all the blame and exorbitant cost of settling or defending any lawsuit falling on that poor schmuck's head. Small sites and national heavyweights alike employed this delightful little codicil to cling safely to the trunk of the tree as they cut off the limb where they'd happily sat next to you on publication.

Stanley, rather, trusted to his wits. He published for the love of it, sheer cussedness and, with maybe fifty thousand readers a day, a little money from some very peculiar advertisers. (Cave-man survivalist crap mixed with 'righteous' micro-zap carriers, and the like, left and right driven around the bend to join hands on the far side of the circle.) HeadFuck and crew rampant, it took guts to poke the big dogs in the ribs whenever someone handed Stan a long enough stick or he dug one out of the weeds himself.

I turned to see an abandoned *New York Dispatch*, still the key shaper of opinion even on such a tabloid-special story as mine; the damn photo was starting to grate, Carole big and brassy above the fold. The décolleté picture, seemingly the only one ever taken of her, leaped out even more surrounded by all that gray. It was like the drawing of a pretty, long-haired girl playing the sousaphone leaping off the dictionary's sober page. Re-cork your tongue, brother, and join in offering a lonely city's concupiscence for her recovery.

The coy headline was perhaps worst of all: "Man Carrying Books, Woman Shot at Penn Station". Fair enough and, depending on the story's speculation as to my intent, perhaps even favorable that they immediately saw the books' significance. But then the headline continued: "Mayor Declares, 'Wider T Link Not Yet Apparent' ". Great. Not that no terror link existed, nor no reason to think me part of some wider plot. But that no link was visible – yet.

Cue the cops' demonization drums, the mayor shaking a tambourine, newsstand guys furiously making change, all bathed in Carole's overripe glory. Nicki said people on the subway were reading a newspaper, of all things. I couldn't wait to see the *Daily Chirp*.

God, I wanted to scream. Why didn't I have a damn job? Then maybe I'd still have a wife I didn't have to e-mail, but could just whisper my plans to. Kind of a big night, she'd had the gall to say, showing up residually boozed at work. What, some Wall Street schmuck who's gotta start despoiling the world at dawn, so he couldn't take her to breakfast like any normal jerk screwing some guy's wife, however estranged? She woke up in her own bed the morning after the night before, no way she was leaving her apartment without breakfast in her belly to soak up the booze. I'd taught her that at least, while also demonstrating its corollary: excessive amounts of food don't compensate for lack of sober sleep. Not really.

Knowing his personal e-mail, I quickly reached Stan the Man to find him stewing over Nicki's note. I asked for his micro-zap, figuring to get home and call him, that a better route to browbeating him into not running something that inadequately explained my motivation at Penn. (Christ, was it really just twenty-five hours before?) Two mangy, self-righteous mutts fighting over scraps, I owed him one, but not this. As Orwell observed: "the squalid farce of left-wing politics."

Stanley wrote back:

> Revealing my phone would violate a security paradigm of long standing, especially with the lens now focused on you, friend. Still, congratulations on the wide coverage your action – not that it's described as such, yet – has received. *WashPost, USA Maybe*. There was even a decent AP account in my local fish-wrapper.
>
> But tell me, friend, how do I know you're not some MoFo trying to finally uncover my location by asking for my micro-zap?

I told him the Minders didn't move in real time on Middling Severity Tiers like mine, so how could anyone but me know Nicki had sent him my e-mail?

> Spooks way beyond the Minders monitor my traffic. But, assuming for a moment that you are you, let's hear some more about 'Nicki' because frankly your relationship appears to be under something of a strain.

Gonna grab a little color on the happy couple, Stan?

I told him to leave my wife out of it and realized my disadvantage not knowing how much of my mawkish crap she'd included in what she'd sent him. Back on my heels, I threw a decent counter-punch that he couldn't have it both ways, pretending it wasn't me and also pumping for info.

He cleverly resolved our little security dilemma so we could then proceed to our real argument. He asked me to name a fact-checker we both happened to know, and I easily remembered his oddball first name: Wrenfield. The shit raining down, he then congratulated me on the marvelous, tattered umbrella our kind offered a discerning, thumb-sucking few.

Stanley! Enough claptrap. You can't run that private e-mail of mine. I'm screwed if that's how it comes out I intended to challenge the cops. It'll color everything and give them room to try to blame me for getting shot in the head.

What's wrong with a laudatory challenge? "Nicki" – if she's not actually a mechanism to fuel your disclosure – did you a favor, friend. Round up the band, the bloggers, dykes on bikes, whoever you can get and march down Fifth Avenue. A lot more people will support your action than you might think.

Stanley, it wasn't an 'action.' As of now, far as anyone knows, I was just walking through Penn Station. The demonization already bad enough, the cops dredging up who knows what wretched excess from my checkered past, I'd just as soon keep it that way for a day or two until I'm able to tell my tale properly. But I need that time to stop being woozy from getting shot in the head. That was a private e-mail to my wife, and you have no freaking right to it.

I could hear him laughing through the screen.

Friend, an e-mail sent to a news site that gets more than approximately 52,312 uniques a day is not exactly private - never mind the MoFos reading it. You certainly don't own it. I doubt that even I own it. Sent unbidden to Naked Opposition for the benefit of its readers, if anyone owns it, they do.

Spare me. I'm not including in an e-mail – cause of you know who – half the stuff that's happened to me over the past 24 hours, and I'm not even home yet. This is off-the-record, damn it, you are NOT allowed to use this. But I was physically prevented from calling my wife to tell her not to send my note out.

As to your coy little reference to the Minders: step on a crack, break your father's back. That is, turn agnostic. It's the only stance that allows soldiering on without whiplash from looking over your shoulder. Really, it's only a matter of time.

What's only a matter of time?

No one knows – that's what makes HeadFuck's America so intriguing.

I'll sue. I'm serious, Stanley.

By all means go right ahead, I could use the diversion. I just hope, fellow traveler that you are, it won't get too, too expensive for you. Either way, I'll enjoy the pro se exercise and use it to drive eyeballs to N. O. Hopefully you'll get your own site (finally) to counterattack, and all in all, the Beast will get fat and happy.

I told him my head was full of mush, that just typing this non-sense was leaving me exhausted, and I was going home.

He said fine, but since he was indeed posting my e-mail to Nicki, he needed to get a couple of things straight.

Let's square this away, and I'll let you go get some rest. I've had four concussions myself over the years, so I know. The last two freed something up in my writing, broke in the gears a bit better somehow.
Anyway, you wrote that you "hope to galoot around enough to spark a search" etc. I don't know that word as a verb, but I guess you were planning on approaching the cops in, according to my dictionary, a foolish manner?

I was goofing around with my wife. You never heard the phrase, big galoot?

So you were using a word ungrammatically because it was not for publication.

Nail the jello to the wall, dude. Could you be any more anal?

For your own protection as well as mine, enough lies soon to be printed about you as it is, brother.

And another thing: what's with the ugliest, skimpiest type I've ever seen? Talk about passive-aggressive.

Saves on archival costs. Until it's printed - and imagine a top-notch site like *N. O.*'s volume of correspondence - I don't consider it saved. But considering where you normally publish, I don't understand this: "Then I'll have a big boffo piece on it for the big bucks."

Damn, I'd been hoping Nick'd had the sense to delete that. Like her "big score" admission to the Dispatch, it was the money quote in all the ways that counted. "That's sarcasm, you dunce."

Like any good reporter, his questions got trickier as he went along, though I would've saved that "boffo" bit for last.

Quoting my e-mail, he wrote:

"So, a real martyr to the Fourth Amendment, maybe.." How did you get the cops to even draw their guns, let alone shoot you? You never impressed me as the reckless type, debating every tiny edit like you do. And finally - says you, not me - how did you know your head is like Wonder Woman's bracelets?

Hell, I was carrying a backpack, and I was going to refuse to submit to a search. So anything was possible. And no, I'm not depressed. Life's peachy. How's by you? You getting enough of whatever rows your boat, I shudder to think?

So the shooting was all just an unfortunate set of circumstances?

Read the damn papers, which I haven't even had the chance to do yet, then flip whatever they say sideways and let your conscience be your guide. My head is swimming, and I'm spending money by the minute on this with you, and I got a long way still to go - and that's not in a taxi - to make it home. Anything else?

You wrote of maybe being a martyr to the Fourth Amendment. Well, my publishing your note will end up making you a martyr of a different sort, a punching bag for the Movement as a whole, the MoFos making an example of you, brother. They know that if refuse-and-resist ever catches on about something like the searches, it might lead to bigger things. And trust that I'm going to do my utmost to boost N. O.'s revelation about your political intent. The greater good demands that I focus on the oak, not the acorn.

If you own a parachute, grab it. Any skeletons in your closet, haul them out into the light yourself, cause a lot of snoops and spooks have you in their crosshairs. Any back taxes, any gun with one of those nasty, multi-burst trigger activators down in the bottom of a real closet (though again, guns don't go with being an effete, strictly rhetorical bomb-thrower), excise them yourself before the skeletons start dancing.

I've tracked down a picture of your lovely wife, which I will not use. (Her name, yes - my responsibilities to N. O.'s readers demand that. But let someone else dunk her pretty face in your lumpy porridge.) Which raises the interesting question of why you have to e-mail her at all to discuss your plans. When I want to talk to my wife, I just roll over. Good luck and try to remember who your friends are.

Stanley scoring points in a flurry with both hands, including rubbing my nose in my obvious estrangement from Nicki. But hell, he's gonna *boost* 'his' revelation my ass. Ah, the Left, so willing to tear each other to shreds.

You finished, Dr. Freud? First off, a true ally would let me tell my story in my own way. A twenty dollar bill falls out of the pocket of someone walking in front of you, you yell - plain and simple. And, given that I got shot in the head yesterday and don't really need to be a punching bag for anyone right now, exactly what 'Movement' you talking about? It's got a name, got leaders, a set of principles or any agenda aside from getting you more attention than you deserve? So screw you and the galoot you rode in on.

That's right - watch out, baby, black power's gonna get your momma. Cause you know damn well what you're doing here is wrong, Stanley, a smart, solidarity-forever, man-the-barricades type like you. A guy who put his body on the line trying to take a stand, someone who's now getting denounced on every front page in town, should have the right to control the raw material of his own story. Control his own damn text - a private note to his wife.

So, should we ever talk again, which I assure you will be too Goddamn soon, spare me your namby-pamby, Kumbaya load. Cause you're nothing but a snake like all the rest,

handing the Swift-Boaters all the fuel they need. I hope
your scrawny ass looks lousy in the wispy, scraggily beard I
assume is all you can grow, since you're not gonna be able
to look yourself in the mirror to shave for a long time. That
I leave you as my curse.

Bruised and abused, damn right it made me feel better to nail
Stanley as the rheumy piece of cheese he was. Though, unfortunately,
he was as sharp and forceful as *N. O.* led me to fear. He'd quickly
realized, for instance, that I hadn't seen Nicki's e-mail. At bottom, I
had little but a personal appeal, just as she'd suggested. Well, screw
him, his galoot and the horse they were spooning on when they
rode in.

Chapter Nineteen

The Hovel's Sheltering Arms

Sticking close to the sidewalk's slow lane abutting the stores, I shambled the couple of blocks to the Queens train, an old hobbler with a four-tipped cane at one point rushing past. I brooded over what Lurch had read from the *Node* and also the dreadful *Dispatch* headline. Wasn't anyone questioning the shootings?

I bought the papers as I hit the subway stairs. Man, my depth perception stank, and I clung to the rail. The post-rush hour brown-out already in force, the train plodded under the river taking folks from all over the world home to Queens. So I had plenty of time to peruse the first rough draft of *my* story, damn it.

The *Dispatch* evinced its usual predilection for official pronounce-ments, starting with the mayor tarring me in that headline. And it quoted the cops high up in the story regarding the silver device I was said to be "brandishing." Saying it was unfortunately lost in the post-shooting melee, the MTA police spokesman added, " 'Whether it was some kind of micro-zap; an old, illegal whole-vid cell phone; an outmoded radio of a rare type no longer in common usage; or a gun or even a detonator is yet to be determined.' "

His stilted reference to what it actually was, a radio, reminded me of when they catch a plagiarist and run both texts. The copy, being a lie, always sounds all-thumbs next to the unself-conscious original. Still, it would take a rare reporter to quiz the cops about this silver embodiment of mutability. The *Dispatch* then quoted the MTA mouthpiece on my " 'antique satchel of East German military design crammed with an inordinate number of printed books which several agencies are subjecting to retroflex analysis to determine their underlying significance.' " What, gonna read 'em?

The article said the police had to delay questioning the "Suspect" – bingo, you bastards, that the *Dispatch'* own term, not quoting any official – since doctors forbade it due to my "grave medical status." That nicely redolent phrase prepared a grieving world for my potential exit stage left. The MTA yapper – country mouse to the NYPD's city mouse – stirred things ever frothier with talk of "an atypical configuration of an unusual amount of semi-perishable food. We're studying whether the subject was self-supplied for a siege of some sort."

Self-supplied. Not catered? Get a MoFo before a cluster of microphones and any fool thing he said, into the paper it went. I weighed – well, in England it'd be a lot of stones – and I had two solid sandwiches. On a normal day moping around the Hovel, let alone out schlepping an "inordinate" library around, that wouldn't last me past three in the afternoon.

Carole, I was happy to read, was expected to make a full recovery after getting her no doubt gorgeous intestines stitched up. From Ridgewood, Queens, the twenty-four-year-old was heading to her job at some big real estate outfit when shot. She was also studying nights at Queens College when not spreading cheer at local hospitals and nursing homes with the rest of her amateur modern dance troop. Carole's fiancé was no slouch in the looks department himself, with a nifty forty-dollar haircut and fireman's de rigueur, rakish mustache. Thank goodness no pictures of me had surfaced, at least there in the *Dispatch*.

The paper spilled some ink interviewing Homeland Control Deputy Chief Undersecretary Diego Smith as well as Wallace Jones, the Alexander M. Palmer Professor of Civil Control at MIT, about the pressures on cops making split-second decisions. Said, Smith, " 'After Manila, we all recognize the importance of targeted kill-shots. At the end of the day, public safety often dictates that the risk the Suspect presents – his guilt, in effect – is established post-neutralization by post-facto neuro-forensics.' " For his part, Jones hoped that, " 'despite the medical odds of a head wound, the Suspect might recover sufficiently to shed light on his motivations, however obscure.' " Shed like a white cat on a black rug, Jones.

The Daily Chirp, bless 'em, had a coy headline framing Carole (who I was definitely getting a little sick of, like your third piece of wedding cake): "Cops Shoot Penn Pair". Below her: "Woman, Man Fight for Life at Bellevue". Inside they had the same MTA garbage about a gun or detonator. But the *Chirp* also harped on whether the police should even draw their guns in Penn Station during rush hour, particularly the machine pistols they increasingly favored. It wondered, "Of the 600,000 who pass through Penn Station daily, how many will now cast a justly fearful eye on the Protectors charged with safeguarding them?" My, my.

But Walk-on-Water Ted instructed *Chirp* readers in no uncertain terms that the (supposedly) random searches, " 'will get the job done and are here to stay on my say-so. Though I don't trouble him with policy specifics, I'm sure I have the mayor's full backing.' " A bit further down, he added, " 'It's no accident that *both* officers – both experienced men and one a Fomenting Hero – felt the need to fire.' "

A third *Chirp* story was headlined: "Penn Protector Called 'Shaky'; Officer Questioned During Sands". It identified the shooter as one Frankie Reisner, a Guardsman and "heroic, four-times Boot." Both he and his partner, Phil Frost, were family men and seasoned MTA officers. However, "The circumstances of Protector Reisner's latest deployment remain cloudy," said the *Chirp* in probably the only real reporting, as opposed to taking dictation, I read that morning. "He has been formally interviewed as a 'person of material interest' regarding an incident with numerous fatalities outside Salakmahest, according to one Army source."

What's more, in an unrelated matter, the MTA had temporarily placed Reisner on desk assignment. This followed " 'a possible T incident, the Protector's weapon drawn but not forced to discharge,' according to a senior MTA leader unauthorized to speak since, he said, 'the matter is before one of those vestigial courts.' " This official regretted Reisner's transfer to Penn Station from the 125th Street Station where the incident occurred. " 'He was doing a bang-up job applying Sands techniques to the people up there.' " Ultimately, Frankie escaped desk-duty and got his gun back about a month before nose met chest.

My man! Head over heels in some Fomenting Democracy mess (what, the wrong warlord's family got slaughtered?), shaky and shell-shocked and carrying it home to rile the folks uptown.

Anton, the National Guardsman accompanying the cops (unlike them, his last name was omitted) got Plunged a few years back from his union electrician job. He then hocked himself to the hilt and bought a car mechanic's shop in rapidly gentrifying East New York only to have his cousin run it into the ground during his last Sands.

I turned the page to find a rapturous study of Carole playing after-work softball. A pitcher, of course, she'd just released the ball and was standing straight, her left arm in a graceful follow-through. A tasty rainbow sherbet in pink sneakers and tall purple socks, even her knees appealed, and how rare is that? But no one would care about knees topped by such a long pour of creamy vanilla thigh, then lemony short-shorts and a cherry tee shirt, *Real Bricks*, the name of her company, stretched tight in chocolate sprinkles. A marvelously intense look was topped by all that platinum whipped cream piled high. The games co-ed, she undoubtedly got numerous strike-three-lookings.

So. The war-vet cop (however compromised), the avuncular, family-man cop, and the pillar of his community, war-vet Boot on the one hand. The heart-of-gold, real-bricks fox on the other. And little old me on a wizened third hand. My instinct to identify myself at Bellevue as Mitch, not my byline's Mitchell, proved sound. Cause none of the papers had connected the dots to my published journalism.

Depending on what Stanley spilled, I still might get to dance on stage in some measure to my own music – once I got it written.

Subways rolled slowly above ground where I lived. Enjoying the AC, I gazed out at what weatherpersons on TV and radio chock-a-block with seven-passenger spewer ads insisted on calling 'haze.' Northwest Queen's low, foreground jumble did nothing to obscure the apartment towers a short leap over the East River. Yet the tall glass towers, curved or jagged, bronze, green or blue – meant to shimmer and dazzle and pronounce about their lofty occupants – were barely visible through the lung-searing smear.

✳✳✳✳✳✳✳✳✳✳✳✳✳✳✳

My stop approaching and the Stuffing giving notice I needed to get horizontal, could I assume refuge behind the polite fiction of my own locked door? Tall, wide and still shabbily handsome, built for some minor shipping magnate in the 1850s, the luxe old pile had been carved into a dog's-breakfast of apartments – cells, really, most of them. Such cramped little cribs hard to find, even in Bumfuckville, at least it was down by the river. Most of its large, shabby peers had been replaced by townhouses whose walls vibrated when struck, their few windows the size of toaster ovens. My home had escaped demolition because, aside from its dicey, ass-end location, the quirky Greek landlord, almost as old as the house itself, refused to sell.

From his enormous, gloomy apartment behind the columned front porch, Mr. Staphilopoulous terrorized the all-male gathering of misfits who lived in the rabbit hutches above. Such was his fierce mien, peering out from under bushy white eyebrows that clashed with his improbable, pomegranaty hair, he even spooked some of the younger kids from the nearby housing project.

What's more, Stap was rich, his fortune resting on the one thing they're making no more of, in his case a vast back yard aswarm with junk. Near the house, a listing, vine-encrusted aboveground swimming pool was missing a few side panels. Further back, a couple of Detroit's finest dinosaurs rusted away, including an ancient, luridly purple Plymouth Road Runner, more's the pity. As to the vast stretch of brambles a long ways back, human foot had not touched ground there for some time.

Nicki lowering the boom right when some schmoe was carried out feet first, I was lucky enough to score one of the few real apartments, mine high up and in back, far from the Greek's prying ears. So Stap and my only tussle was when my friend Ralph dropped by and committed the crime of leaving his bike by the porch while pondering which of the dozen indifferently working bells rigged up by the front door of this ostensibly private home was mine.

I got back in Mr. Staphilopoulous's good graces explaining to him one hot, hot night, the fetid murk pressing down on every crease and cranny, what a presidential vest-pocket veto had been. He'd heard the phrase on TV from a HeadMan partisan, one of the dozens who quickly dominated the airwaves after his installation, once it became clear whose bread was buttered, how, and by whom. HeadMan's stooge argued that Congress allowing itself to be stripped of its subpoena power meant nothing. Why nobody would miss that anymore than they'd miss the vest-pocket veto. And Stap had been driving himself crazy trying to make the phrase parse in his decent English because he couldn't remember any president in his decades in America wearing a vest.

Sometimes amenable to conversation, often not, over time Stap revealed his chief occupations: massaging his almost worthless, post-Plunge shares of ACME Cement and the like; torturing his corrupt city councilman (a yuppie who'd had the nerve to unseat Stap's thieving countryman) with a string of handwritten letters composed with the aid of a well-thumbed Greek-English dictionary; and bemoaning the fortunes of his favorite footballers, AEK Athens.

The entire first floor Stap's faded domain, there were grim single rooms on most of the second and the entire third floors, many with no windows, and all sharing that floor's one kitchen and bath. The Albanians, Chinese, Guatemalans and Mexicans et. al. found them a steal at a measly $650 a month, usually two to a room. The Albanians seemed hard-smoking burn-outs who manned the local produce stores; the Chinese, younger, hard-smoking strivers; and the Latinos, by far the majority, were nonsmoking grunts of all work who blossomed briefly each week from around seven Saturday night through the duration of volleyball Sunday.

Some little whippet of a white guy who favored short-sleeved checked shirts with white pants and went running every morning at six, had long occupied a real apartment on the second floor. Marvin even had sole access to a criminally unused terrace atop the big porch roof. A computer mumbo-jumboist for Chase or Capture or some Despoiler, Marvin saw no need to buddy up to yet another of the losers passing through – especially since Nick tossing me had goosed my usual cleverer-than-thou. Our sole conversation, Marvin mentioned that Saturday night was the house's one night to howl, Mr. Staphilopoulous purposely out. But it wasn't too bad, he prissily assured me, since "the laborers" wanted to be up early for Sunday's catch-and-toss 'volleyball' games in the local school yard. Marvin subsequently greeted my grunts of hello with a vacant stare.

Thus, the fourth-floor, two-room (shower, john and kitchen, of sorts, included) locus of my struggle to inflate my lungs despite the Blue Meanies. The windowless, glorified closet of a bedroom often too hot despite its freakish ten-foot ceiling, I'd make a nest for myself on the floor in the kitchen/rec room/study under my one window and stare at the backyard's towering tree. Yup, my very own Hovel that I was going to learn to love real soon. Click my ruby slippers three times and say it loud.

****

Riding the bus home with the project ladies clutching their shopping bags, I fretted over finding Mr. Staphilopoulos on the porch, waving a copy of *The Daily Chirp* under my nose, my stuff heaped on the front lawn, my landlord yelling about needing no troublemakers. Like most in HeadFuck's politically demobilized land, our conversations hadn't veered to politics (beyond vest pockets). Given Stap's general rules-and-regulations mentality, one could guess his stance. Aside from ancient cars – his own a fossilized barge of a Buick Electra, dark green with burnt-sienna seats – he seemed at an unenthralled remove from most things American. That presumably included such quaint anachronisms as political dissent.

But the porch was empty, Mr. Staphilopoulos perhaps inside brewing another espresso. Far as I could tell, the bitter little cups were his sole sustenance aside from cigarettes, the odd, rich snack (fried eggplant, anchovies, and pearl onions smeared on crackers or pesto spooned straight from the jar) and a genteel sufficiency of Metaxa. I hauled myself four flights up, sending the Stuffing into back flips.

I fired up the machine, glad to see that Stanley was still linking to the same garden-variety scandals as before. Could my tirade have possibly hit home? Ideally, I'd have gotten my side of the story out before he, that twerp Benson at the *Dispatch*, the cops or some haircut on TV heaved another bag of slop my way. But, those four flights up the final blow, the Hovel's walls were going all wavy on me. A cogent and impassioned account not spilling from the Stuffing just then, I was lucky to brush my teeth for the first time in too long. Whatever I wrote getting boatloads of scrutiny, it couldn't be no Dick and Jane.

I decided against a chair wedged under the doorknob. Aside from hardly slowing 'em down, I feared surrendering to that level of paranoia. Plus how would they get in if the Stuffing went south, and I had to crawl to the phone to call an ambulance (assuming I could)?

I unplugged my phone, turned off the micro-zap, and set the alarm for late afternoon to get up and make a stab at "Penn Tale." And feeling like I'd dragged a heavy stone by a strap round my head, out I fell. I had no memory of squelching the alarm, but did recall getting up at some point for a feed and staring at some idiot cop show for fifteen minutes.

Actually, like most, it was far too clever and instructive, teaching that suspects should never demand a lawyer before sparring with the cops. Such behavior-modeling embedded in a TV show's story line is by far the most powerful form of mass inculcation. Hence the struggle every few years over actors smoking in movies and why, leaping into their cars, even the worst desperado and most desperate pursuer fasten their seat belts before burning rubber. Go ahead, start blabbing folks. Don't need no lawyer, cause you're way smarter than the cops.

The room stale and sarcophogeal, I sat there watching the MoFo's easy triumph that Friday evening, dumbly spooning pineapple-laden cottage cheese and wondering how such an oddity arrived in my fridge. After this quarter-hour cultural and gustatory triumph, sleep reclaimed me.

Chapter Twenty

Two Below the Waterline

The vertical coffin's door somehow shut and my pillow drenched, I leaped from my bed too quickly, staggered and clutched at the door, then ran water for three minutes to clear the lead from Stap's 1850's pipes. Five gulped glasses providing some relief, even a lousy breakfast of cereal doused in evaporated milk couldn't wipe off the relative Saturday morning shine of waking up Lurch-less, lord of all I surveyed in two hot little rooms.

Dulling that shine figured to belong to both a certain lefty wanker and to young Benson at *The New York Dispatch*. But first, I spooned away over an article that swam to the top of the kitchen-table pile. It detailed the treatment accorded a certain showpiece Fiend, my brief interlude at Bellevue a day at the beach by comparison. For I'd suffered no long-term sensory deprivation. My windows weren't cloaked, guards hadn't covered my eyes with dark goggles and worn dark visors themselves to prevent ocular intercourse. There were no sound-proof headphones clamped on my ears. Having escaped their 'tests,' I hadn't been rendered "docile as a piece of furniture."

The Stuffing trimmed by caffeine, I logged on to find *Naked Opposition* ballyhooing its "EXCLUSIVE: Wounded Activist-Journalist's Goal to Challenge Illegal Police Searches. Alerted Spouse: His Intent to 'Spark a Search … for a Principled Refusal.' Deemed Arrest 'Likely.' Amid Police Smear, True Patriots Endorse his Planned Action."

So much for *I was just taking them books out to Mom.*

Staking his claim to me as a "stalwart *N.O.* contributor," Stanley led with a properly skeptical description of the shootings and riffed on the unconstitutionality of suspicionless searches. He then echoed the widely held belief that the searches were nothing but security theater designed to flog fear and cow the populace into accepting all manner of abuse. To that end, they're probably even more effective than all the T-apocalyptic TV shows. Getting down to it, he duly anointed me as the standard bearer of some ragtag movement and called for "legions of self-reliant, constitutionally aware citizens to follow this activist's lead."

He moved to "the e-mail exchange with *Naked Opposition* – Fremson's only interview to date since the unwarranted attack by the police." Great. My own pen somehow dry, I chose to tell my tale not to, oh, *The Daily Chirp* or, better yet, news-hound Leslie, but to feisty, little, very obscure *N.O.* Carole Exhibit A (indeed, since puberty), he decried the danger to bystanders in a crowded train station when cops unholster their guns. He said it was a danger I recognized "in a remarkable admission: *'I was carrying a backpack, and I was going to refuse to submit to a search. So anything was possible.'* Bystanders take note when a citizen-activist is willing to put his body on the line to take a stand."

Screw you with an eggbeater, Solidarity Boy. It was a *statement*, not an admission, one that you're flogging to ram home the non-existent shreds of my culpability about my supposed willingness to endanger everyone around me. You got a lawyer picked out for Carole to sue me with yet?

He ran my denial of carrying a weapon and then quoted something that had seemed clever at the time: " *'Read the damn papers … then flip whatever they say sideways and let your conscience be your guide.'* " Shit.

Stan noted my claim to be suffering a concussion and said I seemed, "even through the beclouding, pixeled scrim" – writing with all ten fingers, Stanley! – "to be under considerable stress given the contrast with our previously harmonious relations." So now I was unhinged to boot.

Then he got to my damn e-mail to Nick, starting with my germinating complaint about the searches and the disgust I expressed to her observing them in action: " *'People were just delighted to trot up to have the cops trod all over the Constitution and pretend to paw through their stuff. The cop told a majority of the people to just move on, but maybe a third of those folks – dumb bunnies who'd already been dismissed! – lined up anyway.'* "

Unhinged, but oddly superior.

He let me articulate my plan: " *'[H]ope to galoot around enough to spark a search and then draw myself up in high dudgeon for a principled refusal.'* " But then he channeled his inner schoolmarm. "His granting himself license to employ a noun as a verb is in keeping with – alone among the millions of victims of these police-state tactics – his decision to stick it to the Man." Thanks, I supposed.

As I'd feared, he quoted the impecunious freelancer's optimism about making a few hundred bucks: " *'I'll have a big boffo piece on it for the big bucks. A stunt, yeah, but drawing a line, damn it, with the sort of participatory/observer stuff that's seemingly gone out of style.'* " He compared "a hungry writer conflating himself with the story to walking the railroad tracks searching for lumps of coal tossed from the train."

Whether he or Nicki sanitized it I couldn't say, but at least there was none of my icky, oh-Baby, personal stuff, nor any of my sappiness about Fourth Amendment martyrdom. Nothing about the books, either. But then he quoted my denial of sending him the e-mail myself to surreptitiously disclose my intent to the world. "And that well may be true," he said, running some of the Internet circle-jerk proving – Jesus! – that the cut-and-paste of my original e-mail to Nicki came to him from a veiled Fornix & Foyst account. Man, Nicki was gonna have fourteen different conniption fits – right after she did the boogaloo on my ass. Several attempts to reach her at work proved futile, Stanley said, and a Queens number under her name was recently disconnected. "That may explain the curious tenor of an intra-spousal e-mail."

Bite me. He ended by twisting a guilt-by-association shiv, quoting out of left field (way over by the foul pole), one "Comrade Timmy Refneski, Chief Dogmatist, Bakunin's Rebellion, the Republic of Bushwick." Couldn't reach the Center for Constitutional Rights or the National Lawyers Guild, Stan? After applauding my intent at Penn Station, Comrade Refneski offered this: " 'The police astound me by shooting two so-called Caucasians. Those storm troopers are in obvious need of re-indoctrination.' "

Stan, the master of the smiling screw, tarring me with both Bakunin's brush and this nincompoop, Refneski. Did Timmy even exist, I wondered, or had Stanley conjured him up to add rust to his knife? Timmy got a grand total of twenty-nine google hits, my grandma thirty-years gone probably getting half that. Stanley must have been repaying a debt of some sort plugging *Timmy*, he of the proper, trust-fund revolutionary name. Besides, didn't it take *all* of Brooklyn to constitute a republic?

Stanley ended with another shovelful of purported liability from some twisted sister at an outfit called Citizens' Obligations. An awesome twenty-three googles for her whole organization, Hannah Soledad seemed like she'd be a blast sharing an adult beverage at an appropriately licensed, smoke-free tavern once our IDs were scanned at the door, and we presented affidavits regarding the evening's arbitrated and adumbrated intimacies. Cause she thought my plan at Penn " 'potentially worthwhile, but I would advise against unwarranted soloing. Anyone seeking to properly discharge Citizens' Obligations must inform the police in advance and obtain Commissioner Ted's arrest permit so as to coordinate a legitimate, peaceful arrest with properly accredited media coverage. Deviating from procedure invites at least a tazing and, as this sad case indicates, a young womyn fighting for her life.' "

Arrest permit – darn. Must have missed Walk-on-Water Ted's memo on asking permission to get popped. I'd failed to "coordinate" with the cops, so by Hannah's lights, of course I'd gotten shot. And Stanley's own take on things had me responsible for Carole getting shot too. (And the cops had their guns shooting themselves.) As to accredited media – licensed? – that excluded you, Stanley, you bastard. Quoting these two morons completed his nifty hatchet job, the blood on his shoes all but invisible. Go ahead, lap it up all you other scribblers loading big buckets of slime. Semper Solidarity, Stan – you all comfy with your feet perched on your desk wherever it is you foul the air.

✱✱✱✱✱✱✱✱✱✱✱✱✱✱

The Stuffing throbbing, I swore steadily though without much flair. My last real meal Thursday, two days before, man, I needed to hit the local Chinese. There was one every block or three, the supposedly bulletproof plastic barrier protecting the staff optional. But first to see with how heavy a fist the *Dispatch*'s Benson banged his keys. Eric Keith Benson, I saw, three names crowning the on-line *Dispatch*'s second offering. Second – damn! Tops was the confirmed downing by an RPG of an ancient B-52 accompanied by a link (the *Dispatch* declined to run it itself) to a Pan-T Agency photo of a delirious crowd hammering the huge jet with their shoes.

At least they'd used F&F's PR photo, Nicki looking fine. Any dope like me would be thrilled to have her identified as his wife under the cigarette-while-pumping-gas headline: "Penn Shooting Figure's Wife Wonders if Money Woes Sparked Attack".

There was also that dreaded little tag (if you're the article's focus): *News Analysis*, which meant they gave the writer free rein. It was the only way to justify the front-page treatment, cause Benson had little to hang his ambitious typing on but Nicki's nonsense. After totally sugar-coating the shooting in a quick intro, he went anecdotal, talking of meeting her as she arrived at work. "Asked by means of identification if she was related to the Penn Station shooting figure, his wife immediately replied, 'Why, does he owe you money?' "

It came out of her mouth, so Benson could legitimately write it down and then print it – devil take the hindmost. Almost gleeful, he added that though Nicki "would not confirm how onerous his debts, she did acknowledge that her husband had hit a professional dry spell. She said, 'He has been kind of floundering lately, having trouble getting published. But now, after getting shot, maybe he has a big story, something to use to get himself going again.' Asked to clarify, she said, 'Well of course there's a money angle. Mitch is a writer. That's what he does for a living, if you can call it that.' "

All that a fine start on Richard Jewell-ing or Wen Ho Lee-ing me, time to screw Nick by making sure the Feds made the connection to her agency's new Boots campaign: "A newly minted vice-president and star copywriter at hot ad agency Fornix & Foyst (which recently landed a $67-million U.S. Army minority recruitment account), Ms. Fremson seemed oddly unaware her husband had been shot less than twenty-four hours before. When informed of what still might prove a fatal accident at Penn Station, she declared, 'No, you've got it wrong. Some absurdly stacked blonde is on all the front pages, not my husband.' Finally convinced that he was indeed the attack's Suspect, she protested, 'But nothing was supposed to happen! It was all just a test!' "

Suspect – my *Dispatch* title. Carry a decibel reader around with you, Benson, to justify the exclamation points hung on the Wife?

Mining more Nick ore, Benson wrote, "She seemed to search her mind for a possible explanation of why Mr. Fremson's antique East German military satchel was crammed with an inordinate number of *printed* books: 'Well, Mitch has put on a little weight, and it's very likely he was just getting some exercise carrying them around somewhere, getting out of his little apartment which isn't wired for air conditioning. If he thought it was worth six dollars for the train to

Manhattan and back, he might've ended up in Penn Station just to walk around in its AC.'

"Adding confusion to the Suspect's murky and apparently financially strained circumstances, his spouse refused to clarify their living arrangements or why she referred to it as 'his' apartment."

So: a fat, cheap grifter. I hoped like hell she was still drunk off her ass, cause the Wife didn't even let me roll up my pants leg before shooting me in the knee.

Benson plowed on. "The Suspect's condition is listed as 'grave,' with sources indicating it is likely to deteriorate during an invasive course of intra-cranial diagnosis and treatment. It remains unclear how he managed to ensure the bullet did not prove immediately fatal. One theory was advanced by Dr. Wally R. Littlesmith of Nassau Community University Medical Site. 'I've heard from contacts in our T Community of a new, top-secret, plasticine *super*-Kevlar, if you will, that can be appliquéd to the body. Of course removing it later from the head – required within forty-eight hours lest it painfully shrink whatever anatomical structure it encases – necessitates shaving the scalp. But, at the end of the day, that would seem of little consequence to someone pursuing the extortion scheme you detail in your questions. It all makes sense in the context you provide.' "

Set up the pins and knock 'em down, E. Keith. The police-beat cub added helpfully, "The MTA police still hope to locate the missing 'silver device' the Suspect pointed at Protectors to prompt their discharge, an item the police have identified variously as either a detonator, a gun or perhaps some other weapon."

So, the caveats grew ever fainter in the next-day iteration, no mention – which initially even the cops faintly suggested – that it might be a radio.

Yup, combine the *Dispatch* with *N.O.*, and I emerged as someone who'd set out to dangerously threaten our Heroes' T Paradigm – the basis of all our safety. Plus I'd gotten a classy, no, *iconic*, American broad shot, a fireman's very own. And all for the worst of money-grubbing reasons and nary a word of contradiction from this quarter.

The Stuffing both soggy and oddly light, I plowed through my crappy mail, only an enterprising 187 strangers tracking down my e-mail address. It was actually far less, I saw, since maybe a third of the notes repeated the same awkward slogans, such as "Patriots Obey Protectors" and "Expose the Satchel!" and, my favorite, "Unbuckle, Unzip, De-Latch!" That last'll give B.E.I. a run for its money. So it was probably the same male dork or two mailing them all (women tend to have lives). The vitriol was leavened by inquiries about my health from some reporters and activists I knew, everybody asking way too many questions. And a few folks, eleven, actually, even applauded my intent.

****

Shite, indeed, Maureen. Assuming Carole recovered, and I managed with a compelling (and true) account to deflect the tide of blame rising past my waist, maybe it did come down to taking one for the team. Rather than the usual police fusillade on some late-night corner in a black or brown neighborhood – the circumstances obscure, the investigation contrived, the truth foggy, the outcome fudged, the penalty minimal (a thirty-day suspension without pay for killing a blameless kid on a Brooklyn housing project rooftop because the scaredy-cat cop had his gun out on routine patrol, his brain on hair-trigger) – let the world see that 'weapons discharge' was spreading to Penn Station, to the realm of the white and coiffed.

Time for some five-dollar protein, starch and grease, hopefully in that order, and back upstairs to embark on "Penn Tale." I lifted a twenty from next month's rent, Stap's annoying insistence on cash proving useful. I still had a death-grip on the banister heading four flights down, but my feet didn't flounder quite like the day before.

Chapter Twenty-One

But Mr. DeMille, My Boots Are Muddy, My Spurs Rusty

Sugar-monkey! Down on the porch I heard Mr. Staphilopoulous yelling in far less-accented English than usual. "Hey, News-Man, get that truck from blocking my driveway. Move it before something happens to your windows. We got no news here!" Never mind that Stap's driveway gates were rusted shut.

I'd obviously joined Officer Henderson in floating out by Jupiter's ninth moon, cause it hadn't dawned I'd be prey way out in Bumfuckville. Why, it was a full two days after the shootings, and I'd traveled under an entire river! That should've thrown them off the scent. My phone wasn't listed, and no one but Nicki and my parents knew where I lived. Them and Ralph, damn him if he coughed it up.

I looked down at my work boots, baggy, saggy, *old* cut-off jeans and – the only band shirt I ever bought – my faded, shrunken Hot Tuna tee shirt I'd put on to cheer myself up. If it was a truck, that meant TV and, Mr. DeMille, I was decidedly not ready for my close-up. But, having consumed a muffin and some cottage cheese in the prior 48-hours, my skimpy breakfast hadn't cut it. The floor already going a little wavy on me, attempting four flights back up to change and then four back down was entirely beyond me. Screw it, I wasn't making it to wardrobe.

Nor was I ready to confront my landlord, the Greek presumably furious I'd brought the locusts down on his gritty little patch of paradise. I crept out the long back hall, Stap still yelling out front, got past the swimming pool missing a panel front and back, through the overgrown ramble of a backyard and out a hole in Stap's fence into the neighbor's backyard. The Stuffing's airiness deteriorating to dizziness, I rested a moment in the neighbor's driveway, hands on knees, then slow-mo scooted down the side-walk with barely a glance at the fish-kicking-a-field-goal TV truck on my dreary block. That resurrected Nicki's theory about making out in a dark bar: if you pretend you can't see them, then of course they can't see you.

I did, however, foolishly catch sight of myself in the window of a "Comidas-Soul" joint that had failed despite its valiant effort to appeal to most everyone in the projects. Forget the faded tee shirt struggling to meet its obligations and the disgrace of my shorts. I'd totally forgotten the giant band-aid pasted on my lank, unwashed, thinning, too-long, self-cut former Breck-Boy glory. Jesus, I looked like Cat Wrangler with her skewed lipstick and sister's sock taped to her hand, except I should hope to look half that good.

I hit the bodega for a rare, unhung Dr. Pepper and a two-pack of Lady Linda chocolate cupcakes – the ratio of frosting to cake to filling exactly right – to carry me through the afternoon. Plus some baked beans and bright pink, Dominican hot dogs for dinner, and the *Chirp* and the *Node* that I almost forgot.

Under the headline "Beauty's Miraculous Recovery" the *Node* had Carole leaping off the front page in a pink leotard performing at some hospital a while back. The line below: "City's Prayers Answered". True enough, I for one having joined the chorus. The *Chirp* had the same shot – gotta love it when the tabs got burned like that – only smaller because below Carole was a shot of her chiseled-jawed intended over the headline "Fire Fiancé Demands Answers". I could hope it was answers from the MTA – right after I ran off to join the circus as the bearded lady.

I'd find out after I ordered from the closer, crappier Chinese that served only white rice, rather than the brown-rice joint a block further. Cause I was awfully unsteady on my pins, hopefully at least partly from sheer starvation.

I ordered goop to go and sat watching molecules dance in the murk outside, telling myself it was just a trick of the sun refracted through the smeared window. Only there was no sunlight. (The general hope was someone would catch it someday in a bottle to show little children.) The place deserted that early, the fierce old Boss-Man soon grunted at me. I managed to rise, the Stuffing wobbling just getting to the counter for my Three Kings Displeasures. It seemed I was wolfing down at least one to forestall keeling over on my way back to the Hovel. But man, I did not want any reporter finding me there. Aside from being mentally, physically and sartorially not equal to it, I was Goddamn not in the mood. Hell, anyone getting a regular paycheck would skip this place, its cracked glass door fixed with tape; nothing but the spiffier joint up the block for the likes of them.

I coughed loudly to mask the noise of opening my soda, hid it on the seat and opened the *Node* to bask in a study of Carole. She actually was at the beach, not with the frisbee of my fantasy, but emerging from the surf, her over-matched bikini ajar, hubby-to-be with the photo credit, a scandal in two-dimensions. Only the *Node's* push to canonize her kept it from the front page.

Already feeling steadier for the metallic-tinged pork, I was glad to read she was up and at 'em on her Bellevue ward. I turned to the *Chirp* for some sketchy stuff on me supposedly "absconding" from the hospital. But Carole kept grabbing my eye – an action shot of her running the bases – until the subhead, "Suspect to Face Assault Charges?" got me by the throat.

But the *Chirp* was just musing aloud. According to one MTA honcho, they were " 'waiting on interviewing regrettably absent Protector Reisner before deciding what charges the Suspect will face.' " My demonizing title, but never a notion of suspected of what. I flipped the page to, wow! "Soldier Held Fire, Why Not MTA?" Add this headline to its prior revelation about Frankie's involvement in the Salakmahest cluster-fuck, and the *Chirp* was cooking with gas.

Racing through the article, which initially focused on bystanders' peril, I was interrupted by a young guy lugging a surprisingly compact TV camera festooned with NYONLY logos, a stout chain linking it to his belt. He went to the counter and spoke to Boss-Man in Chinese. His background tough to pin down, hard to say whether he'd learned it at home or in school. Way too thin, with greased, spiky black hair doing a flip off his forehead, he was dressed like *West Side Story*'s Bernardo on his way to the dance in a dark purple shirt, some kind of severely cut black jacket, and pointy-toed Beatle boots Pop would've called them.

Neither shot nor starved, he had no call to sit down at the other greasy table. He said in English to make it to go. Bolting then and there would only trumpet the hounds, so I was glad when he looked right through the Bumfuckville goober bent over his kibble and took to fingering his micro-zap. Feeling slightly more human with each bite and, articles on my mess off-limits, I read about the Yankees' latest blow-up.

My nose buried and mouth working, the restaurant was suddenly flooded with light. The camera on his shoulder boring through me, NYONLY walked up, saying, "You're him, aren't you, the Penn Station Sus – I mean the Penn Station shooting victim? Fremson, right? This officially licensed camera is rolling, by the way."

Done nothing wrong, I had nothing to hide. "Yeah, I'm the guy those cops shot. But I'm eating right now as you can see, my first real meal in days. If you give me your card, I'll be glad to schedule an interview at our mutual convenience. But I'm afraid now is not a good time for me."

And I turned and clutched at the can on the seat and took a long swig, spilling some down my chin. Blind to the napkins at hand, I reached awkwardly to rub my chin on my too short sleeve, a contortion that sent the Stuffing reeling. Adjusting his lens, he spoke excitedly into the top of his camera of "a chance encounter with the man the entire city has been wondering about since he absconded from Bellevue Hospital."

"Just curious: where'd you get my picture?"

He peered over his shoulder at the door, then shrugged and turned off the light. "Let me turn the, uh, *video* off. Not that I have to answer that, but I've got a source in the Commissioner's office who sent me your address and a photo from a Penn Station surveillance camera. They're spreading it around cause there's an ABC truck parked outside your place – no way you own that big house, right? – and I heard FOX was here until he ducked out to get shots of a dry-cleaner explosion up in the Bronx since you're so close to the Giuliani Bridge."

I chewed the Displeasure I'd crammed while he spoke, crazy-nervous and trying to rehab the Stuffing on the fly. And since when did dry cleaners explode?

"Now look," he continued – and why did every schmuck I encountered lately feel free to immediately start barking orders? – "I'm going to turn the video back on in a minute, and I can film you saying nothing and gorging yourself on a lot of nasty food for this hour of the morning. Or I can shoot you running away on up to your front door, which" – he bent down to confirm that the half of me under the table was no more prepossessing than the visible half – "you probably don't want. Or we can do a short interview here, though I would suggest you try to fix your hair a little. No, not the bandage – that gets the sympathy vote, right?"

"So on your exalted say-so, I got no right to tell my own story how and when I want? That is, in prose and whenever I'm damn well ready?"

"Your story's getting told, like it or not. You lost control of it about two minutes after you made that cop shoot you. So how about telling the world what you were really doing in Penn Station. Like somebody said, control what already happened, and you control what's going to happen."

"You mean that somebody named Orwell?"

"Whatever. But I'll tell you what. You hiding any secrets, you better get 'em out now yourself. Put on a jacket and tie – you own a jacket, right? – and come on down to the studio to spill. Cause I guarantee there's a whole lot of cops digging in your dirt right now."

"Ya know, I'm not feeling quite well enough for all this. My head feels like it's made of tapioca – something about getting shot probably. But let me ask you: *I* made that cop shoot me?"

Jesus, I needed to shut up. My faint, dry sarcasm had gotten me into trouble more than once. So I was damn glad he'd turned his camera off.

"Why would a trained police officer – a Protector who's marched through hot Sands defending the Homeland – shoot you if you didn't have a gun or a detonator, right? Let's start with that."

"Do you know any Boots, I mean personally?"

"No, that's not my scene. But which was it, gun or detonator?"

"You drink your Kool-Aid in a sippy-cup?"

"What do you mean?"

"It's an historical reference. Anyway, it ever occur to you that we're competitors in telling *my* story?"

"What, you think you're a *journalist*? Living around here and looking like that? Not for money – no way!"

Nicki been bending his ear? "Now get this: I didn't go to all that trouble lugging that backpack around in this heat to not try to make a chunk of change off it. I mean, you got to pay the rent somehow, right?"

"How much were you hoping to make?"

"A couple of hundred bucks for writing about it. It's called participatory journalism, popular back when you were playing with mud pies."

I'd better be damn careful when this guy turned his camera back on, cause none of this sounded on-target. I could feel it *physically* somehow, my head not firing on all cylinders. And I sure didn't need to be talking about money before discussing my primary concern – that's right, damn it – the searches' assault on civil liberties.

"No, I mean how much were you counting on for getting shot in the head?"

"You ever use your brains for anything but keeping your ears apart? For instance, how did I manage to arrange it that that cop would only graze me? Tell me that, bright boy. Not that it wouldn't be nice to have the MTA pay my rent for a while."

He stared back, and then Boss-Man interrupted to say his shrimp roll was ready. Guess I'd have a TV gig too if all I had for lunch was a damn shrimp roll. He threw two bills on the counter and said, "I'm going to turn on the camera, and you decide your next move."

The bright light caught me delicately finger-combing my hair, the suddenly enormous camera searching for zits from three feet away.

His cool, disaffected drone perked right up. "Tell New York: *You're ... the ... Only... One!*" He then gave a lying little intro about an interview with the man of the moment at a local restaurant I'd chosen. Great, cause that meant I chose to dress like that too. Before I could protest, he launched right in. "So it wasn't just about the money was it? You maintain you had some other purpose involving the police?"

"I'm not quite sure I know what you mean?"

"Is it that you don't know, or is prevarication how you make it through the day?"

Oh spare me, vocabulary-boy. With his Protector-coddling, slice-and-dice sound bites, no way he'd let me challenge the whole search paradigm. But if he'd already read Stanley and caught me fudging about my plans, that'd brand me a liar for good. I fell back until the ropes caught me at the edge of the canvas, the crowd roaring for blood.

"*Prevarication*? You know, I'm just a simple lad who's washed up here in Queens. But that wasn't correct what you said before about me 'absconding' from the hospital. I haven't hid myself away anywhere. I went home because I wasn't happy with the level of care I was receiving at Bellevue. The morning I left – Jesus, yesterday it was – no one even came to as much as take my temperature. So, free, white and over twenty-one – I mean, over twenty-one of any color, of course – I don't need anyone's permission to check out of a lousy hospital."

"OK, let's talk about that. You got yourself discharged?"

"Look, Bellevue's a funny place. A lot of weird stuff happened to me in Bellevue that *I'll* write about myself in my own good time."

"So you got discharged? Got your bill and left?"

Obviously they were disseminating that I skipped on the bill. Well, I'd sound a fool blurting out wild accusations about cops in the next bed, Lurch in his fake uniform, and docs with knock-out drops. I needed something cogent laid out carefully in digital print. Besides, usually only contenting myself with *two* Displeasures at most, this meal he was ruining had cost real money. All I wanted was to eat and lose myself in the sports section for a few minutes before returning home to try, somehow, to pull my chestnuts from the fire – that and maybe a visit from the Wife. Was that asking for the moon?

"Look, unlike revenge, this gourmet offering here is not a meal best served cold. It's my first real meal in – "

"Is that some kind of threat?"

"No, that's Shakespeare – an English playwright."

"Very clever. So what's your response to the engendered discharge that wounded innocent bystander Carole Fiore during your planned encounter with the police?"

"I feel terrible about Carole, obviously, and I'm thrilled to read that she's recovering. You're right, she is an innocent bystander. Me too, someone just putting one foot in front of the other."

"Really? That's what you were doing in Penn Station?"

"I was just going from Point A to Point B as far as those cops who shot Ms. Fiore and myself knew."

"But that's not the whole truth, is it?"

"You tell me. Why, cause I had a backpack?"

"What about your *anti*-anti-Fiend intentions? Because a peculiar website called, *Naked* – "

"Right, of course. *Naked Opposition*. I was about to steer our viewers there myself for background if they were interested. I e-mailed the editor there yesterday a bit about my plans. You might find it useful, yourself."

"You mean useful to know that you set out to obstruct T Containment?"

"Nothing I can do to stop you putting that traction on it if you like. But I would urge folks to go read *Naked Opposition* themselves."

"And you told this site, quote: 'I was carrying a backpack, and I was going to refuse to submit to a search. So anything was possible.' "

"Well, that's right. Someone had to do it. People going about their daily lives cannot be stopped and searched for no reason. Period. Besides, it doesn't work. *Usually*, you can just turn and walk away. Though I've seen that's not always true either. It's no different than the cops racing round town in caravans of fifty to then sit and stew and then race somewhere else, all just to puff themselves up."

"Whatever. But you wrote, 'Anything can happen.' So you were willing for civilians to get shot as well?"

"Civilians *as well*? Does this look like a uniform to you? Hot Tuna?"

"Hot what? Forget that. So you *were* willing?"

"Look, you can play gotcha all you want, but if you don't mind – and even if you do – I'm gonna go home and finish this goop here, cause it doesn't seem you're going to leave me alone." I looked up at the camera. "Folks, I'll be writing about my ordeal as soon as the Stuffing permits. That's, uh, my little pet name for what happened to my head. So, uhm – hi, Mom. All that baloney. And to Ms. Fiore, Godspeed on your recovery."

I stood up, realized I couldn't manage an open soda along with cupcakes, newspapers and the rest of my food, and so drained the

Dr. P. Over at the counter I asked for a plastic bag to dump it all in and suffered Boss-Man's lecture on not sneaking soda in "when I got orange soda like that." I turned to see NYONLY filming my greasy mass of picked-over food. Damn my head for not allowing me to flee when Boss-Man handed breakfast over, cause this was one stone-bad encounter. I retrieved my stuff, banged out the door, hitched up my shorts and trudged off, compounding any number of gaffes by looking (guiltily) over my shoulder to see him standing in the doorway filming away. A wonder I didn't flip him off.

I certainly wasn't disclosing my back-fence route, so I headed straight for the ABC truck by Stap's front gate, finding it blessedly locked and empty. First stroke of luck since meeting Maureen – who seemed of a more innocent time, when all I confronted was murderous cops, not online 'Movement' mavens and boy TV reporters. Thank God his camera was turned off for most of that embarrassment. On the infinitesimal chance he'd use it, I just hoped it was running for my nifty quip about the playwright.

Chapter Twenty-Two

Nickilicious No More

My luck continued to hold as Mr. Staphilopoulos came charging up the hall, his shirt particularly faded for the occasion and his pomegranate hair awry. I braced myself, but he was grinning. "I see you not thief anymore – you use the front door."

"I'm sorry, Stap. I needed something to eat before I could talk to anyone."

"You a tough guy to figure, mister, dressing like a bum, staying up there all day doing whatever you do. Then going out at night with that little radio of yours playing stupid baseball, but going where, still dressed like that? Now it turns out – I have friends with Internet – you some kind of writer. Somebody who tells the government to get lost!"

"Look, Stap, I can explain, or try to anyway. It's all about protecting basic rights. This bit with the subways – "

"I don't know about subways if that's what you mixed in now. I don't ride them, don't care about them. But I asked and my friend, the Turk, found stuff you wrote from years ago – good stuff."

(He'd told me the story: he'd had a fling with the Turk's sister back when dinosaurs roamed. Though properly affronted, the Turk initiated their cats-and-dogs friendship by bowing to the sacred compact among husbands and helping to conceal it from Stap's wife, long since fled on numerous grounds.)

"Oh, that."

"You don't think I understand all that, a man who had to leave Greece, go up a mountain in middle of the night with clothes on my back, no goodbyes to nobody?"

"You mean with the colonels?"

"An American knows about them? So, Mr. Bird-Brains, no more dress like this, you got the TVs after you, OK? And don't worry. When you getting beauty sleep last night, I sent them away?"

"Sent who away?"

"Two men in suits, said they were from the railroad. Shit-hole cops. I told them come back with papers from a judge. Told them I pay a lot of damn taxes on this house. More than anyone around here with that giant backyard no good to nobody till I'm dead. They should look that up before they bother me. Me or my ... my *house-mates* – that's the word."

"You sent them away? What'd they want?"

"They wanted you, 'to talk' – ha! And a woman, dressed nice, *looks* nice. She made me laugh, laughed right in her face when she said she was your wife. Said she was worried about you. No cop, I don't think. Probably newsie, always being a sneak. She wanted to know your bell on the door, said you weren't answering your micro-thing. Like a man like you living here got a wife like her. I said sure, *that's* his bell. I pointed, you know, to all those bells there, and I went inside."

"Stap!"

"She stood ringing those broken bells and then she just yelling your name. A lot of noise out of a skinny girl – not *too* skinny. I stand behind the door, can't believe it, think maybe she climb up, go knock on a window upstairs."

"Jesus, Stap. She – "

"Wait. Then some coloreds, three or four hanging out selling down on the corner, come up cause she's yelling. And they all want to be a big help, but she ignores them. It was almost ten o'clock, and I thought for a minute they were gonna come in my gate, and believe me, I be out there quick with my knife, asking no questions. Not because of news-girl, and not because they colored. But this is *my* house, and they better know that. But she's smart. She sits right down in my chair on the porch and crosses her legs like a cool cookie waiting for a man to come down. And then she left, soon as they go."

"That *was* my wife. Technically we're still married."

"Sure, Big Stuff, whatever you say. You not like my other guys upstairs, right? So listen, no fights over a girl – wife, whatever. You got that? So, OK, I send her up. But I don't think she come here again. She don't like it down here by the river, no yellow taxis every twenty feet."

"Damn. Shit, Stap!"

"That's right. Women: damn shit."

"Maybe it's just as well, cause I'm still in a fog. And thanks about those cops. They said they were MTA?"

"MTA, what's that? They flash a badge two seconds. American cops I don't care about except they sit on my balls. But these damn TVs, their trucks in everybody's spot, the whole block a mess. There were two last night, so Georgos had to park around the corner and walk back alone, old as he is. How long they chase you?"

"Only until I get my story out – write it myself and then they'll lose interest. I'm not so good today, but I'm gonna try to start."

"You got shot, mister. Messing with that blonde I saw her picture on TV – how you do it, a guy like you? That pretty woman you call your wife and now this blonde, a young man's dream? I give you a beer for your secret, a big green bottle like you buy. Walking through train stations with what – a pack? I know you not running away leaving all your stuff upstairs."

"What stuff?"

"Your junk. All those boxes of paper up there."

"What the hell, Stap!"

"I looked in your rooms yesterday. I want to know if you have bombs like they making talk about on TV – what's the word – not *jokes*."

"I don't know. Hints."

"Hints, right. But a man who got nothing don't leave what little he got. Going over mountain late at night not your way. Me? I had a lot in Greece, one time. But that's a separate story."

"Tell me someday. But let me get out of here now before that TV guy parked there shows up again. Meanwhile, if my wife comes back – who knows? – do me a favor and send her up, OK? Her name's Nicki. And Mr. Staphilopoulos, I appreciate all your help, all your guard-dogging. Cause we got colonels over here too."

"You got money? You need ten dollars?"

"Stap, I'm good. Ask me next week."

✳✳✳✳✳✳✳✳✳✳✳✳✳✳✳

Wow, keeper of the keep, Staphilopoulos, refugee and politically astute new friend. Upstairs I saw that *N.O.* was bouncing like a red rubber ball, number six on the day's ranking behind only stuff like the whole-vid of a pre-season quarterback getting his leg snapped, and the global-exclusive from Jacquine's steady limo driver that she's really a he, the itchy-pants driver claiming to know. Christ, number six! Not bad, Stanley, for a piece that, for all its nonsense, did discuss the politics of challenging the searches. So maybe something might come of that *if* the civ-lib aspect didn't get Swift-Boated overboard.

I forced myself to the mirror to contemplate the snug Hot Tuna tee, decades old and an indeterminate color. Man, NYONLY's whole-vid would probably bounce too, the already infamous wastrel scarfing down in a shabby Chinese, talking trash and beating an ignominious retreat. I turned and caught the horror-show band-aid I kept forgetting, and then Frankie loomed up suddenly in his two-handed shooting stance. And I cracked. But only for a second, damn it! A sob, a choke and a single, long, loud "Aaarrrgghhhghhgh!" was all I gave them. Let the buzzards circling low fight over that. That's right. I'd shed not one, single Goddamn tear over Nicki. None of that

194

Tears get in my ears/Lying down crying over you garbage.

Collapsing in the big wing-chair wedged between fridge and window, my refuge since college, my thoughts dragged against my will to our first date when I'd thrown my sole, time-tested seduction strategy out the window. (Kiss her till both your jaws ache on the first date, but touch nothing covered by a bikini. Not foolproof, of course, but the gentlemanly lack of a clothed grope blossomed and soon typically rendered the party of the second part horizontal.) Rather, a few first kisses in, I'd startled myself – certainly not Nickilicious – by reaching out for her succulent right breast on the street by her apartment. My left hand the one wired to the pleasure center, therefore her right breast. Sitting there in my chair, I couldn't figure how to re-spark a flame that for most of the last nine years she'd fanned right along.

Pushing noon, I was entitled to call. She'd journeyed to Bumfuckville the night before, so she'd just have to return, come sit an hour in my kitchen looking askance. That and hugging me twice, damn it – coming and going. And then I could think of facing the future, would be forced to by how she turned to offer her cheek where once she'd melted at the end of a tentative left hand.

No answer at home. Dialing her micro-zap, I realized she'd have some reaction to Stanley and Benson's beat-downs, so best to have my print-outs at hand when she started yelling. Low and intense and angrier probably than even the night she smashed the Christmas tree ornaments, the Wife poured molten ice in my ear.

"Did you see what they did, your absurd friend Stanley, and of course that prick at the *Dispatch*? What – Charley? Forget Charley. Padwick himself is going to shit a cow that F&F got dragged into your nonsense. That twerp at the *Dispatch* knew exactly what he was doing mentioning my promotion and all that Army money in the same sentence. Everybody knew I was going to be the lead writer on that. A $67-million-dollar ad buy! Do you have any idea how much F&F

creams off the top of that and how much would drip down even to me?"

"Nicki, he had to put in where you work cause that's where he encountered you. And that bit about Army recruitment is just boilerplate on Fornix & Foyst cause it's a big new account. Anyway, where are you?"

"And that damn Stanley putting in all that Internet stuff to prove you contacted me at work about your plans in advance. It's like I'm an accessory before the fact."

"Accessory to what? Come on, you know I wasn't doing anything illegal. Besides, I thought you approved."

"I'll be lucky if they wait till Monday to fire me. And I got a big nut to make now every month in the City."

"They're not going to fire you. Tell them you don't even live with me anymore."

"That'll be the least of it. But look, I came all the way out there to your ridiculous … *home* to see you last night, and your bizarre landlord was no help at all."

"He's OK. He thought you were a reporter, couldn't believe I have so enchanting a wife. Plus he told two MTA DTs to scram if they didn't have a warrant, so I can't complain. So, uh, Nick, what happens when I call you back at home?"

"Why don't you fucking grow up. I don't even know if I'm getting escorted from F&F with just my picture of Otis in my hand in forty-eight hours. They're sure not gonna let me work on what's a hell of a challenge convincing black and brown kids to step up. I already had a tagline working: *Army. Because we ALL bleed red.*"

"Do you ever listen to yourself? Huh, Nicki? Sending kids to a Sands isn't exactly CheeseSpray…. Nicki?" Ah, going all silent – my all-time favorite Nick tactic. "So how is Otis?"

"He's fine, though he doesn't like it that the windows in my new place don't open."

"Smart cat doesn't want to live in a sealed tomb." *Our* cat, torn from my bosom, the clever black and white tuxedo number who Nick appropriated as a matter of course. "Look, Nicki, I know we're down the tubes, but I'd still like to see you today. Some nurse told me that depression kicks in with a head injury, and it's just – things are tough right now."

"I can make it tomorrow, but not tonight."

"What about this afternoon?"

"It's just not a good time today."

"Busy, huh?"

"Look, tomorrow I'll be able to tell you all about the great theatrical sensation. Someone scalped tickets for like five-hundred each – and he was lucky to get them – for *Abu Ghraib, the Musical.* You know, the one that Jacquine dropped out of over artistic differences about her nude scene."

Someone. I let it alone cause what was the point. Besides, like everyone else, I was distracted by Jacquine. Some thought the musical's subject a bit outré. But, so many years later, the argument that sufficient time had passed to allow for a light-hearted reconsideration carried the day. Especially after the producers circulated opening-night pictures of HeadMan's brittle, waxen girlfriend cackling away in the eighth row, most folks surprised she could move her face enough to laugh.

Its first-half-closer, featuring hundreds of little lights winking out in the backdrop, represented the fate of Boots and maybe even Fiends (it was said). Then the second act opened with an aircraft carrier steaming on stage, hurrahs turning to horror as it catapulted little souvenir metal planes out into the audience. The Sands come to Broadway, the tickets with the same waivers in infinitesimal print that baseball tickets had about foul balls.

Two female guards did a competitive striptease in front of the chorus of prisoners, and a mousey female guard's first-half flirtation with a tough-guy mercenary blossomed into a precarious, love-conquers-all romance in the second half. But the noose tightening, the brute turned state's evidence against her, and she tragically chose not to head home to her family in disgrace. The mercenary's bathos-laden, self-lacerating closing lament was all over the radio for about three weeks until it was pulled one day – sometimes in mid-song – never to return. All in all a boffo show with hen's-teeth tickets despite its dependence on drum machines.

"Yeah, well, I hope one of those little planes gets him. So, you told the *Dispatch*, now I'm supposedly fat as well as a scam artist too cheap to cough up train fare."

"I told you that creep shocked the shit out of me telling me you were the other shooting victim. I was back on my heels the entire time. I know you're just big boned even if your head alone weighs thirty-seven pounds. But even you must know you have bigger problems than your stupid vanity, cause they're saying you had a detonator or a gun."

"And you believe that?"

"Of course not. I know that's not your deal."

"What you don't realize is that *Naked Opposition* is the more important story. Wait – listen! That's cause it gives some idea, in my words and, yeah, in Stanley's too, of the civ-lib context to what I was doing."

"It ever occur to you that that kind of twisted thinking is why your career never took off, thinking that some stupid, lefty blog is more important than a front-page story in *The New York* fucking *Dispatch*!"

"Look, I'm gonna get the truth out on Penn Station, but I'm kinda foggy and can't really write right now."

"How about you skip the writing and call a lawyer. Your father probably still knows a real one."

"Did you punt all the personal stuff from my e-mail you forwarded, or did Stanley delete it out of the goodness of his heart?"

"I deleted it. That Stanley is a joke. Miss Universe gets shot, and he's worried about you using goofy verbs in an e-mail."

"Uh – I believe *two* people got shot. But I am so screwed. Look at that freaking headline in the *Dispatch*: 'Wife Wonders if Money Woes Sparked Attack….' " I could hear her shushing someone, her new Mr. Right-All-The-Time. "I could catch Moby Dick in my hat next week, and that headline is all people would remember. I gotta go. Gotta go 'flounder' my way through another 'professional dry spell.' Or so I hear tell."

"I'll call you tomorrow to let you know what time I can come over."

"Yeah, well, hopefully he'll kick you out of bed by noon."

"Bye."

And she hung up, like I was the one messing up. Hell, maybe I was and for a long time too, the past week just icing. A thousand freaking dollars to go to a show, the Wife had a hot thang going with some moneybags and couldn't be bothered to hide it. I could just hope MoneyBags hadn't discovered that special little live-wire spot on her lower back yet.

✳✳✳✳✳✳✳✳✳✳✳✳✳✳✳

Work my best refuge, the stakes weren't high. Just clearing my name. Man, the going was slow, searching for words and fumbling details. Surprised I didn't have to look at the keyboard. After a rough hour, my head started pitching forward towards the machine. I was hitting the hay or the hay was hitting me. I printed out a couple of pages of scrambled notes – Stan the Man right again: until it's on paper, it ain't saved, not really – and called it a start.

Slipping off, something that had rankled since my first exchange with Stanley propelled itself to the surface, its subcutaneous tickle finally breaking through. Both he and that NYONLY slickster had warned me in no uncertain terms to boot any skeletons from my closet. And, yup, I did have bones to kick to the curb, bones so new, bits of flesh had yet to fall. I wrote *Indiana* on my palm and fell instantly asleep.

The phone jangled after what felt like a long time, Pop sans pre-liminaries. "You did it for money? Why didn't you come to me if you needed a couple of hundred dollars?"

"Sure, Pop, I did it for the money – a lot more than a couple of hundred dollars. The only problem is I won't see it for like two years. Pop, that's ridiculous. How in the world could I know that cop would only graze me?"

"So you're being sarcastic. I get it. Your being so clever, boy, is gonna turn around someday and bite you in the ass."

Some might say at Penn Station it sorta already had. We didn't talk long. Too dazed to work, a snooze topped off my main nap till hunger drove me to those Dominican pups, a fine, tasteless platform for mustard and ketchup.

I tried committing further halting words, but damn tough to concentrate with that ink on my palm. Heck, any claim to being a regular Joe had flown out the window through the barrel of a gun two days before. So go ahead and empty my closet before someone else did? Not that the two bastards with their own skeletons – twins to mine – would be so inclined. Short and sweet and don't even try to get paid for such a confession. Just hope the damage would be out-weighed in a day or two by the sheer news heft of "Penn Tale." Or, rather, "Embarking on an Exemplary Refusal." Or simply, "A Sad Farce."

I started musing happily on where to publish... "Shot by a Nose." *Blackboard*? Nah, they'd chop it off at the knees with the ripe non-sense that no one read more than four-hundred words online. *Defiant Obeisance* or *Big Buckets of Hail*? Shoot, aim big: *Morning Dyspepsia* and be done with it.

In the meantime, I still had a boringly sober, soberly etc. Saturday evening to get through, both baseball teams having played day games. The walls closing in (not far to go), I ventured out to the hall around ten, the house feeling oddly like the locked, 3:00 a.m. study-room in a college library. This a Saturday, the one night Stap granted license to howl, yet there was no salsa (it was all 'salsa' to me) throbbing up from the third floor. Heading to the stairs, I heard no feet pounding from room to room, no calls in Spanish or faint phisst! of a pop-top. Two guys down there were *whispering* for some bizarre reason.

Gazing mournfully out the hall window to the towers lost in murk across the nearby East River, I gave Otis a wave in case he was futilely trying to sniff some 'air.' Beyond, despite vast expenditures of candle-power, the Times Square behemoths merely hinted their presence, the Despoilers paying big for something barely seen. Finding little solace gazing west, I went to the opposite window to sneer at another damn TV truck – late to the party, boys – and look out over the low rooftops to the planes stacked up over Cheney International.

Soon curled defensively on my side, I peered up at the vertical coffin's ceiling far above. Hell, we'd had a good run and such larks as I'd probably not see again. Turning forty had hit Nicki like a ton of bricks just as her career took flight, what with her string of quirky successes de scandale. And clients with nothing to lose (fifth or sixth in their category) soon beat down the door at a fusty old F&F gone unexpectedly edgy. Rejuvenated man-about-town Ernesto Padwick had gladly bid adieu to the old fogey who'd quit in disgust, especially since the latter's main client, a blue-blood private bank, had been recently gobbled up by a South Korean maker of manufactured steel buildings.

With her every outrage and subsequent raise, Nicki seemed to regard ours as some sort of morganatic marriage. I kept walking that plank pointed Left till eventually the Big Town stole her away. No, we weren't destined to grow old together.

I snuffed the light and rolled on my back to summon visions of succor (not daring to aim for true happiness) that began with a bowl of coffee-shop soup and *preceded* the crushing, Neil LaButian revelation of Maureen's true intent.

Chapter Twenty-Three

The Frying Pan Flips

The Stuffing felt darn good come Sunday morning, and I lay there pondering a downgrade to Breadcrumbs. Approaching an age when you don't wake regretting having had five too few, my satisfaction at such *Saturday*-night virtue was tempered by foreboding over the day's Indiana confession.

Heeding Stap's advice, I threw on some slacks (absurd in the heat) and a real shirt, and caught sight of myself on the way out. Oddly enough – not that the poor bastard made it that far – it was Orwell who noted you wake up at fifty with the face you deserve. But then, water unavailable, he'd shave with wine during the Spanish Civil War. The dawn of fifty no longer dozens of years off, I wasn't exactly hollow-cheeked, but the past days of irregular eating and no beering lent a nicely gaunt(ish) look.

So a relatively cheery lad was I heading out for the *Node* and *Daily Chirp* (Not wanting to muddy its feet, the *Dispatch* wasn't sold within a mile of the Hovel) and an egg sandwich, never mind the Wonder Bread the bodega couldn't transcend. Still before eight on a Sunday, hopefully it was too early for any newsies downstairs, or perhaps they'd even lost interest, NYONLY having beaten them to the punch. Assuming he wasn't sitting on it, I'd check out Bernardo's story online after breakfast.

Sweating some in the idiot long pants down stairs that stayed largely in place beneath my feet, I passed a couple of Latino dudes sweating their way up. They met my grunt of a greeting with angry stares. Word had obviously gone round that I was responsible for the cop cars cruising outside, the Fuji blimp no doubt overhead to immortalize all our features for the new Domesday Book. (Back before people grew so politically demoralized and demobilized, Fuji let the NYPD use its blimp to observe and presumably record demonstrators down in the streets below. After resolving some of the niggling little issues haunting my life, I needed to organize the boycott Fuji so richly deserved.)

I tossed a goofy grin at the plain-clothes with a crew cut lounging in the dark Ford out front, a cluster of electronics under the dash. Turd-Touch spooking the Latinos (hence the hush on the third floor the night before), had I also halted the reefer trade by the projects a block away? How soon before everyone, including Stap's buddies objecting to the TV trucks usurping their parking spots, united to pressure the Greek to throw my disruptive ass out? Rather than nodding appreciatively at my geek duds, the cop just eye-fucked me, then reached for his radio. Which raised the question of why the Red Squad bothered with an unmarked car. Less theoretically, how did I know he even was a state security MoFo rather than a private goon – and which was worse, assuming any difference?

At the bodega, my buddy the counterman interrupted my gasping dash through the pages of the *Node*. "My friend, we give big thanks to you for all the TV people here with Manhattan money. Cops too. Many cigarettes and coffee and soda and even food we sell because you a big star."

"Big freaking star – right here on the front page, my whole life down the crapper."

"We see that this morning and big surprise, yes. But any story in newspapers is good for business. Tell me, more TV people today – what do you think? I need to know how much bacon to cook."

"Who knows. Maybe there'll be a funeral instead, and all my friends will come – big eaters and drinkers all three of 'em."

"No, no – no funeral, I *personally* will see to that. A young man like you, many women ahead, now you a star. You know already, that's why you dressed up today."

"OK, you personally guarantee no funeral. That I'll take. Thank you in advance." He made me a damn nice sandwich.

I stumbled home staring at the *Node*'s front-page surveillance camera photo of Ms. Hubba-Hubba striding down that Penn Station corridor "seconds before the engendered shot" said the caption. But even Carole paled before the headline picking my bones clean.

PENN SUSPECT A HITLER FAN WITH A CRIMINAL PAST MONEY-SCHEME WITH AD-BIG WIFE AT ARMY AGENCY

Something was as rotten as could be. Forget the photos gracing the page 4/page 5 spread: my ancient, chock-full-of-nerd high school yearbook photo, and the (sexy) drunken-slattern shot of Nicki laughing uproariously that she was afraid would surface. Cause five cherry-picking, *Node* typists, led by one Nathan E. Tredwell, had culled details of my e-mails, incoming and outgoing both, along with my phone call the day before to Pop. And that wasn't supposed to happen, one of the Data's selling points (way back when HeadFuck liked to pretend he cared about such things) being that the government was supposed to harvest and control everything. Supposed to keep all its spooking and peeping clutched nice and tight solely to its own bosom for its own burrowing MoFo secret purposes. Apparently not.

BARMY BACKPACKER COURTED DANGER

By Nathan E. Tredwell

According to a host of officials who must remain nameless so as to escape censure for prejudicing the jury pool, Mitchell Fremson, the Backpack

Bungler who caused a defensive police shooting on a jammed Penn Station concourse Thursday, staged it as a "stunt" to, he admitted, make the "big bucks." What's more, he showed a shocking indifference to innocent-bystander casualties; has both Nazi and communist East German Army linkages; plotted the attack with his wife, an executive at an advertising agency crucial to American military readiness; and is freighted with a tawdry legal history suggesting a vendetta against mass transit Protectors.

The *Node* has also learned he refers to his fellow New Yorkers as "dumb bunnies" for following proper, lawful orders from the front-line Heroes who daily keep us safe.

Conferring by phone with an unknown colleague and potential paymaster who he referred to as 'Pop,' the Penn Station shooting Suspect was heard to say on Saturday, two days after the near-massacre, "Sure, Pop, I did it for the money – a lot more than a couple of hundred dollars. The only problem is I won't see it for like two years."

T officials are still working to uncover the projected use for any money obtained in what appears to be, as one put it, "A deliberate, find a broken sidewalk, trip-and-sue scheme." What's more, several issues remain to be clarified. For instance, noted one senior police commander, "How did he know to be lurking in that Penn Station corridor just as the officers and their National Guard escort rounded the corner?"

Another source feared the worst: that any eventual court award might have been slated for a neo-Nazi campaign since, shockingly, the Suspect carried a copy of Adolf Hitler's hate-book, *Mein Kampf*. In a communiqué prior to the incident with his wife, the Suspect referred to Hitler's officially condemned hate-screed as "a necessary document."

A subsequent source wondered at the training that enabled the Suspect to dodge his head so precisely to ensure a non-fatal grazing after eliciting Thursday's weapons discharge. "That's treading a fine line, and that sort of expertise doesn't come cheap and it doesn't come easy," this close-arms combat veteran said. He added ominously, "I doubt it's even American in origin."

In a statement somehow captured by a marginal cable 'news' outlet, the Suspect thundered, "Not that it wouldn't be nice to have the MTA pay my rent for a while. Just get this: I didn't go to all that trouble lugging that backpack around in this heat to not try to make a chunk of change off it. I mean, you got to pay the rent somehow, right?"

This was Fremson's admission of a direct, mercenary plan to challenge the lawful *random* search paradigm so beloved by the public. As subway rider Denis Naufrasen of Tidal Basin, Brooklyn put it, "When no one has any rights, we're all equal. I just thank God for Commissioner Ted and hope to be voting for him for higher office soon."

TAWDRY AND ALARMING CRIMINAL HISTORY

The *Node* has also learned of the Suspect's criminal record, a history both alarming and tawdry that he himself recognizes as a liability. In an e-mail to his confederate, one Stanley Netherhall, whose obscure blog has published a number of his musings, the Knapsack Knucklehead expressed concern about "the cops dredging up who knows what wretched excess from my checkered past."

Whoever was stuffing my life down Tredwell's maw fed him my couple of quotidian, standard-issue open container violations on city subways, plus, wrote Tredwell, the "pending offense involving foul language directed at the person of an official MTA Public Facilitator. These malfactions on the trains may indicate the source of some sort of personal vendetta against transport Protectors."

The *Node* then slammed into Nicki at top speed, discussing her work for the Army's minority enlistment campaign.

Given the manifest need for patriotic replacements to plug holes in the T Campaign's overseas defensive projections, the Pentagon is anxious for new initiatives to drive enlistment. The previous nonwhite campaign – *Shoot Someone Over There Cause You Can't Kill Them Here* – was initially praised for its off-beat charm, yet it was discontinued when, at the end of the day, only 117 African-Descents stepped up to the plate last year.

Then there was this:

The Normative Forensic Diagnostician on the case, whose name is being withheld since he lives with his mother, is still researching the import of the Backpack Bungler's statement, "My head feels like it's made of tapioca." The Endowed NFD theorized, "Is he so delusional that he believes his head is constructed of a pudding? Or is he signaling co-conspirators about liquid explosives hidden in a lavatory – that is, the 'head?' "

The Diagnostician did admit to total bafflement trying to decode this instruction from what he termed a driven antiestablishmentarian: "Spare me your namby-pamby, Kumbaya load." The reference may be to "some sort of new threat we've not yet seen," the NFD warned. He added, "I can only hope the authorities follow HeadMan's leadership in remaining Bold, Extolled, Impregnable!"

I was eventually linked to Communism, anarchism, illegal weapons, East Germany and pyromania. Everything but the sinking of the *Maine*.

Not bad, not bad at all I concluded, daintily smearing a morsel of egg from my lips with the back of my hand. A single phone call and a few woefully unguarded e-mails – sent a day or three before, in more innocent times when I foolishly dared think of them as solely the Minders' domain and therefore off-limits to the press – were all that the *Node* needed to chop-suey my life. Voila, America, your latest violent, delusional psychopath.

All that, yet Tredwell couldn't find room for a word on my civ-lib concerns. Nothing of my statement to Nicki that it was high time someone took a stand. And certainly no mention of Stanley's musings that resisting the searches just might spark something bigger. Nor was there anything of my muttering to Stanley about being physically restrained in Bellevue. A neat bit of stove-piping indeed, both Nick and I flipped from the pan to a flame turned high.

I pictured poor Nicki sitting across from an apoplectic, permanently tanned Ernesto come Monday morning. No ad agency got the fifteen percent commission on media buys that was standard in days of yore. For the sake of argument, halve that and say that F&F got 7.5% – an assumption – of the $67-million campaign. Something north of $5 million, right, Ernesto? If I somehow ever spoke to the Wife again, I'd just have to say she'll be far better off growing radishes. I sent the damn e-mail to her job just to make sure she read it. I didn't mean anything malicious.

Nor did it sound remotely good about NYONLY. Time to see the damn thing, which I'd certainly been in no mood for while my useless Saturday unspooled. I sprang to the machine – that is, turned slightly in my chair – and, what the hell: "Access Denied." How could I not freaking get a cable channel's home page? I beat my head against a couple of digital doors and finally pried one a crack to see that *my* machine was specifically denied. It referenced the Net gobbledygook address of the box on my kitchen table. I threw it across the room.

****

No I didn't. Man, the *Node* was gonna suck all the air out of the room, leaving none for some actually positive *Daily Chirp* articles. One was an exclusive with the slinky girl from Penn Station and her boyfriend, the big Asian dude. They said I'd been holding a simple transistor radio which they whole-vided minutes after I'd gotten shot. But that was minutes before the cops confiscated their legal, college-sanctioned whole-vid. His name was Marko (as I maybe recalled her saying), and she was Bethany, both of them film students at Brooklyn College. They'd contacted the *Chirp* to demand the MTA return their camera and everything it contained. Marko had stored a semester's worth of work in two courses in it and Bethany one – courses that neither could afford to flunk.

The cops let them have it, citing their prior disorderly conduct arrests for 'unauthorized documentation' of that infamous veg-an-rights Demo that turned ugly when the lamb that protesters symbolically released spooked a police horse. The intrepid pair had whole-vided a cop tazing the lamb. Plus, like me, they had their own frictional costs of riding the trains. Marko had the standard, late-night open container ticket besmirching his record, while Bethany had been caught smoking a cigarette on one of the elevated plat-forms out in Brooklyn.

For pity's sake, hide the children and the old folks.

The *Chirp*'s next page featured Carole in her high school cheer-leading outfit, pompoms aflutter, next to the welcome news that, such was the outpouring of restorative love from the entire city, she was feeling well enough to probably be released on Tuesday. The TV chat-fests were already making competing offers for her first inter-view – a bout of penetrating political analysis surely on tap.

Worse was the article on my vanishing from Bellevue, which they pinned on a desire to skip out on the bill. But "The Backpack Bungler apparently miscalculated on this as on so much else since Bellevue had already verified that his address in Queens is...." Then big as life – heads-up every disaffected looney in town – came my Bumfuckville address. Screw the *Chirp* and its nonexistent pretext for printing my address. So much for the Hovel as haven, Goddamn it!

My best, my *only* hope was to offer "Penn Tale" to history near the start of the week's news cycle. For Maureen's sake, I'd have to fudge my escape from Bellevue. Finagle it, somehow, or maybe just include that part out – an interesting technical challenge. Speaking of *technical* challenges, beyond speaking loud enough for the wire she'd wear, was I really pursuing Maureen hoping to get horizontal?

I actually got to stringing a few words together when, of course, the phone rang. Some politician, no doubt, offering big bucks to say I once dated his opponent.

Chapter Twenty-Four

Corporate Spook

But it was Ralph, falling all over himself that I'd been brought so low. "Nice shorts you got."

"And why do you care?"

"You haven't seen it, haven't seen yourself on NYONLY yet, have you? I forgot. You're the only person in New York who doesn't have cable even though you get nothing but ghosts on your TV."

"I tried to get NYONLY online, but it's blocked on my computer – my *specific* machine. You believe that?"

"They got you by the nuts, dude."

"Maybe, maybe not. But what about my shorts?"

"You mean the world's oldest, baggiest, somebody-shat-in-them-and-died, blue-jeans shorts you got on. Throw in them boots you wear even in the middle of August, and some tee shirt that's way too small and so old I couldn't begin to tell you what color it used to be. And that's with my new Osmosis-Screen I been telling you about."

"So I was dressed like a bum going out for ten minutes for Chrissakes. The guy ambushed me. But what did that jerk say about me getting shot? And – why, yes, thank you – my head is feeling better."

"Wait. So the best part is when he ends his report saying something like your path forward remains uncertain given all the trouble you're in. And there's this long, zooming-in shot as you shuffle off down this crappy block of you in those shorts. First all of you, then just focusing right in on this, this *remnant* that you're wearing that you really should burn except that the EPA – if HeadFuck still had it – would come after you."

"Think you should be calling him that on my phone given the trouble I'm in?"

"Right, uh…Minders…uhm "

"Anyway, Ralph, I promise to call you for sartorial advice before leaving the house from here on out."

"Suit yourself, wiseass. But what were you eating, man? It looks like, I don't know, pig vomit or something. All greasy and dull at the same time, and you couldn't identify any of the ingredients even when he pulled in real tight. That was the other thing he kept the camera on. Oh, and that bandage on your head. He loved that too."

"So he screwed me every way he could just to show the world how clever and superior he is. I should've stolen his damn change off the counter."

"Don't steal anything, man. You need to be clean as a whistle, buddy-boy. And wash your hair, for Christ's sake."

"Look, Ralph, for the last time: I was starving and I stupidly went out without bothering to think. It'd been less than forty-eight hours since I got shot – in the head! – and I snuck out the back hoping they'd miss me. But this turkey showed up to get a damn shrimp roll. That's all he freaking ate for lunch was one shrimp roll!"

"Well, you are well and truly fucked. And they're saying there's gonna be some kind of whole-vid of you casing Penn Station released later today. Apparently shots of you carrying that backpack in this heat."

That weird pain started up again on the side of my head *away* from the abrasion.

"So what were you doing in Penn Station," Ralph continued. "Looking for the right cop to shoot you, but almost miss?"

"That's it, exactly. How come I never recognized before how gosh-darn clever you are."

"Yeah, and I'm sure it's a good time to piss off your friends. But you know, it was weird."

"Weird how?"

"Weird that his camera was busted or something. Cause he kept jumping to himself back in the studio with this smirk on his puss listening to you just talk, no picture. Then he'd jump to shots of you in that Chinese, the audio and video both on. He kept flip-flopping like his camera was fritzing in and out."

"What a minute, what was I saying during just audio?"

"I don't know, your usual wise-ass."

"*Ralph!*"

"Alright, let me think. The thing that leaps out – and you should've seen his little grin with this – was when you admitted making that cop shoot you."

"What in the world are you talking about?"

"He had you saying, 'I made that cop shoot me.' Though it sounded like you were asking a question. Not that that's not getting lost in the sauce."

Christ, he said his damn camera was off. He made this whole big production about turning– shit! – turning the *video* back on. Lying scum. Goddamn sarcasm. Never, ever resort to sarcasm, the world isn't made for it anymore. "That was sarcasm, Ralph, answering his stupid questions. Jesus, am I fucked. What else?"

"He said you refused to answer whether the device you carried was a gun or a detonator. I almost choked on my sandwich, that a punk like you had a bomb or even a gun. It's like – "

"It was that stupid transistor radio I carry around that you and everyone else find so amusing."

"Well you'd better get a big, big picture of that radio up in Times Square like tomorrow. Another thing – I remember this perfectly cause it just nails your ass so bad – he had you saying something about wouldn't it be nice to have the MTA pay your rent for a while. And then you used one of your phrases, something about making 'a chunk of change' carrying that backpack around in the heat."

"You really think I'm dumb enough to say that? I was talking about getting paid for an article – a lousy couple of hundred bucks – and he just sliced it up any way he wanted. Well, the hell with them, cause it doesn't make any sense. The big hole in this whole smear campaign is how did I make that cop shoot me, but just nick me in the head? Tell me that, Goddamn it!"

"Dude – my ear! You still think logic has anything to do with this? They brand you a 'dirty bomber,' and that's it. It's like the war hero versus the deserter in that election, remember? Only in your case, you got a gorgeous blonde with tits from here to Hoboken – and real by the looks of 'em – shot in the gut, a *fireman's* own personal playpen. Then there's the cops – sorry, our 'Protectors.' And a Boot. On the other side of the equation we got you looking homeless *and* talking about doing it for money. Whatever you were doing, challenging those useless searches that do all of nothing and that nobody cares about except they make you late. Yeah, I read that lefty blog of yours, *Naked Opprobrium* – whatever. The King of fucking Bushwick rushing to your side."

"Like the cops can tell anything patting the outside of your bag for half-a-second."

"People just want to get out of there and get on with their day. Nobody's getting X-rayed or felt-up like at the airport. Just keep your weed in tin foil and don't go near any of their damn dogs waiting to bite your balls off. You think anyone's gonna care NYONLY sliced up your words? Go ahead, prove it. And then get a real big megaphone."

"I am so screwed."

"The fork just fell *outta* your ass, you are so done. But yo, you ever go pay a sympathy visit to that Fiore action, make sure you bring me along. I can be your cousin or something, cause she can butter my toast any way she wants."

"Sure, Ralph. You're first on my list. But I don't think I'll be seeing Carole anytime soon. I gotta go."

"Alright. Make sure you watch the news tonight. That cop whole-vid might even be on your TV."

"Right. Thanks. Bye."

My anchor in the storm.

****

Not knowing where to buy a megaphone, I couldn't think what to do about NYONLY just then. But it was pretty damn clear that if the cops were spoon-feeding my bush-league transgressions to the Tredwells of the world, I'd damn well better usher a certain skeleton into the light myself. Both Stanley and NYONLY had urged that, and neither carried a light load between the ears. Whether the cover-up was worse than the crime depended, probably, on whether the crime stayed blanketed. Bedclothes slipping to the floor, time to bellow and bluff like my betters, only in my case, I'd aim for the truth.

Anyone who made a stink about my little slip-up was a sore loser – get over it and move on! Destroy the village in order to save it. A full recount violates voters' rights. These Boots are made for Fomenting, don't worry about why. War crimes so old-school, we need to look forward as opposed to looking back. Senator, I'm not here to discuss the past, said the ballplayer. Right, and tomorrow's another news cycle, maybe Jacquine will have done something outrageous. Anyone paying attention knew the drill.

So. A couple of months back, at the beginning of June, still joined in connubial bliss – well, still tethered under one roof – I was $287 short on my half of the rent. And, astoundingly, a corporate espionage assignment fell out of the sky, some unidentified big schmoe having need of a newshound with a certain ... *flexibility*. No excuse, of course, but who was to say a chunk of cash might not help preserve what, all in all, had been a pretty slipericious marriage? The dumb thing was, when a Mr. Bettinger of Bettinger, Smoot and Associates called out of the blue, I hadn't a clue what to charge, so I asked for a chump-change fifteen-hundred, when I easily could have doubled that. All I was risking was my byline – my name – a bit faded, sure, but still capable of a spit-shine if I somehow encountered a big score. As the Man for All Seasons observes, "Why … it profits a man nothing to give his soul for the whole world…. But for Wales!" That's right, for a measly fifteen-hundred clams.

So, confess to all this, really? Muddy the waters more, though I couldn't see my feet?

Nicki pretty levelheaded despite her recent flibbertigibbet ways, I would've loved to run it by her. Pop? Part of our problem was he didn't take my work seriously because of the paltry pay, so the journalistic ethics involved would mean little. He'd just start muttering about a lawyer – which I plain did not want to think about. Savvy Maureen would be best, both our heads on the flip-side of the pillow recently under her lovely ass to improve the angle of attack.

If I confessed, it had to be public, and it had to be quick before somebody beat me to it. Not that anyone who knew of this little peccadillo wanted it exposed. Would *The Symington Referendum* even take such a stark announcement? Or what about Bill Syriac's blog on the press, basically a well read bulletin board? He always seemed to have a whiff of the father confessor about him. That was if I didn't just let this mangy dog sleep, hopefully to choke on gristle fallen from an abscessed tooth.

Cause two days after Bettinger called, I found myself flying out to Lester, Indiana under the cover of journalism to attend Heavy-Duty Manufacturing Inc.'s dog-and-pony introducing its next generation, workhorse vehicle for shuttling Boots around. That is, its new, light-tactical death-crate, a giant Jeep of sorts (not that H-DM would ever refer to it as such).

Yup, working for "the competition," as Bettinger said more than once, this reporter was to go spy on H-DM to learn what I could of its new 'Hillbilly Grinder' as it was introduced to the press and Pentagon brass. Hillbilly Grinder was ground-up Boots' near-universal term for H-DM's current, roll-over prone vehicle that needlessly killed so many of them. The pending, decade-long, eight-billion-dollar military contract didn't include the billions more that American males of a certain age might someday fork over for an eventual civilian model. Drivers looking to tumescefy their lives could drape themselves in watered-down élan borrowed from younger, poorer and entirely more virile American fighting men (and women).

America at war – many wars – I was spying for the Germans, cause H-DM's only "competition" for the contract was Chrysler's Jeep. (The Germans had been trying to unload Chrysler for years, but were still searching high and low, Fiat having walked away some time back.) The Pentagon had narrowed it down to a new generation H-DM vehicle on steroids and a new Jeep on human growth hormone. So the German-owned Jeep was striving to replace the H-DM Grinder that had proved so tippy and breakdown-prone in the Sands. Search obscurely online, and you'd read of far too many combat related rollovers – heck, fatal rollovers just driving scared along a riverbank.

But, Christ, didn't Bettinger even google some of my man-the-barricades articles of recent years that should have disqualified me from working for a defense company? I certainly bothered to learn of his tainted background. Maybe he did and figured I was broke enough to be desperate. Maybe he was right. After instructing him that his idiotic request for an e-mailed report was a deal-breaker, he finally agreed I could report in from an Indiana pay phone. I told him he'd have to work out security at his end.

I figured to get in, learn what I could of the H-DM prototype, get out, and then go scrub with lye soap and a wire brush. So I dropped everything, a light load for a longish time, publishers unaccountably not clamoring for my proposed book, *Pernicious and Insidious: The Sub Rosa Subversion that Demands Attention* – a working title only.

Just being lucky out in Indiana two months back, I encountered an H-DM machinist (actually, he encountered me), a disgruntled

Boot who'd dodged round several Sands in the tippy, extant H-DM Grinder. And he dropped a tasty scoop on me that would've had my byline bouncing, except I couldn't publish it without shooting myself in the foot exposing my whole false-flag operation. Pretty ironic, since my client, "the competition," would've obviously been thrilled by any H-DM bad news. Yeah, a scoop that might save a *bunch* of Boots' lives. A scoop that, should I confess on Syriac, I'd then be free to publish. I sat and sweated – I'd been sweating over it, really, since the day I met that damn machinist – my head hurting in ways I couldn't blame on Frankie.

I finally decided to at least write the stupid thing. Get that done and then decide if Syriac should hang my skeleton in his window come Monday morning. One thing was sure: with another whole-vid salvo coming that Sunday evening, the cops weren't letting any grass grow under their trotters.

I actually strung a few words together, but the damn phone rang again, probably someone caught drowning kittens wanting me to testify as a character witness. But it was Pop, informing me that Mom was feeling peaked, and they'd have to come see me in a day or two. Then, "You're right, those searches are dumb. And maybe sometimes it's a dummy who doesn't care about his own neck is what this country needs. See if he can get some other dummies to maybe fall in behind him."

"I guess that was the ultimate idea."

"We'll see. But the main thing is, why the hell did you e-mail Nicki at her job talking about this stuff with the cops? You think maybe that e-mail was … you know, a deliberate little *fuck-you* as, your marriage over, you checked out one way or the other?"

"Pop, what in God's name are you talking about? No. I sent it to her job to make sure she got it because I didn't know what was going to happen with the cops. Any non-work e-mail, Nicki might delete without a glance."

"So this deal in Penn Station was dangerous, but you didn't care what happened messing with men who got more guns than sense?"

"Pop, what're you trying to say?"

"I don't know. Back in my day, you break a cop's nose, they would've just taken you down the alley and got their message across in about sixty seconds. Nowadays, especially somewhere they got cameras everywhere, they can't do that. So everything gets escalated. All the wars we're in, nobody cares about them shooting some big lug who pissed them off. Except for you being white and doing it somewhere full of rich commuters, it happens all the time. Plus you not being a Null, which I assume you ain't, far as anyone knows about that Minder crap."

"I guess I scared that one cop, holding my radio out at them and carrying a pack."

"And why do something so shit-for-brains? No kids or nothing, you're way old enough to do what you want with your life. That's always the big question under every other question, isn't it? Still, a girl dumps you, I say walk away with your head high. Make her wonder if she made a mistake. Don't do this petty shit, screwing her over at her job with an e-mail. That's too easy, just hitting send."

"Pop, you got it all wrong. Jesus, you're starting to sound like one of these damn reporters. Before this happened, before getting shot, Nick and I were *estranged* – that's all. We had some hope, maybe. I mean, she wrote me back that morning before I left for Penn Station and said she missed me."

"Yeah, 'missed you.' But she didn't say anything about wanting to see you, did she? OK, mister, none of my business. But the next dame, leave the damn e-mails alone. Though all these big shots making big money never seem to learn that, do they."

Ours was not a warm goodbye. Shit, e-mailing Nick was basically like swimming somewhere with no lifeguard: you employ the buddy system. With all her cutsey-poo crap about soccer moms in reply, she'd certainly said nothing about not writing her at work. Still, Pop was right about one thing. Yeah, she'd said she missed me, but not a peep about any getting together to ease her pain.

PART FIVE

Chapter Twenty-Five

That'll Knock 'Em Back on their Heels

Pop throwing punches wildly with both hands, but not scoring, damn it. Aside from the odd, arch comment at an F&F party, I'd never messed with Nicki's job. Hell, I'd tweaked her copy for her, helped rub consumers' noses in their own dumb complicity with it all.

I went to my window, but it didn't help, my breath shallower still, and suddenly, no kidding, I needed to get out of there. Head up by the train maybe. Sure, treat myself to my first five-buck coffee concoction at one of those chrome-table joints. See if the Backpack Bungler's new status might sway one of the dead-eyed lovelies up there, a haughty Greek or some snickering Kansas City transplant. Shoot the moon.

As I hit the porch, an NBC truck lumbered round the corner to block Stap's driveway. Damn – just a minute quicker! Cause, in long pants or not, still reeling from Pop's flurry and lacking the head for an *encounter* just then, I fled back upstairs.

I'd missed a call, Nicki saying she wanted to see me before hitting work on Monday, and why didn't we have dinner at our favorite (i.e., less snooty) local Greek. Her treat. We could get some of that grilled calamari we both liked. Gotta be able to make a formal declaration at work, huh, Nicki? Cause that sure sounded like applying our no-breakups-on-the-phone vow that we'd solemnly pledged on our two-month anniversary as a couple: about the time, we both well knew, when inflamed affairs such as ours tended to peter out.

Like condemned-man Barnadine in *Measure for Measure* who declares, "I swear I will not die today," and then, oddly enough, stomps unmolested back to his cell, I was in no mood for the axe. Plus, I had to write Syriac and deal with his potential caveats, make a further stab at "Penn Tale" and cope with, or at least watch, the cops' whole-vid. Not to mention working up the nerve to remove that dead-mouse bandage and wash the grease from my attractively thinning locks. Cause I had prior, pressing business to conduct out in the world on Monday at a court of sorts, Monday the deadline. I was set to handle it Friday except I'd woken up in a hospital bed with a goon barring the door. So no, I was a mite too busy to dissolve my marriage that evening.

Shrinking from calling her micro-zap to interrupt her third? frolic of the day with MoneyBags, he of the little rat eyes scrunched by bloated cheeks, I left Nick a message pleading the Stuffing's exhaustion and proposing she come by Monday night. I then fell to typing my Syriac statement. Actually, still not convinced I'd send it, I switched immediately to a pad and pen. Even with my machine always offline when offline, the MoFos' *retroactive* keystroke monitoring programs were awfully sticky.

Dear Bill:

You may have noticed I've been in the news lately, which came as a shock to me too. I've certainly lost control of my own narrative, but as I discussed with the editor of *Naked Opposition*, I thought it past time that someone stood up to the *non*-random, suspicionless search program here in New York City that, in total violation of the Fourth Amendment, subjects anyone dicey enough to resort to public transportation to an immediate public undressing – metaphorically speaking (for now).

The way the searches have been incorrectly portrayed, passengers are supposedly able to refuse and hoof it to another station though it may be a half-mile away. Never mind that you might be old, or late or traveling with little kids – or all three in a downpour. I'll have more to say on all this when I publish my account of getting shot in Penn Station as I set out to execute a principled refusal to this illegal policy. While I didn't shy from the risk of a civil-liberties protest arrest, I had every reason to expect that would be the worst of it.

Far more luminous individuals, though on issues of perhaps similar import, have been arrested for such non-violent protest. It's a legitimate and worthwhile action, one that I believe should be both endorsed and emulated in these perilous times. Yet I've heard of no one just standing up and saying 'Get-out-of-my-face No!' in a city of almost nine million. As the poet has it, "The best lack all convictions, while the worst are full of passionate intensity."

I did indeed intend to write about it – and expected to earn my normal pittance for my words: a couple of hundred bucks. For what good the tree that falls on deaf ears, what purpose in making my statement of refusal before some few commuters left to wonder what the heck that was all about? It's the sort of old-fashioned, shoe-leather, participant/observer work that most reporters with weekly paychecks feel beneath them these days. They'd rather flog a mouse and call that an investigation. (Half of them don't even know how to work a source on the phone anymore.) So I ended up taking one for the team as a result – my team. Because it's past time to choose sides. You're either on the bus or off the damn bus!

And speaking of those on the wrong side, on whose 'authority' were my private e-mails and a transcript of an obviously private phone call to my father obtained? And then who gave them to the *New York Node* as manna for the absurd fictions it published this Sunday morning? In the midst of all this stove-piping from illegally obtained material, the *Node* failed to mention that these private communications discussed my plan to protest the searches.

But to the impetus for this letter and the reason I hope you can post it forthwith. I'm proud of my intent Thursday in Penn Station and sorry that a simple pedestrian accident rounding a blind corner ended up forestalling it – for now. Let me extend heartfelt best wishes to Ms. Carole Fiore, whom the MTA police also shot that morning, and express my delight that she is apparently well on her way to a full recovery. (As to my head, time will tell.)

I write today driven by a bona fide skeleton in my closet, something well beyond the normal frictional 'transaction costs' of the hardscrabble passage through life (not to mention the city's subways) of someone who – on occasion – finds unmediated, *dry* existence a tad dreary. Those costs represent the human condition rather than a true skeleton, people throughout history having maintained their right to cognitive autonomy despite the sad, sorry advent in Manhattan of the eight-dollar glass of beer.

But there is something I regret, and let me attempt to mitigate its impact by disclosing it here myself.

I dissembled on behalf of Chrysler, my target the soon to be retired Hillbilly Grinder's current manufacturer, Heavy-Duty Manufacturing. As you may know, Chrysler's Jeep and H-DM's Hillbilly Grinder are locked in a stiff competition for the contract to produce the Army's next generation light-tactical vehicle. (Is it too much to hope that new war materiel might prove unnecessary?) I did so at the behest of a Mr. Bettinger of Bettinger, Smoot and Associates.

Though I might maintain that I intended to write about it, nevertheless I am owed a very small sum of money for traveling under the flag of journalism to H-DM's Lester, Indiana factory back in early June to learn what I could of the new vehicle being show-horsed that day to the press and then to report back. Which I did. And yes, it was a fraught experience, both that day and since. That I've yet to be paid is of no consequence to anyone but my landlord.

Funny thing is, I learned something out in Indiana of fairly enormous consequence to our troops when the new vehicle *hits* the road. So now that this stinking cat (skeleton of a cat – no mixed metaphors here) is out of the bag, I will soon tell that tale too and maybe even save some lives in the process. H-DM's new death-crate, the new Grinder, is still far from general production, let alone deployment, so there's no harm in my having tarried these couple of months. That my (near-deathbed) conversion took getting shot in the head and then smeared by every paper in town – well, we are brought into this world far from perfect and try to progress from there.

Somewhat cryptic, Bill, I know. But I managed to make the key point about my misdeed, and I hope, numerous curs nipping at my ankles, you can publish this statement come Monday morning. Thanks a bunch.

Sincerely,
Mitchell Fremson

Having been blasted as a Fiend, I couldn't resist a few rhetorical blandishments in this first self-penned salvo from my bunker. So, type it up and hit send? A cover-up is worse than the crime only when it fails. Easy to write, easier to send – but repent at leisure. Man, who could I ask or, rather, get to tell me what to do? Maybe get Mr. Staphilopoulos to convene his chorus of Greek buddies (and one Turk) down on the porch to sift the entrails. Yeah, confess to something known by only two other men, both of whom wanted it hidden. *That'll* send the MoFos packing!

Still mid-afternoon, I decided to sit on it and, suddenly weary, succumbed to the call of my chair.

****

"Nice shorts," said the voice on the phone that woke me. "So now we gotta be on the lookout for the naked, fat homeless skell you stole 'em from?"

Ralph doing a bad Brooklyn tough-guy? And why was he suddenly obsessed with my nether regions?

"Very funny, bright boy."

"We figured you were the genius. In fact, that's why we're leaving you loose, doing our job so good for us every time you open your mouth or leave that little rat-hole of yours. But we we're still thinking about inviting you down here for a little chat. Informal-like."

Not Ralph. "Look, pal, like Sam Spade said, 'If you want to see me, pinch me or subpoena me, and I'll come in with my lawyer.' And aren't you supposed to identify yourself at the start of the call, maybe be a little professional?"

"I was getting to that. Everyone's in such a hurry these days. You going on *60 Minutes* tonight and gotta make sure to get that filthy bandage changed? We figured – "

I slammed the phone down. It rang again, the jocularity gone. "Hey, *bright boy* – B.E.I., Goddamn it! You ever stop to think, maybe, that T has got this country screwed down pretty tight?"

"What T is that? The kind where somebody whole-vids a factory farm and you call that T? Huh? Ya never know, MoFo, the right stone in the right pond might wash away those guaranteed-overtime searches of yours."

"The wetbacks in that house of yours, maybe three of them legal, making you feel at home, an ass-wipe white boy like you? We'll be shaking that rat-trap pretty good, spreading the word about the happiness you bring wherever you go."

"Your name, cop. I'm counting to five. One, two – "

"Sure, sure thing, punk. DeBrunt. One word, capital D, capital B. Detective, MTA. So tell me, you're just some schmuck they recruited to probe the searches, right? I mean, you gotta be somebody's pawn, arranging that interview with NYONLY looking like something my ex-wife's cat threw up. That supposed to add to your street cred with the maggots already lining up behind you?"

"All over the country, DeBrunt."

"Not for long, with what we got in store for them."

Them – who's them? Cause that was just a dumb line about all over the country.

He went on. "I got two suggestions, punk. First, make the most of the temporary little slice of freedom you got. Probably with a ho since your wife is so *occupied*. And second, I'd watch the local news tonight if I were you. Any channel. We were wondering if we got your good side – with the cameras, not Frankie. We got much better shots than that asshole. Very patient guys, all ages, all sizes, all colors. All hanging around northwest Queens keeping the public safe."

And then the *baanhhnh* of a dead line. Jesus, good old fashioned, bare-knuckles intimidation, the best sign in days. Cause if the MTA thought they had me nailed, they'd feel no need to alert me to their damn whole-vid. They were the ones running scared over a bum shooting.

Chapter Twenty-Six

Artless Fabrication

Alright, what the heck time did the local news come on anyway, before *Belly Up to the Beast Within* or after? The paper said six o'clock on Sundays – in a little while. Of course there was a Nicki voice-mail. Sounding again way too sweet, she said dinner Monday worked cause, "It's been quite a full weekend to tell you the truth, and I'm bushed."

Spare me the details, darling. Going down to the hall window to shoot malevolence Manhattan's way – rise, oceans, rise! – I heard talk from the floor below and scooted down to see two of the friendlier guys coming in. I asked about any 'autos de periodicos en la calle' – newspaper cars in the street. One snarled as they pushed into their room, "You bad. You bring la Migra. They already get two men with children who need food back home. You go to Hell."

Turd-Touch! Turning everything brown and smelly. I went and sat and tried not to think.

Then it was time for the tube, any channel, 'DeBrunt' said. That meant Channel 10, pretty much the only station that came in at all clear since the old citywide television antenna was malignly neglected to dust.

(Damn peculiar after those towers fell that nowhere in New York's hundreds of square miles or on one of the many dozens of remaining tall buildings, not a single spot was deemed suitable to build a new antenna for the biggest TV market in the country. That the miserable reception forced most everyone but me to pay big for cable month after month was no doubt entirely coincidental. Hey, forget Building 7. Forget that they'd shipped ruined steel off to China before it was cool, sold it as scrap right damn quick, never mind it was key evidence from a fairly major crime scene. Forced cable is a conspiracy that'll stick with the public. Spread the word.

So, along with the drinking water they'd made great inroads on, and all those publicly funded private schools, they managed to privatize television as well, never mind the publicly owned airwaves. Amazing how bad a beating you can inflict, the alley dark enough, cause nobody wrote a word about the missing antenna. Like Ralph said, the occasional free-TV basketball game, the court got a mite crowded on my set, everyone shadowed by his ghost, twenty players running around.)

The cop's whole-vid was Channel 10's lead story. "Metropolitan Transportation Authority police have this afternoon released dramatic, never before seen whole-vid of the so-called Penn Station Shooter." Wow, why was DeBrunt wetting his pants over them showing Frankie shooting me? Clutching and grabbing, I knew it wasn't so.

They had maybe forty-five seconds total, the telling bit a nifty mis-spliced fifteen seconds that turned reality inside out. The MoFos having traveled often and far down the mendacity trail, blatant misrepresentation came easy, certainly when dealing with a nobody like me. Well, they misunderestimated me, cause I have truth on my side, with goodness and, and ... beauty right behind.

As reported by Channel 10's Cloud McNamara, the whole-vid started off with a clear view of me talking to the Penn Station cop who'd been jotting down demographics on Wednesday, looking, yes Chilean Cassandra, a little like an aging grad student in my button-down shirt with the sleeves rolled up. They'd helpfully circled my bulging pack, not that you could miss it, and the news puppy allowed as how the cops were "unsure what threat it might have contained since the Suspect was, unfortunately, not apprehended on this the day prior to the shooting."

Big-time threats in that pack, Pup – little black marks on paper.

There was a break in the whole-vid and then a view of me walking past that same cop a second time when I tried to spark a search but the cop didn't bite. "Having probed the Protectors' defensive perimeter, nineteen minutes later the Suspect returned. But he thankfully loses his nerve, or perhaps there was a technical glitch, and he moved on without incident."

Glitch, yeah, the ray beam from the orbiting Mother Ship deflected by a low-flying Fuji blimp's biometric cameras.

He continued. "Stated MTA Deputy Commissioner Walton Everidge, 'If an attack or mandated discharge had occurred in this much more crowded waiting area rather than in the next day's more isolated corridor, I shudder at the consequences.' "

And I quiver, Everidge, at the thought of a particularly righteous meteor crashing through the roof onto your lying head. News-Pup got more breathless still. "Now here's the whole-vid from the actual day of the forced shooting that imperiled commuters and sent hundreds fleeing. Be advised that due to a suspicious technical glitch potentially similar to the previous day's, uh … malfunction, the whole-vid is of poor quality."

That gobbledygook apparently meant I was too incompetent to blow myself and a multitude to high heaven on Wednesday, but somehow possessed the magical power to incapacitate hidden surveillance cameras on Thursday.

"As the whole-vid starts, police advise viewers to observe – there! – the Shooter comes into view."

Which technically speaking was true. The image of much poorer quality, you could see just a touch of blue uniform, Frankie's knee maybe. But I dominated the screen, jerking oddly into view like stage furniture whose guide-wire has suddenly gone haywire. Was it that bald-faced and direct, the phrase 'the Shooter comes into view' justified by Frankie's knee but obviously referring to me, the unarmed, bleeding man rushed off in an ambulance? As with issues more momentous than ruining some mope's life, merely follow Goebbels' infamous advice (whether he actually said it or not): *Just repeat the lie.*

"The whole-vid resumes here, and police instruct Homelanders and others to note the flat silver object in the Suspect's hand – right there! Police sources have theorized about it, given the bulky nature of the Suspect's backpack. But the exact nature of the threat remains to be determined."

There was a brief, grainy, slow-mo shot from the rear of me pointing some kind of … *something*. Though it was again helpfully circled in white, it could be a lump of plutonium, or the Holy Grail, or a used condom dried all stiff or, sure, some kind of very rectangular weapon. Whatever floated your boat.

"Unfortunately, in the melee that followed the tragic engendered discharge Thursday morning, the weapon itself was secreted away, presumably by an as yet unidentified co-assailant. Protectors are asking Homelanders or others with information to report to their local precinct."

Co-assailant – a nifty step up from co-conspirator.

"Fearing for their lives, MTA Protectors felt it necessary to 'mechanically accelerate' the Suspect's East German Army rucksack rather than risk it exploding." Then, of course, came whole-vid of my pack on a tarmac followed by a nice, medium-sized boom and little ball of fire down at Floyd Bennett Field, a big NYPD helicopter parked close by. Knowing the size of the coming explosion, having engineered it themselves, they felt no need to move a multi-million-dollar aircraft. Could I ask for my books back, or did they actually return them to the pack before blowing it up? Either way, they owed me twenty bucks for a new army-surplus pack.

He continued, "Senior MTA officials have ruled out releasing the footage of the actual discharge due to the sensitivities of the Protectors victimized by the incident. However, they were able to provide two other pieces of evidentiary whole-vid that shed light on the Suspect's dastardly attack."

Out of sequence, since they'd already shown me brandishing the Entertainment System, they then showed Frost ministering to Frankie around the corner, the soldier standing in front of the two cops in a defensive crouch. The whole-vid no longer cloudy, blood flowed crimson down Frankie's face.

Betty, let me hear! Always with the questions. The guy had a gun, or something, and the cops had their guns. But they're not gonna show that – they got their reasons. Anyway, he beat up the cop somehow. No, there weren't three cops, one's a soldier. But that T-guy's a big guy. You know, the 'fog of war.' Now, look, my fish sticks got cold watching this. Be a doll and nuke 'em for me."

Violence the main course, they offered some cheesecake for dessert.

"MTA specialists, aided by federal, state and private agencies, have carefully reviewed literally tens of thousands of feet of whole-vid from Penn Station's 284 cameras, searching for co-assailants. And, I'm happy to say, they unearthed a last bit of whole-vid that speaks for itself: never before seen candid shots of someone who at this point certainly needs no introduction. Ladies and Gentlemen, by generous permission of the MTA police department, permit Cloud McNamara to proudly present Miss Carole Fiore!" .

And a well-hinged and very determined Carole (I remembered the clackity-clack of her high heels) came rushing down that corridor prior to the shooting in that tight, alarmingly green dress, her gorgeous, morning-commute game-face on: *stare if you must, but out of my way.* They ran it twice, the second time with just a tasteful touch of slow-mo.

"Betty! Get in here and look at this cupcake. That lucky-stiff fireman, I hope none of the good parts got shot."

Cloud wrapped up with security-camera footage of ambulances and cop cars tying up traffic on Seventh Avenue. But, despite capturing Carole for the ages, they had nothing of me walking that same corridor seconds before, nor of the two dummies' collision round that corner.

Just me leaping into the frame as "the Shooter" and then pointing that silver thing.

It was shown that Sunday evening on every channel in New York. But, its job done, what came to be referred to as the "Silver Weapon" whole-vid was deemed too "disconcerting" to ever broadcast again. It's not self-censorship, man! Some sights – a rolled, burning Hillbilly Grinder, for instance, or steel magically imploding – are just too darn fraught to inflict on a fragile public. The hens might stop laying. Never mind that Boots were shown daily on TV in every country but their own doing horrible and having horrible done (or vice versa).

Sorry that I'd waited all afternoon to write Syriac and his audience of scribblers (plus the bounce), I typed my letter off that legal pad, inserting this right before my confession about spying on H-DM:

> And just now the TV news aired an obviously manipulated and out of sequence set of surveillance whole-vids that seek to place me in the worst possible light as I walked through Penn Station carrying a back-pack full of books (*quel horror*) hoping to spark a search so I could just say no. Just say, in effect – to cite an ostensibly spontaneous, but similarly planned action – that I wasn't moving to the back of the bus.
>
> Of course, having blown up my backpack – which they now owe me for – explosive residue coats whatever remains. It ain't rocket science. At Bellevue, a 'cop' wearing absolutely no identifying insignia knew all the titles I carried, mentioning them one by one. So they didn't have to explode my pack, they'd already opened it.
>
> The narration I heard on my local station, Channel 10, referred to me as the "Shooter," though I was unarmed and rushed to the hospital bleeding from a bullet to the head. Let me state categorically: I had no gun and no detonator. The citizen's responsibility to keep an ear on events is more crucial than ever in today's fractious political climate. To that end, I was carrying a silver transistor radio that was audibly playing. It rested under my shirt on my shoulder where I could hear it. The man who shot me remarked on the content of the news, and its presence was attested to by two independent eyewitnesses in Sunday's *New York Daily Chirp*.

The MTA was able to supply a whole-vid of Carole Fiore, Thursday's other cop-shot, walking down the same corridor I'd traversed seconds before. (As mentioned, I certainly do wish Ms. Fiore a speedy and complete recovery.) But they somehow had no footage of me in that corridor from that same camera. Providing it would harm their fabricated and, let me reiterate, out of sequence whole-vid narrative that magically tars me as the 'Shooter.' Nor did they show the blameless collision round a blind corner where I inadvertently bloodied the nose of the short cop who shot me, Officer Reisner.

Finally, most crucially, the MTA withheld the whole-vid of the "bullets' actual discharge." (Apparently they leaped out of the cops' guns of their own accord.) According to Channel 10's Cloud McNamara, this was supposedly "due to the sensitivities of the Protectors victimized by the incident." The MTA is obviously floundering. Otherwise why release such a botched job destined to turn and bite them in the elbow?

Sure, this would steal some thunder from "Penn Tale," but this whole-vid had to be refuted and quick. Focused on what I'd just written rather than the crucial confession I'd penned earlier about spying on H-DM, I pretended to think about it, then cried havoc and hit send. And another scrumptious meal cobbled together from a can of curried kidney beans and a block of ice-encrusted peas over some couscous I found.

One heck of a Sunday: lies in the paper, confessing to the world, my marriage kaput, Pop's nasty accusation, a cop calling with threats and, finally, the MTA's whole-vid, an artless indictment dropping me off Stap's tall roof. Hell, I no longer batted an eye at cops anchored downstairs monitoring my comings and goings. Not that I had anywhere to go. Shoot, deal with it tomorrow, all of it and all of them, happy at least that my head seemed better, and the week – one heck of a *week* – was finally over as long as no one came crashing through my door before the clock struck twelve.

Chapter Twenty-Seven

Syriac Swollen, Stap Primed

I woke with a jolt from a combustible mix: the Sunday *Node's* mention, stolen from my e-mail to Nicki, of an incident with a cat and a cop on the LIRR that left me "bruised and breathless"; the cheap malice of the *Daily Chirp* printing my address; and the MTA fairy-tale whole-vid featuring my pretty mug. Mix, season and bake for twenty-two minutes at 612 mega-Hertz and Statie would have no problem wrapping his warped brain around two plus two equaled me. In fact, any of the louts chanting USA! USA! in that LIRR car could link little old blameless me to an attack on a Protector *before* Penn Station.

Screw it. Should the LIRR riot surface somehow, I'd cope with my usual knife-thrust alacrity. My appearance, motives, work, finances and the remnants of my marriage lay in tatters on a Times Square sidewalk. Yet getting shot was strangely liberating. Lightning never striking twice, it wasn't like they could just plain shoot me again. *Can't Touch Me*, got that DeBrunt? Plus, Penn Station five days prior and the cops with the weekend to think about it, if I didn't get arrested as Monday played itself out, time to back-burner all the legal threats the press pondered so lovingly.

First, I needed to confirm that Syriac had played his part in my exceedingly odd rope-a-dope rehabilitation. Then I'd hightail it off to Brooklyn so they couldn't arrest me on a weeks-old HateCrime ticket whose witching hour was nigh. Then back to the Hovel to finally polish off "Penn Tale" and send it off to three different news sites – and heck with 'em if they couldn't cope with a simultaneous submission from the man of the hour. (Much to Nicki's disgust, I never held editors up for money. Unseemly, somehow, disseminating Truth, so whoever responded first snared the prize.) Then noodle around for reaction to my Syriac confession, followed by a beer or three to hornswoggle things properly for Divorce-Dinner with the Wife. That'd make a day.

Syriac's note leaped out of my mail's queue of garbage and abuse, the fanciful, daily barrage of "Minder-Savvy Tier Reduction" offers. He said the Net nuts-and-bolts ferrying my letter matched the two e-mails I'd sent him back when. And that satisfied his vetting. He'd posted early to garner the maximum exposure. And thanks for thinking of him – for free! – despite my new notoriety. Right. Eschewing payment for a confession was the sort of dumb squeamishness that helped explain landing in the Hovel at my ripe, lonely age.

The way of it these days: the writer calling up a screen to see what the world saw *as* it sees it. No e-mailed confirmation from Syriac or, heavens, phone call, no massaging of the text or consideration of any liability. OK, Bill, fine. I wrote it, and sent it and, yeah, take responsibility for probably the weightiest prose I'd ever committed. At least he ran my letter unmolested below his backhanded intro:

> Mitchell Fremson's byline has been flitting hither and inconsequentially yon for years. Then, last Thursday, as readers know, his name exploded (so to speak) in very peculiar circumstances. He maintains he was seeking to resurrect the shady old practice of participant/observer journalism. Due to its disastrous outcome, his Penn Station prank has achieved wide notice. But he apparently preceded sans assignment, doing it on 'spec' as it were. And no wonder, for no professional editor would approve of setting out to challenge a practice

that stands between us and perdition: state control of our movements. Worse, he aimed to publicize his stunt with an eye towards emulation! 'Spec' as in *spectacularly* brain-locked!

Armed with a bulky backpack, he sought to balk at the random (but still fully clothed) searches that keep all New Yorkers fearful, especially, one hopes, those seeking to embrace Perdition. He states that he was carrying, oddly secured on his person, a small ... transistor radio is probably the term. This contention – however harmful to an economy dependent on churning through generations of gadgets – was corroborated by eyewitnesses professionally quoted in yesterday's *New York Daily Chirp*.

This much is known: Fremson was shot in the head. That has not impacted his capacity to generate the workmanlike prose that I generously provide room for below. (Donation buttons scattered throughout this site.) As to what might be termed his statement of 'guilt' – a difficult concept post-Plunge – I remain agnostic. As long as it's done delicately, there's room for a certain, oh, *stretchiness* of standards, B.E.I. Mere subterfuge to provide simple competitive information to a private client, a respected Democracy Fomenter – well, to coin a phrase, no blood, no biggie.

As the Continental Op might tell poor, bedraggled Mitch: "*You talked too much, son. You were too damn anxious to make your life an open book for me. That's a way you amateur criminals have. You've always got to overdo the frank and open business.*"

I didn't know whether to take comfort from Syriac pooh-poohing any thought of wrongdoing, or see his license as confirming my transgression.

Stanley also weighed in in his normal, inimitable fashion:

Comrade:
    You should know that I'm thinking of dropping the periods in the logo,

236

closing it up and adding an underscore. Thus: _NO_, Build on the updraft in traffic as it were. Though why solicit your opinion on graphics or anything else? Nothing but silence from your quarter – and after I gave you such a boost running our interview. You should know that Bakunin's Rebellion's Comrade Refneski might well have proved an ally. But your failure to reach out to him after he went to bat for you in my story Saturday has cost you his support. A simple courtesy note would have preserved your access to his ability to stage a countervailing whole-vid to the cartoon the MTA released last night. I'm sure you've seen his devastating work regarding the Gnome of Greenpoint, the little fellow born with no arms from the decades-old oil spill fouling Brooklyn's water. Yes, _that_ Refneski.

Admittedly, I do applaud your little disclosure on Syriac today. By all means hobble the global armaments elite with any monkey wrench in the works you can grab. Get all the monkeys clawing and biting, and if it takes destroying a once perfectly good byline to do so, I at least am among the few who appreciate that you're looking at the bigger picture.

Have you considered a pen name? Keep your first name, thus: Mitchell Hill. I've always thought Hill would be a good moniker. Short, sweet and you never have to spell it. Of course, it might be tough to establish a new byline at your age. In fact, I was a little surprised at the cops' whole-vid of you. Frankly, you write younger.
Stanley

****

I was none too thrilled with the prospect of prying off my gnarly gray bandage. What if little bits of Stuffing came with it? But last Thursday five sticky days past, this boy was taking a shower, no ifs or buts. I couldn't then just leave it there, a sodden, congealing mass. Besides, didn't the wound demand a look-see? Prolong the agony by removing it slowly and carefully, or peel it off with a roar to mask the pain? A little worried what might accompany it if I yanked, I chose the former.

And it didn't look too bad. Inside the little crop circle of hair that Dr. Hwang had harvested lay the inconsequential mark, about the size of a small wooly worm, of a gun fired from fifteen feet. Damn lucky, even if the upshot was a job grading manure under an assumed name.

Eating the seed corn stashed away for Stap's rent, I grabbed fifty

237

bucks to (hopefully not) pay the HateCrime ticket and another forty because who knew what might befall before night fell; shat-showered-shaved (in correct order); covered the wooly worm with the ugly, *orangey* band-aid that was all I had; ran a damp paper towel over my slightly dressier black boots; pocketed a paperback and a slim reporter's notebook; made the requisite sandwich; thought to also pocket the 'assignment memo' Bettinger had foolishly sent me in case some reporter demanded proof of my corporate espionage; headed on out.

Spiffed as I was in a pair of black chinos and a *laundered* blue shirt over a sweat-barrier black tee, I hoped to find a reporter downstairs so I could denounce the MTA's fairy-tale whole-vid. Usually open in the heat, Mr. Staphilopoulos's door was closed as I crept by. You'd sometimes see him across a dark expanse of living room seated by a window on a wooden folding chair reading the local Greek newspaper. At first I'd wave, thinking it ruder not to, but he'd just stare, enforcing the invisible privacy-curtain that hung at his open door. The morning's closed door meant hope Stap was out, cause I wanted to let things at least marginally calm down – yeah, hold my freaking breath – before we spoke again, and he could toss the troublemaker on out. But he was out on his porch in nothing but an ancient pair of khakis and an even older pair of sandals, a surprisingly good chest for a guy probably over eighty, with most of the curly hairs still black.

"Ah, Mr. Staphilopoulos, taking the air this lovely morning."

A slow grin spread over a face that had seen too much sun. "You take it, Mr. Excitement Man. I don't like this air. An animal coming from a deep hole don't like this air. You make it better with a snap of your fingers."

"That's me: control the weather when I'm not making the world spin."

"You did *something*, wise guy, I not do all my years in this house, not with all my yellings. Your friends parked here babysitting you mean the project boys don't bring their dogs to shit on my sidewalk no more. That's good."

He pointed to the MTA cruiser I'd been trying to ignore, its cherry top oscillating red and blue, the bored guy behind the wheel fond of toys. "Stap, I'm sorry. But look at that idiot with his lights just in case the whole block can't see him."

"Hey, this best excitement here since the lady across the street got sick in her head and kept running around with her dress off. And that was way back with the President who dyed his hair."

A couple of third-floor men slunk out and pushed past, one of them jostling me roughly though there was plenty of room on the huge porch. Stap chided them. "Hey, what's the matter with you guys? Don't you know we got a big fish living here now?"

One kept walking, but the other made a big deal of turning on the walk and staring first at Mr. Staphilopoulos, then me, shaking his head all the while and then spitting showily on the step below where I stood.

"Hey, mister!" Stap yelled, loud but still amazingly sanguine. "You want to spit on him, I don't care. You're all big boys, do what you want. But out the other side of my gate. No fighting upstairs and no spitting on my house, the house you living in. You got that, amigo?"

"OK. You the boss in this house. But tell him no more Migra. They in this street every day, and already two men gone. Some stay upstairs, scared. So they lose their jobs. All cause of this big pendejo."

"Look, pal," I told him. "It's not my fault if the cops are going nuts. That's what they do in this country. Your country too. But look at that car. It says 'Metropolitan Transportation Authority.' That means it's railroad cops. Got it: *el train*. They don't care about you. All they care about is me."

Looking up at us and shading his eyes with both hands for some reason, the sun as usual oppressive but unseen, he spat again, only this time off on Stap's rocks and weeds. "It's your problem, you fix it. Before somebody fix it for you. OK, *pal*?"

They left. So the South American Syndicate was after me too. Pile on the teetering heap with the rest, boys.

Stap started laughing low. "Mr. Popularity – you got big talent make people happy."

"I'm glad you find it funny."

"I like funny at my age. I don't get much funny. I told you before, I like a guy mess with cops. Nobody does that since HeadFuck came in. Long as things not get too crazy, you OK here."

"Thanks, Stap. It's good to know I have a home."

"So what you dressed all nice for? You going to a lawyer? You want good Greek lawyer, very expensive, all the judges in Queens in his pocket?"

"I'll let you know."

I stuck out my mitt and we shook and, holy mackerel, he palmed me a ten-spot. Not a lot of rope thrown my way, who was I to insult the man whose roof sheltered me?

The MTA was tossing money around too, cause along with the standard-issue big glowerer behind the wheel, a female cop sat in the passenger seat, exhaling cigarette smoke out the window like it was her last act upright. And the sheer dingbatism of their flat-footed stalking rose up my throat and out.

"Hey, officers, thanks so much for the extra security. The whole block appreciates it. Since there's even less for you busy guys – pardon, Ma'am: guy and gal – to do once I leave, how about a ride to the subway in this heat so I don't get my nice clean shirt all sweaty. Maybe I'll start blabbing, and you can crack the case."

I was blabbing already, the request for a ride impulsive, silly and almost genuine once I realized how beastly it was out on the naked sidewalk, nary a tree the mile to the train's AC this dodgy part of Queens. Besides, what the heck was the point of their syrupy intimidation? The woman, too jaded to be really cute, took another drag, and the glowerer just shook his copy of the day's Kangaroo Krap at me and disappeared behind it. Guess it was a bum assignment, sitting there to no purpose, few folks drifting by to break the monotony.

But still an affront every time I opened Stap's front door. "Come on, how 'bout a ride? You guys are public servants, and you got a member of the public here looking for a little servicing. Whadiya say, Sunshine?"

The object of this last tossed her smoke and blasted the siren so sudden and so loud, I yelped and staggered back. I sure didn't like giving them that satisfaction though, unlike when Statie's club connected, these two couldn't hear my cry. Christ, it was a *lot* louder than a normal siren – a twin, almost, to the aural weapon Nicki and I encountered donkey-years ago, the cops using a fake ambulance to break up an anti-war Demo blocking a Manhattan street. I fell further back, holding my ears and crouching down as if that would make it hurt less. Holding his ears too, Mr. Staphilopoulos charged down the steps, his eyebrow tufts primed for battle. The sonic assault lasted a long moment; then we stood there twitching, its aftershock concrete.

Finally able to open the gate, Stap laughed. "More Mr. Popularity, huh?" He hitched up his beltless pants and then yelled far louder than was necessary, maybe from the clamor in his head.

"Hey you cocksuckers! I pay taxes here, you got that? I know people – I'm talking Mister Bigs for the City. So be nice, you want to sit all day in front of my house in *my* spot. Or maybe time for you to go get coffee. Charge it to Staphilopoulos. Charge it anywhere, they all know me. S-T-A-P-H-I-L-O-P-O-U-L-O-S. You got that? Write it down! And then you go fart on my balls."

The dude stared, then disappeared behind his paper again, while the siren-queen curled her lip. Stap said something unpleasant in Greek, hitched his pants back up, turned and marched up his porch steps and in.

Cocksuckers – wow – not to mention that farting bit I'd never heard before. In all my tangles with authority, I'd never had the guts for such endearments. HeadFuck ascendant, Stap still thought his old-school connections counted for something. In Queens, maybe they did.

Left alone, I half expected the cops to spring out after me, but there was just the barricade of newspaper and the flashing lights. Across the street, one of Stap's Merry Men stood on his porch shaking his head and wagging his outstretched finger at me. But I wasn't worried about my landlord. If he was pissed at me, he would've said something right then. He always did. Besides, yelling at those cops was the most fun he'd had in weeks.

Chapter Twenty-Eight

Hate Crime

Some drivers collect speeding tickets like lint in a fat man's belly button. Riding the Iron Horse, I accumulated my own frictional transportation costs, including this new HateCrime hogwash I had to beat or pay by that Monday's close of business. Otherwise there was nothing to stop them from issuing a delinquent-ticket warrant and showing up at my door that evening and off to the land of stale baloney sandwiches and its attendant thrills. So, no, I wasn't fleeing a bigger, more intractable problem (like a defaming police whole-vid) by heading to Brooklyn on something I could actually wrap my hands around.

It hadn't been my proudest moment, chiding a deliberately balky civil servant a couple of months back, back at the beginning of the summer, when Nicki and I were still slightly ensconced. An anti-incarceration, harm-reduction maven who ran a quality drug-policy boutique was looking for a director of research. There was a chance he'd be glad to get a stickler. It paid more than twice what I was scratching out freelance and, though I shrank from the thought until too late, yeah, my marriage probably was at stake. Emasculating, really, to quit reporting and be a flower girl carrying this guy's train, but I'd worry about that after I got the job.

Running late for the interview, I saw the nose of the train appear far down the elevated tracks and motivated the last block to the station. Though I'd emptied my MetroCard the day before, if no one had the gall to be on line ahead of me, I could thrust six soggy singles at the clerk, grab a MetroCard and levitate to the platform, the train doors closing on my butt. No time to limp-noodle all those bills into a machine.

I hauled up the stairs to the mezzanine, the train's rumble ever closer, and yes! no one on line. I thrust the bills in the slot, held up two fingers and half-danced a little importuning jig like a kid afraid he can't hold it any longer. My jitterbugging yielding nothing, it came time to venture a little encouragement.

"Come on, buddy. Train's coming! There's the money."

Doing some bookkeeping, the man behind the glass ignored me. He shouldered a tough, relentless job for not much money and less respect, serving us rushed schmoes while keeping his totals straight. I invested a full third of the available time in silent propitiation. No avail. So, almost wagging my tail to get the clerk to spend a second on a customer, "Come on, pal! There's six bucks. All I need is a two-trip."

By rule, three token clerks later separately told me, they're required to stop their bookkeeping for a customer, and usually the clerks do everything they can to help you make the train. This guy finished with a pile of money and jotted down the total, his cue to dispense with me. Never looking up, he reached for a fresh stack of bills. The stairs down from the platform full of whoosh, I glanced at the turnstiles to make sure they weren't jammed with people, noticed a cop on the other side and turned back for a last-chance plea to this willful obstructionist.

Picking up that fresh stack of bills his Rubicon, I met him midstream. "For Christ's sake, you're doing this deliberately. Can I just get my damn MetroCard? The train's coming!"

Immune to insult as well as plea, the sneering clerk all-thumbs inched his way through a very simple transaction. They can seem to comply, fumbling just enough to scotch any hope. I finally grabbed the MetroCard and dashed, still with a glimmer of a ghost of a chance.

But not with my path blocked by the authoritarian in blue.

"Get over there, sir. Stand over there now!" The cop ordered me to one side.

"For what – the train's pulling in!"

We argued over where we would stand for the ensuing argument. The third time he told me to move, he puffed up and started reaching for his radio. The train starting up, I groaned and moved ten feet, staring at a young, with-it, skinny transit cop sporting a fine Frankie Valli duck's-ass and ink on his forearm of a face crowned by thorns.

I reached for pen and paper and peered for his name and badge number. He recited them proudly, did Officer Brian Malone, and then demanded, "Is that courteous, raising your voice like that?"

"I was talking in a perfectly normal tone."

"But was that courteous, talking to the clerk that way?"

"Look, being rude isn't against the law. I don't need to listen to this."

"So you admit you were rude?"

"What the hell is this all about, your ticket quota?" Kiss any hope of that job good-bye, I missed a second train. I took a step forward, he held his ground, pointed his leather ticket book at me and ordered me to stay where I was.

"That's precisely what we're talking about: profanity. And you're just digging a deeper hole for yourself with more."

"What profanity? What the heck are you talking about?"

"Sir, the booth surveillance system has recorded you taking our Lord's name in vain, and – "

"What're you talking about – *whose* Lord?"

Was I gonna have to call my prospective boss and tell him I was delayed wrangling over free speech? It wouldn't exactly improve my odds with that dour soul to hear I couldn't make it into Manhattan without tripping over the cops.

Perhaps not wanting to answer broad, theological questions, he said, "Sir, it's everyone's responsibility to remain aware of changes in the Regs governing Homelanders/others' behavior. Hate leads to T – that's been proven on both sides of the coin. Are you not aware of the latest HateCrime Regs?"

"Cop, I got somewhere to be. What the heck are you talking about?"

"Jesus Christ" – the good little First-Communion boy bowed his head – "is revered by Christians and respected by all other religions. A higher percentage of Americans define themselves as Christians than Israelis do as religious Jews. Therefore, assuming that clerk is a believer, he shouldn't have his beliefs spat on while serving the public. Under Public Reg 19-038, written by the Commissioner himself and signed by the Mayor last month, any offense to an on-duty City employee's beliefs is a Class Three offense punishable by a fine of up to three hundred dollars."

"Three hundred dollars – you're out of your cotton-picking mind! What the hell – "

"Sir, I'm warning you. I will not tolerate any more such talk in the performance of my duties. As I was about to say, I follow His path as best I can and practice forgiveness. Since you were ignorant of the new Reg, I will fine you only fifty dollars. Now hand over your identification."

"You're the one fining me? Since there's no judge involved, maybe I should just pay you directly."

"If that's an offer of a bribe, this can turn real serious very quickly. I'm talking a likely Boosting."

"Bite me, pal. Though that's probably a bribe for you as well."

"I'm going to ignore that, and follow His path as best I'm able. But you should know the fine is the last part of the ticket I fill out. Now give me your ID or I'm calling for back-up. Which is it?"

I coughed up my papers and as he bent to write, said, "I'll fight it, I'll drag you to court."

"Fine. Do it on my day off so I get the overtime."

He then asked for my Social Security number. I told him he had my ID, he didn't need that. He primly pointed to a space on the ticket for it, a box to be filled. I refused and managed, astoundingly, to make it stick. Then it was my work address and phone number, just so they could mess with your livelihood then – and with your SS number – for the rest of your life if they wanted. I told him I was self-employed but didn't say how.

Up on the platform, lucky not to have missed another train, I swore satisfyingly for real, though none too loudly, and read that in Officer Malone's opinion I'd committed a 1050.7(r) offense. As his short narrative explained, I'd been "observed by PO being loud and boisterous and using religious hate speech." Boisterous: a classy, infinitely elastic word.

Being late for the interview and how that spoke to my "maturity" hadn't helped, my policy maven subsequently sniffed in a turn-down phone call, a call that came a day before spymaster Bettinger surprised me with his clandestine assignment out in Indiana. Failure to get the job a straw dropped on an arthritic camel, Nicki pulled the plug shortly after my day-trip spying on H-DM. So much for trashing my byline trying to save my marriage. I should've left for the damn job interview five minutes earlier, should've had a valid MetroCard. Shoulda done a lot of things.

Chapter Twenty-Nine

Know-It-All Al

Amidst the weeks of intermittent fuming before the deadline to pay or fight the idiot ticket, sporadic googling unearthed a spoonful of mention of the City expanding HateCrime. But the text of the Reg remained as elusive as the verbiage of all the other new Regs dropped on our heads. Was it so ridiculously broad that the phrase "For Christ's sake" qualified? I'd planned on a last attempt to uncover its Swiss-cheese legal basis on Friday. But I was tied up, so couldn't just march into the local cop-shop and demand to read it (yeah, right). Here a Monday morning and my one o'clock court appearance fast upon me, I managed to make it to the Transit Adjudication Bureau in downtown Brooklyn without offending anyone.

But there was no Reg to read to measure my boisterous offense, so they said, just a ten-page pamphlet, the official Rules of Conduct, pried from the unwilling receptionist's grasp. Chock-full of prohibitions and circumlocutions, the brochure gave the cops innumerable excuses to fatten the City's coffers. Just sitting on the stairs waiting interminably on a train, a late-night practice for generations willing to sully their pants, could cost two-hundred bucks.

It was a cautious little instrument in some respects, taking five dense paragraphs to define who could use a guide dog and how. But it also reached for the stars. Section 1050.7(i) read: No one shall "conduct himself or herself in any manner which may cause or tend to cause annoyance, alarm or inconvenience to a reasonable person...." That tie with that shirt, sir, truly alarming. Seventy-five bucks! Moving your lips while reading, Ma'am: fifty. If someone's boom box blared away in an otherwise empty subway car, would he be liable for a hundred-dollar tendency? But the brochure stopped at .7(i); my (r) offense indicated more recent progress.

I quit the Adjudication Bureau in favor of Transit Authority headquarters a few blocks distant, twelve stories of glossy stone. Telling the guy in reception I needed a copy of the Reg, he said customer service was up on the third floor. He then leaned forward to whisper about the law library on twelve that he doubted I'd access. But I was required to *leave* my driver's license to even go up to customer service, an awfully strong hint to just get lost.

No indication of where customers were served, two guys soon appeared, one with an unlit butt already in hand. Surface Transportation occupied the whole third floor, they said, but they knew of no customer service or public affairs department. They hadn't heard of the new HateCrime and, career civil servants, wouldn't opine on the ticket's validity. But they encouraged my quest for information and started musing about this one guy, Al, over in Bronx buses who knew just about everything. They led me around a corner to a bunch of cubicles and a youngish Al, who I'd assumed was some graybeard. Four or five people gathered round, glad of the extreme novelty of someone attempting to run the City to ground.

Al said customer service used to be on the third floor, but it had been disbanded in light of the Current P. Crisis, not that anyone bothered to tell the lobby receptionist. Crappy little stores offered a customer service window, but this sage knew of none for us millions of riders. I assured them I'd never seen any of them (Minders Turn Elsewhere!) and said I hoped to make it up to the Bronx for a bus ride real soon.

As I stared at the numbers over the elevators, someone whispered my name. Al said, "I thought that was you, Fremson, but I didn't want to say anything in front of the others. Listen, my girlfriend works upstairs for one of the MTA big Kahunas. And she says they've been working overtime to smear you."

"That's just the newspapers carrying the cops' water like usual. And TV – who cares? Here today, gone tomorrow."

"Really? Cause that NYONLY clip of you wearing those shorts from beyond the grave is bouncing all over. What were you thinking, man?" His shirt crisp and his hair wavy, he sported the sort of rimless glasses that add twenty points IQ. "Anyway, *some* people in this building are behind you, however subterraneously. There's some weird stuff going on, if you catch my drift."

"Well sure. I mean, no."

"OK, look. Obviously you're not some kind of weird HeadFuck agent I can't say boo to. Cause no way a government agent lets himself get shot in the head, right?"

"That's the truss missing from their whole dumb story, the hole I almost got in my head."

"Right. Not to mention no way an agent would wear that absurd outfit of yours leaving that Chinese joint; even undercover, he wouldn't stoop to that."

Give it a rest, people! "So you're covered. Goody-goody. Me – guess I'll just have to take what you say with a grain of salt, Al."

"That works. So, have you ever heard of an MTA police deputy commissioner named Walton Everidge?"

"Yeah. On TV."

"All over TV last night commenting on that ridiculously fake whole-vid they worked up on you. You know, 'the shooter' without a gun who gets a head wound."

"I am really glad to hear you say that about that whole-vid. I was hoping it was obvious to anyone who saw it."

"You got 'em panicked, man. A guy getting shot just walking through Penn Station with a backpack – even someone like you – threatens their whole scheme. So they demonize the shit out of the guy, not least with whole-vid of him with some kind of, quote, 'weapon.' I doubt you were pointing anything dangerous at two cops and a soldier."

"That's me, Mister Milquetoast. It was a little radio, just like *The Daily Chirp* quoted those two kids saying."

"You mean a transistor radio? They still make them?"

Jesus. "Al – what scheme?"

"Alright. Listen and get this good. Everidge – "

The elevator I'd called popped open with a ring, and we both froze and stared obliviously up at the numbers. Empty.

"Everidge is slated for a big-ticket job with something called ASPIC."

"The outfit run by that nut-job who keeps marrying twenty-year-olds in order to save them from a life of sin? Got their hands in every security-MoFo pie there is. Drug-testing and bounty hunting, right? Plus mercenaries and private space-flight. And they got this facial recognition scanner that IDs you from the other side of a football stadium."

"I pegged you for a prairie dog, Fremson. Up on your haunches, scanning the horizon. They pack that scanner in a drone's nose so HeadFuck can target the right guy – you know, the Fiend with a *beard* in the crowd at the market, or maybe the man just carrying a tainted micro-zap."

"Like John Doe in that movie says, 'The world's been shaved by a drunken barber.' "

He grimaced, put off by me trying to be clever too. "Look, you have no idea the risk I'm taking talking to you with what's going on upstairs. They'd nail me for conspiracy. From the Latin, *conspirare*: breathing the same air. Then they make it up from there."

"I appreciate it. I gotta tell you – "

"Alright! Now ASPIC has the ball rolling for a huge new five-year contract to privatize the MTA's – quote, unquote – 'random' searches, which are totally useless, by the way. And Everidge is their soon-to-retire tool on the inside. They've got a sweetheart, no-bid deal pending, with some MTA board member's wife supposedly getting a big cut as a 'consultant.' All so ASPIC can jack up the whole program for like $159-million a year. Then multiply that by five years. Which is insane since right now the MTA is doing our little sham pretend-searches for something like $9-million a year."

"Jesus, Al. Wait, that's like – "

"Just short of 800-million bucks."

"No wonder they were gonna scramble my brains. So what's the board member's wife's name?"

"I don't know. Sorry. But you have no idea what a relief it is to get this off my chest to somebody besides my girlfriend."

"At least you got somebody to talk to, and not just e-mailing your ex-wife."

"Right. But even lining a lot of pockets, for that kind of money, they'll still have to turbo-charge the whole program. So they'll be searching huge numbers of people, way more than now, and doing facial and/or iris scans right on the spot, anybody they want to."

"Using one of those hand-held *Gotcha!* machines, huh?"

"Fremson, the MoFos – HeadFuck just the MoFo-in-chief – are constantly looking to get folks in the system *and* get 'em comfortable having their biometrics read. Like in *The Handmaid's Tale:* 'Ordinary is what you are used to. This may not seem ordinary to you now, but after a time it will.' It's not like a fingerprint, right? Doesn't leave a stain, doesn't even physically touch you. Like any of that matters, because it's worse."

"The NYPD has a saying: If you can see the Chrysler Building, we can see you."

"Dominance and control, buddy – plus Walk-on-Water's pure ego. And it's not just the cops. The New York Public Library, the research one with the lions where nothing ever leaves the building, they're – "

"I used to use that all the time."

"I had to walk out," Al said. "About two months ago because they wanted a digital photo and your birth date – the month and the year only, like that slick little subterfuge matters when they have your name, address and face. Just for looking at a book right there that never leaves or using their computers. It's all about getting as many people as possible, in this case, the 'problematical' sort of person who uses sophisticated libraries, into their giant mug-shot file."

"What, the MoFos back-alley search their library records?"

"You think way too small, man. That's good. That's what it takes to walk around with a backpack to challenge this T-crap from the ground up. You're not naive, exactly, but you are willing to look foolish. Or maybe you just don't care. Like Huxley said, 'What fun it would be if one didn't have to think about happiness!' "

Freaking show-off. "Happiness ain't been much on my radar lately, Al."

"That's good, man. *That's* what it takes! Except then you end up leaving the house looking homeless the day after you're on every front page in town."

"Let it alone, man."

"Maybe. But what if your anti-search effort catches fire? That's why they got 800-million reasons to come down on you like a ton of bricks." With a rueful grimace, he met my gaze for the first time. "Let me finish about ASPIC, brother, before someone comes. ASPIC has all these bonuses built into their prospective contract to grab illegal aliens, deadbeat dads, registered sex offenders too far from home. Plus all these stealthy new offenses to get you into the database like your HateCrime nonsense."

"Just exactly whose Lord did I offend is what I want to know."

"Anybody's Lord, man. It doesn't matter. Whatever it takes to get us all processed into the Mug-Shot File. Plus the ASPIC contract authorizes some real black-boot stuff, their guys – private contractors – tootling around with submachine guns and full powers of arrest and initial detention in this huge warehouse they got cheap at the Brooklyn Navy Yard. Then they run your name and face through the mill till something pops."

"They perfect it in the Sands and then bring it on home."

"And they're private, so no names on their uniform or number on their badges. They kick your ass, go ahead and prove which one did it."

He stared up at the elevator numbers as two women yakking away walked past behind us. "Those two wouldn't see us if we fell out of a window at their feet. You know, Fremson, people are all over the map on you since you got shot, some on the left trashing your 'ill-considered' action, some libertarians jumping to your defense. Either way, the Barmy Bibliophile Bomber – a Nazi, right? – helps scare everyone into accepting the searches that ASPIC and a bunch of newly retired train cops are gonna get rich on real soon."

"No wonder they were acting like that in Bellevue."

"Do yourself a favor, Mitch. Stay squeaky-clean as long as this lasts – hell, long as *you* last. No open-container bullshit, pay any back taxes."

Still before lunch, thank God he hadn't run across my Syriac confession yet. I smiled, wondering his reaction when he stumbled across that.

"Laugh if you want. And a haircut wouldn't hurt either. You cut it yourself?"

"You don't mess around do you, Al?"

"Look, you represent something bigger than yourself right now, so act like it."

"People keep trying to draft me into some kinda 'Movement,' but they never can tell me much about it. I got nobody. I don't need anybody. Me against Them."

"Rebel without a clue, huh? Just try not to be a four-flusher, that's all. Look, brother, go take care of their stupid HateCrime ticket. You got money for it?"

He reached into his pocket as I nodded.

"You know, your chances of looking at the new Reg with the Gorgon running the law library are slim and none, and Slim just fell in the river with rocks in his pocket. I couldn't find the Reg's text anywhere online. And, believe me, I looked."

"Yeah, pretty damn weird. I spent about an hour looking, but still...."

"Well I spent over two, and with a Masters in public administration, I like to think I know what I'm doing."

"So, Al, a young dude like you with a masters degree, fire in the belly, on the right side of the barricades – talking of *Gorgons* for crying out loud – I mean, what the hell you doing?"

"Bronx bus routes? Simple. My ex-wife and I have a five-year-old daughter with brain damage. Fucking says it in four-point type right in the combination vaccine's product literature: *may cause brain damage* because they give you so many disease agents in one needle."

"That's terrible!"

"She only gets one life – one, total – and now it's fucked. I got Plunged from this Equitable/Sustainable policy outfit and needed a job. Even these days, City health benefits are still decent. With my daughter, end of story."

"Jesus, Al."

"Yeah, well, obsessing over it is one reason we got divorced. So, my girlfriend's name is Elaine Livingston. Not 'stone.' She's even angrier than me about ASPIC getting this big sweetheart contract. She was already planning on contacting a reporter, once she found one with guts. Then you got shot, and, last night, after we saw the MTA's nonsense on TV, I told her it'd be poetic justice to pick you despite all your baggage. She was on the fence about you, but look, here you are. Kismet."

"All the luck in the world."

"All you really need for a story is a copy of the ASPIC contract, and" – his whisper fell even further – "she's already got that. The girl's got balls, cause now she's trying to get ahold of Everidge or her boss's employment contract with ASPIC too. But that's gravy. Call her tomorrow, Tuesday. Maybe she'll agree you haven't been too compromised by your recent travails."

"Not too compromised, hunh, to put *my* name on top of the article for *another* fucking Boosting! You got any idea how Goddamn close I am to RoundUp already?"

He held both hands up. "No one really knows what that means."

"Looks like I'm the one about to find out. But first I gotta get a haircut, hunh Al?"

"Suit yourself, man." And he turned to go.

"Wait! I call her *here*?"

"Are you nuts? No, at night. Call her – " and a man in a sharp suit strode down from the far corridor, one arm pumping, the other holding the papers he studied. Without a glance, he marched up and hit Down; I'd punched Up when he appeared. Down came home a winner under my heavy whip, and I turned to where Al had scurried down the hall.

"Brooklyn," he whispered. "There's only two Elaine Living*ston*s. Tuesday evening – and from a pay phone if they haven't shut them all down by tomorrow."

Chapter Thirty

The Major Knows *What?*

The bell rang for Up, and I got in and pressed 12. Maureen said she'd never seen so heavy a hammer on a cop-shot, but an ASPIC dollar sign fronting almost 800-million smackers explained a lot. If Lurch was an ASPIC thug, that's why the cops, mere public servants, were afraid of him. The pending ASPIC deal also helped explain why news of the LIRR riot was suppressed since Cat Wrangler objecting to a search sparked that whole conflagration. Showing that it was conceivable to refuse? No, no, no, nix that news.

Yup, on the very day my idiot Syriac confession shredded my hard-won (and very low profile) credibility, a source swimming among the big fish of the MTA had potentially offered a whale of a document. Hell, just say Indiana was to make some money, not that I'd seen any. That floated any boat these days. No: I did it to write about. Having irrevocably confessed, just brazen it out like everyone else.

Three suits and a white-shirt cop crowded on the elevator on eight, and I faded into the back wall. My shooting would provide the wham-bang anecdotal beginning to an article on big-bucks corruption and the private thugs soon to be toting submachine guns on the trains. And my incarceration at Bellevue would be "Penn Tale's" perfect fulcrum. From personal atrocity to systemic corruption, a three-headed monster of a scoop as long as Elaine fed me that contract.

Getting out on 12 at the lawyers' plush lair, my incipient tantrum went nowhere. What chance would someone *not* professionally accustomed to flailing away against officialdom, or without English as her native tongue, or someone with a nine-to-five have had? Most people would have sworn loudly, perhaps boisterously, and mailed in a check. And so our rights eroded as the MoFos gorged on bitterness, fines and arrests. Back on the street, I sat and ate my sandwich over a sports section someone had tossed. The Yankees were one-and-nine over their last ten, and the paper hinted primly at revelations to come involving a blimp pilot and a ball girl.

✲✲✲✲✲✲✲✲✲✲✲✲✲✲✲

Upstairs at the TAB for my one o'clock hearing, I was taken aback to see the little sign hidden way over in a corner: Civil Court of the City of New York. Maybe the ticket referred to the Transit Adjudication Bureau so people took it less seriously, not realizing (Social Security number and all) the potential real consequences down the road when trying for a job, a loan or an apartment. Some sixty blue plastic chairs filled the room, and another sign commanded: "Please Remove Your Hat." Two dozen people were scattered around, three of us white, the rest brown or black, the median age two decades less than mine.

None looking gleeful and a few quite glum, folks emerged from the hearing rooms in back where they'd been ushered by one of the three administrative law judges. So, did I prefer Hate adjudicated by the pale, orthodox Jewish man – probably not, given my offense – a black woman in foreboding glasses, or, as it turned out, Administrative Law Judge Judith Fennerly, a tall, hawkish dame with a certain brittle appeal dressed in a loose purple sweater and straight red skirt?

"Well, Judge," I intoned, barely room to cross my legs sitting in her 'court,' "I hope you'll agree that today's case has nothing to do with what happened to me last week. And I also hope we can discuss this cockamamie new religious HateCrime Reg, which I'd never heard of, and which sounds like a gross violation of the separation of church and state."

"First, let me say I'm glad to see you can dress appropriately when

258

you feel the need. But tell me one thing, Mr. Fremson. It's obvious you think you're clever. But that doesn't mean you're a Nazi like the papers say, right?"

"Judge, come on! I was carrying a bunch of books, books that deal with the sin of over-arching state control. The MoFos – I mean the cops – have chosen to emphasize only one. But Judge, they're pawing through our bags any time, any place, anyhow. And now this new Reg I'm here on today is about controlling how we think. I mean, how did that cop know when I told the token clerk: 'For Christ's sake, give me a MetroCard,' that I didn't mean it literally? That I wasn't late on my way to go preach somewhere?"

"The narrative is bare-bones, but then the police are told to write as little as possible since at least nine in ten New Yorkers just mail in a check. The less written, the less people have to dispute. Are you sure that's all you said?"

I nodded.

"As much as I might like to dismiss this ticket by highlighting your challenge to the underlying Reg, I can't. Wait, Mr. Fremson! Luckily for me, Officer Malone has written it so poorly, I'm taking almost no risk in just dismissing it. Way down at this level, well, out of sight, out of mind. On the federal bench…."

She held her smile a beat too long, wrote a moment, tore off my stenciled copy, then picked up the next case from the tall pile near her elbow and bid me gone.

Wow. I hoped she eventually met the right misdemeanant who'd let her slap down this new Reg from her very low perch. The ticket garbage on a technicality, Judge Fennerly had written: "The NOV [Notice of Violation] does not state a prima facie case since it alleges only that RESP[ondent] was observed by PO [i.e., MoFo] being loud, boisterous and 'hateful.' It describes but does not identify the city employee allegedly impacted. Therefore, on its face, it does not allege sufficient facts to state a violation."

The coming evening with the Wife obviously my last, I'd get my first good meal in days, maybe even a few laughs with Nicki over old times. Anything had to be better than her death by a thousand cuts. Just freaking get it over with – or better, make a scene, knock over a glass and storm out. What, and skip dessert on her dime?

Mooning over a broken heart, the sudden, sickening realization slammed home with such force I was lucky the elevator cable didn't snap. Surprised I didn't hit the Stop button to dangle in space awhile to get my bearings. Jousting over the idiot ticket, I'd been fleeing buried doubts about my Syriac confession all day. No, not about its necessity. But, enjoying my cleverness crafting prose to address Bill and the world, I hadn't forced a halt to examine my basic premise. Beyond dumb – cause it was 'only' a letter to Syriac – to not exercise the due diligence a regular article demanded.

In other words, 'Who else could it be?' wasn't nearly enough of a justification for such a stark accusation against Chrysler, that it had hired me through Bettinger. Not even close.

I staggered out of the TAB building and collapsed on the same bench where I'd read the sports section, back when still anticipating my next triumphant whirl on the merry-go-round. That's right, Al and Elaine, the boffo reporter is at your door, hand over that ASPIC contract. You can count on me. Never mind I may have botched basic shit like who'd hired me to spook.

That cookie, Bettinger, had intimated his ass all over the lot, mentioning the Hillbilly Grinder's "competition" at least three times. Right, but he'd never specifically named our client. Damn, I wouldn't have made such a cavalier accusation in a real article. That, or some editor (certainly Stan the stickler) would've sheep-dogged me to prove it. My stomach lurched, and for a moment I thought I might foul the sidewalk right there, maybe spatter my shoes as a fitting commentary on my recent accomplishments. But who the hell else could it be but Chrysler? The Army had already limited the competition to the Grinder versus Jeep.

The online function on my antediluvian micro-zap went on the fritz back before Nicki and I had. Concentrating on fluff like storing some rent away, I hadn't replaced it. Recalling a cyber-café two blocks from the TAB, I raced there ignoring an ankle at that stubborn stage where, the easy healing done, the rest was going to take a while.

Syriac, I saw, had helpfully linked to Heavy-Duty Manufacturing's denunciation of me and demand for an explanation. As its statement put it, "If these disturbing allegations from this peculiar individual in New York have any basis in fact, the Germans need to address them quickly. Such tactics, if true, only underscore the American-made Terminator's [H-DM's official name for the Grinder] overall battlefield superiority in a wide range of theaters from the Sands to any remaining Snow. Only a full disclosure of their relationship can allow the Dept. of Defense to properly award a contract that's crucial to America's Heroes Fomenting Democracy – and suppressing T – on so many fronts worldwide."

This did little but turn up the heat. Mid-afternoon and no word yet from Chrysler, I entertained the hope that my rash unbosoming might hold water. Who *else* could it have been? Syriac's comments page didn't shy from those decrying "journalists debasing themselves by dissembling." Still, about half of the comments joined Syriac in exonerating me.

Most of my personal e-mail I deleted unopened based on the malevolent subject headings. One tricked me, though, with what appeared to be a threatening reference to Nicki. But opening, "As soon as able get Money from Wife," revealed the same bilge I'd been punting for days:

Fremson, Mike Tyson was right, the only thing to do with toilet waste like you is to "eat your children." That's assuming you found some hoe to rut with. If you got no kids, me and Arthur will make other arrangements. You don't know Arthur, but that's okay. He does what I tell him – mostly. Sometimes he gets a little excited & then things get MESSY. But that's okay to because by then we're always way deep in the woods. Way, way back cause Arthur is real strong at dragging things, even kicking and screaming things. We don't never worry about cleaning up the mess. After me and Arthur get done – and that can take all kinds of time - the bigger animals take care of the big parts, the weasels take care of the smaller stuff & then the bugs clean up the rest real good. Leastwise, that is how it works so far.

So, you piece of twat, before you can mess with any more MEN putting their balls on the line keeping us safe from T-scum like you, me and Arthur will be making the trip up to Queens real soon. Right as soon as we can make Arthur's wife turn over her disability check for gas money.

And this is signed, so even on the computer you know it's for real - Me & Arthur.

Another one I foolishly opened praised *The Daily Chirp* for printing my address as "a public service." It got down to business quickly, something about extension cords that I didn't bother to finish.

Then the subject heading from a gobbledygook Dutch pirate address jabbed me in the throat: "I've got the real deal on Chrysler. Call me."

Nothing but two phone numbers with 703 area codes (DC's Virginia suburbs), one with a 1:00 pm time, the other at 2:00 pm. Plus the command to "Call securely." I'd long since missed the one-o'clock window and would have to hustle to make the two o'clock. I jotted down both numbers, reached under to unplug the computer and ran, the café dude screaming at me in Urdu or some such.

A half-full phone card in my wallet, I started racing to the corner when I realized it was already compromised by old calls to the listed number Nick and I once shared. I turned for the bodega the other way and it all magically fell into place three minutes before two at the pay phone by the bodega, the name of my unattainable fourth-grade crush my PIN on my new phone card.

First surprise: she was a she. "It's me, Miss. I certainly appreciate your contacting me. Plus this is a secure call on my end."

"Good. Not that we're talking long. My name is Lois – not that you can refer to me in any way in print, not by gender or anything else. This is all on a not-for-attribution basis. Agreed?"

Second surprise: she sounded black, though with more than a touch of the South in her speech, it was hard to say.

"You have my promise … Lois. You're pretty experienced dealing with the press if you say not-for-attribution, rather than the useless 'off-the-record' that's been twisted and abused into meaning absolutely nothing."

"Actually, no. This is my first time, and I'm not happy about it. But I had to contact you rather than let my thief of a boss enrich himself while my brothers and sisters under arms are getting blown to pieces all over the world."

"You're in the military?"

"Major, United States Army – a fact that is most certainly off-limits. But to get down to it: Yes, you were hired to spy on the new Grinder, which, rumor has it, may be as much of a death-crate as the old one. I encountered your letter to that Syriac site today, but Chrysler was not – repeat, not – the client. I know who did hire you, and I can give you the e-mail to prove it."

Shit-fuck.

"I wish you would. Cause, assuming you're right – and I do – I really messed up. And I don't need that in my life right now. It would really help if I could rectify that ASAP."

"I have the documents. How you're able to use them is up to you. But you did mess up, which is surprising. Because it was the quality of your work that got you hired to check out the Grinder in the first place."

"It was?"

263

"Two points: I have what you need to prove where your assignment came from. Whether you contact that individual for his bullshit denial is up to you. Either way, my second point: things are going to get hot for you up in New York because of your Syriac posting. That means today, as of now. I have no idea how far he might take it, but he can be a snake when cornered."

"So I got to add someone else to the list of crazy bastards out to do me harm? Sure, make it an even half-dozen, what's the difference?"

"Listen to me, Fremson. This is some serious shit you've got yourself involved in, with barrels of DoD procurement money at stake. Your best bet safeguarding yourself is to publicize this man's involvement with you – like tomorrow. Go stay somewhere else tonight, cause I would think twice about going home."

"You're serious, huh?"

"In an operational context like this, I am tied down tight at all times. Something you might want to copy. Now look, I'm only saying this once, and then I'm terminating this call. Tomorrow, Tuesday, I will be in the northwest quadrant of Farragut Square, a park in downtown Washington just north of the White House. Northwest – like the only part of DC that matters to most people, that's how to remember the quadrant. I'll recognize you, but have a copy of *The Washington Times* on the bench next to you. I'll be there at 0800 hours and again at 1730. For your sake I hope you make it there by morning. You know north from south, right? And dress decently because you'll need to move around DC inconspicuously. Leave those nasty shorts at home."

"Wait. This is an awful lot to take in at once. What – "

"Farragut Square, tomorrow morning at eight. Like the man said, the journey of a thousand miles begins with a single step."

"You really think I'm in some kind of danger."

"About eighty percent probability. I can give this story to somebody else if you want. But, having screwed up on Chrysler, you need

it more, and there's something to be said for that. And Fremson –
well, there's something else, something regarding you specifically,
that I'll explain when I see you."

"Well, OK. I guess – "

Baanhhnh, the line went dead.

Chapter Thirty-One

Short Leg Goes Pfhifft!

S o Chrysler wasn't the client said a voice on the phone.

****

D eep down, I'd always known I'd end up swelling my prostate inching a cab around midtown. Hard to conjure a worse time for a galloping assumption leading to the worst mistake by far of my so-called career. Self-publishing even a grocery list on the Net, you gotta, gotta, gotta self-edit. And then sit on it and then cogitate some more. Forget a second source, I had no affirmative statements of any kind. All I had was Bettinger's wink and a nod, misdirection from someone I didn't know from beans. Me who'd always made that extra call, always been willing to further annoy a source.

Maybe just track down Statie or Frankie or DeBrunt to finish the job the first two botched. Or finance Me & Arthur's trip with the rent money I'd no longer need and spare the purse of Arthur's long-suffering wife. Meet them up in Van Cortland Park at the top of the Bronx, the densest forest in the city, to save pack-mule Arthur some wear and tear.

Or take my rope-a-dope stab at redemption on Syriac a step further by exposing what sounded like a big-shot Army officer who had hired Bettinger, who'd then hired me. A story on that, plus "Penn/Bellevue/ASPIC," would make a nice one-two punch since apparently I'd just agreed to drop everything and race off to DC.

Absurd to jump right quick just because a voice beckoned,

someone speaking of a mistake, and then a threat and its containment – which she just happened to possess. She built a nice, scary straw man, herself with a lighter at hand. A *woman*, a maybe African-American Army officer, with something "specific" to relate – about me! – and she from a milieu totally foreign to my own. If a trap, a damn intriguing one. Hell, everyone knew where I lived since Sunday's *Daily Chirp*, so they could damn well trouble themselves to get it done on my turf. Too unsporting, surely, to lure me to DC solely for their convenience.

So, take Lois's warning about going home seriously, skip the divorce dinner on tap, and head to Chinatown and one of those cheapo buses, a sketchy driver with two fingers on the wheel? Followed by a night in some flea-bag motel if I could even find one in ever-glossier, money-swollen DC, the local industry going great-guns.

Go ahead, Major, lengthen the list of those on my tail but, please, whoever claimed the prize, do your damn job right. Don't leave me pissing in a bag, a nip bottle or three secreted away in my wheelchair, trying to rouse images of the Crimson Nurse – what the heck was her name? – the last woman I kissed while still a man.

****

Mind still whirling, I rounded my corner to see nary a news truck or even cop car in sight. Had fortune propelled me off the radar, my shoals already plumbed by liars and cheats? Marvin, the self-satisfied computer geek with the criminally unused second-floor balcony, stood by the front gate talking with some bald doofus in a sack of a green suit. With a garish, orange tie askew, his glasses with masking tape at the hinge and a mole sprouting hairs on his chubby cheek, he looked too ill-stitched to be a cop.

A reporter, obviously. He'd prove easy enough to blow off, though I couldn't stop him getting some nasty quotes from Marvin, my unloved neighbor. I had half a mind to stride up snarling incantations and drawing symbols in the air – give his readers their money's worth. Neither scrawny Marvin nor the bulky stranger moved out of my way by the gate. I waited a moment, then brushed past with downcast eyes so as not to crack the door to conversation. The guy had an odd twist to his foot and was wearing the built-up shoe of someone with a shorter leg.

Marvin said, "Right, that's him. See what kind of jerk he is like I was telling you."

Great. That not auguring a pleasant chat, using the front door risked rubbing Mr. Staphilopoulos's nose in the fact that Trouble leaving that morning was Annoyance coming home. I veered off across the grit and weeds that passed for his lawn and headed around back.

And the stranger asked, "You're sure, absolutely one-hundred-percent sure, that's Mitchell Fremson?"

Marvin said, "Do I look like a man to make reckless statements? He's the newbie who thinks he's a big wheel around here. But he'll get taken down a peg or two before too long."

Some might say, Marv, that I'd recently been knocked down a fair number of pegs. I motivated around the side of the house, confident that with that foot, the reporter wasn't catching up to fire any questions.

A few steps on, I turned to see he was moving fast himself and with some kind of long-barreled pistol out, held low against his body but clearly visible when his arm swung out to compensate for his leg.

Christ, Statie! My address got published, and it took him all of one day to get this sweaty joker on me, only he didn't look like he was joking. I grabbed at the back of the house with both hands, wheeling through the turn as one of the little windows in Stap's tumble-down garage shattered, scattering several of the rats-with-wings who lived there. Christ! Not joking at all and a silencer to boot. The back door fortified by a rusty lock, the one key good front and back, I couldn't risk fumbling with it.

Where? What the fuck where?

I dashed through the broken front panel and into the wreck of a pool, almost slipping into the swamp low in the middle.

And, kicking his leg oddly, he ran past the open panel, stopping to pound on the locked back door. Thank goodness it was locked so he couldn't get in to accost Stap and the lads.

Shit, go on in, pal. Roam up one hall and down the next and look under each and every one of all those beds on the second and third floors. Let me flee to my new life washing cars in some broke-down western Massachusetts mill town.

He stopped pounding and took to kicking with that built-up shoe, bellowing in a husky wheeze, "Fremson, an atheist like you isn't disrupting our plans. You hear me? We deserve it, we've been waiting so long. So get down here and open this door now!"

Atheist? I peeked over the edge of the pool and saw him with his ear up against the door, one hand clawing at it softly, the other holding the gun straight down against his leg.

"Fremson – let the Devil take you! This one is guaranteed to have no white hairs in its tail. You get down here now – and with that semen!"

Say what?

The hole in Stap's fence, the one I'd used Saturday morning sneaking out to get Chinese! I turned and again almost skidded into the swamp before edging around to the pool's missing panel in back. Pressing his ear against the door, the gun dangling, he was almost moaning it sounded like. He reached up and pounded on it softly. I scurried across the *long* patch of weeds and made it behind the one big tree to look again. He was peering up at the sky muttering.

Praying myself that the oddball bloodhound stayed fixated on the door where he thought the trail led, I scrunched through the fence. With any luck, I'd get across the neighbor's yard and then up her driveway to head for the hills. His muttering grew louder till he declared, "And Amen!" His big dome visible over the fence, a light bulb appeared just above, and he turned to Stap's pool with an odd, strangled cry and stormed in. Good, fall in the swamp while Lois appeared overhead in her Army chopper, Maureen at the door lowering a rope ladder and ready to hand me a Ballantine.

I scooted across most of the neighbor's yard before cracking that stick. Should've known to Goddamn wear my moccasins leaving the house that morning. Short Leg popped his head up over the wall of the pool and our eyes locked over the fence. His slow, slobbery grin led to a triumphant "Ha!" as he moved to the wall of the pool to steady his gun hand. "Pfhifft!" He grinned again and waved me closer, a cat toying with its prey.

I leaped to the neighbor's back door as another "Pfhifft!" splintered the side of her house. Hey, Up There, any deal you want, long as the back door was open to race blindly through *and* I could make the front door work without a key. Through a kitchen window I spotted the clunky, compensatory shoe scrabbling at the top of the five-foot fence, a fleshy athlete not to be denied.

I reeled down the dark back hall, bellowing. "Hey, whoever lives here – it's me, a guy from Mr. Staphilopoulos's house next door. I'm just passing through real quick. Don't worry about me!"

I shot a look into the empty dining room. "Yo, wait, that's not fair! There's a guy with a gun! Dressed in a green suit. I think he's after only me, but if you're here somewhere, get behind a locked door and call the cops! Though he might be an off-duty cop himself, I don't know. Bye!"

Best I could do. I took way too much time fumbling with the front door's two locks till flinging it open. I screeched to a halt on the porch, but he wasn't lurking in the threadbare little bushes that dotted the front yard.

Down the steps and … to the projects? Not that they'd daunt this kook, but the buildings' zigzag footprint offered slightly better prospects than the right-angle grid of baked, treeless streets the other way. Maybe get through the projects' maze to find a loitering gypsy cab on the other side and then where, the local cop-shop?

Well sure, mister. We'll take a report. What color suit you say this gunman's wearing? Look, don't get excited. We'll send a car down there as soon as one frees up. Stop yelling, I said. So why don't you catch a bus, go to the movies or something. Or maybe you should avoid public transportation, huh, wise guy?

Crashing through the neighbor's front gate, I got such a pain in my chest I had to stop. But the count of five found me running for the projects. I kept waiting for the final "Pfhifft!" but made it to the corner. I looked back to see him coming out of the yard the far side of Stap's house clutching some kid's scooter. He saw me, beckoned again with his goofy insinuation and then bent over to pump the scooter.

OK, make him shoot me in front of a bunch of people. I dashed the half-block to my local bodega to burst through the door gasping for air. Everyone startled, including the two cops in uniform who must've strayed in for a soda or cigarettes, people on the clock eating better than that.

"Officers! There's a man with a gun. He's after me. In a green suit. He's already fired like three shots and he's not trying to hide it. Though he's got a silencer. A green suit, bald, glasses and one of those built-up shoes when one leg is short."

One cop got on his radio and the other drew his gun and took a defensive position by the Lady Lindas' display, peering over it out the window.

"Green suit? How tall? What's he after you for," one yelled.

The other yelled, "You're that crazy fuck, right, the one in those shorts that's messing with MTA cops?"

"I don't know what he wants – not too short, chunky. But I gotta go, cause he's not fooling. He stole a kid's scooter, and he'll be here in a second, so – "

"Mister!" It was my buddy, the counterman who'd foretold good fortune with women. "Come on!"

One cop yelled, "Hey, wait!" and turned and pointed his gun at me. And the other stopped barking into his radio and yelled, "Rick, here he fucking comes, gun in his *right* hand!"

The Bodega Dude grabbed my wrist and jerked me through a slippery kitchen and out back where he bent to boost me over the tall fence into someone's back yard. Not knowing I could still do such a thing, I scratched and scrambled up and over and – Christ! – down far below, though my good foot took most of it. He yelled "Run!" and I turned to thank him. But he'd already grabbed a mop and was racing back into his store.

PART SIX

Chapter Thirty-Two

Heading South

I heard no shots as I ran up the driveway. And with all the sirens that rent the air as I ran, then jogged, then strolled, whistling, through Bumfuckville's surprisingly nice little riverside park, and then zigzagged to the subway station *two* stops down the line, there was no way to distinguish the sound of any ambulances.

The Hovel inhospitable, might as well head to Washington to see about Lois's 'evidence.' Waiting on a train to Penn Station, a picture loomed up of the assassin beckoning with his gun, wearing the demented grin of a father finally getting his toddler off to bed, mom out late. The gunman obviously not caring about getting caught, was I such damaged goods he had license to all but sit and have tea with Marvin, my twit of a housemate?

And I was suddenly driven to crouch down behind a trash bin up on that elevated subway platform. Peering round it, my viscera squashed, I reared up unable to breathe. Man, that queered things, Short Leg wearing orange to my Bambi. That long stretch under the river to Manhattan, I forced my breath to slow and tried to divine who lusted so to see me cold. Speaking of which, why was I heading straight for Penn Station – DeBrunt *and* Statie's lair – Short Leg certainly unhinged enough to be one of Statie's running buddies? Nope, I needed to take the back-alley PATH train to Newark to catch the Amtrak to DC.

Out in Manhattan, I hit the sleepiest of the several PATH stations and, yikes, look at all the soldiers and not a cop in sight. Ten! soldiers all on their lonesome searching bags at this rinky-dink PATH station, American cities the defeated, Reconstruction South.

Having seen plenty of soldiers scattered all over Manhattan in recent years, I should have taken this detachment in stride. But already shaky, I crossed the street and lurked by a panel truck to watch a military squad shunt folks into their circle to be searched. *Not* NYPD-devil-may-care, two soldiers stood close, their eyes fixed on people's hands; two others flanked the station entrance, their gaze rotating, the tips of their rifles nosing curiously forward.

I stuck a foot out to test the waters in the street between us, got halfway and froze. A honking car materialized, and I leaped back to the far curb by the truck, my head throbbing again. I needed to calm my damn breathing, stroll through the soldiers and get to Newark to fall out on the train to DC. Get out of Dodge before those two cops in the bodega put out an APB on me as a Concerted Witness or some such – assuming they still could. Short Leg a chubby, older white dude in a suit, could I hope that improved everyone's odds of maintaining the number of holes they came with at birth?

It was a *bunch* of soldiers out on their own recognizance, not just one or two palling around with the cops as usual, the latter at least offering a fig leaf of local civilian authority. The pistol on the hip of the sergeant running things was somehow more puissant than any three cops' exact same gun. None of the Jerseyites heading home said a word, neither the few picked for the plucking, nor the majority shuffling along staring at the ground as I'd done at Coney Island. Happy couples chatting side by side were stricken silent and alone. *Do it to her. No, him.* One guy stage-whispered, "This better not turn into another Penn Station, when that asshole went nuts attacking that Protector." Hoist with his own, misinformed petard, he was chosen for sticking his head up even those few inches, though he had no bag.

I donned a far-off stare over a slack mouth, hunched down in on myself and, thus disguised, made it through the soldiers. Downstairs, shaky hands kept jamming wet-noodle singles into a machine that spat them back. I tried to stiffen my bills cause, no, I wasn't using my credit card. Some chippie in a hurry behind me basically grabbed my inadequate funds and swiped me through on her card. There was no mention of the sixty! cents change.

In Newark, the cops were busy with a woman with skin stretched painfully over her face, plus her drunk companion wearing many socks but no shoes. She kept screaming, "I got a check coming Wednesday. Talk to me then." Newark with enough homegrown issues, I caught the DC train no problem.

****

Safe, perhaps, for a couple of hours, I grabbed a window seat to groove on some fine decaying infrastructure as we rattled and thumped our way south. Even pre-Plunge, it'd been too effete, somehow, for a country swamped with spewers to maintain a decent national railroad. The moon cloaked like the sun, Mother Ocean would offer her inky embrace south of Philly, dark water racing up to nestle the train.

Drooling there at Stap's back door, what had Short Leg bellowed, something about me not screwing up their plans? That they've been waiting so long, they deserve it. What – some top MTA cops about to hook up with ASPIC money? Al pegged himself as so damn smart, yet there he stood mouthing off in an MTA hallway. Yeah, right after I'd left my license down in the lobby pegging me as me.

But what about Short Leg's other nonsense, something about no white hairs in the tail? And I had to get down there with *semen*? Though not exactly my type, as little as I'd been getting lately (i.e., none), the fat bastard didn't have to come after me with a gun. A lot to think about on a parched throat, not to mention I was suddenly starving. To the snack car for a beer and some pretzels, the eleven-dollar sandwiches out of my league.

Swaying to the rhythm of the rails with my two-buck-extra bottle of National Bohemian (a splurge since I hadn't seen one in years), a voice rang out "Yo, Fremson!" and I almost dumped the beer on the slinky woman I was admiring. It was a kid and look at him, with his blonde tints, lime-green polo shirt with the collar turned up just so and Nantucket-Red pants looking extra-fetishy on someone so young.

I kept going, but he said, "Yo, I thought I recognized you with that orange band-aid on your head. You're the dude getting Boosted sticking your nose in T-control."

Jesus, bellowing about a potential Boosting right out loud on the train, something normally barely whispered to your honey at the kitchen table. No wonder a lady bolted up and pushed past me to another car. "Getting out of town, man? I don't blame you bro, whole-vid flying all over of you in those shorts looking like a Null."

"I have some business down in, ah … away. Why would I need to leave town?"

"You tell me, messing with New York's Finest, even if only the train cops. But dude, where's your entourage? You're like famous, all the stuff they're saying about Metal Head. My girlfriend – we're in this special pre-Capitol Hill program down at Georgetown – said people were talking about you and this anti-search crap of yours at a party last night. And that's unheard of. Nobody at Georgetown talks about *current* stuff, not in pre-Hill. All political talk can do is ruin your chances."

I drank in the idiot flip-flops – Jeeze, his ankles were enormous – the buttery leather shoulder bag and matching suitcase scattered over three seats, the copy of *MAXIMUS* open to a comparison of picking up a girl to picking up a bowling ball, the absurd pants, the muscles and the tints, not to mention a laptop frozen on an improbable woman writhing on a stone altar.

That rarity, a laptop! Cause with Lois and Short Leg running over my day and then backing their vehicles up for another go, I hadn't a clue as to Chrysler's response to my confession. Not with my Net-unabled micro-zap basically reduced to an ancient cell phone. So, "Politics have grown a bit problematical, haven't they. But, tell you what, friend. There's a piece of news I gotta check out, so if I could maybe look at your machine a minute, I'd appreciate it."

"Why don't you just use smoke signals? *I'll* tell you what: fifteen minutes online for that beer. That little dictator behind the counter – I should have him fired – got all high and mighty on me when I gave him my step-brother's ID that says I'm only like thirty-two. I guess that boy's got an attitude problem, cause it works all over Georgetown."

Damn! I reluctantly handed over the seven-buck Natty Bo. He complained he thought it was an Amstel and half-tossed me his open computer. Laughing hard mid-swallow at my fumbling – I'd never had occasion to catch an open laptop on a moving train before – some beer foamed from his nose. He quickly wiped it with his upturned collar (so that's why they wear them up like that) and said, "Dude, that puppy's stone-ground military spec, its hard-drive *encased* in fossilized amber. You couldn't dent it if you dropped it from a plane." And with that he buried his nose in *MAXIMUS*, the skin mag that dry-hump showed no real skin.

Syriac was linking to the befuddlement emanating from the

Germans' North American headquarters. The meat of it made some thin sense a second time through:

> We state adjudicatedly that no corporate officer here or abroad authorized, participated in or was even fully aware of any attempt that specific day in June to breach the security of our partners in the Greater Global Fomenting Campaign. Homelander corporate staff met with surprise the 'blogged' claims made today by one Mitchell Fremson, an individual so marginalized as to be unworthy of comment. In fact, a person recently exposed as **opposed** to Protectors' T-measures!!!
>
> However, stated Marilyn Aubuchon, Senior Externality Chief, "The product launch for the Hillbilly Grinder (as H-DM's second-rate platform is popularly called by Heroes of the Sands) was in fact a public meeting at which some twenty-three authorized journalists filed reports.
>
> Officials at Chrysler, a company held for now within our corporate family stated from Auburn Hills, Michigan that "as of now" they had no knowledge of any passive harvesting of competition data points."
>
> The head of Chrysler's Washington Disbursement Office, Walter Pantly was unavailable for comment. His deputy, who declined to give his/her name pending authorization from Mr. Pantly, said in a statement that the office could not formally comment at this time. However, sources within the W.D.O. office declared a "a senior leader in a rogue operation that interfaced with the Disbursement Office" to be of interest. Said one asset close to the investigation. "Sure the lever was in place – that didn't cost us anything. But no one in this shop had seen the need to pull it as yet. Frankly, the tippy Grinder's stability is so poor, even that minimal extra expense seemed unwarranted at day's end.
>
> We wish to ensure our 17,312.5 contingent employees worldwide that we are studying the import of a remark we hasten to note emerged from the W.D.O. office anonymously off the record.
>
> Finally, to return to the scruilous individual who lodged today's unproven allegation, a Suspect, it should be noted, whose temperate actions "engendered"the tragedy upon an innocent bystander. An examination of his so-called 'career' casts a long shadow on any statement he might make.

At the end of the day, ultimately nothing stated by this Fremson person – who, for reasons rooted in a obviously deep pathology, opts for extreme shabbiness when being interviewed by a New York cable outlet – should be granted any weight.

Finally, as a matter of personal concession, the members of the Office of Externality solemnly express our affirmation and avow that we know nothing of any of this. Yet, our study of the matter will indeed garner no rest until we unearth the Truth. Boots deserve no more."

Surely "extreme shabbiness" was a bit harsh; wouldn't mere *remarkable sloppiness* have served? Syriac also linked to Heavy-Duty Manufacturing's conniption fit in reply. H-DM concluded with, "Since the Germans admit 'the lever was in place,' they should pull it to produce Pantly to explain the 'rogue operation.' That or withdraw their inferior, foreign vehicle as unworthy of transporting America's Heroic Fomenters."

I resisted the impulse to toss the pup's laptop back, thanked him and ignored the nonsense he spouted as I switched cars. Had Chrysler hired me or not? Should I be encouraged by its waffling non-denial/denial? What did that mean, the lever was in place? *The Moon is round, lads, but sail on the ebb tide.* They're studying the matter? Wallowing in it chest-deep more like it.

Needing to say something before the sun set, the Germans promulgated crap, crap so mutable as to be twisted any way they liked depending on how things unfolded. Twist slowly, slowly schmucks, cause there was a certain Army major giving me the goods to nail somebody, whether Chrysler directly or as collateral damage, my assignation in Farragut Square would tell. Master of a crowded editorial calendar and the low-three-figure fee, I needed to publish quick to resuscitate my byline and raise my profile too high – *way* over the foxhole's lip – to shoot.

Chapter Thirty-Three

Indiana Wants Me

Man, I didn't need to pay extra for that Natty Bo just to give it away. I glared at the morose face mooning back from the dark window and searched for meaning in the Germans' weasel-words.

My false-flag trip to Lester, Indiana a couple of months back in June was supposed to be quick and clean. H-DM had been supplying the Army and Marines with their main light tactical vehicle for many years. But the current Grinder had proved so fatally unstable, that a mere five years after its introduction – lightening speed by military standards – the Army had had enough of the rollovers. Here in the new contract's final round, after prototypes from such Fomentingly plump death merchants as Lockheed and Grumman had fallen by the wayside, it came down to Daimler (i.e., Mercedes)/Chrysler's Jeep Repulser versus H-DM's not quite new enough Terminator.

Bettinger had hired me for a pittance (a mere six or seven times the fee for a typical article) to get in to H-DM's dog-and-pony show introducing its contender, get out and report in by phone to someone unnamed. Call him Mr. X. Cash the fetid check at a check-cashing joint rather than my bank, and go scrub myself all over, the money salvaging my marriage for another month or two. Maybe.

For some dunderheaded reason, Bettinger had insisted on faxing me my marching orders *on* his letterhead. Maybe, such a dubious enterprise, he clutched for some kind of authority. Or, maybe he was too distracted with such matters as his firm helping to quash that big immigrant uprising at the meatpacker outside Sioux City, Iowa. (Three-thousand brown folks totally trashing a giant facility – and reported only *deep* on-line.)

In any event, I was to snoop on the Germans' presumed behalf in three areas: whether the Grinder had any hidden foreign content (for obvious reasons); had the prior model's woefully inadequate engine, transmission and suspension been improved; and, third, was its armor still so mismatched to the underlying vehicle that the damn thing rolled over unless driven – at war, often on roads that barely deserved the name – like it was tootling around Mayberry for a quart of milk.

Flat-backing a mattress for money, I'd treated myself to a Zounder. A final desperate grab for a lifeline, it was the last new Lincoln ever made. Clunky for a two-door and cobbled together from mismatched parts from Ford Europe, they sat untouched on dealers' back lots for years before being dumped on bottom-feeding outfits like the Rent-a-Heap at the airport. I was just as glad to have no time to master the 53-channel TV embedded in the steering wheel.

Amusing myself that morning pressing buttons on the Zounder's dash to no discernable effect, I wondered if I'd even get past the front gate. H-DM's in-house PR, a Mr. Faxil, was decidedly vague when deigning to take the fourth call from one Preston Lestwick, who I said was doing a story with important T-logistics implications for *Untoward Vitiation*. And why yes, Mr. Faxil, it was on spec, just a further indication of the story's significance that I was risking my own time and money. *Untoward Vitiation*'s editor, a rat far glossier than I whom I'd met once or twice, us both scrambling for cheese, would've busted a gut should, heaven forfend, he ever hear I went to Indiana on a nuts-and-bolts defense procurement piece for his glossy scandal sheet.

Out in Indiana, Preston had some business cards in my pocket identifying me as *Untoward Vitiation*'s Senior Econometrician; a *very* occasional contributor, I'd failed to crack the masthead. I was clad econometrically in a tight, mostly green plaid jacket, yellow shirt and brown slacks unearthed from deep in my closet. Thus costumed, the time was soon upon me to smile my way inside a defense plant with nothing but a homemade business card. Sweaty palms gripped the Zounder's wheel pulling up to the

H-DM gate. It featured a guard tower and enough fencing and razor wire to safeguard the $1,700-an-ounce gold in Ft. Knox – whatever little was left.

The several guards wore the standard-issue stompers and goggle-like black shades, plus silver and black baseball caps. No name or insignia adorned gray uniforms that seemed to shimmer somehow as they moved. One slung a machine pistol over his shoulder and approached my window with a clipboard. Another went to the passenger side with the same gun cradled in the crook of his elbow, a mirror on a pole in his other hand.

The first had Preston's name on a long list – one hurdle cleared! – and, icily polite, told me to pop the trunk and hood. Blinding lights switched on at ground-level as the other guard busied himself with his mirror under the car. I found the little latch for the hood, but for the life of me couldn't find the trunk latch. Cars backing up behind, I importuned with a look. Frost forming on my glasses as he spoke, the guard advised that the morning's presentation would wait until everyone was "situated." Almost pushing him with the door, I eventually got out to stand blinking in the fierce light, then bend for a better look under the dash. But no. He finally reached in and found it in a nonce, a damn *button* up under the dash, not a latch like the hood's.

Best to know my own name, there was a moment's panic signing in on whether Lestwick had an 'e' on the end. I offered an indeterminate scrawl and was ushered into a cavernous presentation area, the working part of the factory curtained off. Among the couple of hundred people milling around were a bunch in dark suits and maybe twenty in dress-blue uniforms. Engineering types in khakis and short-sleeves trailed the officers. Numerous workers in jeans clustered back by the refreshment tables laden with soda, chips, cookies and untouched fruit, competent-looking men with serious arms, some with serious bellies. The very few women wore skirts to the knee, not a pants suit among them, their blouses featuring a concealing frill or bow.

Up front, there were rows of chairs before two long, draped tables with name cards. The hulking guest of honor graced the gap between the tables so as to appear in any shot of the speaker at the low podium. Painted in camouflage, the new Terminator wasn't much bigger than the current Grinder, just a lot angrier. It's windows opaque for some reason, I was glad to see one parked in back with its doors open for the assembled press to sit inside and play soldier.

I skirted one of the scrums around the competing local-TV beauty queens (no concealing frills or bows whatsoever) and looked around for someone to chisel, an engineering type with a tongue loose from too much soda. Ah-ha, *there* was my guy. His double chin ill-shaved, his enormous red and white checked shirt stolen from a scarecrow, his darting eyes pleaded for relief from standing there alone. Yup, a pocket slide rule nestled among the pens. Math. That meant he knew … something. OK, my standard ice-breaker from the good old days.

"So, whadiya think of all this wretched excess?"

Wrong move. He wasn't some lissome lovely at a crowded party I was trying to maneuver out to the fire escape for a private chat. Hell, the two of us would probably tear any fire escape from its moorings. He looked at me uncertainly, swiped an oily nose with a meaty hand, but said nothing.

"I mean all these cookies and stuff. TV-girls – generals, for crying out loud! Some of those guys gotta be generals, right?"

"I only had seven cookies. We got an e-mail about minding our manners. So I asked Mr. Kearney, and he said there was no strict *numerical* limit as long as we were polite and didn't stuff our pockets."

"Well, I had ten myself, but they can't touch me. I'm a guest."

"The peanut butter ones don't look it, but they're really the best."

"Plain old chocolate chip for me, my man." Jee-zus – next! But all I saw was a sea of backs; talking to the young cookie monster hadn't raised my meager stock. Besides, he had that slide rule.

"Just looking at it, it's obvious that your Terminator is going to wipe the floor with Jeep's Repulser."

"You've *seen* the Repulser?"

"No. How? I mean, isn't Jeep – hah, that's a laugh. Aren't the Germans showcasing it next month?" He nodded. "I guess I was thinking of Raytheon's new APC." No point harboring my scant lingo.

"*Raytheon* is doing a new armored personnel carrier?"

"Yup. Very hush-hush on the QT. Shouldn't even have mentioned it, so if you could forget you heard it, that'd be great. They don't want to tip, uhm … Mack Trucks to their plans."

"*Mack Trucks?*"

I shushed him with a finger to my mouth as he fished a cookie out from among the pens and chewed in obvious befuddlement at the shocking competitive info I'd so casually let slip. Why the freak couldn't Mack make an APC, they put their minds to it – or Studebaker for that matter?

"So, that Terminator, that's a beautiful hunk of metal."

"Metal's the key component," he declared. "But I don't know about all that *dark* green in the camo. I sent a couple of section chiefs an e-mail on it and got a rather rude reply about sticking to my area. One even grabbed me in the cafeteria and said just cause I have a Ph.D. doesn't mean I know everything."

Wound up, he waved a hand around clutching another cookie from who knew where. Plucked it from my ear perhaps, though I was the one dressed like a vaudevillian. He complained sensibly enough about that color green not working well in the Sands.

I cocked an eyebrow at him. "Maybe it's not meant for the Sands."

"Is *Norway* our next pre-emption? I mean Fomenting. It's not like there's many Christmas trees in any of the Sands, right?" Giggling at his own joke, he choked loudly on the cookie, and several heads turned our way. Damn!

"So what is your area of expertise, Doctor?"

"The most important of all, the bottom hull."

"Of course."

"The half of the bomb that makes a big hole in the ground we don't care about. It's the half of the bomb that goes up, where the soldiers are riding, that counts. And if stupid HR, not an advanced degree in the whole bunch of 'em, would just leave me alone to do my work, I might be able to save soldiers' lives!"

More heads turned at his outburst. "It's always the visionaries," I comforted him, "who suffer with marbles at their feet." Come on doll-face, let something slip before they drop a net on you.

"And that stupid Indian transmission. The bean counters, who don't come close to understanding my work, are insisting on it. Something about a whorled gear. All I know is it bumps out and totally messes up my hull coating performance. Transmissions are mechanical – you can bend them if you have to. You can't *bend* metallurgy. Besides, who cares how much it costs the Indians to reconfigure. Let them charge us an extra $270 per vehicle."

Of course the Plunge had hit their casinos hard. But since when did Indians make transmissions? I tried to ask, but he had a full head of steam.

"IED transverse penetration causes even more fatalities than all our rollovers. And aren't rollovers one of the main reasons the Army canceled us after only five years? Well, *that*'s not my area, thank goodness."

Spotting a tall, fit man in a blazer striding our way, "Yeah, rollovers. What's the deal – "

But steam was leaking from his nose by then. "If they'd only listen about my reversed-ion, tungsten hull coating. I've achieved a 27 percent improvement in blast dispersal in the third quadrant of the hull alone. An extra $4,000 per Terminator is *not* that much. The Army's got to see that. When you compare it to the medical costs of somebody with no legs for the ten-year care-allotment they get under the new Enlistment Regs. I don't – "

"Wilson! Introduce me to our new friend here."

The man in the blazer was smiling so hard, he made *my* teeth hurt. You could set your clock by the part in his hair, and the crease in his slacks was sharp enough to be illegal on airplanes. So much for getting any more out of Wilson, and a damn shame, cause his sugar-high had really kicked in.

"Can't, Mr. Kearney. He never said his name." For a big man, Wilson sure shrank in on himself pretty small.

Preston shook hands with Wilson damply and Kearney wincingly.

"So, Wilson, what have you been telling our friend Preston with such gusto?"

"My usual, Mr. Kearney. Reversed-ion tungsten. You know that's all I talk about to anyone who'll listen. That and Purdue girls tennis."

Picturing Wilson slavering from the front row over the young lovelies on the court, I hastened to assure Kearney we hadn't gotten to the tennis yet.

"Of course, Wilson. But I thought we agreed, after that unfortunate incident with that Marine colonel, that your tungsten wasn't quite ready for public discussion." He turned to me with his fierce smile. "Don't want to push it out of the nest before it's ready to fly."

"I know, Mr. Kearney. But the more people who know about it, that's more who can bring pressure on the Army. You get those ions hot enough, and once they start reversing – "

"Wilson! Zip it, now! Talk of ions with a guest is way out of bounds."

"That's OK, Mr. Kearney. *Look* at him. He won't understand any of it."

"Wilson, remember the e-mail from Mr. Samuelson himself on decorum with our guests. Now, have you – have you had any cookies yet? What? Good. Try the peanut butter, I hear they're best."

"Oh, I have, Mr. Kearney."

"Well go have some more. No – bye-bye, Wilson. I'd like to have a little chat with Preston here."

Kearney watched Wilson's broad back a moment, then turned to me a second before pasting on his smile.

Chapter Thirty-Four

Windows You Can't See Out

"He's a brilliant metallurgist, you know," Kearney informed me. "Set the entire department at Purdue on its head getting his Ph.D. there. Some kerfuffle involving that tungsten of his. We're lucky to have him, of course. But Wilson's not quite ready for public consumption, not after we cut his meds cause he kept lying down on his lab bench. Not ready for – I assume you're press."

I admitted as much as various muckety-mucks started to drift over towards the two tables with the name cards. Not wanting to fry Wilson's considerable bacon any more by linking him to my crucial question on rollovers, I temporized with something he'd said that made no sense. "So, Native Americans are making transmissions now? That's a nice, solid piece of business. That's down in … Oklahoma somewhere?" They had Indians there, right?

"The Germans did what? Really – you've heard that? Son of a gun, going all affirmative action on us."

What? I almost fished for a cookie in my own pocket. "No, for you guys, for H-DM."

"Boy, that's news to me. I wasn't aware that Native Americans did that kind of manufacturing." He beckoned with his eyes to someone over my shoulder.

"Neither was I. I guess there's a lot of crony-capitalism floating around these days, you get the right representation in DC." I gave him a complicit smile.

"Well, Native Americans can bid on that piece of business like anyone else. Bring it on."

The silence went from awkward to tortured pretty quick, both of us waiting the other out. I cracked first, trying to worm my way to any foreign content. "So, you guys dropped a Volvo engine in there?"

"Volvo? You've got some funny ideas, friend. No. We're sticking with the tried and true, a hard-working, fuel-sipping General Motors V-8."

Of course your ideas get funny, plucking them from air. "A V-8 works OK, a vehicle that heavy, long as you keep it under 50 miles an hour, huh?"

He grimaced and smiled and again importuned someone over my shoulder. "It's worked fine for years. With the right down-road security projection, there's no need for our Heroes to exceed 50 m.p.h."

Un-huh. Bettinger was interested in whether they'd beefed up the power plant. "You ever think about going with a Caterpillar engine or a Detroit Diesel or something with some oomph that truckers use?"

"If you had any notion of this category, you'd know that the Krauts own Cat and that Detroit Diesel is also foreign owned. Post-Plunge, our heavy manufacturing isn't what it was, or haven't you heard? But we're glad to offer a – well, that's right, a 100-percent American vehicle."

"All home-grown?"

"Like I said, various GM V-8s have been working just fine for us for decades now."

"Quite an advantage that, fighting for a defense contract. Wouldn't want our Heroes riding around in foreign metal. So, 100-percent American, huh?"

"Ah, Colonel, there you are. Have you met our new friend, Preston Lestwick – a *special* friend, Colonel. I wanted to make sure you two met."

I turned and was confronted by a ball of wire that rendered the exceedingly crisp Kearney a rag doll by comparison. His hatchet of a jaw aimed way too close at my Adam's apple, he grabbed my elbow to pull me even closer as he abused my hand.

"Ah, the military perspective we've been lacking, Colonel...."

"Kubark," he growled. "I saw you talking to that brilliant young Wilson a moment ago. Just generalities, I trust."

"Wilson and I plumbed deep platitudes, Colonel Kubark. And under Mr. Kearney's tutelage, I've forgotten them already."

"I'm surprised Wilson was allowed to attend this event, Kearney," he said, staring dead at me. "So, Lestwick. What exactly are you looking for a military perspective on?"

"Now that you mention it, those windows on the Terminator there. Not to put too fine a point on it – but can troops see out of them? See where they're going?"

"Damn glad you asked that, cause that *has* come up for discussion. But we've got seven cameras mounted strategically round the Terminator's exterior. Catch you picking your nose a mile away, Lestwick. Upload your picture to Florida, and with Fused Intelligence's real-time, biometric enhancements, we'll kinetically *know* it's you in just over forty seconds. They're heat sensitive and provide night vision and motion detection. Plus, now we're able to interface a Target's whole-vid history from up to ninety meters. That means we can ID any micro-zap out there with prior T-Fiend use. No need to even exit the vehicle. And with that, under the new C. P. Crisis Regs, we don't really worry too much who the Target is. The Target's just a platform for a guilty phone."

"Wait a minute. Somebody borrows his uncle's micro-zap not knowing about the wrong-number call he got six months back – and that's it? Lights out?"

Kubark gave me the smile of someone who's just let one loose in church and is about to turn and glare at the old lady behind him. But all he said was, "Given those capabilities, we went for the full blast protection instead of mere unaided human vision. The naked eye is for the last war, not the *next* Fomenting Democracy on tap, right Kearney?"

"Whatever our Heroes need on the full-spectrum battlefield,"

Kearney affirmed. "And you can bet the Chi-Coms are playing catch-up as we speak."

Reporters never actually questioned the a priori need for the next Fomenting "on tap." So (and this was bad enough), "That must cost a pretty penny, seven cameras."

The colonel snarled, "You going to be the one to tell her *her* Hero has gone to his Reward because the Army decided to save a measly $37K a vehicle?"

"No, sir, not me. But if you can't see out, why not just metal it over entirely?"

"The glass is PR, you come right down to it, for the populations we're Fomenting – plus the Army's ever expanding Homeland duties."

An alarmed Kearney said, "Don't you think it best, Colonel, that we focus overseas, what with American Heroes currently conducting three Democracy Fomentations and one Pre-emption."

The colonel coughed, but remained intent on four very shiny shoes, plus mine. "Ah, currently, that's *two* Fomentations, one Pre-emption. One, the hoped for surge petered out, and it's been downgraded to a Holding Action."

Holy mackerel! HeadFuck had bowed to the obvious, and thrown in the towel on one of the Sands? But which one? I wasn't even sure which were full-blown Fomentations and which a Pre-emption. Us so chummy, I almost asked Kubark, but before I could get it out, he said, "So, Lestwick – *Preston* Lestwick. I thought I was familiar with all the reporters – sorry, journalists – on the wheeled-vehicle procurement beat. But that's a name I haven't heard."

"Well, my magazine thought it would be interesting to approach such a crucial topic from an econometric point of view."

"And what magazine did you say you're doing this for?"

A particularly interested Kearney leaned closer.

"And how, for instance, that meshes with defense contractors' typical distribution of work among key congressional districts.

Building, of course, on the pioneering work of Styron and ... Cheever regarding the defense budget's failure to intersect with the country's overlaying macros and never – it seemingly off-limits – a discussion of any ongoing rationale. Post-Plunge, you know. In fact, I think your Terminator here represents a very specific iteration with its innovative camera configuration that obsoletes unaided optics."

That understandably left them gasping for more, but always leave your audience hungry. Finally, Kubark said, "And you're working for who exactly?"

"Oh – ah, *Untoward Vitiation*." A gossip rag, one with pretensions, but still.

"*Untoward ...*"

"*Vitiation*. It's a technical journal, well that and with a bit of celebrity gloss to carry the freight, of course. Its influence far exceeds its modest circulation."

"New to me. I'll be very interested to check that out." He again thrust his chin at my neck.

Kubark was getting more steamed and Kearney more pained with every breath I took. People drifting towards the rows of seats, I flung caution aside. "Does it still roll?" They stared, four lips pressed tight. "I mean, of course it rolls. It's not like it's tracked."

"What the devil are you talking about," demanded the colonel.

But I couldn't bring myself to utter the offending phrase, *roll over*. "I mean, does it still tip, the new one?"

Kearney stared me down. "You mean *over*?"

"Yeah, like on its side, down the bank and into a river, Heroes laden with equipment gasping their life's breath away?"

Formerly unflappable, Kearney exploded. "That trial at Aberdeen was biased. Everyone knows that. A tree stump would've rolled, the way she was driving it! Besides, that is highly classified info – *toxic* in the wrong hands. *Directly* toxic to the hands holding it. You follow me, bud?"

A whole bunch of heads turned our way. Licking his chops and trying to remember where he'd left his knife and fork, Kubark said, "Kearney, I'm just glad it's you, a patriotic private Homelander, and not the United States Army instructing this … person on what is what."

Aberdeen. What, the proving ground, where apparently a woman had rolled a Grinder? And wouldn't Mr. X like to know. So, "Well: Aberdeen. I don't have to tell you how big a place that is, all kinds of people there. Why, I heard – "

"Alright. Listen up maggot, and you listen good." A beet-red Kubark was all up in my face talking low. "That test-range perimeter was as tight as a drum. I'm security for this entire program, and when I say it was locked down, that means it was clean enough to cook a grilled-cheese sandwich on its ass. I don't care about that damn hill – which is *nine* kilometers out. So if anything got out, it came from inside. Which means it's only a matter of time before I'm breathing down that traitor's neck with full T-enhancement. You tell your source that!"

I would, soon as I met him. "Why, Colonel, I'm sure I don't know what you mean." I batted mint-julep lashes at him. "I see the union rep is free. Let me grab him while I can. Labor's view can be quite telling, econometrically speaking. G'day, gentlemen." I turned so quick, Kubark flailed at air, Kearney grabbing him by the arm.

Jim Kowalski, president of Local 3 of the United Electrical, Farm, Service Workers Amalgamated – a rump, military offshoot of an eviscerated United Auto Workers – scurried off to one of the TV-girls just as I was getting him all warm and squishy for the kill on rollovers. Then someone tapped the microphone for us to take our seats, and I barely had time before the shilling started to grab not nearly enough cookies to keep the demons at bay. (The chocolate chip beat the peanut butter by a nose.) I plopped down in back, my notebook propped on my knee like a good pup, a hard wedge of a man in uniform who I'd seen huddled with Kubark glaring from across the aisle.

I'd come all this way on assignment, damn it, a professional who didn't like to disappoint. And while I could offer Mr. X. a few frayed strings to tug, I had nothing conclusive. Man, I should've caught the five a.m. plane Nicki had pushed and gotten in some more schmooze time. Cause I got nothing from Congressman Howdy Doody and Colonel Hosanna but happy talk about "the 100 percent all-American Terminator from the tires on up, a USA-united vehicle from right here in the heart of the Homeland." At that, the workers clustered in back got the TV cameras turned their way with some less than spontaneous chants of USA! USA! Never mind that the Repulser was made a couple of hundred miles away.

Luckily, the H-DM boss invited guests to get a closer look at the two Grinders on display, so we weren't hustled right out. That a consequential gent with white hair was chatting up a terrified looking Wilson (Turd-Touch strikes again!) when I trolled by was moot since Kubark's bullet-headed subordinate trailed me closely. I joined the crowd of workers, engineering types and military men milling round the Grinder in back. But any time I ventured a hello, my new shadow was breathing down my neck. So all I got were versions of "Rah, team, here in the heart of the Homeland."

Once that became all too plain, I figured to at least sit in the monstrosity like everyone else was doing. I could offer Mr. X the pivotal Intel that the cabin had nine screens, five gauges and eleven dials. Oh, and a steering wheel – probably. I stood in line, but gosh if they didn't shut it down right when I was next. Too bad, cause it looked chock-full in there, enough doo-dads to fly the Chinese moon mission. Despite my protest, they made it quite clear – what with all the Fomenting, not to mention Pre-empting – they had to get back to work. Yes, at that exact moment. And thunk went the doors. The two young reporters behind me made not a peep, one reassuring the other they could make do with the handouts.

And that was meagerly that. Welp, time to fake it with Mr. X.

Time to see if the campaign to supply pay phones to the post-Plunge fifth of the populace without a phone or micro-zap to use to call an ambulance had gained any traction in Lester, Indiana.

Rinsing my hands in the men's room – what the hell! – someone jostled me from behind. This subway rider instinctively clutched his wallet as a hand slipped something into my jacket pocket. I turned with an oath to see a well put together worker with a finger to his lips." A good one," he whispered and strolled out, laughing to himself.

The deft precision of the hand-drawn map, coupled with his confident air, convinced me to follow his directions out to the fields a few miles from town. That and the promised "SCANDAL" – just the one word in block letters below the map. I could hope it was both about the Grinder and passed the smell test. If so, Mr. X would be glad of the delay.

Chapter Thirty-Five

The Man Who Doesn't Give Two Shits

Standing on a baking back-country road, I tried not to gulp the blessedly cold beer mystery man slapped in my mitt when I went to shake. Still looking like he was laughing to himself when I pulled up to the crossroads in the fields, he was leaning on a small, dust-encrusted, baby station wagon, so ancient it was a Datsun rather than the Nissan they changed it to donkey years ago.

"I figured, instead of a voice from the dash leading you by the nose, you were old enough to know how to read a map." He was a little younger and just a little shorter, with jackhammer forearms, a drinker's loose, skinny face, and a tired, assertive voice, not too deep despite his size.

"I got that left turn by the water tower, so I was OK. But, Jesus, a Genny Cream Ale, man. How'd you find them out here in bum-fuck Indiana?"

"Indiana's not so bad a place if you got to be from somewhere."

"No, of course not. I mean – "

"You're from where, New York? Guy in We're-Fuckedistan talked like you. A real zero, but I guess somebody's got to be from there too. Genny Cream, they're all I drink – when I'm drinking beer. Developed a taste for 'em way back, when I was active-duty at Fort Drum. Just a kid then, I guess I liked piss-water beer."

"Still in at your age, you Guard or Reserve?"

"Guard. You never served your country, did you?"

I shook my head and introduced myself, unthinkingly using my real name. Christ – so much for the day's stage name. He crushed a hand still sore from Kubark and said, "Everett."

"It's your dime Everett, cause I got fish to fry."

"Trust you on the fly, hunh, Mitch? Fine. My life insurance is paid up for the rest of the year. And my H-DM job – forget my job. Except for losing that, I don't see this coming back on my wife and daughter. And they'll cope. She's got a big family that grows a lot of their own food."

"Guess that's pretty crucial these days, you got a kid."

"Look, nothing worse can happen to me – not with what I've seen and done. There's no point sitting in the back of a Grinder with both your hands hid behind a ceramic vest and your gun at your feet. Not over in a Sands. And not here neither."

Not liking talk of life insurance and that the worst has already happened, I said, "Sounds like you got it sewed up tight."

He gave that the grunt it deserved. "OK, let's do it. I was enjoying the legs on that TV-girl all the bosses were elbowing each other to talk to. The brunette, not the blonde. And the weirdest thing is, ever since I got my blast concussion, my balance is shot, my memory's not so great, and I get 'fogged-in,' I call it. Oh, and my wife and little girl love the mood-swings. But my hearing's been like 20-20. Better."

"I'm sorry about your head injury. I can imagine. I mean, nothing's ever happened to my head, thank God. We all certainly appreciate your – "

"Can that shit. So I'm staring at the TV-girl, hoping she'll drop that little gold pen she's waving around. And I hear you getting under Kearney and that colonel's skin about our new Grinder. About the Indian transmission that's supposed to be this big secret till we get the new contract. Even though it's not half-bad. Better than the Allison spider trap we're using now, anyway."

"Indians, right. Why are Indians making something like transmissions? I mean who even knew they did that?"

"What are you talking about, all those billions of people over there. But wait. No, wait! So that shit-hole dictator, Kearney – who likes abusing anyone who can't talk back, especially that fat scientist who ain't all there – and that colonel had a cow when you started asking about how the Grinder is still way too top-heavy. Which is why I brought you out here. You see – ”

“Look – *you* wait.” I was finally able to interrupt. “This is a conversation, not a lecture, or I’m out of here. If you won’t let me ask questions, I can’t do my job. OK?” (Never mind that it was a whole other job than what he thought.) His stare so long and pointed, I almost fell back a step. Finally he nodded.

“What kind of Indians are making your transmissions? From where?”

“From over next to We’re-Fuckedistan. You know, the people put chutney on their curry. What, you thought they set up a tranny plant out in South Dakota somewhere?”

“So that’s why Kearney freaked when I asked about that. Come to think of it, he never did answer my question about it being one-hundred percent American. The more foreign content H-DM’s got, the less you can wave the American flag about Mercedes owning Jeep.”

“No shit, Shirley. But that whole ‘home-grown’ argument is shot, or it should be, with how many foreign *aspirants*, they call ‘em, we got in the regular Army. Anyway, I start wondering about you asking about the transmission and especially about the Grinder still being tippy. Most of those reporters back there look mighty comfortable at the trough. But you look like maybe you gotta elbow your way in from around back.”

And, finishing the rest of his beer in a single, smooth swallow, he squinted at me for an answer. Out there in farm country, there was even some sun this city boy hadn’t seen in many a moon. “Everett, I figure coming the wrong way to the trough is what this trip is all about.”

“Good, cause I need a reporter, and they don’t run in my circles.” He started ripping the label off his empty bottle. “My wife taught me this trick. Peel the label all the way off before getting another beer. Probably doesn’t make any difference in the total come the end of the night, but it slows you down a little.”

"There's nights I can use that."

He looked at me hard. "Barbara's her name. She says this whole thing is because I'm mad the Guard is charging me 595-bucks for losing my helmet. Shit like that happens when the lead vehicle rolls over in the middle of an ambush. So I grabbed Willie's helmet. He didn't need it anymore. And that's what I wore cause we didn't exactly police the motherfucking area getting out of there. Who knew the Guard was going to check serial numbers on the helmet they got back. Never did the first couple of times."

"I'm sorry about Willie."

"So's Willie. Anyway, I'm freezing my ass off up on top of this mountain drinking water out of a bottle. They're sniping us, we're shooting back – nothing for miles around but this piss-hole we built ourselves. It don't mean shit. Turns out they bottle the water in Colorado and ship it clear round the other side of the world in these little plastic bottles."

"What do they say: strategy is for amateurs, logistics for professionals. We might as well bore a hole through the earth and drop it down."

"Costs a million bucks a year to keep a Boots in your average Sands. They got hash, sure, some of them. But not much booze, and almost no hookers, but plenty of Big Macs and ice cream. Kids who didn't have money in their pocket for that crap at home go to war and get fat."

"Welp, war sucks, so I hear. But what can I do you for, Everett?"

"You're not as bad a wiseass. But you're still like that other damn New Yorker. Alright, the whole-vid I'm gonna give you might even make it on *Up Yours Truly* or *Breakfast Raunch*."

"Right. Cause you got some whole-vid that neither you nor anyone you know is willing to put their name on under the new Regs – but it's perfect for me. Whadiya got, HeadFuck and the Pope getting it on, one in a dress, the other in a chicken suit?"

Man, his stare creeped me out. "I got one way and one way only to protect my brothers-in-arms from out here in 'bum-fuck Indiana.'

And that's to see that H-DM, which I've been working for for seventeen years, doesn't win the new Grinder contract."

"How you gonna do that?"

"I'm not. You are, with the whole-vid I'll be *mailing* you – like from the Post Office – starring the Secretary of Defense. Remember a while back when she showed up with a big band-aid on her chin and joked to some reporters that she cut herself shaving. You might've heard about it because some guy on TV worked up a spoof showing her shaving. So they fired him for HateCrime cause of all the talk about her being dyke."

I admitted to some vague familiarity.

"It wasn't shaving, not that band-aid, anyway. Nope, she rolled our prototype going barely 35 miles an hour. I mean, she could hardly see over the steering wheel. She ended up jerking the wheel – a little, not a lot – to avoid embarrassing herself driving over an orange cone on the course – "

"At Aberdeen!" Showing that you already knew stuff was one of the best ways to cultivate a source, even if you're only playing reporter.

"You knew about Aberdeen, or did you hear it today? Cause it ain't exactly the world's best kept secret around here."

"And you have a whole-vid of this?" Even play-acting, I still got that tingly feeling.

"Course I got it. You think I'd risk getting fired going AWOL from work just to chat? The way jobs are around here? Look, I'm sorry about your name going on top, but something like this, you gotta follow the Regs to get it out there. At least you'll get a hell of a scoop out of it."

Shit, would embarrassing the Secretary of Defense, PC figurehead that she was, earn an Elevation to RoundUp? Not that I was actually doing the story. "It all falls on my shoulders, huh – Minders Turn Elsewhere!"

Everett would remain good looking till the Genny took its toll down the road, but he got real ugly real quick. "Screw the Data. This is the real world we're talking about here, men's lives at stake. Besides, I don't think the fuckers even exist. You know anyone the Minders have messed with?"

"There's this one guy, but that was probably mostly back taxes."

"It ain't happening to the boys I'm drinking with after work – or anybody any of us knows. Let the Minders worm their way down deep, have a party for all I care. Cause *I* don't feel 'em."

"I still need some sense of where you got the whole-vid. I mean, all the Regs on whole-vid cameras now, how'd a guy like – "

"You mean how'd a nobody-autoworker get ahold of a whole-vid of the SecDef herfuckingself proving the new Grinder's gonna chew Boots up as bad as the old one? And she wasn't some scared, lead-foot kid in-theater. She was driving slow."

"Yeah, a guy like you or any other source, you come right down to it. I haven't made a career-threatening mistake yet. But you're only as good as your last story, especially a freelancer like me." What the heck was I talking about? I was just stringing Everett along fishing for details to phone in to Mr. X.

Ignoring my sourcing question, he said, "It's funny as shit if you don't think about what it means. First you see the SecDef hiking her skirt up to her butt so she can haul herself *way* up into the Grinder. Legs that should not see the full light of day. She finally gets it in gear, and then she's just driving for a minute, which they can edit out."

"I don't know if you want to edit it any, so they can't accuse you of anything."

"Maybe, maybe not, given people's attention spans these days. Anyway, then she does this little jog to her left – nothing big, not at all. But over she tips, sliding on the driver's side. She was going so slow, she didn't flip all the way over. And all hell breaks loose. Three emergency vehicles come roaring up, and a fire suppression team sprays this aqueous-film foam all over it. And they're running around putting a chain on it to pull it back over. But then a bunch of grunts just go push it over, and she's flopping around inside cause she's taken her seatbelt off. That's when she cut her chin; you get to see the blood dripping pretty good when they finally haul her out. So it'll bounce pretty high."

"Who wears a skirt to Aberdeen?"

"Gotcha. As to how we got the whole-vid – come on! We make the damn thing. Don't you think we had some folks babysitting it, going to Aberdeen and back? Some ex-military with access to all kinds of equipment, including spy-cams." His bottle stripped, the label peels at his feet marking our rendezvous, he whirled and tossed it far.

"Great. So now some kid's gonna get broken glass in his corn flakes after the combine gets ahold of that."

"I doubt it, seeing as how that's sorghum." Rasping his hollow laugh, he turned abruptly for his truck. What, I'd screwed the pooch ragging him about littering? He rummaged around under the front seat for two more Gennys and sneered mightily when I declined a second. "Can't drive on two, a big guy like you?"

"No. It's just that as a reporter, I got to keep my wits about me."

"Unlike the dumb-ass who spends his day messing with machines that'll take your arm as quick as look at you?"

"Were you always this pissed off?"

He took a step towards me, stopped and stared. "You always such an arrogant prick? But Barbara'd tell you no about always being this pissed off. She told me flat out she wouldn't have married the guy who came back, not from that last tour."

"It was worse?"

"My first two Sands were SOP death-and-destruction. But we took so many casualties that last one, the officers lost control, and things got ugly up on that mountain. Some things you can't really imagine how they'll hit you till you see them for yourself. Like the fountain of blood when a man's head gets cut from his body. That was after we found three of ours from the neck down."

"Jesus, Everett."

"Never heard about that, did you? Theirs or ours. Anyway, all I did was watch, but I could've left. A lot of nights now, when I finally fall asleep, I wish like fuck I had. So, no, I don't give two shits anymore – except about my family."

No way I interrupted the silence that dropped on him. Finally he looked up. "Somebody's gotta try to protect the boys HeadFuck's gonna send out Fomenting next in that thing. I've seen at least six dumb-as-dirt rollovers myself. Put all the Sands together, we're getting hundreds of fatalities a year. It's so fucking bad, the Army built these shake-and-bake things they call HEAT – Humvee Egress Assistance Trainers – and trucked 'em all over to teach you how to 'survive' a rollover."

"They built some kind of carnival ride so you knew what it was like to roll?"

"Right. Except not 'was' – *is*. We threw 2,600 pounds of armor on the one we've been making the last five years, so when it's not flipping like a coin, the transmission or suspension fail. Or the motherfucker sinks to the axles in any kind of mud. And there you sit with a bull's-eye big as life. And the payload is so skimpy, you get blown up twice making two trips instead of one."

He peeled his label a minute, then said, "You fed up enough, Mitch, with what's going on – from HeadFuck on down to the bully with a badge down on your corner? Has your life reached the point that you don't give enough of a shit?"

While I pondered that, he stumbled and almost fell, and I made the mistake of stepping forward, asking if he was OK.

He slapped my hand away hard. "I am *not* drunk, damn it! That's my first two of the day, right there in front of you. That's the damn blast-concussion messing up my balance. I'm heading for face-first into a machine press, and that'll be that."

"I'm sorry about your injury."

"An *injury's* something you get playing ball. Mine is a war wound, damn it, a simple little IED that didn't leave a scratch. But the blast-wave hits you at 1600-feet a second. Then all the air that got moved out rushes back in at pretty much the same speed and clobbers you again. And so your brain gets so shook – first one way, then the other – it ain't the same for a long time, if ever. I know I'm not close to getting it back. Not yet."

"I'm real sorry to hear that, man."

"The Army says, oh, it's just a concussion like you get in football. Got your bell rung. Or, oh, you were depressed and woozy before you even signed up. Though how they know that they never say. No treatment or compensation, and sure as hell no Purple Heart cause your skull stays intact."

"I thought they decided to give Purple Hearts for that."

"Nope. HeadFuck rescinded it. Didn't hear about that either, did you? They try to pin it on stress or depression and slap you on the ass out the door with a happy-pill. And all *that* does is turn you into a limp-dick tub of lard so you really got something to be depressed about. My deal ain't from me freaking out cause I killed some people who were trying to kill me. It's because my damn brain got put in a blender! Got it?"

Jesus, he was scary. He stared off somewhere, then grabbed my arm. "The main thing is stopping the new H-DM Grinder. It's one thing to get shot up in a fire-fight. That was another big difference in We're-Fuckedistan, them finally going toe-to-toe. Or even to buy it from a bomb in a goat lying on the road. Spam in a Can ain't much, but it's something. But to get killed cause your own stupid vehicle can't take a curve over 55 miles-an-hour, that's just sad."

"Alright already. Send me the Goddamn whole-vid. I'll see what I can do."

"Both of us'll be interested in seeing what you can do. Look at it as your contribution as a civilian – a big one, I know, with the Reg about your name."

Un-huh. But I gave him my bricks-and-mortar post-office box. Sure, that was a Data-screwed thing to do. But standing there in the stupid *sorghum*, it wasn't like I could start up a pirate Dutch anonymizing address, one of those supposedly stealth jobbies that usually last about ten days before they got shut down.

We had drifted over by his absurd little station wagon, and he leaned in and took a picture off the visor. "Let's get this shit done, and you come on back sometime after the damn Germans get their contract. Then, maybe a year after it all blows over, assuming we're *both* still breathing air – come out for a visit, long as you drive. No flying coming to see my family. See a little bit of the country before they stop you crossing state lines."

"You mean me, or everybody?"

"You tell me. Anyway, I'll let you meet Barbara and my daughter."

He handed me the photo, and I gave a sincere whistle. Yellow-haired wife and daughter, sunburnt and pretty, solid looking inside and out. Some might say Barbara paled before the wraiths of Manhattan – and she looked all the better for it.

"Ain't she a honey after all our years together? You notice I don't say my daughter's name. You gotta earn that. After sixteen months of me falling off that stinking mountain, she was scared of me at first when I got home. That broke my heart more than anything. She went from a toddler to a little girl, and I missed every second of it. And you don't get it back."

"That's horrible, man. I give soldiers props like everyone else, but…. All these wars, where's the Demos? We used to do 'em, hundreds of thousands of people freezing their asses off. Any Demo now, it's over getting abortion rights restored, or college kids worrying about their janitors' pay."

"So, you in or you out?"

"You're asking a lot, dude."

"OK. So we won't shake on it – for now. In the meantime, I got to get back to work. Look, the wife makes a mean beef stew. We'll drink some Gennys. They're a fuck-lot better than Hose-'Em anyway. "

"Hose-'Em?"

"Hoosier. They dropped the regular beer, and all they're selling now is Hoosier-Dried-Ice, Hoosier-Clam Juice, Hoosier-Meth – whatever they call that one. Wash your dog in it maybe, but don't let it pass your lips."

We parted such friends, I fired up the Zounder wondering what his little girl's name was and not where I'd toss the envelope soon to hit my post-office box.

****

Mr. X was pissed I called so late. He said he'd heard the presentation had ended by 11:30, so why was it pushing one o'clock? Then he surprised me saying he didn't like being away from his desk so long to be at that number. I hadn't thought of him with a regular-type job. But I mollified him with news of the Indian transmission and especially the VIP rollover. He got so excited about that, I finally told him it was the "SecDef herfuckingself," and he just about swooned. I figured, what the hell, maybe Everett's scoop would see the light through this unlikely channel.

X was also intrigued to hear of the Christmas-tree camouflage, but he already knew about the substitution of cameras for windows. I decided at the last minute not to mention Wilson's tungsten, which sounded like it might actually help protect Boots someday. No problem, cause the tranny and the SecDef sure stewed his prunes. Hanging up, I realized there was a sibilant little 'S' in his speech when he got excited telling me what excellent work I'd done, and that he'd tell Bettinger to cut a check that afternoon. Not that that freaking happened.

Chapter Thirty-Six

Nick Spills Beans

Musing on Indiana, sheer nervous exhaustion eventually over-came me as the train clickity-soothing-clacked down to DC. No rest for the wicked, my jangling micro-zap pulled me awake and away from my dream of Everett's groaning board. Forks in hand, Barbara, he and their handsome daughter – introduced as Betty – had all been laughing nastily, the child harsh beyond her years, at my tale of leaping long ago over a rat in a subway tunnel. Not growing up pressing their nose to a subway's greasy window during trips to town from Long Island, they didn't grasp the tracks' dark allure, punctu-ated by mysterious lights of many colors, cryptic signs and the very occasional ghost station. They'd never sat astride a local, flogging hopelessly as an express cantered up, toyed with us a moment and then galloped by. The other train's adults flickered into view, first one then another framed perfectly for a moment as my local gave her all, and then quickly past, all of them oddly unmoved by the desperate race. I tried to explain to my phantasmagorical hosts about encountering that rat. How late of an evening, setting off through the tunnel for the next station's half-moon of light was a drunken, manly scaling of the only Everest at hand.

Unable to remember the last call with good news, I was tempted to ignore my micro-zap and seek a different dream, perhaps discover-ing if Maureen had an appendix scar. But it was an old friend calling, Nicki on familiar ground – angry rather than her recent patronizing over-solicitousness.

"Damn it, Mitchell. I'm paying a fortune in rent so I could quit riding out to Queens. Where the hell are you? It ever occur to you our meeting tonight might be a little, oh, important – to me if not to you?"

My dulcet-toned wife, a little tipsy by the sound of it and a lot furious. "I'm on the train. Something happened, and I had – "

"The train? So you're late, and I should just meet you up by the subway? You get a kick out of me sweating my way all the way down here giving a hundred creeps *another* opportunity to comment on each and every part of me? Just because I wore that yellow dress you always liked for our little whatever the hell it is, *ceremony*, tonight. That and having to flaunt it at work today after how you've fucked me over. That dress is probably the only reason Ernesto the slime overruled basically the entire rest of the agency who wanted to fire me on the spot."

Ah, the clingy yellow number, normally reserved for rats-chasing-cheese parties, not plucking Bumfuckville's strings. That she came so sculpted to highlight my loss thrilled me no end. "Listen, I'm on a real train, headed – well, never mind where I'm headed. I'm sorry about your job. I really am. But I got a hot tip on fixing a bum steer."

"You're still funny, you know. I hope you don't lose that, all the shit going on with you. It's your most appealing quality."

"Advice on ensuring your successor is worthy of a dress that – *bright*, Nicki? ... So did you happen to catch Syriac today?"

"Syriac? What are you talking about, with the world falling down on your head?"

"Something happened, something bad. So I'm headed to DC to fix what I can." Shit, I should not have said that right out loud.

"Something bad – something new bad? Or the same old bad as five days ago when you threw your life in the toilet and pulled me in after you?"

"Something new. And it's not good."

"And I'm supposed to care that Syriac, the great and powerful, added his two cents about you, like that's going to change anything?

Will you please get real and maybe worry about what the cops are saying about you on *television*, for Chrissakes?"

"That is not something I'm worried about, not even a little. The man with no gun and a bloody head who's called the shooter. No, it's something I wrote on Syriac, not vice versa. Anyway, look, I'm on to a couple of big scores – and no, that does *not* mean money – out of all this. So maybe it all happened for a reason, long as Carole gets better."

"She's better. She's going on *Breakfast Raunch* or whatever that new macro-transmission is for something like ten-grand on Wednesday. She'll probably be wrapped in cellophane. But wait a Goddamn minute. What do you mean all this happened for a reason? I'm probably getting fired from a hot agency's vice-presidency, when less than two years ago I was a glorified secretary living with you on rice and beans."

"Nicki, look, it – "

"But it's all OK cause you're getting some lousy little civ-lib articles out of it? The Minders are the only ones reading them, the crap places you publish. Times have changed, Mitchell, since HeadMan clawed his way in. It's not like during his first few months when maybe we had a chance. I mean, F&F found out you're flirting with RoundUp as it is."

"Not on the phone!"

"Sorry – sorry about that. But I was doing pretty good, captain of my own keyboard, until you dropped your stink bomb on me."

"I'm sorry about Fornix & Foyst. But I had to tell someone what was going on before I set out last Thursday to challenge the searches. Just in case. Jesus, I don't know who's more suspicious, you or Pop."

"Your father's a smart cookie. If he were you, he'd be making some money elbowing Fiore aside on *Breakfast Raunch* so fast her boobs would spin. Car alarms would be going off for six blocks."

"How drunk are you? Cause this is the most honest conversation we've had in a long time."

"Not nearly drunk enough. So what? I wasn't exactly looking

forward to this evening, long-time coming or not. Plus I had to mollify someone pretty pissed off I was seeing you at all."

"Ah-ha! The yellow dress's true target revealed."

"He's gotten awfully ... proprietary awfully quickly. It must go with money. *Noblesse spoiled rotten* or something. He got ugly, yelling I should call you and do it by phone. I think he's worried about one for the road, but I told him you've got too much self-respect for that."

"Don't be so sure in that do-me dress."

"I wish the hell he was here now so I could get out of here. He offered to drive me, but he'd probably get car-jacked down here in his ridiculous heap of metal. Though I do like the baby kangaroo-hide seats. You know, 'outrage' as a prestige thing that was so big right before the Plunge. But him driving ran the risk of you two meeting."

"Kick his ass for him."

"Probably. I haven't had two boys scrapping in the dirt over me since high school, though it'd never do for him to see where you live. I still wish he was here now to drive us home."

'*Us.*' '*Home.*' "Why, where are you now?"

"On your damn porch where I spend half my life these days."

"Jesus, are you? Look, Nicki – seriously, if you run in to some fat doofus in a green suit with one leg shorter than the other, keep going. Fast. He's bad news, real bad news. Don't talk to him, for real. And for God's sake don't tell him we're – that we know each other. He's dangerous."

"I haven't seen anyone like that. And who wears a green suit? I'm sitting here in one of these nasty chairs waiting for these two jerks on the sidewalk to get bored staring at me so I can get out of here. I called the two car services whose numbers I remembered, and they both said there was too much craziness on your block right now."

"Why, what's going on? Aren't there any cops sitting around scratching?"

"Nope. Just some remarkably unfriendly Spanish guys in and out.

Oh, and your landlord, Mr. Stapapoopous. We had quite the conversation. A very subtle, old-world visual undressing."

"Nicki, you're hot, OK? All of Bumfuckville is in a tizzy. I got it. I sorta discovered that myself a long time ago, remember. Jesus – what's gotten in to you?"

"Maybe I just decided to live a little after hibernating so long. So, hey, you're coming in really clear. Did you get a new micro-zap so you can finally get back online? Or is it still that same old dinosaur with no Internet and the fuzzy GPS that leaves you floating out in space?"

"The old one."

"OK. So no accurate GPS. Anyway, Stapapoopous – "

"Just call him Stap like everyone but me does."

"Oh, only *you* can master his name, you who grabs success by the throat and feasts on it? Mr. Poopous and I got to talking after I demanded he take me up to your 'apartment' let's generously call it. You didn't answer either phone, and I really did, you know, want to see you. I mean, I haven't even seen you since you got shot."

"Your concern knows no bounds."

"I didn't know if you were up there worshipping an open stove or what. So I got Poopous – who really is kind of sweet, bringing me an espresso and almost getting me to try one of his nasty little Greek cigarettes – to take me up there. So now you're fleeing all your problems running to DC to do some story for three-hundred bucks?"

"Yeah. No. Just go read Syriac." Jesus, I shouldn't have freaking said that either. "Let's just say I had to leave in a hurry. So, look – walk the other way, you see that guy in the green suit."

"OK, no green suit. But, Mitch, you gotta get some plants up there or a Farah Fawcett poster or something. Living like that, no wonder you're running around messing with the cops, looking to get shot."

"Nick – for the last freaking time: I was walking through Penn Station minding my business when they shot me. That's important, OK, for your next sterling encounter with the jackals of the press."

"So that was all just your idea, right – all that with the searches? Nobody else involved … *feeding* you the concept?"

"What? You know I work alone. What the hell's gotten into you?"

"And our bed. It looks absurd, that big bed crammed into that little room. You can't even put your feet on the other side, all those stupid boxes you have up there. For what? No one's suing you over a story from five years ago."

"*Our* bed? Look, the narrow little bed of nails I ordered is still getting sharpened."

"So … what're you working on going to DC?"

"Nothing."

"Come on, Mitchell, you know I've always supported your work."

"You should remember one of the keys to our former happiness: you're a terrible liar."

"Screw you! Cause of you, I'm off the Army's African-descents – "

"Nicki!"

"That's what the Pentagon calls them now. F&F's big plum, *my* big plum. Plain off it. Not even any behind-the-scenes tweaking the copy."

"I'm sorry. No, I am. What do you want me to say? I never thought I'd get shot refusing a search. Not really."

"So what freaking happened here tonight? Stapapoopous assumed it was 'Mr. Popularity.' Cop cars were screaming up to the bodega from every direction, he doesn't know why."

Where's Stap now?"

"Inside using the john. That's why I'm calling now."

"Did he say anything about any cop getting – *injured*, or a bodega guy?"

"No. For Christ's sake, Mitchell! You get mixed up in any more shit, just tie a rock around your neck and jump off the roof here into the river. So what happened?"

"Nothing. Don't worry about it. Look, just get Mr. Staphilopoulos to give you a ride. He's probably happy to do it."

"Too happy. So, come on, you won't tell your wife what you're working on in Washington?"

"Nope."

"Well, where're you staying? That old dump we stayed in when we were down there playing tourist, the Harrisburg?"

"Yeah, probably. Ah, Nicki" – and damn me if I didn't almost lose it – "those were the days, huh? Hearing your voice, even so pissed off and asking all these weird questions like I don't know what – it's tough."

"Look on the bright side, dude. You're getting out of town, your luck's due for a change. Can't get any worse, right? And the Harrisburg's not so bad. Just bring your own towel."

"Will you stop Goddamn mentioning it. It's not like I need to broadcast where I'm staying, some maniac taking shots at me."

"So the craziness here was you tonight. There's a shock. Some guy was shooting at you – what does he look like? I mean, I'm curious. Plus I gotta make sure I don't run into him. Height, hair color, anything special, any – what do they call it – distinguishing characteristics?"

"What the hell kind of Kool-Aid is in that drink of yours? You haven't even asked me if I'm OK."

"Somebody shooting at my husband, a girl gets curious. But you're OK, right?

"Pretty shook, but OK."

"So can we stop being quite so self-important about this dumb call. Like with all the T out there – supposedly – all the *chatter* anyway, the Minders are wasting an actual live human listening in on you in real time to hear where you're staying in a couple of hours."

"Draw 'em a map, why don't you. Christ!"

"Hey, you there listening! Send a chopper quick to airlift me out of Bumfuckville. Yoo-hoo!"

"You saw the Goddamn *New York Node* yesterday, with details of my calls and e-mail. Or were you too busy yesterday."

"I was busy, thank you. I saw it very early this morning, or heard it, Ernesto reading most of it to me. I couldn't follow it all, he was so mad, but I do know that like *half* was about me. So read *Sy-ri-ac*, huh? That's easy enough to spell, right? That's what you're going down to DC for?"

"What the fuck's this all about, worrying about my micro-zap's messed up GPS and everything? You know how to spell Syriac's name. You're the one who freaking turned me on to him in the first place, *Nicki!*"

"So enjoy the Harrisburg. I mean it's right downtown, right? I – "

I hung up. So they flipped her, must've scared the shit out of her. Or maybe somebody leaned on Ernesto about his big Army account and instructed him to let her keep her precious job if she pumped me for info. God, the way her voice went all cotton-candy: *Aren't you going to tell Wifey-poo why you're going to DC?* Pretty damn surprised I didn't. Because angry, tipsy and dancing me round the floor to who knew whose tune, Nicki still had me rapt tight, though, Lord knows, the rope should've broke a long time ago.

Forget her *and* MoneyBags' damn kangaroo hides. Had I been elevated to RoundUp and its real-time spookery rather than Middling Severity's standard passive harvesting? Screw it – Harrisburg here I came, come what may. Yet another in a string of long, lousy days, digging out another place to sleep in Imperium Central was beyond me – my wallet and all the rest of me too. If they wanted to mess with me, they knew the Hovel's address, and they hadn't yet.

I stared out the window to see an inlet racing towards me, a canoe perched on a dock, a new life washing dishes in some shore town a paddle away. Stop the train! Shave my head and sprout a beard. Was it possible to still disappear in America, start anew in a room over a garage – assuming I could beat out the locals hungry for a subsistence job? Like Maureen said, maybe 'going to ground' was gone. For where was the town with no cameras grabbing eyeballs?

313

Chapter Thirty-Seven

No Blonde in a Red Dress

No way to spot a tail in the crowd or on the Metro, I cast my lot with the Harrisburg of Nicki's antic mention. I'd lumber out from under their net the next morning – sure thing.

My (post-Plunge) fifty-six-dollar room was as I remembered from Nicki and my stay. There was the rod that opened the vent for the air conditioning, whatever temperature management decreed. Threadbare towels – check; lumpy plaster walls – check; no shampoo; old-fashioned walk-in closet with a dime-store mirror hanging on a nail; the riot of miscellaneous hangers; the window shade that recoiled with a snap; the dark, heavy furniture made of real wood; the sagging bed with the nubby, pale pink bedspread; the indifferent TV: all check.

I wrestled the bureau up against the door – laughing somewhere, were you Maureen? – and took out the micro-zap the Wife had turned Judas. Removing the battery achieves all of nothing since, even inert, its homing-device heart still silently beats. The damn thing old and there-fore built to last, I repeatedly slammed the real-wood bureau drawer home on it to no effect. The closet door just scuffed it. My eyes suddenly fuzzy over her betrayal, I went bat-shit, swearing from way down deep. Finally smashing it on the tub, I emerged shaken but victorious from the Battle of the Phone, pieces resting on a carpet mottled with stains, my palm bleeding only slightly. I flushed what I could down the john.

Breathing ragged, I sat and waited for the thump on the door that never came. Screw 'em. Statie got slammed, Frankie's bullet bounced, the papers smeared as much egg on themselves as on me, the MTA's obviously fabricated whole-vid fell flat, Short Leg's only casualty was

Stap's garage window, Carole was on the mend and Turncoat Wife was naught but a cinder growing cool. Sure, I'd nicked myself with Chrysler. But the only one who'd scored a real hit was that damn NYONLY chippie, a *sartorial* hit. The rest of you bastards, get your skank selves behind that buried electronic fence with the Garden City guard dog who struck out the night Statie got stomped. That's right, MoFos, *Can't Touch Me!*

Boy, I was hungry. A cabbie lolling by the entrance had said I'd be lucky to get some over-priced gristle at the one joint open within blocks. Yup, downtown a little after eleven in what was laughably still called the capital of the Free World, God forbid there should be a deli open to get a cheap egg-salad hero.

Stomach grumbling, I fell asleep watching flickering Dodgers (I half expected to wake up to a test pattern on the H-burg TV) taking a lead on the White Sox on a walk, a balk, a squibbler and then a monstrous three-run homer by an emergency call-up second baseman in his sixteenth major league at-bat at age thirty-one.

****

Abroad in the glossy, shuttered downtown at six and no coffee for love nor rue. Why hadn't folks from any number of far-off lands gotten rich fixing that, and why did the locals tolerate it? Only the closest of friends ever wondered aloud how their government had gone so wrong. But last night's proffered plate of gristle and the morning's forced fast made it clear: folks with any sense or standards stayed far, far away.

So, off to meet an undoubtedly beautiful Army major armed with the documents to shift my chestnuts to a much cooler fire. No big black spewer with tinted windows following me at five m.p.h., I cast searching looks at the cab and truck drivers, the porters hosing down the sidewalks, the odd office worker getting an early start, the many homeless just starting to stir from the ledges they'd found for the night. No one looked back but the guy I handed some change. "May the Tail be red," he intoned. Right – fresh from a spanking.

Jeeze, it was hot already. I had to flee *south*? Waiting on a light, a staring, crew-cut man spooked me onto a bus at the last second. Fifteen minutes north and then the subway back, no blonde in a red dress dogged my heels far as I could tell. Can't Touch Me! Strolling with one eye in the back of my head towards Farragut Square, I finally encountered some food, its over-priced drabness (powdered eggs?) mitigated by its skimpiness. That some grinning bozo greeted me with wild enthusiasm at the door and pointed me to the counter five feet ahead did nothing to redeem it.

The eagle-eyed oaf darted into a Metro station, then out a different way. And I finally noticed the American flags everywhere. Leaving the Harrisburg an hour before, I'd been too wigged about spooks to notice them draped over office building doorways and taped to the inside of windows up above, as bunting in store windows, as street furniture on poles at corners, and plastered as ads on the sides of buses, a credit line thanking one of the nation's chief Despoilers.

Such my normally circumscribed haunts, it *was* good to be walking round a far-off town, however thin an excuse for a city. Not allowed to over-awe the Washington Monument, the office buildings marched down K Street in lockstep height of a dozen or so stories, and this New Yorker enjoyed the gray expanse of visible murk overhead. Slices of bread in a stale loaf, many of the buildings echoed the government marble and limestone, with beige, khaki and tan facades amidst the glass and metal skin.

Cripes, that *was* a gun on the hip of the private guard outside that private office building, then another guard packing a half-block on. The Disruption, after all, had started a few miles away in that first food riot in Chevy Chase, of all places. Alright, focus on my meeting with Lois. Keep my eye on the prize – and my hands clearly visible.

Farragut proved a pleasing spot of green surrounded by a bevy of red, white and blue. Almost 7:40, I decided to sit and try to relax rather than running around aping sweaty 'tradecraft.' I grabbed a *New York Node* from one of the many boxes on the corner, intending to check on my progress and, heck, Carole's too, no matter the marbles she'd soon roll my way on *Breakfast Raunch*. But I merely sat in the southeast corner of the park, catty-corner to my assigned, northwest quadrant, the one in DC itself where the white people hang. That's what Lois pretty much said, so what did that say about her? I'd find out soon enough, that and her boss's rank.

The traffic was mild and unhurried – until sirens announced one of the regular caravans of spewers, their lights dancing for the emergency of ushering some muckety-muck to his desk. At one point, three seven-ton camo trucks lumbered to a stop as a bus stalled up ahead. Momentarily mired in traffic, ten soldiers leaped out in vests and helmets and all kinds of unfathomable gear, pointing their M-36s every which way. They scrambled back up only as the trucks were moving. No one but me as much as blinked.

A mess of people – tuna-on-white, extra celery and mayo – headed early to their desks to paper over cracks in the Imperium or siphon money from its maintenance. Most wore two or even three plastic ID badges around their neck. The men, many of them former captains of their homeroom intramural volleyball team, sported short sleeve shirts, baggy slacks and, for some reason, garish ties infantilized with old-school VW Bugs or little hula girls in grass skirts or the like. Perhaps a subconscious comment on their day.

The women tended towards the vaguely appealing in that they were young, clean-scrubbed and healthy, and wore clothes that offered few palpable hints. Echoing the buildings' pale palette, their knee-length dresses featured complicated, concealing bust-lines. They looked like former powers in the French club or debate team, and a vast number were pregnant I soon noticed.

My mind drifted to the Wife's betrayal nattering on endlessly about, "You're sure you're staying at the *Harrisburg*?" When would I stop calling her the Wife? Forget MoneyBags. Her parroting the MoFos' questions in her icky, new, insinuating manner – that settled it. I wrestled off my inscribed band of once cherished gold, symbol of my life's main accomplishment, spit lubricating it painfully over the knuckle, and parked it with the pocket lint.

La-de-fucking-da … the day beckoned, Lois beckoned.

****

I strolled to my assigned sector, passing an entrenched encampment (that was a bookcase full of books) of eight or nine homeless folks right in the middle of this small park surrounded by deluxe office buildings. They were of a piece with the homeless all over the place, visible but unseen and apparently unmolested. Unlike the strident defense of any horizontal surface in Manhattan, the DC ledges and cubbies they slept on were unspiked. Gripped by money and 'policy' and failed conquest and clamping down – and money – the local Deciders and Despoilers' sole contact with the street (unlike in Manhattan, were they *might* conceivably walk a few blocks from office to restaurant) was three steps from spewer back seat to guarded front door.

I felt slick picking a bench commanding a view of anyone approaching from basically anywhere in the park. Three minutes past eight a passerby said, but no sign of her. My major was so damn military-precise, she'd punted our meeting as I was coming up the walk?

Her contralto from behind made me jump.

PART SEVEN

Chapter Thirty-Eight

A Fan Led this Lamb to Slaughter

"Fremson, I told you to display a *Washington Times*, not that even worse garbage. This won't work if you can't manage basic operational coherence regarding a very simple order."

Was I supposed to jump up and salute? I turned in my seat and gaped, not because she was indeed black, but because whatever I'd expected, Lois wasn't it. Her broad, appealing face under short, spiky processed hair was set off well by oblong, almost-green glasses that any gay graphic artist would be proud to wear. Tall – really tall – she was perhaps just starting to benefit from slightly slacking off years of intense physical conditioning. She came around, sat down and, yeah, another damn soldier made this typist wince when we shook.

"You can close your mouth Fremson, or did you not pick up on me preparing you for the shock of a black female officer. Speak up – you're supposed to be good with words."

"I, uh, no – nothing."

"Relax. Since getting moved from Intel to Procurement, professional glad-handers who make a lot more than you get all flustered meeting me." She gave a little laugh. "Alright. You know, it's a shame really, you messed up on Jeep, cause I don't know if H-DM's new Grinder is any better than the one they got chewing our boys up now."

"You hear what happened at Aberdeen?"

"Suppose you tell me."

Yeah, tell the security MoFo – not *unfathomably* gorgeous, but certainly a foxy, formidable woman sent to lure me out. "How about you show me yours first?"

"Watch your tongue, Fremson. I am not in the mood, taking who knows what risk meeting you here. Not that I care all that much anymore. I'm never making lieutenant colonel, not with the pious fakers running the Army like it was a high school clique. I have three short years till my twenty, so let them come after me. Still, do you have any idea if you were followed here?"

"I wasted some time taking a bus north and doubling back by subway. Getting off the bus by myself up where it was pretty empty, I didn't see anyone."

"Hopefully no one from that out of control T-Squad run by a thug named Cummings. If half of what you hear of Cummings' back room is true, it's no wonder most of the DC *cops* are afraid of him. Even if he's not Red Calf, though he's gotta be, a job like that."

"Scared cops. That worked out well for me in Penn Station."

"Maybe it did – for the rest of us. At least your public declarations aren't just hot air, like so many."

"No – right. But how?"

"No government agent lets himself get shot in the head. That's another reason I called you down to DC: you're safe. I actually know where you stand. And you're at least peeking your head up out of the foxhole to see what's going on."

"Isn't that how heads get shot?"

"You're going to die anyway, mister, or didn't you get that memo?

320

A man like you, no kids, right? Act like it's already happened and keep moving."

What the hell did that mean, a man like me and no kids? "I thought I was pulling on my end of the rope OK. It's not like it's crowded, that end of the rope."

"It's not, I'll give you that." She sighed, then looked up with a *very* nice smile. "OK, the clown you came down here to nail, General Parnell Whitaker – "

"Your boss is a general, not just a colonel? That's great, that means our story will bounce higher."

She slowly let out a lot of air. "Nothing *ours* about it, like I told you. You got that, Fremson – your name only on top." Her stare pinning me down, I nodded. "Whitaker is big in this Red Calf crap that's flourishing up and down every corridor of the Pentagon. And I got ahold of a couple of his e-mails to your crook up in New York, Bettinger."

"Your guy and Bettinger – how?"

"Be a good boy and don't interrupt, and maybe I'll tell you why I feel guilty in regard to you and Bettinger. Anyway, yesterday morning Whitaker was bellowing into the phone like usual – like he's six beers into watching football – something about a website called Syriac. Imagine my surprise when I went there, and it turned out to be you on it."

"Why surprised? Cause it involves a nobody like me?"

"Negatory. Because it involves a *somebody* like you – which you need to start acting like and *dressing* like. Anyway, yesterday, Whitaker stormed out like a headless chicken, and I took the risk to root around this private laptop he doesn't even lock in his desk. That's how self-involved and reckless he is."

"Yeah, well – our leaders in spades."

"Thank God it was a private computer, not a superior officer's Army machine, but I found the e-mail where he introduced you to Bettinger."

"Whitaker introduced me? You know, it never made sense how the hell Bettinger got to me. You've got the e-mail?"

She patted her camo shirt pocket with another one of those smiles. "But here's the screwy part: I was the one who introduced Whitaker to you."

"Get out of here."

"It was his doing, really. It was a couple of weeks after I got involuntarily transferred to Procurement, which is as slimy as you might imagine. Transferring sucked, cause after my last Sands, I had a dream job in Intel using my masters from Hopkins – "

"Where you no doubt drank buckets of Fomenting Kool-Aid."

"Big tubs of it sloshing around, which I tried to avoid. Look, so you know where I'm coming from – literally: an Army career wasn't exactly in my plans until I blew my knee out in a pre-season scrimmage against Elizabeth Seton, those proper young prep-school ladies doing us a favor even showing up on the same court as Anacostia High School. That was before I got to play a single damn game my senior year. And that was going to be my year! I already had three scholarships on the table from mid-majors, plus a Missouri assistant coach got *real* friendly after a playoff game junior year where I had 34 points, and the hot-shot I was guarding had six before she fouled out. All that went bye-bye when that Seton pig pushed me under the basket."

"Guard or forward?"

"Shooting guard. Just give me the ball! After that Seton gorilla blind-sided my ACL to smithereens, I didn't like where my life was headed, senior year pretty much a waste, and I'm not just talking about the crutches. So six weeks after barely graduating – me with straight A's the first three years – I was doing push-ups at Fort Jackson."

"The military the only option at hand, huh?"

"My brothers and I grew up solid, my father working for the District. But joining the military wasn't in the cards till that rich white girl wiped out a basketball scholarship. And then the Army put me through undergraduate in dribs and drabs, and then full-time through Hopkins. Now with HeadFuck and way too many

322

Sands, some of us with some sense have to stay in to try to keep the Army from going entirely off the rails."

Head*Fuck* from this officer in uniform. "That's a heavy load."

"Uh-huh. It was getting all Bohica this Spring, when we were massing troops in our little puppet, Kyrgyzstan, so we could menace Kazakhstan."

"And where's Bohica?"

"Nowhere. That's Army for: Bend Over, Here It Comes Again. They had a big natural gas discovery in Kazakhstan, and the Russians were freaking out cause it looked like we were going to invite ourselves in. Create some sort of pretext *again*."

"That would be Sands number what since HeadMan burrowed his way to the top?"

"Five or six depending on how you count. HeadFuck's buddies pay a lot of retired generals to go on TV and fan that confusion. Anyway, it's a *lot* of natural gas. And it came to my Intel shop's attention that a certain Russian blog, supposedly private, but well connected and full of retired officers, was putting out some very sophisticated analysis of our troop deployments in Kyrgyzstan getting ready to go over the border into Kazakhstan. Probably mostly just Russian satellite imaging, but someone was dumping high-quality Intel into this blog called *Asian Sovereignty Alert*."

"Just like the Russians did way back during one of those first Sands, the one in Iraq."

"Right. Iraq II, not Iraq III. Doing historical research, I came across your old article on the real-time Intel the Russians were giving on U.S. tactics and strategy *during* the Iraq II invasion. My lieutenant colonel and I started making noise about the Russians doing the same thing this Spring, pre-invasion of Kazakhstan. And your story was part of the proof."

"Imagine that."

"Open source textual analysis: half the time that's all you need. So my boss and I made some waves – not the first time for that, either – and it rubbed a big bull two-star the wrong way."

"Honor among thieves, huh, him and the Russians?"

"Maybe. Either way, my lieutenant colonel got shipped out to Fort Hood, overseas his next stop, soon as they figure out who needs Fomenting next. I'd just got back home, so, technically, they couldn't order me. But working for Whitaker became my only option, even if I know nothing about Procurement you can't learn in a PX. Five combat tours and a masters in international relations, if the Army wants to waste all that…. Three more years and I'm gone."

"And so, Major, mad at me for obscure reasons of your own, you sicced Whitaker on me?"

Man, she could flash some choppers. "No. Shortly after getting to Procurement, I had your article up on the screen still just kind of wondering if there was anything I could do to help our boys massing on the Kazakhstan border. And Whitaker came up behind me and put his dead-fish hand on my shoulder and bent way too close and asked what I was reading. I scrubbed for a week to get his stain off a uniform that I've worked damn hard to wear, including this major's oak leaf."

"You wear it well. No – Major. I mean, it obviously means a lot to you."

"Uh-huh. I told him if he ever touched me again I'd file charges so fast his desk would spin. That I hadn't slept overseas with a knife in my hand for a total of 66 months – fifteen months twice, fourteen months, twelve and ten – to put up with any part of that Stateside. And surely not from some rear-echelon stooge like him."

"So those stories we hear are true?"

"The mortars, the IEDs, the women in black working their way close to explode – forget all that. The worst was sleeping with that knife. Some women wore adult diapers so they wouldn't have to go pee too late at night. Hot as it was, I'd risk dehydration every night having nothing to drink after 1800-hours."

"That's terrible."

"Affirmative. Anyway, Whitaker started pretending he'd just been bending close to see what I was reading because it didn't look like anything to do with seven-ton axels, and he ordered me to e-mail him your article. I tried to laugh him off, that it was just obvious nonsense that someone had sent around as a joke."

"Now, now, Major."

"But he made clear it was an order. That was months ago. Then yesterday, I heard him bellowing leaving someone a voice-mail, presumably Bettinger, about your Syriac post. Your writing is a little fancy there, don't you think?"

Everyone's a critic. God only knew what Elaine, keeper of the ASPIC documents, thought of it. "It had been a long weekend."

"Maybe that chow you were eating in that Chinese place went to your head." She laughed. "Your little stunt was tactically poor, not to mention dangerous, marching round train stations with a loaded backpack looking to tell off the cops. But from a psy-ops standpoint not so bad."

"Shout it from the rooftops."

"You never know where a Demo might lead, even one that doesn't get off the ground. But, listen: this isn't easy cause I am *not* used to apologizing to civilians." She stopped and worked the gravel with her boot. "But I am truly sorry for the trouble that's found you because I sent shit-magnet Whitaker your article."

"Hey, no one put a gun to my head to go to Indiana." I looked up to see two more very young, very pregnant women walk by dressed all dowdy like the others.

"Isn't New York overrun with post-adolescents dressed all Sunday-go-to-meeting and churning out Christian warriors?"

"Not in my part of Queens. But wait. What kind of insanity is your general capable of? Cause I'm afraid you were right saying I was in danger last night." And I told her about Short Leg.

"That's Whitaker's bag-man for his petty little Red Calf schemes. I didn't know he did wet work too. I hope you hurt him."

"No, just melted away – more my style. What's his name?"

"That I don't know. But in the few minutes I had on Whitaker's laptop, I did find three e-mails: one was him introducing you to Bettinger. Plus another to Bettinger on the foreign content and rollovers he wanted you to focus on at the H-DM plant. And finally, a summary of your phoned-in report that he sent to the Chrysler lobbyist, Pantly, talking about the Indian transmission and hinting at some catastrophe during the Grinder's test at Aberdeen. *Something* happened there that they've managed to keep quiet. It sounds like you did OK for someone who doesn't come from this world. Your hair was shorter then, I guess." And she gave that grin I was really starting to like.

"So how in blazes did you hack Whitaker's e-mail?"

"His wife's dog's name is his password, a name written on the back of a photo on his desk. He was braying over the phone about it in that voice of his to his girlfriend. So what happened at Aberdeen?"

In deep enough, I decided to spill. "Just the SecDef herfreaking-self rolled a Grinder at low speed trying not to hit an orange cone."

"So that's what all the hush-hush was about with that bit about her 'shaving.' Going slow, you're sure? And that's after we cancelled the old H-DM contract – unheard of – because the damn rollovers are causing hundreds of casualties a year."

"Yup, slow."

"So how do you know about the SecDef? My end of Procurement, nobody seems to know, they're holding it so close."

"I've seen a whole-vid of it. Somebody showed it to me."

"Somebody not up in New York. Who had it out in Indiana?"

"A gentleman never tells, Lois. Besides, wouldn't it make more sense that somebody at Aberdeen had it."

After it arrived in my post office box, I'd hidden Everett's whole-vid under the kitchen sink, and, yeah, that'll stymie 'em for entire minutes. Everett barraged my stealth Dutch e-mail address with six or seven increasingly blistering harangues to get the damn thing out. I read them – for five bucks a pop! – on a supposedly Minder-proof, illegal machine behind a curtain in a Bumfuckville laundromat. But I never gave Everett the false hope of a reply.

Awfully damn slick with her sneaky little smiles setting me up to finger Everett. Who the hell had mentioned Aberdeen first, Lois or me? Me, the idiot show-off trying to impress her? Had the Army caught on to me from Everett's end, or was it just pulling on the loose string of my ridiculous Syriac posting, fool that I was?

Whether to help or to knock me further back on my heels, Lois (Abernathy, it said on her shirt, for whatever little that was worth with a potential DoD MoFo) handed me the latest H-DM statement that she'd printed out at home that morning. Its salient guts:

> In accordance with the *Protect-the-Protectors* prohibition on unlicensed visual recordings, U.S. Army T Regs prohibit filming of its personnel, either by standard methods or overtly. However, once T-Irregularities are ruled present – such as a visitor to a H-DM General Readiness facility refusing to fully yield his vehicle – Army Regs encourage any and all imaging short of capturing our Heroes' biometrics.
> H-DM believes it has Whole-Vided™ the German spy entering its facility. The company's security enhancers have bio-densed our Whole-Vid™ in conjunction with the tape issued by New York Protectors regarding this individual who calls himself Mitchell Fremson AKA, as 'Preston Lestwick.'
> The amateurish nature of the New York imaging, however, rules out full Bio-Meshing™. Homeland Control Transport authorities are currently confirming this individual's rental of the vehicle seen here entering our South outer perimeter."

A bemused Lois said, "You know, they don't actually need lights that bright. In fact, their dark glasses cut them by sixty percent. It's just done to disorient the target. Which by the look of you standing there chewing spit, they could've done with a flashlight."

She gave me her most devastating smile yet as I hauled out Bettinger's assignment memo, his firm's logo up top particularly catching her eye. It was an overwrought, mystical hodge-podge with an elaborately spoked wheel, a cross, tongues of fire, six or seven candlesticks, a unicorn springing free from a slathering pack of dogs and an insipid looking baby cow.

"Bettinger doesn't have any of this stuff on his bare-bones web site," she said. "I guess it's just for insiders like you who've earned paper-based communication. It uses some of the same elements as the graffiti that Army bible-thumpers have been painting on walls all over the world. The candlesticks for instance, and this calf here – she's red, by the way."

"That's like the third time you've mentioned a red calf."

"What rock you been living under, you don't know what it takes for the Messiah to stoop to returning to this lousy old world? First off, they have to rebuild the temple on Jerusalem's Temple Mount – the one the Romans destroyed. But the guy driving the excavator can't start digging the foundation until he's been purified with a dab of the ashes of an all-red cow. And though they've been trying for years and years, always a couple of white hairs sprout out somewhere before the cow reaches age three as required. Meanwhile, people who *pretend* to believe this mumbo-jumbo are taking over all over DC."

"No real believers?"

"Some of them, sure. Mostly it's just a fancy way of them iden-tifying who's up for one hand washing the other. But enough background Intel, cause we need to get out of this park, Mitch. Look, first take this ticket to the big Defense-Theft Association – whatever it's called – party tonight up at the top of the Hart Senate office build-ing. Whitaker will be there, and you need to pound home how your fates are linked. How anything happens to you, he's busted."

"A party. Good, it's been a while."

"A party where you'll be *working*, mister. Here's his direct line, though I wouldn't be too eager to call him any more than you have to. He's a snake underneath it all." She wrote and ripped a page from a little notebook. "Basically, do a reporter's bare necessities, and get your story published linking him tight to you. That's the only way Short Leg, or more likely someone a lot worse, doesn't hound you for the rest of your very short life."

"Maybe. But being boat-loads more famous and powerful than me didn't stop G. Gordon Liddy from offering to kill Jack Anderson."

"Liddy I know. They teach him at Hopkins. Never heard of Anderson. You got a better idea for staying left of the Boom? Gonna go to the cops? Move to Fiji? Look, go to the party and tell Whitaker you have him nailed. You have his e-mails, end of story. Tell him you got them at the other end – up in New York."

"I guess I'll spot him from that weird 'S' in his voice when he talks."

"Ah-ha. You did report in by phone. Plus he's not hard to pick out; he'll be one of the few in uniform who look, I don't know, kind of *doughy*."

"This one hell of a shindig tonight?"

"Not for you. Have one drink, two tops – that's an order, Fremson! You occupy the high ground, or so both you and Parnell should come away thinking. You can enjoy yourself without getting drunk like the rest of them, right? You married?"

"You come right down to it, I got an *ex*-wife, I guess. She's gone – moved to Manhattan."

"Un-huh. Tonight there'll be lots of females nodding and grinning their fool heads off and ... you'll see. These booze-fests get pretty raunchy."

"In a Senate office building?"

"Especially in Hart for some reason, crowded with the sort of field-rejects I've spent my whole career avoiding. I don't suppose you brought a suit and tie, or even a sports coat?"

"Lois, I jumped over a fence fleeing an imbecile with a gun. I didn't pack for the trip. Am I going to be able to fit in at all?"

"No. But without a jacket, you'll look like a chicken scratching

329

itself. I've got a fancy one haunting my closet, two actually, and a couple of ties. Left there by someone who got a little too stuck on himself. The sleeves will probably be a little long, but…. Get to my place by 1700-hours. We'll have a fashion show. Plus you'll probably benefit from a hosing down by then."

She wrote and ripped and handed me directions to an address in Southeast. "That's Anacostia. First metro stop on the other side of the river. Paint the right look on your face – you can do that, New York? – and it'll be early enough nobody should mess with you."

I stared at the paper till she laughed. "You look like a recruit I just ordered to go get a can of striped paint. But look, enough of this talk. You've got real work to do, and I've got some seven-ton axels Humpty Dumpty pushed off the wall."

"Humpty Dumpty should kick ass for once, all the King's Horses and all the King's Men lying in a pile instead."

"Maybe someday he will. Someday, Mitchell."

She gave me a look, then rose suddenly and strode off. I hissed, "The e-mails!" She sat back down, slipped some folded papers to the bench by my leg, said "1700-hours," rose and cut fast through the civilians.

Chapter Thirty-Nine

A Great Capital Worthy of its People

She could whip my potatoes anytime. Five combat tours! Though, sad to say, that number had become fairly standard. Could I even conceive of what she's seen and done? *Lois*. Have to ask how she acquired such a white-bread name when we met for our date later. Sure it was a date: we were meeting in the evening at an assigned time and place. Her place. Never mind it was just to borrow a jacket with extra long sleeves. And exactly how humongous was her ex, someone with so many jackets he could afford to mark his territory abandoning not one, but two?

Whitaker's e-mail introducing me to Bettinger was, face it, probably all too accurate. For while he praised me as a dogged reporter – "a plugger" – who could probably handle the dissembling required out in Indiana, he also declared me "small-fry enough to be desperate enough to do it." His second note to Bettinger instructed what to emphasize in Indiana. Last came his boast to the Germans' lobbyist, Pantly: "What one of my most trusted operatives unearthed at Aberdeen makes me tingle. As we'll discuss in person, he represents the sort of flexible insider I've nurtured over my twenty-five year career that might prove invaluable to your shop."

Most trusted. Right. All three e-mail featured his automatic office signature big as life, with its gobbledygook about his rank, unit and internal Pentagon address. Was it just the plain, dumb conviction you're somehow beyond getting caught?

It'd be a short, wire-servicey article – the truth, wrinkle-free and stain-resistant and nailing him but good. I pocketed the three print-outs and flipped open the *NY Node* to find a puff piece on Carole hyping her appearance on *Breakfast Raunch* on the morrow, Wednesday. I threw it down in disgust and vowed it was the last paper I read till I left DC. That's right, boycott their asses. I gave it to a passing homeless guy.

A bus belched by, a single ad on its side amidst the flags: "*T is the threat. Complacency is the accomplice. Silence makes YOU guilty too! Be aware and speak up. Doubt is no one's friend.*" Darn tooting. Doubt and I were motherhumping estranged. Time to find a computer at some informal, local outfit that took cash. Failing that, I vowed not to worry about Whitaker's henchmen alerting on my credit card at some brand-name joint. Yeah, my own plain, dumb conviction: Can't Touch Me!

Three Washington go-get-'em types strolled up, two nodding at the tall one with his hair parted in the middle and particularly fierce glasses. They actually responded to my Hail-and-Deliver, the shortest one with the biggest briefcase pleased as punch to spout the locations of two nearby Unfettered Desks, complete with his hand signals indicating the required left and right turns. But no, he didn't know of any café or mom-and-pop place that might, as I incautiously put it, "be casual about those Regs that some folks get all caught up in renting out computers."

"This is the nation's capital," he said with a start when he realized what I'd asked. He took a step back, hid his briefcase behind him and planted his feet squarely, as if I might rush the three of them. "We go for the tried and true national brands here, B.E.I. An unsanctioned machine – that's barking up the wrong tree, bud." The tall one swore and took to polishing his glasses on a tie featuring frogs morphing M. C. Escher-style into greenbacks. I counted seven credentials around three necks before beating my retreat.

A dude old for his skateboard said, nope, he'd never encountered an "informal net café." Neither did a long-haired lass in one of those old-school peasant blouses that offer so much opaque intrigue, nor a

Rasta man know of such a place. The latter said, "Maybe you find one, you look hard somewhere like Forestville or District Heights over in Maryland. But you need some luck there, looking pale like you do."

Alright, they constituted an offbeat enough sample to decide that a big chain was the only option at hand. Eight bucks, credit card only, for twenty minutes at a Deskless, which I stumbled upon heading to Unfettered Desk.

I willy-nilly punted the day's queue of abuse, opening only Stanley's demand for something for *NO* given the higher server costs I'd caused. Plus a fond note of appreciation for my "efforts at the front lines of patriotism" from Millie the librarian. And Al on an anonymous Dutch-server looking forward to the evening's meeting, his girlfriend (Elaine) onboard. Had to find some safe way to tell him punt that till my return.

Revealing none of my hole cards, I sent off a pointedly vague query to three editors who'd previously ushered my typing to a panting public. Yes, indeed, I'd perpetrated a large boo-boo with Chrysler. But I'd since come into possession of the *documents* to nail the party who'd hired me to spy on H-DM. I just needed to contact this person for his lying response, along with one or two ancillary scoundrels, and we were good to go. My thousand-word *J'accuse, the Retread*, plus the aforementioned evidence, could hit their desk posthaste – by fax.

All three replied with some version of: gee, ain't that interesting, and we'd love to talk about Penn Station as well as subsequent, attendant mysteries, including this little snag with the Hillbilly Grinder. But as to an article under your byline on your peccadilloes out in Indiana, sorry, but the water a bit murky at present, perhaps we should wait to see how (if) it clears. In the meantime, they all wondered if I might sit for an interview; they promised a fair hearing, including discussion of my Fourth Amendment absolutism.

No thanks, schmucks. I dropped down a notch to an outfit I'd read but never graced with my byline. *Off the Warpath* got play –

some – with the right piece, plus they'd actually relish the chance to display a general's dirty undies. Probably pay an entire $200 for a scoop from the man its betters would interview but not publish.

Off the Warpath's Joe Francessa digitally chortled yes to the tune of $250! provided I could swear the e-mails were legit, and I secured some kind of response from Whitaker, no matter how hostile or tangled. Sure, Joe, the e-mails were copacetic; some dame I knew nothing of beyond generous hints of how she filled out a camo uniform had just handed them over. Joe was also amused to hear I was filing by fax; supplying the number, he wrote he'd have to check his machine's paper hadn't turned to dust.

Armed with a publisher's imprimatur, time for some reporting to save my scalp. Time to undress an Army general, confound a big-time, light-weight private spook, and embarrass a lobbyist for the Germans. All from a pay phone, armed with a phone card and buckets of self-inflicted mud. Plus no way for them to call me back, cause I sure wasn't giving up my location to a general who'd already loosed a mad gunman on me.

Leery of confronting Whitaker, I temporized by unplugging the first Deskless computer and cranking out the story's bare bones on a second. Procrastination by writing: a switch. E-mailing myself story drafts for everyone and his brother to read was out, so I bought a cheap, little micro-zip to store it. Sure, they might track down the credit-card powered computer and unearth my work. But, *assuming* – the only way one foot was able to follow the other – I wasn't already in RoundUp's real-time surveillance, quick publication would render that moot.

I put the stamp-sized micro-zip in my wallet (miniaturization-chic having long exceeded its diminishing returns) and decided not to count my cash as I headed out in search of a pay phone. Hell, it was *Whitaker*'s heart I clutched beating weakly in my palm. A truckload of soldiers rolled by, accompanied by three Grinders, two with big guns mounted up top. Clenching from the bottom up, I was again the only pedestrian who gave them a glance.

✳✳✳✳✳✳✳✳✳✳✳✳✳✳✳

"Whitaker speaking."

"General, Mitchell Fremson here. Tell me, how is it possible that an e-mail from you refers to me as 'small fry' and 'desperate,' but that a subsequent e-mail – mere days later to a different recipient – applauds me as one of your 'most trusted operatives?' Frankly, the cognitive dissonance of melding these two wildly disparate characterizations leaves me reeling and uncertain how to categorize them in print."

"What? What e-mails? That's ridiculous, Fremson." Ah, there was my boy's little half-whistle on his 'S's. "I'm sure I did call you small fry and desperate. That e-mail proved an excellent judge of character, I'd say. As for the other I'd have to check my records."

"Thanks, Parnell. That's damn white of you to confirm sending that e-mail," I said, scribbling furiously.

"Wait a minute."

I did.

"Quit your damn fancy talk and tell me how someone like you has this secure Pentagon number."

"Doesn't Bettinger call it regularly. Remember, I've worked for him. It's not like you two are seeing eye to eye at the moment." Nothing like spreading a little chaff.

"Bettinger! I doubt it. But rest certain I'll ask him if he ever answers his phone."

"Yeah, he's running scared too – or trying to. He was foolish enough to send me a fax on his letterhead with your instructions for my trip to Indiana. And you, Parnell, are knee-deep in rapidly drying cement since I'm in possession of three very trenchant e-mails, from you, re me. All, astoundingly enough, featuring your automatic office signature, all emanating from Pentagon room number 3D877. Seems like I've got all the evidence I need, so let's talk motive. Was it all about getting a big-bucks job with the Germans to keep your slick little mistress all comfy in baubles and beads?"

"*Baubles*? I'm a very busy man, Fremson. Do you have any idea how many Fomenting Campaigns we're involved in right now – four or five, I think it is, when you add the imminent to the on-going. And the T, of course. We'll have to speak again in an hour. What number do I reach you at? Perhaps we can work something out, something advantageous to us both."

"Sure, Parnell. Always happy to talk – advantageously. But make it an hour-and-a-half. *I'll* call you. And no Short Leg, got that?"

"Who? Oh, him. I believe he's being detained up in New York. Some little unpleasantness that won't keep him long."

"*Unpleasant* – my ass! The two of us are joined at the hip, Whitaker, so your threatening me is over! Not with the letters I've mailed to three editors, the envelope to be opened only should anything happen to me."

"Believe it or not, Fremson, I actually am busy. So, 11:30. I'll see if I can clear five minutes to deal with you properly. Anything else?"

"Nope."

I then told Pantly's secretary I had an e-mail addressed to him from an Army general offering inside connections. Dripping venom, she said he was "in conference for the balance of the day."

And I promised Bettinger's voice-mail I'd e-mail a couple of questions for an imminent story he'd find of interest. I could hope for his denial if he was foolish enough to lie, then blow it out of the water with his memo and Whitaker's e-mails.

Having tooled around the same area way too long, past time to decamp. Ah, a rare teenager in that corporate/homeless enclave, one happy to help. "Dude, you in luck talking to me. I go to this place – *legit*, man – down Near-East. Down by that half-built baseball stadium that got Plunged. The joint has everything, dude: old-school phone cards, rent-a-computers, race-neutral condoms – shit, maybe even a whole-vid micro-zap, Minders Turn Elsewhere."

"Screw the Minders." He pretty much fled at that, but not before telling me about Connexions, on the corner of First and N Streets SE.

Chapter Forty

Making Connexions

Dodgy, down-market Southeast did not entice, not with its garages and cab companies, smoky power plant, shuttered businesses and, of course, the shells of a couple of partially built, pre-Plunge condos.

Connexions proved a long, low, listing affair that might've started life as a machine shop. The bright sign over the battered wooden door featured a riotously laughing black man in a top hat framed by a red, black and green rainbow. Its one sprawling room was littered with floor lamps resting on worn oriental rugs. A long maroon couch anchored one wall, and beat-up armchairs were scattered about. Three computers sat on tables by the wall opposite the couch. A teenager sat before a big screen noisy with slaughter.

A small Subcontinent guy well used by life raised his gaze reluctantly from his book resting on a dusty glass case displaying novelty beer mugs and old board games. Another case held stacks of magazines, a presumably fake gorilla's head, and an assortment of shrink-wrapped sneakers. Behind him hung a splayed snakeskin tacked to a framed piece of red velvet.

He held up his book. "A history of your civil war. Your fields ran red not so long ago, and yet America, that *exceptional* nation, instructs us all. Good morning. You may call me Zafar."

The machines were seven bucks an hour, cash only, not the Deskless's $24. A great price and no credit-card trail. Break free of your chains, folks, buy local, Minders Go Hump Yourselves! Plus he even had a working fax machine.

I e-mailed Bettinger some straightforward questions about Whitaker and their e-mails, plus one self-indulgence: "Why did you insist on faxing me your advisory memo on my H-DM trip, a document that features your logo, letterhead and signature? Did conscience prick, and you wanted to get caught? Or are you just sloppy?"

I hit send and walked through the story's draft I'd just written, clarifying and curlicuing, adding some atmospherics about the fatuous speeches out in Indiana. Oops! Gotta know when to stop stringing words together – discipline, man! Otherwise no one will read the damn thing. Besides, it was time to go drape a noose round Whitaker's neck and tie the other end round my waist, Lois's route to Left of the Boom.

****

Zafar directed me to a pay phone around the corner "in front of the candy store that sells few candies." Past an empty lot's banner-crop of broken bricks, smashed bottles, crushed cans, old tires and a dishwasher with its door open and dishes still inside, I found Jaimo's Candy and Notions. The two big windows shuttered, a few hard-worn men and women flitted through the smeared glass door. They were of all ages, but one body type: skinny. The phone was plastered with fliers offering "Down-Home Meals from 3 to ten, Friday, Sat & the Lords' Day, $4.95 complete, corn bread too." Using it meant pale, overdressed me standing with my back to all that Jaimo's traffic.

"Whitaker speaking."

"So General, I guess we never discussed those e-mails I have, two from you to Bettinger and one to Pantley, all three involving my trip to Indiana on your behalf."

"Wait a minute, Fremson. I am *not* hanging up on you." His phone disengaged in an odd way without hanging up. Fine, let him record the call, that'd keep me on my toes.

"Got your recorder going," I said when he came back. "Well, I got mine, too. It's called a pen."

"Fremson, in a world with T raining down left and right, do you have any idea the level on which the upper echelons of the United States Army operate? Levels far, far beyond someone like you. For instance, why would Bettinger have faxed you instructions if not for your small role in a very sophisticated, on-going check on vendor security. We had reason to pick you."

"And what – what was that reason?"

"A varied body of work combined with obviously flexible standards."

"Right. Tell it to the Marines."

"The Marines! What the hell do they have to do with this? They are strictly back-seat, mister, this allocation cycle. You got that?"

"That's a – never mind. So now you're telling me, out of all the Army's vast security-MoFo apparatus, there wasn't a single soul you could grab to whistle past the H-DM gate? Not one? Far better to trust this 'sophisticated' operation to someone you didn't know from Adam."

"It was thought best if the H-DM people googled you, they'd come up with some published writing."

"Except I didn't give them my real name, you dolt. And if I had, they'd come up with just the sort of hobble-the-empire writing guaranteed to put a defense contractor at ease."

"Fremson, I – "

"So you presented me to Bettinger, who sicced me on H-DM. Which raises the question of why this *sophisticated*, U. S. Army operation involved Bettinger in the first place. You like mustard on your Swiss cheese, General? Cause everything you say is full of holes."

"Bettinger, now he's a ...."

We plowed through some silence. Then, "He's a what? Hard to say, isn't it. But let's talk about you, General, and those three e-mails you sent. You should know they're going to appear in print immediately, me and you holding hands, draped in infamy. One single hair on my head gets mussed, and the authorities are knocking on your door."

"*Authorities*? What authorities is that marching into the HeadMan's Pentagon? Who's cutting that order, maggot?"

My turn to let my mind race and tongue rest. Finally, "Those e-mails, they supposed to be part of that same 'sting,' Parnell? The one that had you all set to report in to the Germans fifteen minutes after H-DM's product launch?"

"The proper form of address is General Whitaker, Fremson."

"And my proper form is *Mister* Fremson. Or do you try to avoid words with 'S' in them? You know you're going to sound awfully funny on the tape I've got of you soiling your fatigues when I told you about the Grinder's Indian transmission and the SecDef rolling the damn thing on its side." Two could lie as well as one.

"Release that tape and – the Calf help me – see how long you last."

"Just remember those letters to three nationally prominent editor buddies of mine nailing you if anything happens to me." Not that I knew any editors I could really trust except new pal Joe Francessa (hopefully) and, oddly enough, maybe Stan the Man.

"A *letter*. If you were serious, you'd have rented time in an authorized whole-vid parlor."

"Screw that – I'm a print dinosaur, a wordsmith."

"Mailed from Washington, I bet."

"You got the manpower to intercept mail throughout the entire District? Sure you do. That's why you sent a clown like Short Leg up to New York."

"He was itching to go for his own reasons as much as I sent him."

"Right on, General, cause you just admitted to being in league with a failed assassin."

"No such thing and you know it. Fremson, I – "

"You nothing, Parnell! Now – "

Feeling them, I turned to the three guys glaring at me. One said,

"Yo, that's my motherfucking phone, unless you be wanting six more band-aids on your head."

Scrawny, but three of them and entirely their turf ... screw it and screw Nicki too, harping on the Harrisburg. "Looks like a public pay phone to me, gentlemen," I said and gave them my back, come what might.

"Alright, General, let's wrap this up. There wasn't a single soldier you could spare for a day-trip to Indiana, so you plucked me out of the blue to do my part for the Fomenting by testing H-DM's security. Bettinger was involved because, well, he needed the money let's say, and you dated his sister back in college. And you needed a phoned report immediately following H-DM's dog-and-pony because, well, that's the type of take-charge dude you are. Right. You stick to that steaming pile of nonsense, I'll write the truth, staple it to your e-mails, and we'll see who the public lines up behind. Not that it matters, because *my* health and *your* freedom are linked – at the hip! No more Short Legs and no slipping and hitting my head in the shower. Got that, Parnell?"

"You're delusional, Fremson. I didn't even know Bettinger had a sister, let alone dated her in college. Now get this and get it good: the people I am piously aligned with have resources beyond – "

"Yo, Shorts-Man! Your phone call be finished one way or the other." I turned to see a fourth guy, scarier than the others and making meaningful gestures with his hand in his waistband under his shirt. I nodded my compliance.

"Look for the story tomorrow, Parnell. Bye."

"Tomorrow, you say? I – "

I hung up, realizing too late how dangerous it was to let him know he had the rest of the day to play with, and shouldered my way past the four of them. Damn it, checking in with Pantly a second time would have to wait, since it didn't seem like I was using their office phone again. That done, I could fax the fool thing off to *Off the Warpath*, Bettinger no doubt remaining silent.

342

Too bad the kid who'd been slaughtering space-cats who look like Hitler was gone, cause he might have shielded my screen from the big lunk ensconced at one of Connexions' machines. The way he was two-finger pounding the piece-of-fluff keyboard (pounding his default mode by the look of him), I hoped Zafar had a replacement lying around. Though in jeans and tee shirt, from the crew cut up top to the boots down below and all the chiseled slabs of beef in between, everything about him hollered hooah! Damn, Whitaker was lightning-quick tracking me at that phone booth cause bingo! – a Boot on the ground. (Wasn't like there were any other shops nearby renting out computer time.) Of course that explained his odd little machination at the start of our call, not recording it as I'd foolishly thought. Forget getting quoted correctly, Whitaker was gonna ensure our little chat and especially his e-mails never saw print at all.

I sat down next to a grin from a tanned open face not particularly marred by an undulating nose. I nodded hello and – heck with it – micro-zipped my story up on my screen to insert Whitaker's lies.

"Nothing like a nice clean, no-tell-motel kind of computer to keep up with your buddies," he said.

"Unlike the ones where they get your DNA first."

"Riki-tik, friend." He looked me over, then said, "Let JSOC prove it was me using the Dutch e-mail. Cause this boy is gonna find out if his squad's got any casualties. And nothing but the crotch-rot Swanson was born with."

JSOC – Joint Special Operations Command – damn! "Glad to hear about the no casualties. We certainly appreciate your service."

"*We*? Oh, you mean all them people going shopping. How about you send my wife a case of peanut butter instead. We got two boys gonna be bigger than me sometime next month the way them ingrates are scarfing it down. Or maybe just put a *magnet* yellow ribbon on your car bumper cause a bumper sticker would be too big a commitment."

"So you don't care if they catch you e-mailing?"

"Do I look like I give a shit, my college-boy lieutenant e-mailing frat bunnies all over North Carolina, sending 'em *pictures* of himself standing with his shirt off in front of our fire base, for fuck's sake."

"He's not worried about the pictures going viral?"

"We're hanging it way over the line on a daily basis, people's heads – enemies and friendlies – like pumpkins sitting on a fence. So a pissant order from some numb-nuts in Florida who gets to change his socks every morning ain't gonna stop you from checking up on your wife or girlfriend – or both." He grinned again.

"You got both, I'd bet."

"Me? Boy, we be nothing but ghosts where I been, hush-hush up the ass. So any vows this side of the ocean don't carry no weight over there. But we kill enough of 'em, then buy off the rest, get somebody running things who's got his mind right, we won't even need an official Sands." This tumbled out in a syrupy, good-old-boy rush.

"That'd be good, cause we got how many Sands going right now?"

"Three official, two probably never gonna be official, where we're using proxies and mercenaries – the only difference being the proxies' color and the mercenaries' pay. And I don't know how many hush-hush jobs to prop things up like the one I was in for 140 days and would still be there except for the wrong damn NATO field-reject."

"Yeah, what happened?"

"Army says I got the yips from pulling the trigger too much. Like a little shooting is gonna ruin my sleep. Ain't nothing but politics – international relations – them saying I need to calm my ass down. That NATO scum-sucker I walked away from after he pulled his weapon on me, he's *calm*, you got that shit right. They're saying how I could've killed him. Like if I wanted him dead he wouldn't be stiff right now."

Him getting excited, I said, "Hey, my name's, uhm, Nick."

He smirked. "OK, uhm-Nick. How about you call me Mac. So what boogalooed your ass down to the shady side?"

So, brass-tacks time instead of the nonsense he was spinning to soften me up. "Trying to get some stuff out, down here off the beaten track where nobody'd bother me."

"I hear that."

"And you don't worry about the Minders messing with you for e-mailing your squad?"

He met my inquiring look. "The hidden tip of the spear, man! All the HeadFuck water we're carrying, snake-eaters do not waste their time worrying about the shit Homelanders got to worry about."

Jesus H., no wonder. Cause, I finally noticed, the whites of his eyes encircled his irises 360-degrees. Like the thin circle of sun all the way around during a solar eclipse. Looking permanently fierce and alarmed since birth and, voila, a stone-killer Whitaker sent to Connexions to attend to a little spot of bother on the side. Damn, I had to tip Whitaker to my location, *had* to do my job right calling him though I'd probably never write for even a supermarket shopper ever again. Hopefully Mac wouldn't mess with Zafar too, listening avidly as he pretended to read. "Lucky you, dude," I said and turned back to my screen. Make him blindside me.

My scrawled notes held up, and I plugged in Whitaker's crap. Good that it was wire-servicey, cause waiting for Mac – pounding away there at arm's length – to make his move didn't exactly facilitate my usual chaste web of prose.

I hit print before it dawned I had no idea if Zafar had a printer, but a dinosaur of an ink-jet began chugging away over by his display cases. I thought about grabbing it and gone, but, Deskless faxless, where else to find a fax before Mac rendered me room temperature? Zafar made it moot, saying, "I see you have printed – ah, only two pages single-spaced. They're on the house. Now for a fax, which no one has asked for in many a moon."

I smoothed out the e-mails and Bettinger's memo on the display case and gave him *Warpath*'s fax number.

"Doing business way down in Near-East DC, I am able to shrug off most official burdens – Minders Turn Elsewhere!" Zafar said with a smile. "It took but a short time after purchasing Connexions from Mr. Howard's widow to appreciate the local advantages. But, since this fax machine is still registered, I *think*, may I glance at your material? Homeland Control Regs, you know."

I hesitated, but hell, getting it out to the world was the whole point. Zafar recoiled after studying Whitaker's e-mails with their bold heading: "For Official Use by Authorized U.S. Army Personnel Only" and his auto-signature at the bottom. "You are into it deep, faxing private U.S. Army e-mails from a *general*!"

"Could you please shush!" I said, indicating Mac with my finger pointing back through my chest.

"Him? He is no worry. This is his fourth time here – nothing to do with you. We see much worse than him in my country."

I turned to see Mac lounging back in his chair, his hands laced behind his head. He stood up. Bigger than me where it counted, younger, someone who turned heads to jelly! He ambled up and said, "Most business this guy's had in weeks, at least the times I've been here."

He turned to perusing the dusty display cases as Zafir said OK, he'd fax my stuff – just this once. With a shrug, he added, "I'll plead the rigors of age and just say I forgot to review them."

I thanked him and handed over a twenty rather than the ten-spot I'd been holding, and sat back down to scroll through the day's abuse to confirm that Bettinger remained his usual silent self.

A tall, skinny, almost albino-looking guy dressed in fatigues burst through the door. His small eyes set in a pale, squinty face, there was nothing washed-out about his intent. I logged off before he was on me, but couldn't pull the plug. No talk, no shilly-shallying, he grabbed my wrist and sore shoulder and hissed, "Get up! Playtime's over. You're coming with me!"

I made myself heavy in the chair and flailed away as Mac rushed up. Two of them, Christ, time's up. I looked to Zafar, and he held the faxes up and signaled OK. Why in the world had Mac let all that sail through to *Off the Warpath*?

Jabbing my attacker sideways in the knee as he dragged me up got a grunt but no more. No matter, cause he never saw Mac grown huge, his face a snarl. Mac hit him in the neck, and down he went neat and clean, Mac catching his head before it hit. He groaned and started to rise, but Mac did something I didn't quite catch, and he slumped down and stayed there.

"Jesus, did you kill him?"

"Fuck no. For what? Cause you owe him thirty dollars for bending over his wife? You've never come close to killing anyone, so trust me: you better have a reason – or an officer to hang it on. Let's go."

"Where? What? I mean, where?"

"Out of here. Or do you want to be here when Twinkie wakes up? He's not gonna be any too happy, and you weren't exactly kicking ass before he got mad."

"I don't – "

He grabbed me by the arm, but I shook him off. "I'm tired of you people putting hands on me, damn it!"

"I just assaulted an officer in uniform. So you ain't got much to say about what happens next." He looked down. "Shit – you see this rear-echelon motherhunchie's tattoo?" He pointed to a red animal of some sort on Twinkie's forearm. "Probably some numb-nuts Academy-boy. They're big-time Calfers. That means *double* you're coming with me, cause I am not leaving you wandering around out here to tell the Calfers about the guy who saved your ass. Vamos, got it?"

More Red Calf shit. So, leave with my ostensible savior? Would

Mac really have caught the guy's head like that if they weren't on the same team? He reached under the table and yanked the electric cords to his and my machines, rose, pulled some bills out of his jeans, and in two strides was at Zafar's counter.

"Sorry about unplugging the machines, friend. I hope this takes care of that – and Sleeping Beauty there." He threw the money down and picked up my papers sight unseen. "He won't be out long, so your best bet is call 911 and say he fainted. Don't worry, *you're* not the issue. Let's go, tough guy, no fooling." He pushed my work at me and then pushed me out the door.

Chapter Forty-One

Home on the Home Front

We jogged two blocks to a tall pickup with a workmanlike gleam inside and out. I made the compass and the radar detector, but the four or five extra gizmos mounted here and there eluded me. My craven ass having just been saved by another damn soldier, I didn't feel like small talk about his toys. Mac grabbed a "CAT Machine" baseball cap to shield his face from light-pole cameras and tossed me a grimy brown one smeared with the name of some unpronounceable cattle drug.

He drove hard, more intent on his mirrors than the windshield. Finally encountering a red light at an intersection too busy to run, he pounded the steering wheel and give a whoop. "First action in weeks!" He punched a button, and some twangy, pained country singer started up loud about "*I'm too damn tired for how hard it is to fix you anymore.*"

"I'm glad you enjoyed it," I yelled. "No, I mean, thanks a million, man."

"No problemo. Anyone sending out a general's e-mail, I got their back. That is some deep shit. So you a blackmailer or just some reporter?"

"A reporter. Doing a corruption story about – "

"Shut it! If it affects me or my squad, I'll hear about it when they cut my orders. Otherwise, who cares. Either way, I got deniability."

"Okay. So where we going?"

"We're getting the hell off the streets – that means both of us – until Twinkie back there wakes up enough to get back wherever he came from. Me, I ain't worried. If he had back-up, they would've jumped in. Plus he's not calling any kind of cop, I don't think. As to you, we're gonna hang out long enough for me to assess your threat-status and you to forget you ever met me."

"So where we going?"

"My house."

"You *live* around here?"

"Sure, my crib. Do a little relaxing."

Great. What, this guy wanted his pound of flesh for saving my bacon? We drove past a giant, half-completed shell, which Mac took great pleasure in pointing out as the Washington Nationals' attempt at a new stadium before that all went to hash, and they stayed in that old dishpan on the other side of town, (the former) RFK Memorial. The new one had been delayed by defective concrete, a big scandal when a ramp failed during construction, killing three workers and exposing a bribed inspector. That delayed it a year, and the Plunge did the rest.

We crossed over into Southwest, which featured run-down residential blocks sprinkled among various shed-like little businesses whose best days were long gone. Down on First and R, down by where you fall off the edge of the world into the Anacostia River, he steamed to a stop by a surprisingly ramshackle little ranch house whose shabbiness didn't match his or his pickup's crisp air. Burying his face in his chest under his hat, he strode through the wreck of a yard and waved his hand behind him to lock a truck which didn't beep back.

We kicked through the dust by the side of the house, but kept going rather than turning towards a back door reached by a couple of stacked cinderblocks. He warned of dog shit in the baked swamp of naked dirt. On cue, a large, sloppy mutt stirred himself from the hole he'd dug under the yard's one tree and came up snapping and growling till Mac snarled and raised his hand. We passed through some bare bushes into a neat backyard with grass and flowers and then through a bright red back door.

Inside the sunny yellow kitchen I was surprised by the framed portraits of Malcolm and Martin; in the living room Martin and JFK hung amidst the chintz. A big, flat-screen TV was over in a corner, its giant packing box in the corner opposite. I drank in the red-roses couch encased in plastic, the blinding yellow carpet, the dried flowers overflowing a vase on the table, the Beatrix Potter bunnies here, the coffee-table antiques books there and looked at Mac and his muscles and laughed and said, "I'm sorry. But all this crap isn't exactly what I expected."

"It's not my house, shit-brains. Look here."

Deep red curtains blanketing the living room windows, he pulled one slightly ajar. Across the street, a long expanse of weathered brick wall stretched out of sight in both directions. A little to our left, the two halves of a hurricane-fence gate were so askew, anyone could have crawled underneath. Beyond lay an expanse of tall scrubby weeds. I said, "What's that, an old TB hospital they've closed down?"

"You'd never know it from here, but that's Fort McNair, home to the Capital Region Homeland Defense Battalion. Twenty-three-hundred grunts sitting on their asses waiting to lock down a rebellion. The Army should move them up to Baltimore, the shit going down up there, packs of dogs gone feral roaming the streets. But HeadFuck wants them here. Wonder what he knows he ain't saying. Anyway, the best way to stay out of sight is right under the Army's nose."

"What're you, AWOL?"

He was on me quick, grabbing a fistful of the shirt I needed to wear that night to confront Whitaker. "Do I look like somebody who'd go AWOL, the men I'm supposed to be getting home safe getting shot at four times a week? That the kind of staff sergeant I look like to you, you sonofabitch?"

"No, of course not. It's just I…."

"Just you what?"

Doing nothing for my nerves, he did a quick frisk, released me and stared his weird stare, then went over to the couch and started fiddling with something in a drawer in the coffee table. "You a drop-kick dog, dude? One of them dogs going through life getting punted into one wall after another?"

Was I? An interesting question I normally eschewed, I shook my head.

"Un-huh. Somebody who likes to hitchhike with a piano? There's a brother in my squad in-country – where I'd fucking be right now if the Army had any balls. This is his momma's house. For twelve-hundred bucks for the time I got to report to Walter Reed three days a week, she figured she could go live with her sister."

"What's happening at Walter Reed?"

"You know what PTSD is, that the shit-for-brains newspapers are always yelling about whenever a soldier punches a door or has a DWI. You know what it stands for?"

I nodded.

"Wrong! It stands for Pussies and Titty-Sucking Douchebags. The whole damn deal was cause of this college-boy lieutenant, not mine, but this asshole from The Citadel – fuck him very much – walking way out of his way to tell me about needing to shave if you can fucking believe it. Me with thirteen years in to his thirteen months, and us *deep* in-country and my 'beard' like a week old."

He stopped a second and stared hard. "One of our own had got dusted the day before and, basically, I had asshole's shirt up over his head and his hands behind his back before he could spit."

"But you didn't hurt him?"

"Only a little. If he was a Red Calfer, I'd be sitting in a cell right now. Then there was wiping the floor with that NATO dick who took his side-arm out at the wrong party. So now I'm sitting around singing Campfire-Girl songs to calm my ass down so I can go back and shoot Fiends – the same ones we'll be 'mentoring' a month later, after we buy off the long-beard running their tribe."

"Asymetric warfare, huh?"

"Look, America's not at war. America's at the mall, feeling for the money that used to be in our pockets. That's what, almost 340-million of you to get your ass kicked or to fuck a soldier on a Saturday night, depending."

"And pay the tab."

"And you're paying your tab for Twinkie back there by being amusing. Got that? While I relax. Then, a step up from you Homelanders, you got Air Force, Navy, Cub Scouts – that shit. The Marines, whatever. Then you get your roll-around-in-the-mud regular grunt, good and bad both, even all the foreigners wearing my flag on their shoulder. Finally, up top, there's the little slice of men that do what I do, the snake-eating tip of the motherfucking spear."

"Special Ops."

"Even the dumb-ass Army knows we gotta get regular maintenance. Years back, we'd get a short hop to Greece or Spain or someplace to raise some hell. Shit, had me one of my best times ever in Crete – if you ever heard of that. Everything, and I'm talking *everything*, was dirt-cheap in Crete. But now, that's too 'dangerous,' American personnel on everybody's shit-list with HeadFuck making friends all over the map."

"You think he's more hated here or overseas?"

"Both. For a supposed to be 'caretaker' president, HeadFuck's dug his self in pretty damn deep. Anyway, instead of sitting with German broads going topless on a beach in Majorca, I'm at Walter Reed talking about my *feelings* since the Army says it's got too much invested in an experienced Special Ops staff sergeant to flush me down the toilet. The Goddamn psychologist, a civilian who couldn't find his ass in the dark with both hands, says I gotta talk out my *issues*. And here you are, motherhunchie – to talk."

Get talked at, more like it. "So you came to the hood to chill."

"I had to get that one homie's mind right, the one down the block wanted to know why I'd kicked Boo-Right's Momma out. Like he ain't been scaring her white for years. Boo-Right was just like him.

Then, two months in my squad, and he was riki-tik A-OK. Especially the time he basically saved all twelve of us when they were shaving our monkey good in We're-Fuckedistan. We put him up for a Bronze Star, until that butt-fuck colonel blocked it, saying his first Bronze Star in a Sands that big was going to a Calfer."

"So all the Sands we got going, the Army's taking all comers now?"

"Look, the Plunge means most of the grunts we do take got their shit tied down tight. But every recruiter's still got a bottle of urine-flush to wipe the weed away. Or the kid's got some kind of legal trouble. Or they're White Power, in it for the weapons training. The skinheads are OK, you get their attention. But they get all embarrassed and secret and stuff, you catch 'em in a group talking their 'Blood and Earth' shit."

"They play nice with all the foreign grunts?"

"Negatory. But that's another joke. Two deployments back, I was helping babysit some regular Army in a jacked-up sector of We're-Fuckedistan. And I needed a translator to re-give the order I was giving to a kid with an American flag on his arm. You believe that? That's about as fubared as them Navy cocksuckers figuring out if an engine or something is broke by throwing it overboard. If it floats, it ain't broke. What the hell you grinning at?"

"What you said – about the Navy. Sorry, it took me a minute."

"The whole company was half-foreign – Guatemala, Philippines, you name it – one hell of a mix with all the hillbillies like me. Some company down the road had a Goddamn Russian wearing our flag. They kick ass, some of the foreigners, once you got 'em pointed in the right direction, but shit."

"And they're the ones that are always on-point."

"Damn right. You gotta be lucky, and you got to be good to end up with USA stamped on your ass. Unless it's posthumous, which just means paying off the grunt's kids growing up eating tacos somewhere. Give 'em that, shit yeah, growing up with no daddy. It's only money. The same money my two are gonna burn through, the way things are going. At least they're mostly growed, the thirteen-year-old anyway – so the motherhunchie likes to think."

"So where's your wife and kids live?"

"Away. Out in the country three hours from here. We're pretending the gas three times a week to Walter Reed and back cost too much. But fuck it, I left. Had to or I was gonna kill the big one: little, uh, Mac, Jr."

"Thirteen's a tough age. I mean, I would imagine."

"How'd I know your sorry ass ain't reproduced itself? Anyway, he's into death metal, so he'll fit right in the regular Army till he gets his head blowed off when it's his turn. Only by then he'll be fighting over water."

"Gotta fill them plastic bottles, man."

"He better have his mother signed up for the Army death benefit and not some twenty-year-old gash telling him her third baby is his. Problem is, I been away so much, he's got hair down to his ass now, and his mother says that's his *prerogative*. Like you give it a fancy name, that means it's OK."

"The right obfuscation covers up a lot in this country."

"*Clever* – not too clever. But let the kid go queer with that hair. Like I give a shit. Right before I left, what set the fuse, he comes down one Saturday morning with a candy-ass *bracelet* on, and that is where I drew the motherfucking line. He tried telling me I should like it. That it's a warrior thing."

"What'd you do?"

"What you think – I took it off him. He was a strong little motherhunchie, stronger than I would've thought. So that's something. Plus we were out in the backyard, so the only thing got broke was her damn rose bushes. Plus the beer bottle he broke and came after me with. Give him credit for that. Even with having to pay Boo-Right's Momma rent, my wife said I needed to get away, do some thinking about what's important to me."

Mac looking ready to snap something in half, I tried to switch gears. "So what is important to you?"

"It sure ain't the fucking extra life insurance she was on my ass to get, saying the Army death benefit isn't enough to feed them two ingrates on. I needed her to co-sign a pipsqueak sixteen-grand loan to buy a new truck. That one around the corner is eight-years old even if it doesn't look it cause I'm never home long enough to put any miles on it. I tried to tell her buying a new one was as good as life insurance, she could just sell it when my time came."

"Come on, Mac. You're indestructible, you know that. You're gonna end up sitting in a rocking chair with your knees hurting, trying to remember where you put your teeth."

"She thinks with me being away so much, she's calling her own tune now. But I showed her ass. Took my re-enlistment cash that I was gonna buy the new truck with. I had it all picked out, color and everything, and would've locked that money away sitting on rubber in the driveway. But, no, she wouldn't co-sign that itty-bitty loan. So, fuck her, that money ended up here with me, what's left of it, anyway."

"Whadiya mean, what's left?"

"Don't forget my present to Boo-Right's Momma." He pointed to the new TV. "No way I was up here for weeks watching her little toaster oven. Not that there's anything on to give a shit about. Fake laughing, fake explosions, fake tits – it all goes blank, the shit I've seen. Baseball once in a while. I like how the manager has to get up out of the dugout to go talk to the pitcher, not the other way round."

"Who you root for?"

"Been gone so much, I kinda lost touch. The Indians, probably, before they moved down to, where'd they go after the Disruption – Knoxville? Whoever's winning, I guess. I gotta pee."

I fought the sheer nervous impulse to walk around the room and look at Momma's tchotchkes. He came back and started messing again with something in the drawer in the coffee table. Eventually he looked up and said, "Till our day comes, yo, we do got to amuse ourselves. And guess what, I found something here, right here on Boo-Right's Momma's block, helps power-up all that important-type thinking my wife's so worried about."

He pulled something half-way out of the drawer and stopped. "If you and Twinkie back there are setting me up cause I got sloppy e-mailing too many times from Connexions, then you, mother-hunchie, are the most squirrel-nuts JSOC investigator ever been born. Or you're just damn good with this little doofus act of yours. Either way, you got no weapon on you."

Chapter Forty-Two

Twisted Mac Tries Crack to Relax

And Mac brought out a little glass pipe along with a plastic lighter and lit up and sat back, holding in smoke with a rictus grin. He exhaled, not that much came out, reached into the drawer for another few pebbles for his bowl and made them disappear. Crack. That'll calm him down. It had loosened his tongue, that's for damn sure.

"Unless you personally been under fire, I am taking no motherfucking looks from the likes of you."

"Hey, knock yourself out."

"We got six-hundred-and-twelve Special Ops wrapping up that gas pipeline dust-up I was in. The one they say ain't worth shipping me back for. It gets blown up into an official Sands, time for the regular Army to go splash in mud puddles. Either way, the Army says I'm headed to West Timor in a couple of months." He fired up again.

"East Timor. I didn't know we were there."

"Pay attention, damn it. I said West Timor. And we won't be there either, not least anybody owns up to. We gotta … *take out* – that's what the pistol-packin' cowboys call it on TV – forty-two Fiends. That's the last count, though they always up it once we get there. Do it *and* get out, I get to sit on my ass and drink for one solid year. Twelve whole months, they can't fucking touch me!"

"A year on the beach."

"That's if I make it back to my wife's loving arms – the ones getting a workout while I'm gone. A job like West Timor, you got a one-in-five chance of getting dusted. That means a candy-ass like you can't say shit about how I relax."

The gun he took out of the drawer and laid on the coffee table was big and thick and had the usual dull gleam. "Don't mind Henrietta there. She helps me relax too. You want some of this?"

An armed, unhinged, garrulous killer on the pipe – I was so freaking glad he rescued me. "Uh, no. Not my scene, man."

"All this is is plain old cocaine. Not all that strong, but they sure boil it down. Makes no difference if you're smoking it. That's just white-boy thumb-up-your-ass, thinking you're better if you're snorting it and get your nose chewed up. Your lungs will grow back. They're a wet organ. Your nose ain't gonna fix itself."

I sat there staring at him, him and Henrietta. "So I asked you a question, Squirrel-Nuts," he said on the exhale.

"I'm sorry, Mac. What's the question?"

"Yo, don't go squirrelly on me, Squirrel-Nuts, just cause a cold-blooded killer in the Secret Army of Northern Virginia is enjoying a little cocaine. I've got 56 assigned hits. Extremists, Insurgents, Fiends – fucking *Bad Guys* – whatever they're calling them this week. Maybe time to bring Commie back too. Check the T-box, squeeze the trigger soft, and bingo, Miller Time. We call it the Propaganda of the Dead. Works real well keeping the locals in line."

"You don't have to put any heads on stakes?"

"It's civilized, man. They don't know till it's over. And that's not counting who knows how many I've done up on a ridge under the moon spraying on full automatic. But all them airstrikes I called in ain't on my head. No way. You drop the ordnance, they're yours, flyboy. And I've never killed a kid in my life, he ain't shot at me first. I don't care what they say about that one maggot, him supposed to be fifteen and had a beard Abraham Lincoln would die for. Shit, I'd have had more confirmed kills except for that whole stretch before HeadFuck, when they went nuts with the damn drones. That's important, Squirrel-Nuts, cause now you get promoted based on your number of kills. They used to fudge it. Never came right out and said it. But now with HeadFuck turning us loose, they got a formula."

"Promoted based on the number of kills – doesn't that creep you out?"

"They're *Bad Guys*, man! It's just my damn job. If they had the same promotion ladder going all along, I'd be a master sergeant right about now. That's what you get for sixty confirmed kills, and believe me, I'd've found me four more. Be rolling in dough and taking no shit from anybody under a major. Drones blow up dudes up in the mountains because the idiot borrowed his cousin's micro-zap, and the cousin called somebody's uncle the week before. Then some nerd contractor in Utah – who can't change a flat tire driving home – drops a bomb on the guy. That kind of fubar is another reason to hate the drones, even when they ain't taking one of my squad's good honest kills.

He stopped for another bowl. How much damn rock did he have in that drawer, and how twisted was he gonna get?

"All this Homeland T they drum up is bullshit, anyway," he said on the exhale. "Homelanders are more likely to die in the bathtub. Especially you, dude. Anyway, work was slow for a few years till they loaded the drones up with so much shit – geospatials and electronically scanned array radar and satellite uploads – that now they cost more than a hunter-killer team of Boots."

"For real?"

"Some JSOC major got ahold of a secret memo on the actual dollars-and-cents – death benefits versus replacement cost for a kick-ass drone. Our food and fuel versus the cost of securing a runway. That's the big one: runways, us wearing out our welcome everywhere we go. Anyway, they all got stage fright once their toys got so expensive. That and then the Chi-Coms started using drones to bomb those monks – whatever they were – up in Nepal. So me and my guys were back in business."

"Raining death from the skies doesn't cut it quite so much anymore?"

"Doesn't matter how many bombs you drop, Numb-Nuts. Ever hear of a little skirmish called Vietnam? Punk-ass Air Force ain't never won a war, and it never will. So let us do our thing, kill or get killed, and leave us the fuck alone."

He had another hit and held it, polecat-white circumnavigating his eyes.

"So, Mac, why am I more likely to die in my bathtub?"

"You don't think faxing out some general's e-mail don't lead to getting dizzy in the shower? Under HeadFuck? And don't answer that, Squirrel-Nuts. I do not want to be thinking about you naked."

He flared the lighter again. It seemed like he held it in a bit longer each hit. "World War II, they say less than one in four soldiers *under fire* shot back. Now think about what I do. That means the Army made me who I am. I didn't torture the neighbors' cats as a kid. I didn't even go hunting – too boring, nobody shooting back. So now I'm supposed to quit the Army and what? Go sell Chinese cars, that Caddy knock-off they got for like sixteen grand?"

"You got a beer, man?"

"You should get yourself some of that Seroquel the Army gives out like candy – you crush it and snort it. All I got is some bourbon in the kitchen. Give you a hit for every hit you take off this shit here."

I shook my head as he fired up again, Henrietta plopped in his lap. "So, uhm, you know what time it is?" I looked around for a clock. "Cause I got somewhere I gotta be, and I'm not quite sure how to get there from down the ass-end of wherever we are."

He'd been exhaling up towards the ceiling all that time, but this time gave me a nasty face-full of cat-pee/burning-solvent smoke. "Wherever it is, you got plenty of time cause I'll drive you. Right now your job is to sit there and shut the fuck up and be clever. But, just to prove I ain't a hard-ass, you can have some bourbon if you want."

"That's damn white of you, man." Right: time to emphasize our shared heritage. "But I still got some reporting to do later – face to face. The guy'll smell it on me."

"It's against the law, having a drink? Or are you worried the cunt-sucking *Minders* might find out? Speaking of which, I ain't even told you about my wife. That's all she wants now. Don't get me wrong, I don't mind munching a little carpet once in a while – fair's fair, change of pace. All that shit. But that's *all* she wants. Said I was too rough fucking her. She used to like it rough, but what, her new boyfriend's a lapper, so now that's all she wants?"

He stood up, sat back down, turned and put his feet up on the couch.

"And when I wasn't too rough, she said them pills they had me on at Walter Reed till I tossed 'em, were messing me up – *me*, who's fucked his way all up and down the Irrawaddy and back again."

There was no way I was encouraging this alarming heightening of our intimacy, him prone and fiddling with a pistol. "Hey, uh, maybe a hit of bourbon would go down good."

"Forget the bourbon, Reporter-Man. You don't deserve it. Not the way people like you have fucked everything up. The damn Army lost its way when we stopped feeding ourselves. Living in dorm rooms half the time, for Christ's sake, the regular grunts going out on shifts like they're punching a clock, some third-country national smiling at you, loading your plate, pushing cake on you so you can't move quick, spitting in your food in the kitchen. That's what happens when you 'occupy' a country – try to fucking *build* it – instead of beating it down and moving on."

"Can't leave till we got the pipelines laid in the right direction."

"Sit and crack two-thousand eggs in an hour, like way back when, you figure stuff out. Maybe that's why they got the damn Filipinos in the kitchen now, to make sure nobody has any time to think. That and privatizing everything that ain't nailed down, people sitting on their fat asses making big money. Half the dudes you run into in your typical Sands ain't military, the geek Americans the worst."

"How's that?"

"Fucking think they know what they're doing cause they sat in a cubicle somewhere mapping *tendencies* versus *actualities* or some shit. Tracking micro-zaps cause it ain't the bad guy anymore, it's their phone. Their phone's the target now. The Army's so hard up for specialized Boots, they slap six weeks of training on them and call 'em interrogators. I could do better. Hell, I have done better, the only thing I got up my sleeve is a couple of Marlboros that – don't you be giving me no look – I give 'em to *smoke*. Your average raghead goes bat-shit for a Marlboro. Not that sympathy is my big play."

"I don't know, man. I can see the milk of human kindness flowing through your veins."

"Ain't no doubt a bullet in a Bad Guy can solve you a lot of problems. The courts weren't taking them, and when they do, they say too much shit right out in the open, motherhunchie *reporters* sitting there half the time. Plus jailing 'em for life costs too much. But sometimes you gotta grab somebody cause you think you can get some Intel. And these dim-bulb contractors, when they're not shooting at shadows, they got no sense of how to fake friendship with a raghead. Unless they're ex-special forces. Then I won't even talk to the motherfuckers, selling out their unit for buckets of cash."

"Never tempted?"

"You shoot somebody, but you're not under oath and wearing that flag on your arm, then you're just a fucking killer – no more, no less."

"Serious shit, huh?"

"You think? Shit, they call it 'simulated drowning,' but there's nothing simulated about it. It's *interrupted* drowning. The bastard is drowning. Freaks you the fuck out. Freaked me out a little, just standing in a corner watching. That's the price we pay for crawling out of the sea: can't stand to have water in our lungs no more."

"Mac! You believe in evolution."

"One of the few, buddy boy. Don't get me started on the End-

Times cult they got running the Army now. My Spec4, sometimes, real quiet, wonders if HeadFuck's a Calfer too, or is he just looking the other way while everybody lines their pockets?"

He ejected Henrietta's clip, lined it up next to the pipe, took another clip from his pocket and rammed it home. I couldn't sit there anymore. Waiting. With all the people out to get me – and I hadn't even published the damn SecDef whole-vid yet – a crying shame to have it fall to some cracked killer offing me from sheer ennui though he didn't know my real name. I got up.

"That front door is nailed shut. And no way you're making it out the back door. So walk around, have a party. Just be amusing, damn it. And then tell me why the Army don't know that snake-eaters like me need to be hunting and killing, that's it. Charlie-Mike, son: continue mission. Kinetic operations. F3: Find, Fix, Finish. Shift all this nation-building shit – 'clear, hold and build,' my ass – to the hold-your-hand-crossing-the-street regular Army. 'Hearts and minds.' Shit, tits and ass as close as I'm getting to any of that. We pay 'em to turn in their weapons, and they give you some piece of crud Thomas Jefferson shot his first moose with."

"They gotta make room for the truckloads of new guns we're shipping in."

"Plus the Army wants us to get blowed up making sure somebody's finger ain't painted purple twice? Like it matters who they 'vote' for – any more than here in the Homeland. If they're not on Uncle Sam's payroll yet, they just need to torch a couple of Grinders, and they will be. If they burn 'em before they roll over. But don't get me started on the motherfucking Grinders killing grunts."

"So that's true about the Hillbilly Grinders rolling?"

He stared his fierce weird stare, then had another hit, but at least exhaled towards the ceiling this time. "You didn't hear: Don't get me started? But I'll tell you a natural fact. I will get my own damn leg blowed off – below the knee, no biggie. I know just how, guaranteed below the knee. Spend my days sitting on the porch before I let them send me back to the crybaby regular Army like that damn psychologist was threatening me with my last Campfire-Girls up at Walter Reed."

"Look, Mac, I still gotta go." Whatever time it was, I *had* to leave.

"Fine, go! Cause you're being very un-riki-tik. You want Henrietta's little sister to deal with Twinkie or whoever your general deploys next? She's small enough you could probably handle her without blowing your foot off. Please tell me you know how to handle a nice clean little Beretta."

"Thanks, pal. But no guns. I've known for a long-time I ever get my hands on one, I'd hurt myself some kind of way."

"Another surprise. Alright, let's go. That crack-ho down the block's been sniffing around long enough. This shit" – he held up the pipe – "your first time, it's like sex at seventeen times ten. After that one first hit, you're hoping maybe the next bowl or the one after that equals it."

"You know you're never gonna find it. You've been on it what, a week?" He nodded. "That's long enough to know. What happened, some guy down the block gave you a taste or two for free – you know, to thank you for your service?"

"It wasn't so Goddamned easy coming off the Army speed this time back. Maybe cause we were so far in-country they gave us more than usual. Plus I got pulled out of theater so quick after rearranging that broke-dick NATO field-reject. Usually we *try* to taper off before going home. I figured this shit'd ease me off it."

"Medicinal crack – cool."

He threw his feet on the floor, and Henrietta, who'd been resting in his lap, shifted to his hand. "Screw you, Squirrel-Nuts. I've spent less than two-grand on this shit. That means I have got myself locked down. And if I go through the eight-grand I got left, well, fuck her too. Less for her to get when she files for divorce. That's money she could've had sitting safe in my driveway."

"That's a lot of money, man."

"And you are definitely tip-fucking-top of my list for handing out advice. Alright. I need me some rubbers, cause I am definitely wrapping my pile driver before I let that skank neighbor of mine touch it with any part of her that gets wet. Or maybe not. That'd give Mrs. Mother-of-my-Brats something to bitch about."

"You know it's only a matter of time till you flunk a drug test and boom: crybaby regular Army if not dishonorable discharge."

"You think I give a rat-fuck about bad paper? It ever occur to you maybe I don't want to get motherfucking *dead*? That maybe there's a bunch more women I need to get naked with. Ever think maybe I used up my quota of luck, the last little crumb of it sliding down the side of a mountain chasing a Toyota in a Grinder got an engine like a golf cart? I got thirteen years in. What's the Goddamn odds rolling the dice for another seven with HeadFuck deploying the judge/jury/executioner Secret Army of Northern Virginia like he was tossing empties out his truck window? Huh? What's the odds, motherhunchie?"

A noise outside, he rushed the window and raised that big pistol. I made out the sharp ping of an over-inflated basketball hitting the sidewalk. It faded down the block, and he turned to me, still pointing the gun.

"Late one night, all of us tanked, this major let slip that all snake-eaters combined have done something like 68,000 'executive actions' worldwide."

"Executive. Like from the dudes wearing suits."

"Affirmative. All I know, you pull the trigger enough times, it all kind of blends in together and you put it over in one little corner of your brain – where you better well Goddamn keep it. You don't, you're seeing shit on your eyelids in the middle of the night. So – "

"No matter how much Seroquel you got."

He grunted at that. "It's the other shit you remember. The ho with the butter lips after you been up in the mountains for months. How cold it got that one January. The cake Martinez's mom shipped us, or the day Swanson butchered and cooked a whole cow we acquisitioned."

"Don't need any steak sauce, meat that fresh."

"Just a little salt. Now do I need to repeat my question?" Henrietta nosed inquiringly forward.

"Uh, no."

"No, what?"

"No, I never thought about the odds."

"*My* Goddamn odds over the next seven long years seeing the world killing for HeadFuck and whoever's actually running him. Him with only three years in, you know he's taking another five if he don't get sick. Cause he wasn't looking any too healthy the last time I saw him on TV."

"He has been looking weird lately."

"And you, looking like you couldn't make it through a regular Army Search-and-Avoid mission parking your vehicle in a field all day, you don't have to consider them odds, do you Squirrel-Nuts? I see you're not wearing a ring. So maybe you ain't got nobody. Me, I got two boys to raise. The younger one ain't past all hope. So I do not need to be hearing about bad paper from somebody never worn the flag on his arm in his life. You got that?"

"Sure, Mac. You're the king of you."

"Riki-tic, son. Now I am getting me some cocaine, some rubbers and the skankiest ho I can find."

Henrietta pointed the way.

Chapter Forty-Three

Across a Slow River

"You want me to drive since you've had a couple of bowls. You know, no offense."

"The day ain't dawned yet I can't operate a vehicle cause of a little cocaine. Besides, I got plans, motherhunchie, so we're just going to the local Metro stop so you can hop a train back to the World without getting your candy-ass handed to you on a plate."

Telling him I was actually headed across the river to Anacostia knocked him back on his heels the first and only of our little sojourn. He allowed as how he'd drive me there since he could maybe score some cheaper crack, then waved away my carping about the idiocy of two big white guys trolling Anacostia in a loud, look-at-me truck. This time, the twangy singer was wailing about *"Folks coast to coast letting those in the know protect our libertieeees!"*

We drove past tidy, two-story brick homes painted in various pastel shades, a colorful counterpoint to tired looking Ft. McNair. Sailing through *another* red light, a cab on my side had to screech to a halt, and I lost it. "Look, man, I'm going to a lot of trouble pursuing Truth and shit so I can maybe have a better life expectancy than your average Ramone. Now what happens when I ask to get out at the corner there by that bus garage?"

Fishing out the little Beretta from his waistband and nestling it in his crotch, he blew off a third red light. OK, we were skipping that particular corner.

"Running red lights go with a gun in your lap, Mac?"

"You think I'm worried about some punk DC cop? Bring it on!" He fondled the smart little pistol, but did stop at the next light. Trying to keep it light, I asked if he was curious about my errand across the river.

"Look, Broke-Dick, you're at least double age twenty-one. So go chase after whoever you want. We can compare notes later." He made the song even louder, something about *"Our queers round here think the closet's fine by them."*

The hot shank of a hot day, the truck door burned my dangling arm as I scanned the cross-streets for cop cars and barked to make him heed a stop sign. And then we were on the Frederick Douglass Bridge, the Anacostia sluggish, dirty and low in its banks there in late summer. And thank God for a little speed and breeze.

Sliding by a tangle of freeways, we passed a threadbare park, and within a couple of blocks we'd accomplished the journey from Boo Right's Momma's scrappy, spare-parts neighborhood – but on the right side of the river – to a wide-porched, broke-down southern town, many of the houses leaning, their yards overrun. Trees cooled some side streets, and the faded awnings over some windows helped as well. Then came blocks of grim two-story brick bunkers, a bunch with plywood windows.

Sullen, curious people stared at the white men in the loud truck, the one with short hair chewing his teeth. If cops, they were sure flaunting. If not, then who, what and why? We cruised the main drag past empty lots behind wire-topped fences, past check cashing joints, a big Baptist church, abandoned storefronts and at least two take-outs promising an improbable cornucopia of Subs, Chinese, barbecue, fried chicken and – the topper – *fresh* fish. Torn and faded We Buy Houses signs clung to poles.

Mac eased to a stop in a bus stop, rousing a clump of teens across the street all arrayed in some program's blue tee shirts. He shot me the genuine grin – not crack-grimace – pretty much missing since back at Connexions.

"Sorry, motherhunchie, about not having any beer. Me a snake-eater on leave, word of that got out, shit'd be bouncing off my back awhile. So, look: don't let 'em catch you down here with nobody else around. You sure you don't want to borrow Henrietta's little sister? A good Boy Scout like you never got your prints captured, right? Not too many people my line of work even still got their prints. Anyway, this Beretta's clean – like my conscience. Got that, Reporter-Man? Ain't no stains on me. Clean, so you can get somebody's mind right and just drop her as you walk away. Walking slow. Not that you're gonna blend in down here before his homie shoots you in the back. But at least you make your mark long as you remember to never give up your gun hand."

I shook my head.

"Alright. Give me the hat. Gotta toss 'em both now after Twinkie, and too bad about the CAT Machine. But tell you what. I was boring my balls off bouncing off the walls there in Momma's living room. At least you didn't go all wuss on me, so we're free and clear."

"Well thanks, Mac. That's a damn good deal cause, you come right down to it, I guess you might've saved my life. Maybe. So, you know, thanks."

"My name's not Mac."

"I know. Mine ain't Nick."

"No shit. Now make tracks before this gets too disgusting."

*＊＊＊＊＊＊＊＊＊＊＊＊＊

A couple of the staring teens sidling my way, I motivated a block, and in that heat they weren't all that interested. A block on, I came upon Best Booze, a thriving establishment with heavily barred windows. And lookey-there, a pay phone embedded in its fortifications to go the extra mile and call Pantly a second time. His reptilian secretary informed me, "Mr. Pantly is unavailable until next week. You can try to schedule an appointment for mid-week – provided you appear in person with *micro-embedded* credentials from an approved publication."

I told her I'd take that as a no-comment.

Lois's directions easy enough, I turned on a relatively leafy block and then another and soon found myself before her small two-story home with a neat lawn and porch on Mount View Place. The first floor was newly painted a cheery yellow, the second story remained a faded pea-green.

And hello, Lois, returning from circling the track at her old high school dressed in gym shorts, sneakers and an Army tee shirt. She'd also shed the goofy glasses. Curves outdueled muscles – and she had a lot of muscles. She shook my hand and said, "You're early, Mitchell. So I won't apologize for my informality. I was so depressed when I got transferred to Procurement, I did nothing for weeks but sit around and eat chocolate. No exercise at all. But I'll get it back. Anyway, come inside. We've given Old Lady Gaston on her porch there enough gossip for a week. Hi, Mrs. Gaston. You drinking enough water in this heat?"

Inside, the brightly refurbished mixed with various shades of grime, the kitchen with a gleaming new sink, but a fridge that would've felt at home in the Hovel. Following my glance, she said, "That's piece-meal redecorating on an Army salary. I only moved in a few months ago."

"Actually, I was looking at the map. I don't get it." Taped to the refrigerator door was a map of DC with a bunch of big white spaces scattered around. In an empty space towards the bottom, an arrow pointed to a ballpoint drawing of a house labeled *Home Sweet Home*.

"There lie monsters – Negroes. They don't put Anacostia on the official DC tourist maps. Still, this is *my* Home Sweet Home, a bona fide detached house cause I've lived in enough pre-fab barracks to last a lifetime. Girlfriends were telling me why did I want some fix-it-upper in the hood instead of one of those new plastic townhouses in the Buppie ghetto down by the Maryland border. But they're just barracks someone put a skirt on. You drive in and out and nod hello. Live there for years and know three people's names."

"Come on, Whitaker does something dumb, don't you want to be able to come home and punch a hole through your bathroom door? I mean look at your door there – you couldn't get through it with an axe."

"Basically, after all the years overseas, it was time to come home. My mother still lives eight blocks away. My two brothers are OK. Never been arrested either one, amazing for males around here. They got out, one of 'em all the way up to Alaska, you believe that? And my baby sister's still running the streets eight blocks up the other way. She's young, so the jury is still out, maybe. It looking like I'm not getting any young minds of my own to mold, maybe I can show the kids around here how to do push-ups right."

"Come on, a young woman like you."

She snorted. "So, your day: report. You didn't hurt anyone with one of your fancy words?"

I almost blurted out about the albino, but then Mac would end up introduced into the equation, who I'd merely allowed to drive me within blocks of her home. Instead, "I pissed Whitaker off, that's for sure. But that was safely from a pay phone. Otherwise, mostly pretty busy sweating the story."

"You don't sound entirely sure."

"It's not easy doing a story in a day, not reporting from a pay phone." I gazed around her kitchen till she let it pass.

"Well, it's good you're early, even if you are catching me all sweaty. Given the complexity of the mission – making you presentable – it's not like we have all kinds of extra time. You saw the two jackets hanging there in the dining room; I say the blue, not the reddish one. No man over the age of twelve should wear red, not even one with skin as dark as his."

I brandished the Whitaker article to elbow Long-Arms off-stage. She frowned down at the print-out, allowing me to map her contours unimpeded. If that wasn't reward enough, she flashed a big smile. "Pretty good for a rush-job, Mitch. Till I was halfway through

Maryland, formal writing came slow. That's what comes from DC schools followed by years of Army-speak."

She advised me to shoot down Whitaker's assertion that his three e-mails were part of a private check on vendor security; as a main actor in the procurement process, no way he'd float such an operation on his own. And why in the world pick me rather than someone with a security background? Plus, I needed to wed him more strongly to any future trauma visited upon me. Needed to basically make him responsible for my safety, she said.

"I was hoping that assignment would fall to you, Lois."

"I pick my own assignments in my own kitchen, thank you." She tossed the article aside and came towards me, reaching her hand out high – the better to reach for a kiss? Yeah, writing was supposed to save me, but I hadn't dared contemplate this outcome, not really. Man, I could use a glass of water first.

"Ah, Lois, I – "

"Wait, before I get to that band-aid on your head, who'd you send it to?"

"Not the biggest outfit in the world, but well respected."

"Where, Mitchell!"

"Uh – *Off the Warpath*."

"Where? Oh Lord, I can imagine. But the article's tight. Theoretically, that's what counts. I'll get a friend to start it bouncing round the Building, and hopefully your publisher won't matter since you have those e-mails. You included them?"

"Faxed them out with the story."

"*Facsimile* – my man. OK, it'll bounce out the Pentagon door to some political site and then another and then we'll see."

"I just need to punch up those couple of points you want emphasized. Oh, and Pantly's no-comment that I just got. Plus whatever I get from Parnell tonight. So, uh, Lois, where were we?"

"I was about to address that nasty band-aid of yours. Get over by the sink where the light's good and sit down. You were shot on Thursday, right? Writing that today, you're obviously over any concussion and, unless something bad is happening under the band-aid, the outside of your head should be OK too. You don't whimper too much, you might even get your hair washed. It needs … something."

"Fertilizer. The Harrisburg gives you nothing but deodorant soap, which this former Breck Boy did not use on his hair."

So smooth I barely noticed her removing the band-aid, she then took my head in strong hands to tilt it to the light and said, "It's crusting over nicely. Nothing to do but keep it clean and dry and hope the hair grows back around it. Now take your blue shirt off, which, no, Aunt Jemima is not going to iron for you. But keep your tee shirt on. We don't need things getting crazy like back in Korea."

She went to work with the little dish-sprayer hose, me in a chair and leaning back over the sink, and told me of her freelance barbering before her promotion to sergeant. That she'd basically sent her whole, skimpy corporal's paycheck home after her father had his stroke. Men who'd had their fuzz buzzed the week before would line up to flirt for five minutes. Fun times, the peace-time Army. Joining up, she never dreamed she'd pull a career *or* make it to major. And it certainly never dawned that she'd get just that one peace-time stretch at the start. Then the talk turned to me.

"You've gotten a good whacking lately, haven't you, Mitch? Incoming from all sides. So maybe a little treat isn't out of line. Talk is the odds are good tonight."

She refused to elaborate, asking instead whether the SecDef whole-vid was clear or blurry and could I get ahold of it again. I fed her thin trash about a chance encounter I doubted I could replicate. Eyes closed while she worked the lather, I ignored the harrumphs that nonsense elicited.

Leaning back with my neck bared right by the big knife in the drainer, I certainly trusted the woman plying warm, soothing water over my weary head. But I still wasn't giving up that whole-vid till

374

I loosed it on the world myself on, yeah, *Morning Dyspepsia*. That'd be the ticket to the top of its home page, if *MD* and I both had the stomach for it. Not that it wasn't a moot point just then, the damn thing thankfully stashed hundreds of miles away.

The silence lingered till she finally said, "Well something's got to be done, cause the bastards you'll meet at Hart tonight are riding way too high. Everyone is so damn triumphant in this town. And based on what, aside from the fact that it's 'unpatriotic' to question the military? Think about it: we haven't actually *won* a war – I don't count buying a victory in Turkmenistan – since Truman was president. But don't worry, we'll get it right the next Sands say the retired generals on TV. But nobody ever says why there always, always has to be a next one."

"What about West Timor?"

"West Timor! How the hell do you know about that so far off? Who're you working for, mister?"

"Me? No one. I mean, just myself. *Scraping by*, that's my motto."

"Uh-huh. But maybe not scraping by, cause your one-man Demo protesting the searches might have actually sparked something. I know my neighbors are furious about the dogs slobbering on them on the Metro."

"It's been creeping up on us on little cat feet in steps big and small since long before HeadFuck."

Suddenly angry, "I was in mufti the other week on the Metro, and a MoFo clomes up with his dog wanting to stick his nose in my lap. Said the dog had 'alerted' on me. I didn't see the dog do anything but react to his handler trying to get his mind around a black female doing some writing on the train."

"He was worried you were taking notes on what he was doing."

"This old political scientist at Princeton, a guy named Wolin, called it sleight-of-hand, smiley-face, fascism-lite."

"Not so damn smiley – or slight."

"Wolin figured it's rooted in that original seizure of power down in Florida. They got away with that without a murmur of protest. Nothing. *Just get over it, that's so last week* we were told. Florida showed them what they could get away with when people *accept* something as true even if they don't agree that it is."

"Sounds like half the people I know."

"It's the majority in the military. Going to Sands after Sands, even a Spec. Four learns a thing or two. But we don't talk about it. Charlie Mike: complete the mission. After Florida and then them looking the other way to let the Towers come down, time for Grinders to start turning tires-up in Asia."

That – the great Taboo – just wasn't said in HeadFuck's America. Incredulous, I said, "You mean that about the Towers?"

"Shush, boy! Those two Supremes who recused themselves to let HeadFuck in – right all the way to the grave. All people care about now is their family and their 'life' on a screen. And maybe a few friends. Three houses down they won't even wave at the old lady on the porch cause she's not part of their world. So they sure don't care if there's soldiers with automatic weapons three blocks away."

"Just get home and lock the doors."

"That still an option for you, Mitchell? Or are you heading out west to pick apples? Live outside the Bar Code?"

"Nah. I got a story coming out tomorrow that's gonna bounce, plus make me two-hundred-and-fifty smackers."

"Two-fifty. Jesus, you should enlist. You're worse off than the grunts with kids who qualify for food stamps." She mused about wanting to give me a trim, except my head presented the two fields virgin to her scissors of long and thinning hair. Rinsing off the conditioner, her nail caught the wooly worm Frankie gave me.

Jolted, I jerked violently, dislodging the sprayer from her hand, wetting her shirt and propelling my face into her chest. She'd been leaning close to reach around and get the hair down my neck.

"Mother Hubbard! Sorry about your head, Mitch. That takes me back, cause you could teach those GIs in Korea a thing or two."

Speechless, I offered the towel covering my shoulders. She started patting herself down, but seeing me watching, tossed it in my face and told me to dry off while she went in search of a brush because a comb might catch in a way I couldn't afford. She surprised me not changing a now even more munificent shirt, and handed me a brush and pointed to the mirror. Then, channeling her inner Cheshire Cat, Lois led me in to the jackets, ablutions over, the fashion show to start.

But first I had to laugh at her dining room. That and the living room were largely refurbished, all creamy off-white walls and floors buffed within an inch of their lives. And, yes, she'd done it all herself, learning as she went, she said. But the living room had a lot of empty floor space, nothing but a couch, a chair, a well stocked bookcase and a poor excuse for a TV. The dining room was worse, just six stately chairs arrayed around a missing table.

My snicker grew, and then she was laughing too. "I guess I got used to how odd this must look. Count your blessings you won't see the rooms upstairs with the wallpaper with the brown roses. No one but my mother's been over here since I ran into the chairs at a yard sale out in Maryland. She's just thrilled I bought in Anacostia, though she worries about the place being empty when I deploy God knows where sometime next year. Keeps telling me, now that I have a house, time to fix the empty part. Just go down to the bank like I did with the mortgage and apply for a man who maybe won't get his fool self killed being a hero."

A choke caught her, and I stayed shut up. "I normally eat in the kitchen. But I sat in here the other night with a plate in my lap and my wine glass on the floor, imagining someone at the other end and maybe even a kid or two on either side. And if a little tipsy role-playing is as nuts as I get after slinging Intel through five combat tours,

377

I'll count myself lucky."

"Wouldn't you need four kids to fill up the chairs?"

"Like I need to be churning out kids at my age. Anyway, I've decided you're not getting this ridiculous red jacket. I didn't go to town on your head like that to turn you into a fire truck."

Fine by me because the blue one was gorgeous, some kind of weightless worsted or silk or both, for all I knew, an almost imperceptible pattern of dark and darker little blue checks. As to the ties, even Lois's *ex*-dude (that's right!) wasn't immune to the unmanly silliness. Both expensive shimmery silk, one featured a cartoonish giraffe crammed into a little car and driving with his neck and head popping out of the moon roof. The other had several realistic World War I biplanes darting between clouds, one spiraling down in flames. A bit martial for my taste, it would go over well that evening.

The jacket fit fine, except for the damn sleeves which were a whisker shy of having to be rolled up. It was by far the richest piece of fabric that had ever graced my frame. "I appreciate the loan," I said.

"I don't care if I ever see it again. I've asked him to get his stuff three times, the last time saying I was going to throw it out. And he had the gall to say he'd get them when he was good and ready. That he wasn't driving all of five miles here until it was convenient."

Acrimony! But time to reclaim the stage. "So what's a fella got to do to get a drink around here? I haven't been bibulous in a while."

"Nothing – whatever that means, show-off. You're showing up sober. This is important tonight between you and Parnell."

On that ominous note she went to change her wet shirt to drive me to the train. Lois introduced the wizened neighbor on the side opposite Mrs. Gaston's to her "friend from work," then pointed me to an old dark blue Chevy Impala. She said she wanted an American car with some size so as not to get pushed around playing the bare-knuckles dodgeball common to DC's highways. "A sergeant about to deploy had nowhere to park her cause he was getting

378

divorced. So he didn't mind some cash for some last-minute par-
tying heading out right when We're-Fuckedistan started heating up
that first time. Forty-eight hundred bucks later – for under 60,000
miles since he was never home to drive it – she was all mine. And I
hope like hell he spent it all, cause it was his last party."

"I'm sorry."

"So's he."

"No, Lois, I mean it. It never really registered with me before –
before I got, I don't know, mixed up with soldiers."

"Yeah, well, can that shit. He doesn't need anyone's empty words,
and neither do I."

Taken aback by her vehemence, "So, what's the car's name? You
know, like a boat? It needs a name to make it yours."

"Have to make it some old-fashioned, oddball name like what my
parents gave me. Trying to get your feet pointed in the right direction, was all they'd say the couple of times I asked. My brothers too:
Calvin and Henry. Henry used to say he was glad it wasn't Herman.
I get it now – *Lois* – but boy did I hate it coming up. I ever get a dog,
have to name him Otto."

Stopped at a red light, two young bloods in a flash car with shiny,
oversized wheels stared from five feet away, everyone's windows down.
Making a gun of his fingers, the driver coolly shot me point-blank in the
head as his passenger leaned across to yell over the music, "That's right,
bitch! Take that boy back over the river 'fore the same thing fucking
happens to you!" They peeled out laughing their nasty little heads off.

She said, "Just the way the top dogs like it: all of us in our own
little pots on different burners boiling away to nothing."

That shit killing conversation, we pulled too soon into the Metro's
little drop-off area. She turned to me and said, "Be careful of flabby
old Parnell. He's not as pitiful as he seems."

"He warned me about his 'resources' when I spoke to him today."

"Just tell him he's guilty, like your article says. Darn, I left it on my kitchen table. Have to rip it in little pieces and flush it down."

"The standard reaction to my work."

"And forget hinting to Parnell about your source for the e-mails. Just *tell* him you got them at the other end, from Bettinger, and it's time for him to ride off into the sunset with his dumb-bunny wife or dumber girlfriend if either one'll still have him now that his days as an Army big shot are over. You can tell him he's looking at charges of fraudulent concealment, obstructing contract proceedings – that's half the town – and defrauding the United States of his honest services and the right to have its business conducted without improper influence. Tell him all that and put it in your article too. You need me to repeat it?"

I did and she did. "Then tell him there's still a few real judges left, even in DC, and he's going to be too busy defending himself to mess with little old you."

"And off *I* ride into the sunset. But Lois, I gotta thank you. This has really cheered me up – the most fun time I've had with a person in a while."

"You mean with a woman. But hey, you're fun too, Mitch – deep down."

"Whatever that might mean. So, uhm …."

She leaned towards me, and at the last second I closed my eyes for her kiss. They opened with alarm as I felt her fumbling around down by my lap. She undid the seat belt, opened the door, pushed me out and drove off with a smile and a wave, not a word about our next where or when. I didn't even know if she liked coffee-shop soup.

Chapter Forty-Four

A Feather in Their Caps

Crestfallen, I clutched at the sense memory of Lois lifting slowly off my face after nicking the wooly worm, and rode the long Metro escalator past competing H-DM and Jeep Grinder ads (ads to influence federal spending common in DC). They were followed by one for the new cheapo Chinese 'Cadillac' with the headline "A strong want is a justifiable need."

At the first stop back in 'DC proper,' two cops and a particularly unfortunate German Shepherd came aboard. Enormous in the head and chest, the dog's back sloped horribly to the breed's often inadequate hindquarters. A weasel on ice, he slunk forward, his long purple tongue lolling and dripping. Pants tucked into black boots and hands crammed into those horrible tight gloves, the dog handler was short and pretty with a ponytail begging for a tug; her large, red-faced partner glared at everyone all at once and cradled a stubby, complicated gun.

My heart thumping from carrying a general's purloined e-mail, I tried to ratchet things down to deflect the dog. I stopped myself reaching for my book the better to bury my nose. Dogs sense fear, was it as simple as that? The trio advanced towards the middle of the car, the dog calling the shots. The handler flicked his leash to get his attention and nodded towards a slight, dark-skinned kid about twenty sporting an afro, spiked leather bracelets on both wrists and a tee shirt adorned with a garish cartoon of a man with a similar afro pointing a gun. *Yeah – he'll do. Take him!*

Ignoring the dog, the kid eye-fucked the cops. But the boss kept plodding forward, his hind legs slipping on the slick floor. The dog looking the other way as he and the cop passed, I couldn't help but see that her man-tailored uniform pants did her no favors. Bored, the dog stopped, sat, then plopped, nose on paws. Prodded by a boot, his nails clattering for purchase, he turned and caught me sneering. At least I hadn't bloodied his nose. His lip lifting in a snarl, my gaze drifted ever so slowly off over his shoulder to alight on the male cop's gun. Hopefully that wouldn't alert on me.

A plump, older black woman across the aisle foolishly eyed the dog to beat the band. He stared balefully back as she started picking at her face and breathing fast and shallow. That's right, lady, stare at him wide-eyed. What's all that junk in that big bag by your feet anyway – huh, lady? *Take her!* The white boy over here in the slick jacket and stupid tie is riding proper: nothing that doesn't fit in his pockets, including a few radioactive e-mails.

Intrigued by her attention, the dog hunkered down and edged closer. Whimpering, the woman jerked her bag off the floor away from him. Growl met whimper as the dog pocketed his tongue and lunged. She screamed and thrust her bag to ward him off, the short cop bracing both feet and yanking his chain barely in time. Straining furiously, the dog dragged the cop off balance and got perilously close till her partner grabbed the leash and jerked. Down the car, a woman shouted, "No, don't!" His front paws dancing in air, the dog growled and snapped and slavered two feet from the quivering, wheezing woman. Sobbing behind her inadequate bag, she kept gulping out variants of "Do what you want, do whatever you want with me! But Mother of God! get that animal away from me. Please, Jesus, make him stop!"

Mission accomplished, the two white cops together managed to drag the dog towards the door, and the man spoke into the radio on his shoulder. "Search and Suppression Team 23. Official canine alert, center-mass full lunge, bag present. Time: 18:42, approaching Waterfront Station." There was a staticy question off his shoulder, and he said, "That's a negative, Central. No back-up requested."

More garbled talk from Central, then, "Look, Central. This ain't nothing. Maybe got to get a car cleaner here, this lady's so scared. But the dog did his thing. Unmistakable. Like to take her head off. And the car's whole-vid caught it." Mumbled Static. "Affirmative. Start of shift, Johnson warned us that this train's cameras got tape. So Reynolds here, right?" – he looked at his partner, who nodded – "and me, neither one of us is willing to just whistle down the car. We'll take her off at Waterfront, pace out fifty steps, Reynolds'll keep everyone behind that, and I'll clear her stupid bag – which these people have got to get the message through their thick skulls to stop carrying." More static. "Affirmative, Central. Her bag will be cleared under a 13-37." Static. "10-4."

He turned to the woman desperately trying to catch her breath. "OK, Lady. You play ball, and I can fix it so I don't need any more guidance from our canine sensor. Alright? We get off at this stop, I look in your bag a second, and we run your ID through a couple of databases. Nothing on you, right? No skeletons, an old dame like you? You got your papers, right?"

Moaning yes, yes, just keep the dog away – though she was going to be late for her job cleaning offices – just please, Jesus, keep that dog under control, the woman stood up, shielding her most vulnerable parts with the bag. That kicked the dog into gear again, and he leaped the length of his leash, his handler just equal to the task. A woman down the car started praying loudly.

"OK, Lady, let's – "

"Yo, cop!" The kid with the spikey afro started laughing and pointing at the female cop. "You wearing some kind of quilted diaper or what?"

She whirled, yanking the dog, who crouched, rumbling low in his throat, eager to confront a young male like himself.

"What the fuck did you just say?"

"I forget," the kid said, grinning. "But this shit ain't right. That lady don't have a damn bomb and you both know it. Yo, your partner said it right on his radio. You got your thumb on us so heavy, you don't even care what you say right in front of us no more."

The big cop barged up. "You always such a wise-ass? Huh, kid?"

"*Kid*? Yo, I'm twenty-two years old. I'm grown, so that's the way you need to be talking to me."

The man looked to his partner, who was busy looking over her shoulder trying to catch her reflection in a door window. "Alright, *mister*, let's go! Off at the next stop. Won't take me long to find a warrant on you – something – if you even got papers on you. What's that in your right pocket?"

"None of your business. I ain't gave you no just-cause by insulting your female. And I'm damn sure not consenting to a search."

"Cross *my* turnstiles, Mr. Constitution, and you've consented. You'll see, once I get you off this train."

"Yo, People! This shit ain't right, searching this lady cause she's afraid of dogs." The train started slowing. "People be pissed, and we need to be representing on this shit. Like that white dude up in New York said, that freak in them shorts. Word. The bullshit's been rolling downhill too long."

The doors opened and the male cop hustled a truly decent kid out the door, dog and handler following. Better him than the lady, who did not look at all well, sweating freely despite the AC and struggling for air. I smiled and said, "You're gonna be OK." And the woman who'd shouted out, *no, don't!* came and sat next to her and stroked her arm talking low.

And HeadFuck and a top Fiend clinked glasses somewhere, the whole fearsome, expensive exercise a feather in their caps.

****

Goosing my nerve for the coming confrontation, I switched trains and was soon up on the street amidst the spiffed Capitol Hill types flitting past tourists occupying chunks of space. On some secret signal, they'd suddenly halt five-abreast to stare up at that Dome full of hot air. Dogs and their humans lounged everywhere, soldiers too, only half content with mere pistols. A couple of Grinders with machine guns up top were parked unattended.

I waved my Defense-Theft Association ticket at the white mustachioed guard and his half-dozen comrades at Hart's front door. The old gent said, "Sir, this is a public building. Folks don't need tickets to enter – just for that *party* upstairs, if you want to call it that."

Hart was one of those waste-space buildings with an enormous interior courtyard and floor after floor of office windows peering down on an entirely *safe* Calder sculpture plopped down to consume some of that empty space. Steeling myself, I circled the bright, content-less pile of metal, giving the many cameras a shot of my yet to be identified best side.

Christ, look at her and oh my goodness, *her*. I saw that on the Hill, single ID cards had migrated south to women's waistbands, and there was a decided absence of concealing bows or flowing Amish dresses. Nothing but tight silk shirts and tighter skirts for the tall, slender, buxom young women with drop-dead – you, not them – exquisite faces and casually complicated hair. Their legs went from here all the way down to there, ending in those pointy witch shoes that I somehow never saw on the subway in Queens. Men, who came in various sizes, shapes and ages and wore boxy summer suits, did almost all the hiring on the Hill during HeadFuck. So res ipsa loquitur: the thing speaks for itself.

Was I really hitting that elevator there and on up? Lois called her boss a fumbler, but she hated him. Of all the various scoundrels after me, Parnell had clawed his way to the top of the heap by siccing not one, but two weirdoes on me. Hell with it. Cause an Army private, special-ops sergeant and bewitching major had all shown me various stretches of the soldier's rough road, a route untraveled by almost all of a nation on cruise control. Time to confront some of the bastards drawing the map.

Riding up to room SH902 on the ninth floor, I worried about getting in, but there was nothing to it. No one wanted to know, let alone record anything. The no-nonsense silver fox at the reception table inserted my ticket in some whiz-banger which whirred, beeped and lit up and then shredded it on the spot. She waved me in. The three gorillas at the door behind her wore dark, somehow indistinct uniforms with no names or insignia, and one cradled the same slick machine pistol as half the cops outside. My indifferent nod acknowledged their facilitation of the evening's pleasantries.

Chapter Forty-Five

Whitaker at Hart

It was a vast, vulgar room with marble walls framing floor to ceiling windows on three sides, a dark ceiling with sparkly lights unneeded at that hour, and a fruit-salad carpet. The giant spaceship of a Dome menaced the longer wall of windows. Off to the side on a revolving platform, an angel in a poor excuse for a little black dress played, of all things, a harp.

Not that anyone could hear her over the boozy din. Those party goers not braying held a drink to their lips. The women outshone even the beauties downstairs, while the men had sharper haircuts and crisper suits. Of the half not in uniform, many wore those clownish white collars and cuffs with blue, striped, or even pink shirts.

Bosoms heaved and liquor spilled from the glasses of several hundred of America's best and brightest. Waitresses in short, flouncy little noth-ings struggled with their trays as they dipped around large men rooted in the wide stance needed to chew and slurp and bray. Some bellower cut through the clamor, "Hank, you dirt-bag! Never thought I'd see you Stateside, leaving you sliding off that mountain over there. Get over here and hear about the pile of H-27 funding Ray's talking about."

Back-lit by the Dome blazing through the window behind him, an indistinct guard stared my way. I turned to hear a suit pause as he lectured the general he was tugging along. "Look, Garret, all these micro-robotics and neuron sprays and turning their grass-land to desert is fine, far as that goes. But I learned at Mr. Parker's knee, that the real money is always, always in *hardware*; whether we fight or not doesn't really matter. By that time, we're way past my slot in the appropriations cycle. Now I want your shop to generate a report by the middle of next month on three-turret – Nelson! I heard you got back. Is that why there's so many females here tonight? Jesus, you can't swing a dead cat without hitting one in the knockers. Hurt the cat by the look of 'em. You know General Garret, right?" He tugged on the leash, and they strolled on.

Someone tapped me on the shoulder and, jumpy there in the lion's den, I reeled and nearly bowled over a tall young lovely apparently given to speak. Apparently with me. As she apologized for me almost spilling her frightful purple drink, I saw she was merely pretty – no, very pretty – with long dark hair and glasses and a brown, sleeveless dress that actually left something to the imagination. A girl, really, a home-spun beauty and all the better for it amidst the pneumatics.

"Hi. My name's Delores. This is only the second time my boss has let me come to one of these parties. She says I need schooling. But this is such a big one – the Appropriators' Ball we call it – it's all hands on deck. At least I've learned enough to know that no one has a last name. What's your first name?" This tumbled out in a breathless rush.

I told her.

"That's a nice name – *strong*. God, my feet are killing me. My boss, April, runs my firm's entire House Liaison, and she insisted I wear these heels that Mr. Lawson told her to get me."

"Those do look a little rough. Not for me," I said, holding up a glorified black work boot.

"This is the first job I've ever had where I didn't wear sneakers. A colonel in my father's battalion who's friends with Mr. Lawson – they were in I don't know how many Sands together – got it for me after Dad was killed in Were-Fu – you know."

"I'm so sorry. That's terrible. We certainly appreciate his service and mourn your loss."

"No, please. Anyway, it's all so unreal. Everyone wants me to be all broken up. And I *was* for a little while. But it wasn't like my brother and I ever saw him except a couple of weeks a year – when he was even home. My mom divorced him when I was thirteen, he was so crazy every time he got back from a Sands."

"HeadMan asks a lot of our men in uniform *and* their families."

She looked up at me and then remembered to smile. Golly – do that again, please. "So wasn't that great, in the House today, that they passed, I think it was, eight supplementals to the Defense Appropriations bill. All on a voice-vote. They said they wanted to get it done so they could celebrate it here tonight. That really shows that the country is behind our Heroes, right?"

"Passed by acclimation, huh. How much do they all add up to?"

"They're still figuring that out," she said. "So you must be some top-gun scientist or something, am I right?"

"Something, yeah." Trying not to laugh, I had to turn away. Lyricist Sammy Cahn observed: *what is dancing but making love set to music.* But he probably hadn't pictured the amorous water buffalo hunched just so over a short girl with a thousand-yard stare, this to an unheard harp. I turned from the sight as one would from a car wreck to see far across the room some Marines helping two girls up on a table.

"So what aspect of research is your specialty, Mitchell?"

Aspect! Jesus, I had to call Al and Elaine to tell them to hold on to those ASPIC documents for me and not feed them to somebody else. And quick. Al didn't seem like the type to be kept waiting.

"What, did I say something wrong? It's just we're here, me and all these amazing women – I mean, look at her – with certain responsibilities tonight. *Obligations.*"

"Delores, I'm sorry. But I absolutely have to reach someone – duty calls, you know."

"Is it my glasses? I can take them off. I know I shouldn't have worn them, and April wasn't too happy, that's for sure. It's just I have this tiny little infection from my contacts – goodness no, it's not contagious – and I wanted to be able to see to duck if they start throwing glasses like last year. To tell you the truth, I'm a little nervous around soldiers after how my father acted." This last in a whisper.

"Don't be silly. You're scrumptious. But there's one little something. Oh, and then I have to track down some general who's here somewhere for the briefest of chats. Then, I promise, I'm all yours."

"Avoiding bureaucratic formalities is what tonight is all about for the defenders of our freedoms," she recited blankly.

I said I'd hold my breath till we spoke again and left the room to a glare from a guard. I tried to tell myself to ignore them like everyone else was. The Silver Fox at the door assured me she'd remember me. Asked why, she said she was particularly taken with my shoes, the likes of which she had never seen in Hart. Well goody-goody for us both.

A couple of pay phones, dusty relics of a former day, rested over in a corner beyond the elevators. Al and Elaine were less than thrilled, he said, by my Syriac confession *and* my skipping the evening's rendezvous. They'd have to see about things when I got back, which they hoped was soon because something new had surfaced, a specific something.

They started wrangling whether I was worthy, with Al pointing to the value of my fame. *Infamy* more like it, Elaine standing there yelled loud enough to hear. He countered that it wasn't like they had another reporter they could trust waiting in the wings. She loudly reminded him who was taking all the risk, and Al yelled back about the danger of the initial overture he'd made to me. Declaring the call dangerously out of control, Elaine told him to hang up. I tried to mollify Al, but he said Elaine was crying, and he had to go.

Turd-Touch working his magic on their groove-thang, another heaping scoop of uncertainty plopped into my overflowing bowl.

OK, Delores! After I slapped Whitaker down hard. If I could find him.

****

Things had ratcheted up a notch in the enormous room. For one thing, there were six or seven women dancing on tables, not two. They were still clothed – technically – though I couldn't swear for the pair in back who'd attracted the largest, loudest crowd. Some lout yelled at the harpist, "Hey, girl, how about you put that thing away ain't nobody can hear and do some *dancing* on that platform. Or step aside for some gals who will."

Nor had anyone gotten any less drunk in my absence. Slithering through the crowd. I tarried a moment to eavesdrop on an Air Force officer. "If General Allen and his team pick the one I'm crossing my fingers for, the next Sands will be one beaucoup effort, I'll tell you what. About fucking time to let the Air Force loose."

A guy in pinstripes replied, "Throw a dart at the map – sure, sure thing. Keep the Chi-Coms guessing. But I still think we have to keep our focus on Greater Mesopotamia. Natural gas, yeah, I recognize its importance, B.E.I. No doubt. But we still gotta dance with the girl that brung us."

Indeed. Ah, there was my Delores pinned against the long window, looking like she wished the lit-up spaceship hovering outside would beam her aboard, away from the big lug of a soldier waving his drink around as he talked at her. Damn, she looked fine, *especially* in just a normal sexy dress. The back of one wrist fluttered to her mouth as she pretended to laugh at some sledge-hammer witticism. All right, you've laughed enough, darling.

Feeling my stare, she dodged from behind the crew-cut slab to give me a teeny smile and the briefest of nods to meet her *over there*. The trained assessor of the field of battle turned quick to catch my 'one-minute' finger. He ground me into the ridiculous fruit-salad carpet as I beat a strategic retreat for Lois's second and last sanctioned beer and then off to find Parnell.

On line at a very busy bar, I turned to watch a soldier, sailor and

Marine with their uniform jackets off engaged in a furious push-ups contest before a loud, profane crowd. So it took a moment to realize I was being addressed by the two suits ahead of me, one older with wavy white hair, the other awfully young for his shiny shaved head. "So whose interests you representing here tonight, cowboy?" the older one asked. He reached out to knead away absentmindedly on my shoulder.

"Careful with the merchandise, pal. You squeeze that melon there too much, you're gonna have to buy it." Ducking awkwardly out from under fingers that grew more painful as he gained purchase, I said, "Gentlemen, I'll tell you cause I like you. But very hush-hush."

"Hey, don't drop any violations on us, cowboy. Not during the Current Permanent Crisis," the older one said. "It's just we've never seen you, or anyone like you, at the Appropriators' Ball." Turning to the younger one, he said, "Am I right, Fenton? No offense – got that, mister?"

Fenton grinning and nodding away, I said, "I certainly appreciate your interest in my affairs. But let me pose a query if I might. Just what is it about me – "

Fenton barked, "Pose a what?"

"An interrogatory, Mr. Fenton. But what is it exactly that marks me as *different*, not that I accept your premise in that regard. Is it the jejune tie? I assume that's the right plane getting shot down."

The older guy grabbed it with hors d'oeuvre-greased fingers for a look. "No, the tie is the one thing that works. Very festive. Look at Fenton's there, not that I'd ever insult someone's beliefs – no profit in it."

"I knew you'd like this one, Mr. Kratos," said a beaming Fenton. His tie had the cutest red cow prancing before some old stone city, a blazing light piercing the clouds above.

"It's interesting what marks you, friend" said Kratos, warming to his topic. "Takes me back to my old field-Intel days. It's not the jacket – perfectly fine for Pimlico. Nor even those shoes – perfectly fine for walking the dog. And the less said about your hair the better.

392

Like all good assessments, mine confirms initial impressions while penetrating to the heart of things. Cause you don't really like people, do you, you self-satisfied prick. These days, Washington is a friendly town – if you've got the right friends."

"Bold. Extolled. Impregnable!" Fenton piped up.

"*Jejune.* How come a smart guy like you can't see that's not the sort of word to use in a crowd like this?"

I stood there dumbfounded as some syrupy, disco-strings version of a Sinatra ballad boomed from hidden speakers, the harpist finally bludgeoned into silence. Had I ever heard this, among the many indictments of my character over the years, that I didn't *like* people? Was that why all my friends were Nicki's? "Well, I certainly appreciate you gentlemen working to help me reform my character."

And Fenton got all chesty all of a sudden. "OK, fella, enough wise-ass. How about you just tell us how you came by such an exclusive ticket."

"Well, gentlemen, strictly entre nous, it all started with my gig as a consultant on Paraguayan deep-sea fishing rights. Complex stuff, the amount of pink dye you're able to put in a catfish to label it salmon and what-not.... What's that, Fenton? Why yes, of course Paraguay is landlocked, now that you mention it. That's what made it such a devilishly tricky assignment. As to tonight, a marquee American firm – which you'll understand I can't name in such a highly charged competitive environment – is seeking to monetize the technology involved. With obvious DoD support, of course. Men, I believe the good barkeep awaits our order."

And though Kratos looked like he'd swallowed something that wriggled on the way down and Fenton turned a sputtering red, I grabbed my beer and sought the cover of the scrum before the dancers. The biggest crowd was drawn by the newest venue, the harpist's revolving platform usurped by the most professional dancers so far.

Elbowing my way forward, I heard it, the slow, slight drawl and sibilant 'S' first heard during my phoned-in report months back in

Indiana. Not talking to anyone in particular, my man Parnell was one of many encouraging the dancers to ever greater depths. Drifting past to look for a name on his dress uniform, I saw the slightly darker oblong where it had been removed. A glance around the room confirmed what I should have already noticed: not a name in sight. *Doughy*, Lois had said, though not by my necessarily more forgiving standards. About five feet ten, with thin hair greased back, his head – his skull, not his face – was somehow fleshy, as were his pink fingers. He had the usual fruit salad pinned to his dress uniform, though less than most, and I tried to imagine what it must be like to have your deeds and character (of a sort) displayed on your chest.

Discarding the notion of cracking my bottle over his head – wouldn't do to waste my second and last beer – I sidled up and said, "Nice party, huh Parnell?"

Sparing not a glance, he gushed, "Better than last year's even! But hold on a minute, and let's see if she gets the one with the superstructure into that chair with her. Goddamn, they'd give those two skinny ones there a run for their money!"

If *they* were skinny, what did that render some of my past stabs at happiness? Alright, time to lay down the law about my personal safety. "I know your wife doesn't mind you choreographing festivities here, tonight, Parnell. Everyone in D ring knows that. But your girlfriend still might."

He turned, crunching ice furiously as a grin took hold. "And your wife, Fremson, it's taking half a Fusion Center to keep track of all the men she's thrown herself at recently, including a tall, young black. Though she seems to have settled on some rich old bastard for a while. You must have had some money when you got married, just short of ten years ago was it? Cause what other reason would a broad like her have to get hitched with someone like you."

So MoneyBags was old. I almost did a little jig.

"What the devil are you smiling at? And how in God's name did you get in here? People all over Washington scheme all year to score a ticket to this gang-bang."

The crowd yelped as two girls took to a divan as the Captain and Tennille's "Muskrat Love" purred from the speakers. And Delores's brute barged up and saluted, the first of those I'd seen all night. "May I be of assistance, sir? Nothing would give me greater pleasure, sir. B.E.I.!"

"B.E.I. But thank you, Major, no. I think we have things well in hand here, don't we, uh, Mitch? Quite a party, don't you think, Major? Enjoy yourself." Whitaker raised his glass vaguely in response to his parting salute, and the major did a nice cha-cha-cha about-face and barged off.

"You know ... Mitch" – God, it pained him, his sudden charm offensive – "you did outstanding work out in Indiana. Her rollover. And that Intel on the Indian transmission was top-notch. Imagine the effort involved in H-DM keeping that from me. I would've thought all that might have borne fruit by now, and you'd be due for some sort of bonus."

"Yeah, what kind of fruit is that?"

"Low-hanging fruit, nothing exotic. Certainly not by the standards of this room tonight."

Man, he wasn't that doughy. And he didn't look nervous at all. Needing to pop something in my mouth, I swiped blindly at a passing tray, snaring a stuffed mushroom.

"That's a fungus – no damn benefit in eating that. During wilderness training, they teach you not to waste time on them. Stick to meat, friend, that's what your body needs. There's some outstanding beef circulating here, I can get them to bring you a plate of it with a knife and fork if you like."

"I'm good. Now whadiya say we stop all this pussyfooting around and get down to business."

"What's the matter, you don't like watching women express their true debased nature? Fine, stare at the floor if you want, but I find it invigorating to occasionally test my self-resolve…." I made to go, so, "Have it your way if you insist. First, that illegally recorded tape you made out in Indiana, what's its price? As we both know, everything has its price, including you."

Tape – what freaking tape? Oh, right. "Not for sale, Parnell." Though of course it theoretically was. "Unless you want to buy one of the six or seven copies I got floating around various places – for your own archival purposes."

"I look at someone like you crawling along on stumps, and I don't think you're making and distributing seven copies of anything, let alone something so inconsequential."

"You mean something that's going a long way towards keeping me alive?"

"Please, such melodrama. Alright, this is fair, more than fair: a thousand for each of the copies, seven grand total. Add that to whatever you got from that crook, Bettinger – I'm figuring ten grand – and a pipsqueak like you is making out OK."

I almost laughed dead in his face. I looked up with a big grin to see Delores drifting by thinking it was for her. She gave a lovely little smile in reply and again cocked an eye to *over there*. I turned and asked Whitaker, "Ten grand – how the hell you figure that?"

"I paid Bettinger $15,000, so I figured the person who took most of the risk must have gotten two-thirds of that."

He stopped for another gulp from his glass. Jesus – this was why I'd come. All on the record unless one of us said otherwise, I had to stifle the urge to whip out my notebook.

"Look at it this way," he said. "Oh, hi, Charlie. Talk to you in a minute. Who's this? Oh, just an old soldier gone bad. You know, a hustling 'consultant' like the rest of you shysters."

Paraguayan fishing rights, Jack! "Soldiers gone bad – takes one to know one, Parnell. To answer your question, Bettinger promised me fifteen-hundred, I haven't seen it, and I wouldn't take a dime now."

"Fifteen-hundred! You're as bad a sucker as I was, just on the flip side. I paid way too much, you charged way too little. But what's a soldier know? I figured big-time corporate operators like Bettinger, that's what they got. I got a damn high overhead these days, and he wiped my checking account clean – the one my wife doesn't know about."

"I bleed for you, Parnell. Now, about your e-mails, you should know – "

"Your crap is coming out tomorrow, you say? " He downed his short drink and then grabbed a half-drunk one that looked somewhat similar off a tray heading to the kitchen. Staring at the four energetic women revolving before us, he knocked back his scavenged drink, tossed both empty glasses to the carpeted floor and took a staggering step towards me. "Twenty-four years in, Fremson, it's time to get out and make some money. Get myself situated for the next ten years."

"So why not a revolving-door job like everyone else here? Why screw around with me?"

He held his hand up and rubbed his first two fingers against his thumb. "I needed an in to maximize my return, something fancy to bring to the table." I committed that to memory as he added, "As the great Rushdoony says, 'All law is a form of warfare.' Well, I'm at war against the ridiculous conflict of interest Regs."

Riding the self-pity train straight downhill, that last drink hadn't done him any good. "Knives are getting sharpened all over town," he whispered. "The jackals that slunk away when the HeadMan first stomped through the water hole are slinking back. It's almost as bad in his circle, I hear, as it is in the Pentagon. You don't get much protection from being even a top Calfer anymore – or a Dominionist, or a Reconstructionist, or Re-establishmentarian or whatever someone chooses to call himself. Not when that's half the senior ranks Building-wide."

His mouth smeared on his face, Parnell drew even closer to share the whiskey fumes. "You know I had to fake a hell of a bout of stomach flu to miss H-DM's new Grinder launch. Made myself throw up all over my desk the day before, and my absence still raised a lot of eyebrows. But I figured with you already out there, I couldn't risk a security whole-vid of us in the same room. Besides, you got people talking and found out more than those H-DM skunks were telling me officially."

This the man who'd sent two weirdo killers after me, I sneered at his shaky attempt to suck up. "Been a reporter a long time, dude."

"Look, mister! The job you signed up for is done. So just stand down!"

"I don't know, Parnell. I kinda promised the guy who gave me the whole-vid of the SecDef tipping the stupid thing that I'd use it – out of concern for our Heroes and all."

Poleaxed, his mouth worked before the words came out way too loud. "You have a *whole-vid* of her tipping a Grinder?"

Yikes! Flashing cards I hadn't decided on playing yet. I stared, the correct response eluding me.

"Fremson, what the hell you worried about little old me for? Save some lives, man! It's not like a one-star procurement manager can stop a program with momentum like this one, everybody yelling about the damn rollover-Grinder we already got. Neither one of those new plat-forms, Jeep or H-DM, is all that fucking stable. Not that the HeadMan cares. He thinks casualties – a lot of Boots foreigners, thank God – work to inflame you Homelanders. Make you more bloodthirsty."

"You're kidding."

He looked at me slyly. "Why do you think that whole-vid got 'leaked' last month, the one where that pretty-young-thing second lieutenant got herself all bloodied?"

I looked up to see Delores's brute talking earnestly to the two guards who'd been eyeing me all along, and damn if here they didn't come. I edged a bit closer to my new friend, Parnell. The taller guard said, "Good evening, General. This guest with you, sir?"

To his credit, the bastard lost his fuzziness round the edges riki-tik. "No, not *with* me, men. Not yet anyway. But I do want to talk to him a moment more."

"You OK, General," the shorter one asked. "Want to sit down a minute, let me get you a ginger ale?"

He stood up straighter, his eyes darting. Christ, was an Army general actually afraid of these private MoFos? "Fine, boys. Never better. Appreciate you looking out for things tonight." And again his casual wave of dismissal.

"Speaking of security," Whitaker continued, charged by the fog-clearing interruption, "there's a certain captain I know. You come right down to it, he's not exactly a big hit with the ladies. The kind of guy who spends Christmas at the movies, but he's not Jewish. Probably why he's so good with extracurricular work."

"All your henchmen are weird somehow, ain't they, Parnell?"

"It's *General* Whitaker. Anyway, he was really looking forward to the evening's, uh, *sure-thing* social opportunities until he had an unfortunate encounter down in a little shop in Southeast. He said he was way too humiliated to come tonight, waking up to a DC EMT shinning a light in his eyes. And he can't figure how you caught him unawares when you were basically putty in his hands."

"Tell him it's simple little, uh, Norwegian move I've mastered. By the way, how's your other crackerjack henchman doing? You know, Short Leg."

"Do you have any idea how much Red-Calf influence I had to spend to get that idiot out of jail? All kinds of promises to a top NYPD Calfer to get an unlicensed gun charge reduced to disorderly conduct."

"I'm supposed to feel bad, he flubbed that particular assignment?" Damn, this time I was the loudmouth, cause even amidst an ever more raucous circle-jerk, several heads turned our way.

"You listen up and you listen good, mister. Our stealth infiltration of government is over. When I look around this room, I see the people born to lead this country. Homelanders will follow us as they're able to perceive the reality we create. Look at the caliber of men here tonight, and then tell me a nonbeliever like you matters two cents."

"You talking about the *reality* involving all the wars we never seem to actually win, no matter how long they last or ragtag the enemy?"

"Technically, some of those wars remain … un-won, when the governments we help to power then stab us in the back by saying Boots don't have immunity for killing the natives. That we can't even conduct independent missions. So we say screw you and get the hell out. But that doesn't mean we *lost*. It's not like you saw any foreign tanks in the streets on your way here tonight."

A roar erupted as some sailors hauled down a soldier trying to join the fun on the revolving stage, which, I noticed, featured the first unabashedly uncovered bosom of the evening. "Alright, Parnell. This little colloquy ain't exactly rowing my boat."

"Listen to how you talk, so full of yourself. And wearing a sports coat to a high-toned affair in a Senate office building." He stumbled closer. "Well get this, sausage-jockey. You're halting publication – making that call on my micro-zap now! Then you're giving up those e-mails and those tapes. All of them. And then you're going off somewhere. Disappear. Go slop pigs. And this whole nightmare will never have happened."

"Don't you think Bettinger gave me those e-mails – out of New York – for reasons of his own? You're the one disappearing, pal, and for a good long while. You're facing" – what the hell had Lois said? – "federal charges of concealment, and, uh, fraudulent contract and, right, defrauding the Army with improper influence."

"Improper influence? What stupid, *old* history book did you get that out of? Look around you here tonight, shit-hole, at who's got their hands on the tiller."

"In the till, you mean. You sure you got the juice to avoid a traditionalist judge, cause there's a few still hanging on, even down here."

"Third time's the charm, Fremson."

"Third time for what?"

"Twice you've slipped past my men. OK, you want a job done

right, you gotta.... Easy as pie, with you already branded as some kinda Fiend for messing with Protectors up in New York. Shit, I'll just plant it here in *The Call* – the editor's a Calfer – that the head of your cell decided he needed to keep you quiet himself."

"Only problem with that is my only co-conspirators are all those independent editors I clued in, tying me to you with a big red bow."

"Nobody gives a shit about you now, so why is anyone going to care once you're toast?"

"Or how about I just jump up with the girls on that table there and make a nice little speech about our joint endeavors?"

He started turning away, and I grabbed him by the arm. "You don't got the sense God gave geese. I go down, you're getting locked up for the next twenty years cause my story – *our* story, Parnell – is getting published in a few hours, and there's not a damn thing you can do about it. And, yes, my publisher already has the e-mails you were stupid enough to send, plus the assignment memo that Bettinger faxed me for some cockamamie reason."

"How about I staple your ass to your mouth. That way, your fellow prisoners can fuck you twice without having to get all sweaty about it. You'd like that, wouldn't you."

Delores trotted up as I fumbled for the right response. She stood baling with her back foot, but still trying to help, bless her. She said hi to me, then asked Parnell if he was enjoying "a very spirited party."

"Beat it, Missy. This pantywaist is toxic, you got that? Off-limits. There's plenty of All-American Heroes here tonight to punch your ticket for you."

He advanced on her and then lunged. Like Lois said, he was doughy, I found, my hands on his chest as I jumped between them. But he was easy to fend off, his target just another glass on a passing tray. And Delores, wow! Her glasses were off and hooked into her neckline, her hands kung-fu cocked.

"A piece of advice, assuming you're physically capable of it." Parnell leaning in confidentially was worst of all. "Little Missy here is certainly fertile, young as she is. I already know you don't have any kids, so given what's happening here in the Homeland – Europe is already lost – you absolutely must breed in whatever short time you have left. Just drop your load, she can always give it up for adoption."

"What the hell are you talking about?"

"It's the white man's burden, even a maggot like you. Or haven't you heard of the HeadMan's Quiverfull incentives to couples who qualify under the new Nascent Minority Reg."

"You take an awful lot for granted, don't you Parnell, talking like this right in front of a young lady I've just met."

Both of them stared incredulously as a bunch of guards rushed off to smother a sudden brawl in the corner. "What's the matter, Missy, somebody in uniform too much *man* for you? You know, Fremson, that's why this little piece of skirt is in to you."

Kratos and his bald brass knuckles came charging up, Fenton basically shoving Delores aside. Kratos said, "Everything OK here, General?"

"Hard to say, men. Maybe, Mr. Kratos, it's time for this boy's rear end to be scraping sidewalk."

"I thought that the moment I laid eyes on him. But first I'd like to know what he's doing here."

"Right. Where'd you get the ticket, mister," said Fenton, all up in my face.

"Your momma gave it to me as a tip. Said I wasn't charging enough."

"Alright, I've heard enough," said Kratos. He deftly deposited his sputtering muscle behind him.

"Just one thing," Whitaker said as four guards materialized from nowhere. "What was that this morning about me dating Bettinger's sister? His *younger* sister? Do you know what she looks like now or where she lives?"

"How 'bout you start worrying about your criminal defense, Parnell. You're going to be a busy boy with that."

Kratos said, "You want him searched, General, before he leaves?"

"It might be interesting to see what kind of … documents he's got on him. But, now that I think of it, probably not. It is, after all, a festive night, gentlemen, and I wouldn't want to put you out. "

"OK, no documents tonight, General," said Kratos.

"I told you, Parnell, those e-mails have already been delivered."

"So what's that make you, the King of Shit Mountain?"

"I was thinking, you desiccated, rear-echelon tool, it made me more like a phoenix rising from the ashes. You know, one of those mythical creatures, like the so-called female orgasm."

"What the devil are you talking about?"

I looked over at Kratos, who stood there sourly letting a general hold the whip, and gave him a big wink. "I should've known you've never encountered one, Parnell."

"Get him out! Out now! Out before I teach him some fucking manners!" The dancers stopped to stare he yelled so loud, even the mostly naked one.

The guards started bellying me towards the door, Kratos and Fenton following. I looked back to see Whitaker striding towards the bar and Delores standing with the back of her wrist covering her mouth, shaking her head slowly back and forth, back and forth. I gave her a shrug and – no doubt inflating my appeal – mouthed "No" at her so she wouldn't follow. Cutting the line, Whitaker ordered a drink and turned and gave me the finger.

I stopped abruptly, a guard running into me. "At the hip, Whitaker!" Then really loud, "Remember, you and me, *General Parnell Whitaker* and *Mitchell Fremson*, joined at the hip!" Along with the *Warpath* article, bellowing it out to that particular crowd would help forge the bond. I gave sweet Delores a last look – damn, I couldn't freaking win! – as the guards started pushing for real, and the room surged towards us with a roar.

Whitaker yelled, "I won't be the horse to your Lady Godiva, Fremson. You hear me, Goddamn it!"

I heard, no problem. A beehive tipped over in the corner would have created less of a commotion. Fenton twitching and clenching, Kratos turned to the Silver Fox serene behind her desk outside and said, "No way to identify this man's ticket, is there, Miss Smythe?"

"No, sir. According to procedure, I'm afraid not."

"Very good, Miss Smythe. That's exactly the answer I was hoping for. Norda, I believe only two of you are needed to escort him out. See him to the sidewalk – that's it. Got it?"

"B.E.I., Mr. Kratos," the tall one said.

"B.E.I. Fenton, attach yourself to General Whitaker. Discretely, Fenton. It's probably time to get him a girl – one of ours, Cynthia'd be best – and a car and driver."

Fenton yelped, "Bold. Extolled. Impregnable!"

"B.E.I.," Kratos sighed again. "You two men, come with me. There's a certain young lady in there I want to talk to. Though she's one of April's, so I doubt she knows this piece of garbage someone tossed into our midst. She was probably just looking for an easy time of it tonight."

Kratos turned and jabbed me hard in the chest, thankfully not on Statie's side. "I ever encounter you again – which, believe me, can be at the drop of a hat – you'll find out I never let someone off so lightly twice. Your kind, your time is done!"

Sparks came off the short guy in the elevator, but the tall one, Norda, reminded him of its cameras. Norda told me, "Don't bother waiting for Chicken Bones upstairs. No guest'll touch her, tainted like she is, so Mr. Kratos'll probably give her to our guy, Lembeau. He likes bringing a piece of fluff to heel."

Delores's evening, if not days and weeks hence, had turned brown and smelly. Turd-Touch in spades!

PART EIGHT

Chapter Forty-Six

Floundering Across that River

Either of Kratos's men able to take me apart, I stifled my normal wise-ass, mentioned *neither* of their mothers and turned on my heel once outside. Delores giving me the sweetest little c'est-la-vie smile on my way out the door, I could not freaking win. A working dog and his glaring minion passed going the other way, and – plain damn sick of it – I barely kept my foot from spasming out to trip one or the other. And I suddenly needed to pee like the devil, stress maybe, not least from that mess of drunken louts in uniform lunging for me at the end up there.

Yeah, a nice outdoor piss as a stone for two birds; no idea where I was laying my head in a couple of hours, why not the DC jail? Wet down those bushes there over by all that white marble? Sure, the Library of Congress the sign said, a fitting comment on my 'career.' Couldn't just ride the subway all night cause it mickey-mouse shut down. Still before nine, there was always a late Chinatown bus back to the Hovel, back to my well known address. Nope, heading home would jump the gun on the morrow's *Off the Warpath* story inoculating me entirely from harm, uh-huh.

Emptying my bladder one way or another, I took a left onto a leafy street. And there, a block on, its name in green neon above the door, was The Bite Boite. Cripes. It proved all dark wood and cozy tables with little lamps with red shades. The man greeting me blanched when I informed him I was meeting, oh, Mr. Hendon (the late, lamented, courageous congressman) and motored past, the men's room thankfully right there in back. Searching futilely for a Hendon on his clipboard, he called out to stop as I reached the door. Jesus, I won't use any soap, OK?

His sputtering louder, I locked the door. Ah, sweet relief marred by banging on the door. "Come on, get the hell out! You're not allowed." Someone with a deeper voice and heavier fist than the greeter.

Unlocking the door and pushing a cautious inch, it was wrenched out of my hand so violently I almost tumbled out into a bellyful of someone in a blue tuxedo shirt, no tie. Behind him stood three Latinos in those checked kitchen pants, two of them grinning broadly, the third slapping a boxy meat tenderizer into his palm. Thirty diners staring, for the second time in ten minutes I was the object of a crowd's hostile curiosity, this crew at least looking slightly less likely to rip me in half. The owner, for that's who he was, said he was sick of riff-raff off the streets abusing his hospitality. "But you have. So now I want to know what you're going to do to fix it."

Riff-raff? And me dressed better than who knew when. "Whadiya mean, am I going to go back in there and *reabsorb* it? By the looks of 'em, most of your customers don't flush. But I'm afraid I did, so you're out of luck. And if you want me to flip you a dollar for the privilege, you can go suck eggs."

"I'll have you arrested for trespassing and libel against my customers. No, for T Crime."

"Yeah, what T is that – for telling you to suck eggs? How do you know the eggs won't enjoy it?"

I brushed past, one of the grinning kitchen workers giving a little bow to usher me out. I mean, which Goddamn pound of flesh did he want? The owner grabbed at my sore shoulder, but I ducked away and turned to see him beckoning for the meat-tenderizer. This for a piss, I was getting damn tired of getting pushed around.

In fact, enough was too freaking much. I grabbed a knife from an empty table's place setting, really not much more than an elongated butter knife, and brandished it wildly. Then Zorro yelled, "OK, pal, you really want blood all over your nice carpet here – yours, mine, maybe both? Tell you what. I'll mail you a dollar for the water and the *one* paper towel I used, go ahead, hold your breath. Now I'm walking out that door there, so come on if you want to."

I felt for the door behind me and got it open. Someone yelled, "Watch it! That's that Fiend from New York, the one in the shorts. He's all dressed up as a disguise!" Great, and me waving a knife around. I tossed it on the carpet and showed them my back. Cause. I. Really. Did. Not. Care. Ruining some Calfer general's life and then breaching his lair to rub his nose in it, I was supposed to quail at a lard-ass restaurateur acting tough?

The Battle of the Bathroom. Hell, wasn't that why Mailer's literary ex-con killed that poor young waiter, Richard Adan? OK, no pee left to earn a place for the night, so where?

****

It took one short block to admit Lois had been my fallback all along. Come on, not changing her wet shirt after our intimacies by the sink, *plus* those shorts? I hadn't been that darn early. What was her saying no one but mom had been to her house for months but the anguished plea of the lonely and bereft?

The cab driving by made my decision for me, though I had to club the driver to understand I wanted him to pull up to the side entrance of Union Station and sit a moment with the meter running while I scanned the street behind. A variant on Deep Throat instructing Woodward to cab it to a hotel, then duck in, out a different entrance, and quick into another cab on his way to the parking garage.

English seemingly his fourth language, the second cabbie at the station's main entrance was even more obtuse when I asked him to scram to the nearest Metro station. He insisted there was one right there. Well, if I didn't want that one, what train was I looking for? What did I mean it didn't matter, just get the hell out of there? My yelling finally motivated him to the nearby Chinatown Green Line stop straight to Anacostia. Security theater for an audience of one – if Lois even opened her door – the cabs were an expensive way to hit her porch in good conscience.

I lingered on the Anacostia platform a moment but spied no one white getting out with me, so figured no tail. Up on the street a cop drove by and then pulled a U to scare off some teenagers who seemed moved to amuse themselves with me. So I made it to Best Booze's wire-meshed door unmolested in search of their absolutely finest nine-buck red.

The hollowed-out, old white clerk in his plastic isolation booth just pointed vaguely to "the wine area." When I pressed him for a recommendation based on my exacting criteria of price and color, he said, "Do I look like I'm getting paid enough to care about some over-dressed jerk coming down here looking to get laid on the cheap cause she's black?" I didn't bother with the unassailable defense that my wine budget applied to women of any color. Nor did I inquire of the booth's second occupant, a glum young dude in a protective vest, blue pants with a yellow stripe down the leg and a gun on his hip. Hoping Lois had some beer on hand for me, I got the only red under ten dollars with a fake cork, not a screw-top. From Norway, how bad could it be?

I braved deserted residential blocks rather than the populated main drag. Zigging and zagging – the more trees, the safer the block, I decided – I pondered my uncertain reception, then woke up enough to stow the tie in a pocket and shed the jacket. Not that carrying it over my shoulder would blend me in. Some old lady hollered down from a porch did I want to come in and call a car service, and two kids from another porch cursed and told me where to go and what to do with myself getting there.

Damn, an upstairs room was all lit up at Lois's, but just a small light downstairs. Subject to an early reveille all these years, she'd apparently retired for the night, though not much past nine. No way round it but mount her porch and ring her bell. Pushing her gate open, a particularly bright motion-sensitive light kicked on. Up on her porch, I could hear Lois pounding down the stairs, so I lunged for the bell before she could find me lurking unannounced.

She flung the door open and stood coiled, *magnificent*, a big bat in one hand, a club of a flashlight in the other. Pointing to the flashlight, I tried to laugh. "How far do you chase me in the dark after I run from the bat?"

She stared at me balefully, pointed the bat at my chest and finally put it down. "You don't have anywhere else to go, do you?"

"I got plenty of places. All kinds of people clamoring for my company. What I don't have is your zip code – you know, to mail this jacket back."

She came out past me holding the bat high, peered around, turned and shoved me roughly inside. Her hand felt good on my back. She was wearing a faded University of Maryland tee shirt, the Terrapin looking mighty smug, gym shorts and nothing else far as I could tell. "Stop staring, boy. Or ain't you never seen a woman ready for bed before? I thought I made it clear I'd seen the last of that jacket. What time is it? You think Anacostia's so dark and scary I won't dare send you packing?"

409

"Lois, I'm sorry. It's just a little after nine. I, uh – look, I brought a bottle of wine." Taking it out of the bag to show her, she caught sight of the label.

"Thanks. I can use that the next time I make spaghetti – in the pot!" She stared as I offered a baleful, palms-up shrug and finally laughed and said, "Trust you, Mitchell, to leave the Appropriators' Ball alone. So, did they start throwing glasses like last year? Any Marines get their asses kicked?"

"All it needed was some lions and Christians. And better music. You wouldn't believe the 1980s-dreck they were playing."

"Most of those rear-echelon clowns are pretty played-out, so that's all they can handle. You didn't get drunk, that's something. So what happened with Whitaker?"

"We both made enough of a commotion – him first – that half the nation's T-Industrial Complex will have no trouble linking our two names. Not after I bellowed them both out, saying we were linked at the hip."

"You did that? Well, it's not like there was any decorum to maintain."

"They were already throwing me out. And don't worry, the lady at the door told head security there was no way to identify my ticket, which they shredded."

"And the e-mail?"

"I stressed that it came from New York. Parnell seemed to buy it."

"Un-huh." She led me into the living room and plopped down right in the center of the smallish couch. I took the chair. A coffee table still in the offing, she reached for the bottle of wine on the floor by her feet, poured herself another glass and raised a mock salute.

"Since you've offered, thanks, Lois. Wine's not my thing – "

"Obviously."

"But I'll take a beer if you've got one."

"Let's see if you've earned it. So did you get anything for our article? I re-read it before flushing, and it's good, but a little skimpy."

"So now it's *our* article. You putting your name up top too?" Watching her sitting there *breathing* at me, wearing the challenging, quizzical look that seemed hers for the evening, the party was all a blur except for Delores's lovely smile and Whitaker's outbursts. "For one thing, I can add the super-dooper atmospherics of dancing on tables and four women getting progressively less dressed and more entwined."

"Dancing on tables – in a Senate office building! Saw it with your own eyes, so in it goes. Too bad it doesn't specifically serve Parnell's head on a platter."

Jesus, of course! "The main thing is he admitted to paying Bettinger $15,000 to hire me. Wiped his checking account clean, he said. So there's a record of it. Plus he told me it was time he quit the Army and made some money."

"That last goes without saying. But he told you about a fifteen-grand check?"

"Yeah, he was pretty shit-faced, flailing around."

"So nobody followed you here, right? You're sure of that?"

I proudly recounted my taxi-machinations and that only black folks coming home tired from work got off the train with me.

"Look at Maxwell Smart! I don't think Parnell has it in him to get a brother working for him, his mind isn't wired that way. But damn! Fifteen-grand for a day's work. And how much did you get, half?"

"Me? Nothing. I was supposed to get the grand total of fif-teen-hundred, but I haven't seen a dime, and I'm certainly not taking any now – not that that's gonna happen. He also said that neither of the new Grinders, H-DM's or Jeep's, is quote: 'all that fucking stable.' I suppose I can quote him. He knows I'm writing an article, and neither one of us said anything about on- or off-the-record. I didn't have a notebook out, but, shoot, *on* is the default assumption."

"He sends some joker to New York to kill you, and you're worried about all that?"

411

"That's not the half of it. Today – "

"Today, what? What the hell happened today?"

Man, she got fierce quick. "Nothing. *Tonight*, just all kinds of, you know, vague threats, stuff about no one caring about me once I'm 'toast.' And he should do the job right himself and get it over with." Lois not buying, not at all, I plowed on. "That's about it for the party. I overheard a lot of stray talk about various weapons systems. Not that I saw any cash changing hands over in a corner." What else, come on. "Oh, and just before getting tossed, I saw my first unabashed bare tit up on this little revolving stage. God only knows what happened after I left."

"First of the evening or first of your life? But you done good, getting Parnell to spill about that check."

"Yup. Confronted him right in the fundament of the T-Industrial Complex."

"You like confronting people. Gonna tell 'em where to stick it when they try to search you, everybody else staring at their shoes. So what are you, a nihilist, a transit recidivist, some weird, lone-wolf loner, or a Fiend like they're saying in the papers up in New York?"

"I guess I didn't get enough hugs as a kid."

She yawned and stretched, her hands high and feet out straight – as if I wasn't already staring every chance I got. "Things are getting ripe in this country, Mitch, HeadFuck on top long enough to wise people up. You can feel little eddies of it starting to move."

"Citizen sovereignty, a concept due for recrudescence. Tonight, it came from some dog and his cops scaring the bejesus out of a woman on the train."

"Let me guess: a black woman, an older black woman?"

"Old enough. Five minutes after we parted, me verklempt – "

"Talk English, show-off!"

"*My mind troubled*. Troubled, OK Lois, from wondering if I was ever going to see you again…. Anyway, this office cleaner just trying to get to work looked like she was gonna keel over right there, she was so scared. The cop even told Dispatch it was nothing, but the dog had 'alerted,' so they had to take her off the train."

"I can't stand 'em, the dogs always trying to sniff you. You don't see them 'alerting' on men."

"So some kid insulted the cops and forced them to take him, not her. Heck of a guy, he gave a little civ-lib speech to the whole car, even mentioned the doofus up in New York talking about search-refusal."

"That whole-vid of you in those shorts is your best friend." She got up to let me watch her journey across to the bookcase to fumble around behind the shelved volumes. What, a joint to goose my nerves even worse?

Chapter Forty-Seven

Not Tonight, Maybe Never

She turned with a book, removing a piece of scrap paper from it. "This is what I was telling you about before. *Democracy Incorporated: Managed Democracy and the Specter of Inverted Totalitarianism.* I also came across this quote from a poet named Auden, who maybe you've heard of. It sheds a nice light on Wolin's book." She read from the paper: " 'Evil is unspectacular and always human/And shares our bed and eats at our own table.' "

"HeadFuck has apparently stopped worrying about being spectacular – have you seen him lately?"

Lois grunted at that and handed the book over. I pretended to study it a moment. "You may want my oven mitts," she said.

"Hot-stuff, huh? Though I doubt that some dusty old political science tome is nearly as transgressive as some of the books I was toting around Penn Station."

"But those were novels. If they're any good, of course they're more true than even the best analysis."

"And just how the hell, Major, do you know they were all novels?"

She started, smiled, and when I didn't smile back, narrowed her face alarmingly. "I don't know what you're trying to insinuate, Mitchell, but whatever it is, I don't like it. After I've let you into my house twice – once, uninvited – with you being all vague about who knows who tailing you all over DC. I just assumed they were novels, based on the type of person you are."

We looked at each other unhappily. Finally she said, "It's just I like talking about books. Tell me one you like that you carried."

"I don't know. I guess one I *like* is called *A Wrinkle in Time*."

"OK. My Wolin for your *Wrinkle*. I don't get the chance to talk about anything but Army procedure manuals that much anymore since my fool got himself killed." She reached for something in the corner of the couch and pulled out a fancy cigarette case and removed a substantial, brown-paper number. She stared down at it a moment, then lit up. "You don't need to be giving me any looks for a *clove* cigarette. The basketball player isn't allowed or something? You know I haven't picked up a ball since that thug destroyed my knee. Sure I could have sat out a year and limped through a career at Drexel or someplace and maybe had some fun."

"More fun than cutting hair in Korea?"

"But it wouldn't have been the same. Drexel ain't Missouri, and neither my first step nor my elevation was ever going to be what I had. Three different doctors told me that."

A long pause, then, "Going to kiss some village elder's ass my last Sands, we got two men killed out of the blue in a village that was supposed to be totally pacified. Bought and paid for. A bunch of new wells, a new school, baksheesh in a lot of pockets. But it had been all shot up that morning, four civilians killed, including two kids. This was our sector. Shit, we weren't supposed to kill a dog without my colonel knowing about it. Turns out the Secret Army of Northern Virginia – "

"Special Ops."

"Right. JSOC had been pursuing one of their private little vendettas without bothering to tell us people were pissed off at Americans, you head south into that next valley there."

"Special Forces living large?"

"If you call that living. The *tip* of the spear, they call themselves. But more and more it's the whole damn thing, the Army turning itself inside-out. They get awfully twisted awfully quick, doing what they do. A law unto themselves, I try to keep me and my guys the hell away from them. In-theater, a Special Ops lieutenant is just as likely to stare right past me as obey an order from a black female major."

She looked around her half-furnished living room a minute, then whispered, "I just wish Marcel was here to talk to about all this."

"You mean Jacket-Man with the arms?"

"That jerk? Please. No. Marcel's dead. He had to get all heroic saving three of his men. They're still alive, though I don't know if one would call it living. And now Marcel's momma's got a Bronze Star framed on her wall. Whoopee."

Nothing what I was supposed to say to that, I said it.

"We met way back in officer candidate school. It wasn't rocket science, us getting together stuck at Fort Benning. We lost touch, and I didn't see him for years and years till our first time in We're-Fuckedistan. He got killed when we were bringing Turkmenistan to heel after they kicked us out that first time. That boy was finally ready to get down on one knee to get both our mommas off his neck. But look."

She waggled her naked left ring finger at me and choked out a laugh. After a while, she shook herself and said, "And can someone please tell me why the Army dropped 'officer,' a perfectly good term it'd been using for hundreds of years, right when this grunt worked her ass off into a commission? Anyway, this *leader* – right – thinks you probably did earn a beer showing up tonight to get in Parnell's face."

She got up and returned with a big green oil can of Fosters ale, not the tasteless blue beer. Rather than hand it over, she leaned against the door jamb scratching her back like a bear on a tree and smiling at the big dummy gaping in her living room. Just a little like a formidable, very *delectable* bear. Seemed like I was gonna have to stand up to get that ale. Neither one of us moved after I managed to cross the room to take it.

I told myself to remember this the next time I aped indifference to my fate, Short Leg spraying shots or an albino grabbing me. Jesus, I was rusty, years with none but Nick. I gulped. Nice, imported ale not normally in my price range.

I just brushed her lips with mine. Then I did it again. She kept her eyes wide open, or at least did until the kiss deepened and I closed mine. Stuck holding that big can, I pulled her close with one hand. She slipped me some tongue, then pulled suddenly away. What? I gave her my best Cary Grant imitating a scolded puppy.

She nodded across the room. Marcel's ghost had materialized? Cause I didn't see anything. "Could we be any more on stage here in my home with that window wide open and all the lights on?"

"They don't have switches, we could cut the cords."

"I've got a better idea." She brushed past me close. I followed to the foot of the stairs where she laughed and dashed up. I stayed to watch. At the top she turned and slowly peeled off her shirt. I whooped and took the stairs two at a time. By the time I caught up to her in her bedroom, only the elegant little art deco bedside lamp was on.

Almost swooning from what Lois was doing to my neck, and my old friend the Stuffing suddenly acting up, I laughed to myself thinking of Mac and our unstated competition that evening. I said almost aloud, *Man, if Mac could see me now.*

Lois stopped fumbling with my shirt buttons and said, "Who's Mac?"

"Uh, nobody. Just some white guy I know who's expressed a certain fondness for black women."

She stopped and held me at arm's length and then slapped my hand away when I reached for her, and no, not kidding. Alright already. Us about to get slippery, maybe it was time to stop lying to Lois. Commence off the good foot and all. I dragged my eyes north. "He's just this soldier – well, this Special Ops killer, you come right down to it, who saved my ass this afternoon. Don't know quite why he did, except he likes spitting in their eye. Plus he's bored."

"Likes spitting in whose eye," she demanded, stepping even further back and catastrophically crossing her arms. "And don't lie to me, mister. You know how many men have tried to lie their way into my bed? I'd have liked to think you were different. I left the Building

417

at lunch to confirm that your wife's moved to Manhattan, so at least you weren't lying about her. Now spill it. You've been lying all along about what happened to you this afternoon, haven't you?"

My hard-on was fading fast. "Alright. After phoning Whitaker – remember, this *general* threatening me, siccing a gunman on me, hiring me to spy, the whole nine yards. So if I've been a little scattered…. Anyway, I'm in this little joint down in Southeast working on our story. A little place off the beaten track that lets you pay cash for a computer. And – "

"Connexions. You found that your first morning here, huh? Does it still have that sign with the fool in a top hat?" I nodded. "And?"

"There was this good-old-boy soldier already there when I got back from a pay phone interviewing Whitaker. Lois, look, I didn't mention either about getting threatened at the phone by the drug boys, one of them acting like he had a gun. I can't keep track anymore. Anyway, this beefalator sergeant was there contacting his unit somewhere they're not supposed to be. Like Gary Cooper on steroids, a real killer if half of what he said was true. Turns out he was ordered home for treatment for the yips. So I do my thing and fax the story and the e-mails to *Warpath*. I'm about to skedaddle when in comes this albino dude."

"Motherfucker, Mitchell! You've come to my house twice now and, idiot that I am, I've let you in. Goddamn standing there grinning on my porch. Albino – you sure?"

"No, I made it up. Not totally albino, but tending that way. He doesn't say much of anything, but just goes after me and tries to drag me out."

"And so you incapacitated him no problem."

"Actually, Mac did."

"So you thanked this Special Ops for taking care of skeazy Captain Bybee – who is one of Parnell's junior Calfers and a very nasty piece of work – and slunk out of Connexions and led them all to my front door? Probably brought Washington's Chief Cummings along for the ride too."

"Jesus, no. Mac and I piled into his vehicle and off to this house he's renting right outside this decrepit old fort down there. We – "

"Fort McNair."

"Right. He relaxed by smoking crack and fondling his gun and messing with my head."

"He got pulled from a JSOC deployment – where, Africa?"

"Probably not, cause he mentioned something about a gas pipeline."

"That could be anywhere. So, no time to taper off the in-theater speed, he comes home and hits the pipe. He's so played out, he's not worried about bad paper?"

"Worse than bad paper, he's worried about getting killed, what with, Mac said, HeadFuck deploying JSOC like he's tossing empties out his truck window. Anyway, he drove me to MLK Avenue up about eight blocks from here, and then he peeled out. No one followed me from there. I promise"

"Says you."

"How? He didn't call anyone. Besides, he didn't even hear about Anacostia till the last minute."

"You ever think of GPS on his vehicle?"

"Lois, you're getting crazy."

"I've seen what these people do. I don't know about you, but I still have a future I'm interested in pursuing once I kiss the Army goodbye. Which, believe me, cannot come a minute too soon." Agitated, she forgot herself and started gesturing with her hands for a wonderful few seconds.

"Look, the guy running Connexions said that Mac had been there like four times before already. So he had nothing to do with me. If it walks like a duck, sometimes it's just a damn duck. Now come on over here."

"What else?"

"What else nothing. I swear. Now let's be nice."

"Look, I won't throw you to the Anacostia wolves, not at this hour. You escaping Bybee, it'd be too damn stupid to catch it from someone who only cared if you got ten bucks in your pocket."

That didn't sound encouraging. And indeed, her shirt out in the hall, she went to her bureau for the damn tee shirt that rang the curtain down. So close. So freaking close! And to think that moments before I'd considered catching her braless in that Terrapin number a bona fide erotic achievement. I sank down on her bed in defeat.

"Get off my bed and come with me."

I grabbed the oil can off the nightstand and, undoubtedly not returning, took a good look around. The most fully realized of her rehab efforts, the walls were a pale yellow, the ceiling cream, the floor gleaming. A classy mirror topped the dark, real-wood bureau, and various framed photos and weird narrative paintings adorned the walls. The paintings were oddly *constructed* somehow, but art appreciation wasn't on her agenda. Considering all the horrible places Lois had slept since her knee got ripped, it made sense this was her home's first truly finished room.

Yeah, they were her paintings she said, leading me down the hall to a room with brown-rose wallpaper half stripped off, a section of floor removed in one corner and a torturous army cot. She came back with a nice pillow, but a rough green blanket and went over and unlocked the window and threw it open.

"Too bad. Cause you're a nice guy, Mitchell. Mostly. You should've been straight with me. Though if you were, I might not have let you in even this afternoon. A shame you couldn't keep your fool mouth shut, cause I'm damn good. Fourteen years since my last white guy, I was looking forward to a change of pace after someone too slick for his own good."

"You *do* say the nicest things."

"I'm sorry. But lying to me about operational security, which you did like three times, is not something I can tolerate at this stage of the game. The bathroom's down the hall. I'll leave you a new toothbrush. I'll also leave you with a question: do I still sleep with a knife under my pillow?" She punched me lightly on the arm, said "too bad" again and left.

Sirens near and far serenading me, I vowed not to freak out come morning wondering where the hell I was, sleeping on such a contraption, my roses gone brown.

Chapter Forty-Eight

Or Maybe Someday

I woke remembering the fiasco of the night before all too well. Had Nicki hexed me cause she'd settled for some rich old bastard? Lois was still an ally, maybe, but I'd sure shred a budding friendship.

Or perhaps not. Exiting the bathroom after some basic sign-of-the-cross ablutions, I smelled bacon cooking. Even better was the lilt of a woman singing some maddeningly familiar little ditty. Had her anger evaporated, or did Lois just like to whistle while she worked?

"The bacon alarm clock worked, huh? Did you sleep OK on that horrible cot?"

"Like a statue – afraid to move in case it collapsed on me."

She grinned and turned back to the stove looking oh so different in her camos and boots than the sight of her at the top of the stairs burned on my retinas. Speaking of which, she wasn't wearing any goofy glasses.

"First time ever cooking bacon in this kitchen. I was surprised I had it buried in the freezer from my old apartment. Jacket-Man always fled as quick as he could. He wasn't making any money sitting around talking. Marcel, of course, never got to see this place."

Maybe last night's mess was for the best, cause she was obviously still deeply grieving. She broke the silence. "I felt a little guilty about that cot and almost came and got you – just to *sleep*. You're still in the penalty box. Though, judging by the way you looked when I put a shirt back on, I don't know how much sleep you would have gotten."

"Oh come on, what's the big deal?"

"Uh-huh. Been lonely since your wife split?" I finally nodded.

"And it's not like things were all warm and cozy before she left."

"Now the single girl is offering me her insights on marriage." She turned abruptly. "Hey, Lois, I'm sorry. I didn't need to say that. You were indeed a sight for sore eyes, who am I kidding? ... So, feels like another sulfurous day on the planet Mercury kicking into gear." Well after eight, I saw. "You're going in late, or does the Army keep bankers' hours now?"

"The day after the Appropriators' Ball, things'll be a little slack any office having anything to do with procurement."

She motioned me to the table and plopped down bacon, eggs, toast, juice and coffee.

"I hope you like your eggs sunny-side down. Done properly, that's considered a great luxury in the Army."

"I like 'em whatever way you fry 'em. My local bodega, you get it on Wonder Bread." Had she possibly forgiven me?

She fell silent, working her fork. Not getting quite enough to eat as a kid, maybe, the six of them carried solely by Dad's municipal paycheck, did she stick to business at the table? Stirring milk into my coffee – what the heck, the spoon's handle was a young girl dressed in an old-times party dress. I looked up to see Lois displaying another one.

"I was waiting for you to notice them. The Dionne Quintuplets. They only come out for special occasions – and, yeah, the first frying of bacon qualifies. Daddy got them as a boy from his Momma, who got them from hers. Boy, did we fight over them as kids. Made eating the same store-brand sugar-flakes year in and year out almost tolerable."

"They're cute. But you better count the spoons before I leave."

"Why, there's only two, Yvonne and Annette, and they're right here."

"Sure. But what about all the silver a desperado like me might steal? You know, the guy who got himself shot in the head for money."

"The silver what? I don't have any jewelry, if that's what you're talking about. Never having a place to call my own till now - not really – I never wanted to worry about it, and then it just seemed, I don't know, not me."

Before blundering awkwardly into explaining the cliché about counting the spoons, this scion of a cramped Mineola split-level said, "So you still have the other three?"

"Nope, we all took one, Momma too, when Daddy died. Only reason I have two is my running-wild sister admitted it was only a matter of time before someone stole it from her to use as a cooker. Not that she's ever messed with smack herself – far as I know."

I busied myself with my plate.

"See," she said, holding up the spoon. "A pole up her butt. That's half the Building, the self-righteous creeps, especially when the lemmings start saluting and marching off the cliff. But they're nervous. HeadMan's not as easy to control as most commanders-in-chief, not as predictable. So they lash out – all the MoFos, on down to dogs on the subway scaring old ladies."

I waved a piece of bacon at her and tried a new tack. "No crypto-doof glasses this morning?"

"Whatever shit this day is going to bring, it's no time for self-effacement. Besides, maybe I don't feel the need to fend anyone off this morning."

She grinned, mopped up some last egg with toast, went to the dining room and returned with the two jackets. Holding up the fancy-schmantzy one, she demanded, "You sure you don't want the blue?"

"I'll be getting a Blue soon enough."

"And for that I'm sorry, OK? Who or whatever they might be, Minders, Go … Jump in the River! But I'm still giving it to the world this morning, no fooling if you don't take it. This ridiculous red one too."

I mounted a vague protest about not tossing something so nice, more static with Jacket-Man fine by me.

"Don't think for a minute I'm not still mad at you for lying to me about maybe bringing a psycho like Bybee right to my door. Since I still have to report for duty today, I have to assume you didn't. But I had a little trouble sleeping myself, thinking about things. You don't have a whole lot of support do you? None of these freaky websites you publish on even know what you look like, right?"

"Not unless they've seen me in those shorts."

"Crazy like a fox, those shorts: you're the guy next door everyone can identify with since no self-respecting Fiend would wear them."

"Another compliment!"

"Look, I've faced some shit in my day – serious hit-the-fan. But I've done so as part of the most lethal organization the planet has ever seen. Never mind that half the time the shit has had U. S. Army stamped all over it. You, on the other hand, operate alone. So that's a kind of pressure I don't know much about."

"It's easier being responsible to no one."

"Maybe. But, seeing as how you're hanging on by your finger-nails all alone in a hurricane, I've decided to cut you some slack. Provided – and try to keep it in your pea brain that you're talking to an experienced Intel analyst who's been lied to by hard, cruel men, warlords and sheiks and murderers all over Pipelineistan – *provided* you never, ever tell me as much as one tiny little fib ever again."

"I promise. I mean, I swear." I held up my right hand. "But you know, I'm not all alone. Like when I was in Bellevue after getting shot, there was this nurse – I mean, a whole bunch of people trying to help." Jesus, concentrate. "An orderly, all kinds of people. And my landlord has shocked the mess out of me watching my back. A little spark is all it takes, maybe, to get something moving. You're Exhibit A, of course."

"No, no, no. I am Exhibit Not-in-the-Alphabet, boy. Now let's saddle up riki-tik before this gets sloppy."

I joined her at the sink with my dishes. "You want me to do these dishes while you, I don't know, water the horses or something?" She turned to me surprised and way too close, and I was lucky not to break the plate clattering it into the sink. "I mean, you cooked, I'll wash."

"Well, look at you. But we do not have time for nonsense like – "

There was nothing tentative about our first kiss of a new day. She finally broke. "Good – nice. Now we are both going to work. You remember what you wanted to add into our article, right, Whitaker's $15,000 check more important than all the tits you saw last night."

****

Leaving, Lois was glad Old Lady Gaston hadn't made it early to her porch. Driving deeper into Anacostia, she apologized for dumping me far from the train. I dismissed that and fell to brooding. Solid and, shit-yeah gonna bounce, our Parnell story was still freighted with a big *say-what*? Man, I had to get "Penn/Bellevue/ASPIC" out into the world, both to bang the drum on search-refusal and to shed some of the weirdness clinging to me.

"Alright, you have the two points you need to hammer home that we discussed yesterday afternoon?"

"Sure," I said. "Link Whitaker preemptively to anything bad happening to yours truly. And … shit – sorry."

"No way he could have run an independent check on vendor security, certainly not using his private e-mail. That kind of freelancing just doesn't happen in the Army. And double-no-way plucking you from deep, deep on the bench."

"Except I nailed the assignment better than nine out of ten GI Joes."

"Maybe so, hot stuff." She eased to the curb, pointed and said the library was four blocks up on the left. "OK, the girl you need to latch on to is Shandre. My age, she's the only one of my teammates who hasn't moved to the Maryland suburbs if not a whole lot further. Including a couple to the next world. I called her this morning, and she's on the look-out. Not that there's going to be a whole lot of other big white guys walking in there. But just in case, tell her that 'Gimme' sent you."

"Gimme being what the boys said when they saw you?"

426

"No. Down two in a playoff game at our gym, time about to expire, my point guard was just standing there dribbling, frozen. So I yelled loud enough to hear in the locker room, 'Gimme the damn ball!' So many people started calling me Gimme, I decided to embrace it."

"And?"

"And what?"

"What the hell happened in the game?"

"Please. Let's just say I made sure both feet were behind the three-point line."

"You're sure you want to involve Shandre? What if they pull the string from the other end, from *Warpath* back to an Anacostia library?"

"You don't think we've thought of that? For instance, Shandre isn't demanding ID before letting you use a computer. Even though they've been requiring that since *four* days after HeadFuck got in. It was like they had it waiting in the wings to implement, because I'd hate to think cracking down on the DC public libraries was tops on his to-do list."

"They've had it in the libraries up in New York for years – way before HeadFuck."

"We're slow here. That, or the District just doesn't have any money, which can be a blessing these days. Anyway, Shandre'll log you on with this Memory-Hole password she's got. And let 'em prove it. What, you couldn't have found your way to an Anacostia library your own pale self? Lots of people cross that river for all kinds of shady reasons. Some of them don't even bother buying cooking wine first."

Man, I liked her smile. "Were you really surprised to find me on your porch?"

"Yes I was. A lot of women who've served are real particular about their personal space, so on any given night that could've gotten ugly. For whatever reason, last night wasn't one of them. Anyway, I got your address from *The Daily Chirp*. Right by the river in Queens – no doubt a happening condo with a swimming pool on the roof."

"Uh, not really"

"I looked online. Some big old house a block from the projects. I can take it from there."

"It's nice enough. For the short term. For a guy who moved quick and didn't care he was so tore up."

"You make it sound so appealing. But OK, Mitchell – *Mitch* – got to decide which I like better. Here's the deal: we both know where we live, so face to face is our next contact. And that does not include tonight or any other time this trip of yours to DC. You got that, mister? No phone and certainly no e-mail, phony Dutch address or not. We both lay low for a while, not that that's an option for you. No contact for two months – no, make it six weeks. Then who knows, I might be willing to give Manhattan another chance, now that I have someone to show me around."

I grinned. I was starting push-ups *tomorrow*. That'd give Stap something to chew over, another scintillating woman crossing his porch in search of my bell, her race the least of it. (Far as I knew, his delight in his fellow creatures lashed everyone equally.)

"Good – so that's settled," she said, like she was talking about inspecting a barracks. "OK, *Off the Warpath* goes live about 1200 hours our time?"

"Pretty much. I'm glad I don't have much to write."

"You mission-ready?"

"Absotively, Major!"

"Uh-huh. We are definitely starting at the bottom of a long steep climb. Still, taking down a corrupt Calfer general is a good day's work. Looking over their shoulders a little might slow them down. Get near the top of that climb, maybe heads will roll. Whether we're there to see it…."

We sat a moment, each of us looking away in turn. She took my hand, drew it to her breast and leaned in to it. I was too agape to make too, too much of it through the heavy camo, tee shirt and bra.

Hey, even muffled, that pleasing weight felt marvelous. But parked on a busy street and Lois looking solemn, it was as much of a bond, maybe, as something strictly sexual. She dropped her hand and, after a good squeeze, so did I.

"So you're not so broke up over last night. I'll be laughing for a while, the look on your face when you collapsed on my bed after realizing Santa got stuck in the chimney. Nice to have someone not take you for granted. Now de-digitate yourself, man. And, Mitch, two things: write real. Ain't no time for show-offery, like my Dad would say."

I nodded and waited till finally she said, "I'm almost reluctant to say this, all the crap already raining down on you. But if you're willing, and that's a real *if*, get that SecDef rollover whole-vid out soon as you can. I think we both know that tomorrow is promised to no man, Mitchell – or woman."

After all that, a kiss would've been anticlimactic. "I'll never wash this hand again," I said, getting out. She smiled and waved and peeled into a U-turn. I stared, joking to myself that she was so stung by tears, she'd side-swipe a parked car. And a block on, she stopped. What, to beckon me to race to her side and away from all this (and her Army pension) to shared bliss living over a live-poultry store, Lois to clean the cages, me to bite off heads? She got out to hang the jackets on a church's iron fence and back in and gone without a look. Six weeks. De-Hovelizing my rooms beyond mere human endeavor, could I at least get Stap to paint the porch?

Chapter Forty-Nine

Teammates

A fine red brick building with a sloped green shingle roof, the library was deserted at that early hour except for an old man and two teenagers pounding computers. Too tall to be the somnolent point guard and more matronly than Lois, Shandre came out from behind the reference desk and asked if she could help. I gaped at the sign posted both on her desk and a pillar behind her: *The Minders have made no inquiries at this Library* today. *Watch closely for removal of this sign.* Laughing, I said, "Uh, Gimme said I might drop by to see you this morning."

"I thought as much, but you can't be too careful these days. How long do you anticipate using my machine?"

"Well under an hour."

"Good. Go to that magazine rack there and look at one a moment. Then go to that 'Staff-Only' door over there." She nodded in the other direction. *Popular Mechanics* – it'd been how many decades? The staff door opened as I reached for it, and I entered a small, immaculate bathroom. I leaned against the door to the throne, Shandre against the sink, maybe a foot between us. A smile at our forced intimacy wouldn't hurt, but one look and I decided not to hold my breath.

"I understand you're inserting a last-minute update." I nodded. "Gimme said your evening had proved fruitful."

It had? "What?"

"Your *reporting* last night. Is it worth the immediate, real-world risk to both of us, my job the least of it, to add it to your story from here?"

"Absolutely. What I got takes it from good to over-the-moon."

"Right. She said she wouldn't bring you here unless she thought it worth the risk. Your editor is expecting it? Good, cause I think once you send it, you should do your full turnaround and be gone from here within ten minutes. Is your editor the sort of person to appreciate that and not swamp you with endless, niggling TKs?"

"I think so."

"Most important question: when you sent her – "

"Uhm, him."

"OK, sent him the bulk of the article yesterday, did you use a Dutch anonymizer?"

My *name* required on top of the story, I hadn't much worried that. I wanted notoriety to fend off Whitaker. Besides, I'd been writing on computers I'd never see again – a luxury denied Shandre. I said, "No. But I just e-mailed once and then faxed the article to him."

"If you e-mailed him even once, that fax was like taking a shower so you don't get pregnant." She sighed and sunk further on the sink. "And this general of hers is a Calfer. OK, not for anyone but Gimme. And also because one of those damn dogs got fresh with me last month on the train – understand?"

"You mean my stillborn anti-search campaign up in New York?"

"Even a stillborn Demo can strike a chord, all the play that yours is starting to get. For both our safety, ten minutes tops from sending it, to closing the story and then pulling the plug on that computer. And then I never saw you. How could I help it you snuck in when I was helping some old man find West Indian cricket scores – Minders Turn Elsewhere!"

Pondering how much Turd-Touch had screwed Zafar with all my machinations at Connexions, I looked up to see Shandre staring expectantly and mumbled, "Minders Turn Elsewhere!"

"Use the computer in the corner opposite the magazines. It's the only one in a study carrel. And look – I read your Syriac confession – save your flowery touches for your Christmas card."

"Jesus, everyone's a critic." Neither one of us was smiling. "Hey, I'd just gotten shot in the head and – well, all kinds of crap was raining down. I felt entitled."

"Gimme and I both sticking our necks way out on this, your entitlement just ended. Give me a nod when you're ready to send, and I'll start my ten-minute clock. Then I'll come tell you how you're to exit the building." As she left, she whispered, "And Mitchell, good luck!"

The computer already up and humming, damn weird not to be able to check my regular e-mail to see if *Warpath* Joe had any problems with the draft from the day before. Anyway:

Dear Joe:

Personal safety – no kidding – requires publication this morning. I'm unable to check my standard e-mail for any *prior* queries from you. After I send this, I can monitor this address for exactly eight minutes for any questions regarding yesterday's or today's material. Anything else, resolve it best you can or excise with a minimal incision. But, yes, IMPERATIVE to publish today.

Today's additions are air-tight – all direct quotes to me or my direct observation.

Joe, relying on this article to save my skin is a thin reed, I know. But it's all I got and, regardless, it'll strike a spark. Don't stint on the headline. And thus the long, steep climb starts. Good luck to us both.

(Byline is) Mitchell

Shoot, I was so Delores-bereft getting thrown out of Hart, and then focused on not getting mugged making it to Lois's, and then not mugged *by* Lois, and then making nice, and then crying in my ale, I never jotted any notes on what Whitaker said. I had his reason for sending me to Indiana nailed: "I needed an in to maximize my return, something fancy to bring to the table." I also had pretty much verbatim his statement about the $15K check to Bettinger cleaning out his account, plus his threats about no one caring I was toast after he finally sliced the bread himself. And this gem I just remembered: "I'm at war against the ridiculous conflict of interest Regs." First time ever crafting words out of someone's mouth with no notes, as Statie said, the situation did contain exigentness.

I beefed up the two points Lois reminded me to emphasize and added a splash of the evening's debauch. Having next to nothing to drink, I could've written awhile, but didn't, restricting myself to some color on the fights, the drunkenness, the cozying up between suit and uniform, even a sneer about the horrible music. The hundreds of circulating women got their due, but the four entwined on the revolving stage were the stars. Oh, and nudity on my way out (and ain't that too telling a phrase). I read it twice, found it actually somewhat restrained, and gave crack-the-whip Shandre the high sign to start her ten minutes.

What was she coming over for, cause I sure wasn't letting her edit it. Pulling up a chair, Shandre ordered, "Move over, please, so I can show you how this program works."

"What are you talking about? I know how –"

"Shush! Are you always so hard-headed, cause I need a reason to come over here. Well go ahead and send so I can start the clock. When you're done, go back to the staff bathroom and – "

"You're crazy if you think I can fit out that little window."

"*And* keep on going down that same hall to the Emergency Only"exit. The alarm hasn't worked since I got here, and I'd hate to admit how many years ago that was. Out that door, go straight to the ladder I just put there over the back fence and climb down the other side as best you can. Do not break an ankle, cause once you get up from this chair, we've never met. You got that?"

"Sure thing, Mata Hari."

"Once you get over the fence, head on through the trees, down the hill, out that house's driveway and do not get caught. Somebody messes with you, flash your wallet at 'em real quick, act official – act *white* – say something about an 'ongoing investigation,' and don't stop until they get you on the ground. Which it's your job to see does not happen. You can do that, New York?"

"Sure thing, like I been saying."

"You know what, the homeowner comes after you, just tell 'em you work for this psycho DC cop named Cummings and watch them run. Then turn left out of the driveway, keep walking, though not *too* fast, and catch the first bus you see going that way. Any bus runs into MLK. You have four singles on you? Please tell me someone doing this knows to always, always carry singles."

"After the cabs I took last night, probably not." She held up some folded bills. "I can't take – "

"Boy, wake up! You can't take a few dollars from a black woman? Whether you give a damn about yourself or not, we are talking about *my* safety here. And I need you off the street, not big as life fumbling around in a store round the corner from my library making change." She jammed the money in my shirt pocket. "If the bus turns right at MLK, stay on, it's going over the bridge to the District. It turns left, stay on too, it's going to the Metro. Got it? Hit send and you have ten minutes."

She solemnly shook my hand, gave it a squeeze and left. I hit send and waited for the screen to go kerflooey because of the recipient, then worried that Joe might be in the john. A long four minutes later, his minimal queries appeared.

From the big chunk of it the day before, he wanted only a rock-solid assurance that I had reported to Whitaker by phone from Indiana following the H-DM presentation. Doing so violated Joe's sense of how a legit investigation would work and therefore helped indict the general. Plus, from the morning's installment, had Whitaker really said that about being at war with the conflict of interest Regs? And had I really seen a nude dancer in a Senate office building, cause he wanted to pump that big. I offered to describe her. He passed "unless she was in some way remarkable." Well, she was, but.

He offered congrats on a boffo piece, said it'd be up in half-an-hour once he ran it by his partner and would bounce big given the "oddities that abound with you right now." And he told me to get the hell gone from wherever I was. Plus he wanted more stories, especially my tale of getting shot. He suggested I clear up the "disturbing rumors" about my stay at Bellevue, rumors traceable to a certain competitor of his. Joe said he could do three-hundred bucks for either article, five hundred for both. Yeah, big bucks, liked I'd bragged to Nicki the week before.

Rumors. Thanks, Stanley, you bitter little man.

OK, half-an-hour till even more infamy magically rendered me all safe and cozy – a thin reed indeed. Leaving, I nodded to Shandre. But she remained focused on her screen. The first hurdle on the journey home was an eight-foot hurricane fence out back, the kind with green lattice strips you can't see through. Sure, Shandre's ladder would get me up, but it might actually hinder the transfer from windward to leeward. I stashed it by the dumpster and decided I'd be too visible from the street at either corner to take advantage of the fence's right angle. Heck, good for what ails you, climbing a tall fence unaided every once in a great while.

I reached up, got a toe in, then slipped badly. Just scale the Goddamn fence. Do it, so I'd get to testify, with full immunity, against Whitaker in some court down the road. And get "Penn/Etc." out, past time to own my own story or kiss it goodbye. Punch MoneyBags in the nose, sue the MTA for a new pack *and* my books, and get that damn SecDef whole-vid out too – probably, maybe. Bumfuckville's Bodega Dude far, far away, just scram before Whitaker's latest henchman, the Man with One Arm, dropped from a tree. Cause I needed to stuff a few alley cats in a sack and haunt the Huntington train in search of Boss Conductor. Not to mention my enigmatic, potential new girlfriend.

Nothing for it but crab my way up, hope my sole wasn't pierced at the top and vault over and down. Almost up, I thought to go get the ladder and peer over for a soft landing spot rather than the discarded Ford Pinto engine I might be heading for. Robbed of momentum, I got my cuff hung up, but kept going, thinking it'd pull free. The cloth ripped only after turning me half-upside down to crash in a heap on soft earth further down than it looked. Competing in the Unaided-by-Bodega-Dude Division, the Republic of Bushwick's was the only judge who scored it above a 2.6.

But no mangled ankle, and the tear in my pants wasn't too glaring if you didn't look. A quick inventory confirmed the three e-mails and Bettinger's memo, my book, wallet, keys, new toothbrush! pen and notebook – enough gear to assault a whole den of Calfers. Shit! Where was my wedding ring, stashed in my pocket the day before? I searched my pockets, then frantically down amidst last year's leaves turning to mud. No dice, damn it. Lost in the sauce somewhere along the way. And no, I couldn't tarry there in whoever's back yard. Guess that meant taking my ring off was more than a dumb gesture, more than a bit of sleaze for Lois's benefit. Screw it – and the wife.

A scamper through the back yard and down the driveway, and a bus soon showed to take me to the Metro rather than over the bridge. A cop car screaming up behind shrank me in my seat but kept going. Happy that the Whitaker story was out of my hands, I also was glad of the folks off and on and on and off on busy MLK, glad to just sit and picture Lois beckoning from the top of her stairs. Sure, I embodied the necessary chutzpah – she liked me. Plus I was different, uh-huh, than her usual.

But one happy puzzle kept intruding: what to make of Shandre's surprise. Sandwiched between her singles were a couple of twenties. Lucky I didn't feed them blindly into the bus lock-box gizmo, cause there was a big sign saying "No Change For Any Reason!"

We'd just have to see about that, MoFos – me and two Anacostians definitely cooking with gas.

Chapter Fifty

Reckless Everett's Stink Bomb

Along with getting sweaty in the Metro's cavernous heat, I had to check that Joe's partner hadn't kiboshed the story, plus answer the note from Pop that Bybee interrupted leaping on me in Connexions. So back downtown to get the digital lay of the land. Then a museum café to polish off "Penn/Etc." and stare at the tourists. Then a stroll to generate a thirst and a couple of beers.

It became apparent that my time to deliver was soon. I rode a few stops and got out at Chinatown, but those crabbed little restaurants weren't conducive. Walking on, I found myself staring up at the Hay-Adams hotel as matters became more precipitate. A venerable old pile, there was no sign in the rococo lobby. I pasted on a purposeful smile and scooted up a staircase to a promenade. Bingo.

Mission accomplished, I encountered another of the many reasons this is indeed a great country. Every time I shifted – gotta shift for access, no other way round it – the toilet's maniacal laser eye concluded I was done rather than pursuing the necessary paperwork.And so it flushed, spraying me with unclean water. If this was progress, I wanted none of it. I ruminated a moment to lull the laser eye asleep, then leaped off before it got me again. Yup, DC in a nutshell.

Out in search of a computer – God, was that willowy brunette up ahead Delores? Cruising up alongside to see, I felt rather than saw some schmuck pass, stop and turn.

"Fremson, is that you? Stop!"

I closed the last step and gracelessly confirmed, nope, not Delores. The startled young beauty whisked away.

"Yo, stop! That's you, I know it is."

Ah, new excitement, his bellicosity demanding to be answered in kind. Hell, with my new girlfriend a *major* in the United States Army, I needed to hold up my end. Enough was freaking enough! He came charging up wearing the same dumb heifer tie Fenton wore, though his also featured an amorphous, dark presence opposing the light coming from the cloud. He pulled out his pacifier as he came, stopped, thumbed it, compared the image to the corporeal reality, and said, "Why are you harassing that fertile young Homelander, Fremson? I'm surprised you're still out on the streets bothering right-minded people."

"I was just inviting her to watch while I sent you packing. Old-hat, sure, but she might find it amusing."

"Not half as funny as you getting tossed from the Appropriators' Ball last night, B.E.I. You should have stuck around, cause kicking you out was just what that party needed. Even better was when they threw out this piece of baggage who looked like a kindergarten teacher. She kept saying that she didn't know you, that you two were just talking. She put up such a fight against like four of our Enablers, some Marines were actually rooting for her. They were going to taze her right there on the floor after they threw her down, teach her what's what. It would've been fun to watch her twitch, but some damn admiral intervened."

Turd-Touch in spades! He caught my distraught look. "Bad news? Like maybe you did know her and infiltrated the party together?"

"Nah. She was just disappointed not to stick around to see you service those soldiers. The way you handled them I saw online this morning – that must take years of priming the pump."

I leaned against one of the countless flagpoles, crossed my arms and grinned as this guy, young and enough of a jerk to have scored a ticket to Hart, took an angry step towards me. Might as well get it over with, cause rolling around on a DC sidewalk was probably where this trip to HeadFuck's seat was headed all along.

But he stopped and started sputtering. "Industry, the lobbyists, my shop – that's Crutchem and Baggit! – not to mention the Army: we're all gunning for you, Fremson. What makes you think you can smear a Red-Calf Plenipotentiary like General Whitaker during the Current Permanent Crisis? Not to mention how pissed off ASPIC is that your nonsense about refusing random T-search is starting to spread. Do you know how much money is at stake in privatizing those searches – here, New York, Boston, who knows where."

"Spread how?"

"How about you tell me." I stared blankly. Finally, with the water-bearer's natural eagerness to display access to inside poop, he almost whispered, "A very confidential, T list-serve, one I'm able to read only looking over a senior Crutchem and Baggit operative's shoulder, said there were fourteen different search-refusals on transit systems around the Homeland yesterday. Buses too. In Oakland and in Madison, Wisconsin, there were like big, organized groups. And chatter indicates there'll be more today."

"Fourteen, huh?"

"It's only a matter of time before we penetrate your T-symp network. A lot of people are wondering how you got that blonde bitch to accompany you down that corridor in Penn Station. Cause she was damn sympathetic to you on *Breakfast Raunch* this morning. Blamed the Protectors. A talented girl like her people were ready to get behind, what a waste."

Carole, really? "What did she say?"

"Like you, or someone a lot smarter, didn't write her script for her. She didn't even show any goodies, dressed like a damn nun, she was."

"Alright, dude, I got smelts to fry."

I turned to go, and he grabbed me by the sore shoulder and twirled me half around as we grappled. I surprised him by suddenly spinning the way he wanted and slamming him hard in the chest with both hands and off me.

Man, that felt good, enough was indeed enough. I upped to him and he fell back, both of us breathing hard. His cow tie askew, I'd touched one and remained unsmote.

"Why are you messing with a general, you T-symp! Calfers are off-limits in this town! I read your *On the Warpath* little nothing. People are laughing so hard, it's bouncing all over even though – you horse's ass – it's like twelve-hundred words! No one's going to believe it'd take more than fifteen dollars to hire scum like you, not fifteen-thousand. Bold. Extolled. Impregnable! Don't you get it?"

Cool, it got published. And it's got legs. "All that cash wasn't for me, pal." Jesus, had Joe screwed up that bad, saying that money was supposedly for me? If the article said I was spying for real money, just pry open the nearest manhole cover and drop me down.

"Don't you move, while I get a Protector here to see about those e-mails you fabricated."

I swore, turned and booked, managing to head north like I'd been. I looked back to see him yapping into his micro-zap and waving his arm. Our article was supposed to protect me from Whitaker, and maybe it would. But what about all his friends, both institutional and institutionalizable? Time to get the hell away from people who might recognize me, though where, pray tell, was that?

A block on, clown-boy not following – I should remember there's nothing like a salutary little two-handed chest slam – two Grinders full of soldiers came barreling round the corner, headed straight towards me, and kept going. He jumped out to flag them down and just barely jumped back as they roared past.

I had to get off the streets till my *Warpath* screed worked its magic. Plus it'd be good to get in front of a screen to ensure Joe hadn't royally screwed up about Whitaker's $15K check to Bettinger. I cut east and ended up zigging and sagging north through a quiet little homeowners' neighborhood as NW eased into NE. A tolerable 96-degrees according to a passing car radio, I considered a walking beer, not quite sure where I was walking to except *away*. Right, pop a beer and round a corner into the arms of a black cop pissed at someone thinking white skin would let him skate in a vestigially black neighborhood. Just hope not to bloody his nose.

I plodded, sweated, thought about Lois keeping her eyes open kissing, had a Little Debbie to confirm her inferiority to Lady Linda, sweated and plodded, got cursed to "get the fuck back to your own country" by some boys young enough to dismiss (probably), and finally came across Connexions' glossier big brother, one ThinkTanked by name.

The kid behind the counter forbade cash. Independent and out-of-the-way, maybe this joint wouldn't prove as spook-friendly as Deskless and its ilk. Or maybe I was plain done turning tail, a *story* saving me. Like I told Lois, I wasn't kicking no squirrels out of their hollow tree to go live off the Bar Code.

****

A nd there it was making a nifty splash on a traffic-slowed *Off the Warpath*. Preceded by "Exclusive" in red, Joe's nice fat headline pulled no punches: "General Admits to $15,000-Corporate Espionage to 'Maximize my Return'; Declares, 'I'm at war against the ridiculous conflict of interest Regs'; Threatens Reporter at Nude-Dancer Capitol Hill Debauch".

I raced through it, and of course Joe had not screwed up about the money. Plus, Whitaker's e-mails and Bettinger's assignment memo all surfaced bold and brassy at a click. So off to the races, you and me, Parnell.

Joe wrote me that it was bouncing higher than anything on *Warpath* in years. *Morning Dyspepsia* was even linking (Joe's first), and several outfits wanted to interview me. Joe told them, truthfully enough he figured, that I was secreted away somewhere for my own safety but he hoped I surfaced soon.

441

There was also a note from Stan the Man, weighing in with "deep disappointment over your betrayal of this site and the Movement both, publishing today on that parvenu's little rag." There was also the usual torrent of threats, abuse, come-ons legal and otherwise, and appeals to fold my "case" into this or that tortured legal skirmish, several supplicants assuring me they had a "real" judge.

And two notes from Pop, Wednesday's stronger than the prior one. What with my "cell phone" (as he still called it) not answering – did I need help with the bill? – and my home answering machine full, he and Mom were so concerned, he'd endured rush-hour traffic driving to the Hovel Tuesday night when I hadn't answered his first note. And he'd encountered Mr. Staphilopoulos:

Your landlord, whatever the hell his name is, is decent enough. He said there were a couple of people sniffing around after you, but no one showed any warrants, so no dice. He finally got convinced I was your father. He said I was too old to be anything else, though I'm in better shape than him with his funny little Greek cancer sticks that he almost got me to try just curious how it tasted. Like I need to start that shit again. The funny thing was, once he figured out who I was, his English got a lot better. Made me laugh cause the old guys used to pull that in Brooklyn all the time.

Hey, I know things were rough during our phone call Sunday, but answer your damn e-mail. If you'd answered yesterday's, it would had saved me a trip to Queens which I really don't need, all those assholes driving like they got to get some-where to save the world.

Schulman down the block called again this morning, asking if we get macro-transmissions, like we're worrying about that crap at our age. He's a little too caught up in your troubles, you ask me. Anyway, turns out the girl who got shot with you was on something called Breakfast Raunch. And Schulman, when I finally got him to stop bitching about her not wearing a see-through shirt or something trying to pretend he's some old goat, said she blamed the cops about you two getting shot. The TV guy tried to say, well sweetie, your memory aint good, the trauma and all. But she wasn't having none of it. A girl like that turns out to have a head on her shoulders too. Go figure.

Look, I know you're in trouble, but just write back four letters
– I'm OK. Your landlord said I should come back, he'll take
me to his little social club to play cards. Even just looking for
new money on the table, nice to get an invite. Spell his name
for me so I can get it. Write back and don't be a jerk cause I
got enough to worry about right now.
Love, Pop.

Again with the *love*, the dude going soft in his dotage. I replied
that I was down in DC, and he should check out a site called *Off
the Warpath* to learn why. Said I wasn't proud of myself, but – bee's
knees! – at least the whys and wherefores of my disgrace appeared
under my own byline. I cut and pasted the article, gave him the
link for Whitaker's e-mailed dirt it was grounded in, and spelled
Staphilopoulos. Them two a team – look out!

Then up scrolled the disaster of the day, a whole new barrel of
trouble. "Lester Genny" was Everett's handle for public consumption, "You Lying Sack of Shit" the subject heading on his note.

All those weeks of bitching at me, Everett had never violated
my idiot, regular e-mail account, its address my idiot name. But,
included at the bottom of dozens of articles, it wasn't hard to find.
And here he'd violated our radio-silence on this of all days, standing
on a chair waving a red flag. He'd obviously decided to forfeit my
claim to continued respiration, a claim I'd staked by so far declining
to smear mud all over the SecDef's flabby legs. His hands darted out
the screen at my throat:

Sack:
Bottom line up top, you boasted in your ridiculous
letter to that Syriac site that you were going to tell what
you learned at the H-DM plant and "maybe even save some
lives in the process." So when the fuck is the whole-vid I sent
you of the SecDef rolling the new H-DM Grinder at Aberdeen
coming out? That's a hell of a lot more important than some
general trying to line his pockets. Like that doesn't happen
every day in Procurement.

You ignore your Dutch address, so using this one is maybe the spark that my ass-kissing through Holland ain't been. I've identified four sites, including Off the Warpath and that weird little uptight Naked Opposition, that say they'll run the whole-vid soon as I find someone to meet the Regs by putting a verifiable name on top. And believe me I've been looking. But no one gets back to me. I'd do it myself except I got this little girl to raise up.

That was supposed to be where you came in – pushing a LIFE-SAVING whole-vid out the door. And now there's a real reason it's got to be you even more than when we met. That's because you can't get in the shit any deeper than you already are by starting up this anti-T-search business. You got nothing more to lose.

News out of Indianapolis this morning, a bunch of black kids who take a public bus to high school sat on the bus and refused to get off after a dog alerted on one of them. Said it wasn't random, and they were targeted right from the start with the cops stopping their bus like that. That the dog was freaking out from the moment it got on the bus. That it basically alerted on everyone there. They started rocking the bus from the inside after the cops took off the adults, plus some white kids sitting up front heading to a different school. Then the cops said they were all arrested. Like the Wobblies say, "Direct action gets the goods!" One kid they interviewed on TV mentioned your blow-hard Syriac letter. Though he wasn't too crazy about you comparing yourself to Rosa Parks.

Look, the cops blew up your pack to say it had explosives – nice Catch-22 – plus they're putting out fake whole-vid that turns you into the shooter, and they apparently already locked you up in Bellevue. So why the hell you worried about putting out my whole-vid, deep, deep in the crapper like you are?

I don't really care about your aborted Penn Station action. Civ-lib is for civilians. I'm trying to save grunts' lives. Cause if the Army awards the Grinder contract to H-DM, that's it, they aint going back. Just fill out the paperwork on hundreds of non-combat deaths a year.

Do the right thing, dude, or I feel a road-trip coming on. Thank you New York Daily Chirp for your fancy address down by the river. You never know when I might catch the sniffles and need a couple of days off. So just get the whole-vid the hell out before either me or some H-DM criminal comes

banging on your door. Cause then it's too late – tomorrow
ain't coming whether you give a shit or not. Do it, man, and
earn yourself a bowl of mean beef stew.
Genny

The man liked that beer. *The whole-vid I ... sent ... you of the
SecDef....* He had screwed me up, down and Blue. Hell, Everett had
been a blast-concussed loose cannon since way before grabbing me
off the H-DM factory floor. He was right, though, that a whole-vid
taking down an eight-billion-dollar program to save hundreds of
lives outweighed hill-of-beans Whitaker by a lot of beans. So, my
prospects so bleak and my loins so shamefully unreproductive,
nothing for it but shine a light on the SecDef rollover that he's too
freaking pristine, with his precious daughter, to shine himself?

I added the SecDef's merry band of MoFos to the posse after me,
turned the simmering H-DM thugs up to a boil, and didn't e-mail
the bastard back. Damn Everett and his whole-vid, which I'd had no
reason to grab as I left the Hovel two mornings back heading out on
that HateCrime ticket.

Tell you what: with fourteen search-refusals the day before, I
really needed to join that party my *next* opportunity.

Warpath Joe would alert me meanwhile if anything devastating
materialized, like an artfully crafted whole-vid of me with baggy,
disgusting shorts round my ankles skewering a red heifer. And suddenly this weird screen sorta *shimmered* into view on top of my mail.
Never seen anything quite like it wavering there so oddly.

Mitch
Get out now! Pull the plug, out the door and keep going.
NOW!
A Friend Inside

The plug out of reach, I flicked the power off and on and split,
just managing to duck behind a cluster of flags across the street as

445

an enormous, candy-apple red, civilian-model Grinder with dark windows roared up and parked all askew. It was one of those nonsensical pickups with a covered bed too small to carry anything but a few cases of cat food. Still ugly as sin, but natty in the threads he favored when not impersonating a cop, Lurch from Bellevue marched into ThinkTanked. I picked north and ran like I hadn't in a long, long time.

Chapter Fifty-One

Ridden Hard, Put Up Wet

I sat in the back of a Mickey-King, the only sit-down joint for many a block, nursing fries and attempting more scribbling on *my* story, damn it. Lurch hot on my tail, obviously I needed more firepower than *Warpath* on Whitaker. Mostly I bobbed and weaved, Lurch's unfortunate mug swimming before me. His unleavened contempt up at Bellevue had pegged him as from DC. But who the hell did he work for in that ill-fitting cop costume and then jacket and tie?

Unwilling to sit and wait for the net to drop, I walked hither then back yon, comfy homes mingling with desolation. Bates Street was spiffy, as was First and O. Down-home DC offered a nice uncluttered feel about things as you'd turn a corner and find an enormous athletic field attached to a school. Suddenly light-headed in the heat, or such was my excuse, I fell into a little cinder-block joint called The Liar's Alibi figuring it'd welcome me with open arms.

But after ignoring me for several minutes, the bartender in gold lame pants and a fiery wig finally came up and demanded proof of age from the likes of me. Not wanting to hand over my ID for any reason, but mostly just beset on all sides, I didn't need such nonsense to sit and gulp a beer. Badly overestimating me, a customer yelled as I left, "That's right – goodbye! Your kind been Plunged, boy! This neighborhood ain't for sale no more."

Despite Washington's lack of hospitality, I was in no hurry to return to the Hovel. Best to let *Warpath* fester overnight, rendering me all snuggly-safe as dawn broke. So, a room for the night for cash. Judge Fennerly dismissing the HateCrime ticket, topped off by Shandre's generosity, my wallet was probably heavy enough. Use a credit card, and I'd still be on my second beer when the MoFos barged in. And then they'd steal the rest of the six-pack. I doubled back a few blocks to a no-tell motel to hear the guy refuse my cash, even when I offered to bring him the room phone so I couldn't stiff him on phone charges.

"What makes you think my customers need a phone, man? Ain't nobody staying here looking to be bothered by the shit they came here to get away from."

He sent me packing to a place eight blocks down, six blocks over, a sweaty trek that wasn't rewarded. Why didn't I have a credit card, the little foreign man there wanted to know before his English deserted him when I waved money under his nose.

At a loss and my dogs barking, I blindly caught a bus heading back downtown. A woman across the aisle was reading one of those ubiquitous free daily papers, slight trash foisted on an indifferent city. I admired the photo on the back of the Oklahoma City Roughneck young phenom, Callaghan-Perez, sliding into second, spikes high. The headline said, "Payback Tonight?" and thus my plan for the evening.

Out in the world but safe, sequestered among many dozens of Washington Nationals' fans – the Roughnecks, sure. They'd stomped all over the Mets three, four weeks back. And after the Nats lost, well, I'd stroll out on the arm of one of the many lonely, morally casual women known to frequent night baseball games.

I quit the bus for the train to the Stadium-Armory stop. And then sat on it wondering about Lois's day amidst hungover Pentagon Calfers. Fleeing such thoughts, I took to scratching with my pen. And some excitable dweeb started and said, "Hey, what are you doing? What are you writing? Who are you to be writing stuff down, here on the Metro? None of us did anything. I've been in this car since before you, and nobody's done a thing!"

I curled my lip, decided against giving him the bird as he kept sputtering, and set to telling of the green-suited greaseball who'd invaded my ambulance. I didn't think that little violation yet graced the scattershot pages hopefully still on my kitchen table awaiting my return.

We pulled into a stop and Dweeby jumped up, declared the whole "incident" preserved by the car's cameras, and announced that he was going for help. Good – lawyers, guns and money, make it snappy, pal. I grinned around at my fellow passengers to elicit confirmation of his evident illness, but everyone just stared at their feet as the train pulled out.

Thirty-six bucks to get in: $27 for the cheapest ticket, $5 for "handling," though I was standing at the Nats' window paying cash, and $4 for "T-enhancement." No searches, oddly enough, but plenty of cameras. Curious, I joshed with the ticket-taker about the lack of a search. He stiffened and said they'd dispensed with them late last season to save money. "Long as you don't try to smuggle in any sandwiches, you're OK. Why, you got some kind of problem? I can arrange for a supervisor to search you real quick if that makes you feel safer."

Me safer? I was about to point out that particular idiocy, but I'd just dropped a lot of money and, besides, had nowhere else to go.

Half the folks scattered in the upper deck behind home plate were dressed in Nationals bright red, including some dame pushing seventy in uniform pants, stirrups, the works. Neat to be off the streets, amidst the few, the loud, the committed, no MoFo coming up on me unawares.

Moving from Cincinnati after things deteriorated there, the OKC Roughnecks were in the National League's new Southern division, the Central having been disbanded once the Disruption hit Cincinnati hard, and then a new owner hightailed the Pirates off to Las Vegas. They were fun to watch scooting all over the field in their lime-green uniforms, the Nats actually pulling their catcher mid-inning after three Roughnecks stole second with embarrassing ease.

Good to galumph my feet over the empty seat in front, slump

way back and groove on a game in an old football stadium making no effort to be anything else, everything distended and far away and out of scale. Even the distance between home and second seemed off somehow. I finally broke down and hailed one of the black vendors who far outnumbered the black fans there in (formerly) Chocolate City. Peanuts, the cheapest offering, a mere eight bucks. Cracking your way to the puny reward took enough time to pretend you got your money's worth.

Around the fifth inning, the dicey little question I'd been smothering raised itself irreducibly: where was I getting horizontal? Sure I'd been catnip to women since getting shot – long as I didn't think about actually getting laid. But the only women remotely approachable in the entire upper deck were the two youngish moms over there yoked with three preadolescent horrors begging for more soda. They could fight over me, the loser saddled with all three kids.

In other words, time to call this editor I knew at a joint I'd published some, *The Monthly Mordancy*. Call to see about a vacancy on Richard's couch, if his micro-zap miraculously hadn't changed, *and* I still had it scrawled on a piece of paper in my wallet from back when people wanted to hang out with me. The stadium so old as to feature actual working pay phones, yup, there was his number, and there was Richard, recognizing my voice at hello. And how the devil was that possible, I asked.

"I guess because we were talking about you at a story meeting today, which had us watching that absolutely classic NYONLY vid. And we were wondering if we should interview you about how that no-search seed of yours is starting to sprout, plus all the curiosities in your life lately. With the proper editorial controls, of course."

"Control under my own byline is what I like best."

"I don't think that would be possible right now."

"Yeah, fine. Already been offered an interview."

"I can imagine. Your *Warpath* story, it'll be interesting to see how it unfolds once they try to walk it back. But it got quite the bounce with those e-mails your general was dumb enough to send. Who knows, maybe things are starting – *starting* – to get a little interesting, not that that's going anywhere. As for you, you better hope your piece stays tight."

"Tight like the rope I got around Whitaker's neck. But anyway, Richard, I was wondering … a little favor. Any chance your couch has a vacancy sign on it for tonight? Just the one night, I promise. But I think I should stay in DC for another day to wrap things up and, well, things have gotten complicated."

"Complicated? Try radioactive in your case. Tonight – right. The very day you took down a big-shot Army Calfer? That's a 'little favor' I'd tell my own mother to stick it."

"It's just, you told me once if I ever needed a favor, not to hesitate to call."

"That was a long time ago, my man. Way, way before the HeadMan. Uhm, B.E.I. The answer is categorically no-way-Jose. I gotta go. Don't call here again." Baanhhnh!

I sat down within hailing distance of the two moms. Hey, one might be single, all the kids belonging to the other. Not that either responded with anything but a grunt and then silence to my friendly, insightful observations about the game, one of their daughters sticking her tongue out at me. A good game, anyway, a Nat having clubbed a three-run homer – that I of course missed! – staking Washington to a one-run lead.

But the Roughnecks' sheer speed and guile tightening the Nat infielders' collars, they manufactured two runs in the top of the ninth as we all knew they would, and the dejected home-nine's last licks were a quiet one-two-three at ten-fifteen, too late for the 10:30 last Chinatown bus home. I followed the half of the crowd heading for the Metro rather than the parking lots, intending what, exactly? Then everyone disappeared down the steps of the station, not a soul beckoning me to follow. I kept walking away from the lights of the city.

I passed a spooky old hospital by the edge of the Anacostia River, then scuttled by an even spookier giant new jail – one old, one new, do the math. Some doggerel was spray-painted on the jail's far outer wall:

MARCHING TO FUTURE DEPTHS,
THE POWERS SEEK NONE OF MORE.
MAD TO REMEMBER, WE PRAY TO FORGET.
MARCHING, SHOUTING, SCURRYING, SHOOTING —
AVAUNT, HORATIO — THE TANKS *!*

That's right, baby, avaunt! The two institutions gave way to a well appointed neighborhood of single-family homes. And what had apparently been my fallback position all along elbowed its oddly liberating way to the fore. It had been gaining momentum since the two sleaze-bag motels declared my cash unclean.

"Radioactive," unfit for human company, it was time to go to ground, time to sleep under the stars like a proper revolutionary. Good for the soul and no one the wiser, what was I afraid of? That I'd find it all too easy? That the Farragut Square lending library wouldn't soon welcome me, though I carried a book to contribute? That I'd regret, as DC's version of Fall came on, round about Christmas, not taking that fancy jacket from the last woman I'd ever kiss. That I'd soon be buttonholing tourists to draw them as close as uncertain hygiene permitted and plead, "I used to be a contender, sure. But right now, buddy, I could use a bite."

I'd been spending like a drunken sailor, a king's ransom for the ball game and my crunchy dinner. Save some money burrowing away on soft lichen. Dismiss the MoFos for the night. Not under that bridge looming there, I wasn't a troll. Not yet. But, yeah, down by the river.

Walking on, yup, a cemetery behind an easy enough thick brick wall. Congressional Cemetery it said. Well, Congress needed one.

Old trees graced the paths meandering through the modest head-stones and disappearing down a gentle slope towards the river. A cemetery, was that good luck or bad? Teenage couples were always fooling around in them – yeah, right before the haint got them. Awfully inviting, the main thing was to get in without being seen. All the houses across sleepy 17th Street were dark except for a room or two with a blue flicker.

The six-foot wall sloped down to under four-feet by the corner of 17th and H and so up and over like gravy, no Bodega Dude neces-sary. I hunched over and scrambled further in, tripped on a broken headstone, then veered closer to the street lamp shining in the land of the living.

Man, was I really doing this? Sure, welcomed by folks who meant me no harm, and where else could I be sure of that? OK, behind that tree looked pretty soft. I went over to seek benediction from the nearest resident, one Fielding Ablegar, 1818 – 1879. Lucky, probably, with the Civil War age-wise, had Fielding found his allotted time sufficient? Shit, the wolf huffing and puffing at my house of straw, sixty-one sounded pretty good to me. His faded epitaph unreadable in the dark, I'd check it come morning. A pastrami hero and a forty would've settled nice, a propitiating sip poured on Fielding's grave. Throw in the Entertainment System for company, and I'd have been in clover – or lichen.

I curled around a root, my standard recent posture alone in my big bed, and gave Lois's toothbrush a workout. Everett, you reckless bastard, though maybe he was right. His e-mail the cherry on top of the free-floating miasma rising above my knees, maybe it did fall to me to get that SecDef whole-vid out. Save a few hundred lives year after year, plus charge a nice fat fee for the few paragraphs I'd write on Grinder non-combat casualties to accompany my top-five, Keystone Kops whole-vid. Except the only news sites with the guts to run it had no money. Sexual indiscretion about the only scandal that paid, if I had something meaningless like the SecDef rutting with one of HeadMan's chief gangsters, sky's the limit.

Speaking of nastiness, was I so far down south I had to worry about snakes and whatnot? Fire ants, poison lichen? Needing someone to examine all my parts for ticks was the emergency that'd send me to Lois's door on the morrow.

I woke up cold still a long way from morning. Cold and feeling awfully exposed, not that I was moving to a darker precinct among the shades. I rolled over, away from the street light I'd been hugging. And what was that way over there? Forgetting to hunch over, I got up and – yo, momma! – a green tarp covering the loose dirt next to a grave dug for the morning's solemnities. Fleeing the open grave, I dragged the tarp back to my spot by Fielding, he and I with a good groove going.

Half the tarp ground cover, half a blanket, I snuggled in and hugged the earth with as much of me as I could, invisible to the living, the dead hospitable.

PART NINE

Chapter Fifty-Two

Two Guys, Lonely but Not Alone

The birds finally drove me into another thrilling day. That was indeed a root gouging my back, but what in the world was I wrapped up in? Suddenly, a foul breath on my face forced my eyes open.

Its muzzle way too close to mine, no telling how big the dog was, not that it mattered, his teeth within striking distance of so many important parts. Growling and snapping, it had me pinned down pretty good, my hands trapped under my green-tarp blanket. A man called out, "Rip, it's just a bum violating our park. Come on boy, let's go."

But Rip was enjoying himself, and from the next "Come on, boy" I could tell his owner had turned away. Trying to bring my hands up under the tarp elicited a couple of even closer snaps. Scared of a haint in the night, I'd slept with my glasses on. So I'd be able to admire the disfigurement of my mouth and nose if he didn't just go for my throat.

"Hey, mister!" I managed to call before the dog silenced me with way too close a feint. No reply. OK. I smashed him in the nose through the tarp, the damn thing yelping as I scrambled up. A wire-haired Jack Russell well capable of biting the mess out of someone lying prone.

His owner came rushing up. "What did you just do?"

"Kept him from going for my throat. You enjoyed that didn't you, pal?"

"Never mind that. If he's damaged right before the Greater Richmond All-Dog Invitational, you will pay, believe me. Members pay $200 a year for the exclusive right to use this dog park. You don't have a dog, not that someone vicious like that to a defenseless animal would even be allowed on our waiting list."

"*Defenseless*?"

"Don't pretend you didn't see the signs prohibiting admittance after dark, because you slept here overnight. You can't deny it. This cemetery is on the National Registration of History Sites, so that makes you a T-Felon!"

"No, no, a T-*Fiend*. Doesn't that make you nervous, cowboy? As to 'defenseless,' he was going for my throat unprovoked. You got no – "

"I stupidly left the house without my micro-zap. Or you'd be running from the Protectors soon enough. Rip, we're leaving!"

"And the horse you rode in on, pal. Jesus H. Christ!"

As if knowing that Fielding was my protector, the nasty little thing darted to lift his leg on his headstone before I could stop him. I bent and stretched, trying to iron out the kinks.

"I've never heard what the 'H' stands for. You wouldn't happen to know, would you?"

I turned to see a big, laughing old guy with shades (not that there was any sun), brush-cut white hair and some faded tattoos on his meaty forearms. "H stands for, 'How the hell do I rid myself of the ass*holery* haunting my life?' I'm sorry – I'm sure you're jake. It's just that twerp was getting his rocks off letting his dog mess with me, and

I've about had my full of lying there taking it. Plus I really don't like this rotten town of yours."

"A visitor? Well, of course, sleeping rough like this. Stupid me. Sorry, I don't get to talk to too many folks, people who talk back, I mean. My name's Pete." And he stepped forward to shake and – heck with it – I gave up my first name.

"I like dogs, don't get me wrong," he said. "But, man, they do not belong in cemeteries. Not one with hundreds of Civil War veterans. Yuppies with their fancy little dogs toss balls, frisbees even, and the dogs trample all over the graves. This is consecrated ground, but the cemetery lets them pay to turn it into a dog run. And don't get me started on the dogs lifting their legs on headstones – or worse."

"Speaking of which, me and Fielding Ablegar there got simpatico during the night. I was curious about his epitaph, which I couldn't read in the dark. Kind of an impromptu sojourn last night, I didn't bring my flashlight."

I started over towards Fielding but, standing behind me, he recited: "Search the World Over, but Find thy True Beacon upon Offering thy Surrender."

"Man, you're really into this cemetery, cause how many head-stones have you memorized?"

"None. My eyesight isn't 20-10 anymore, but it's still good enough to read that. I'd have memorized Matthew Brady's inscription if he had one. Ever since I came by and found dog shit on him – he's right over there – I've been dropping by most mornings to send the dogs over to J. Edgar Hoover."

I studied Fielding's inscription a moment. He said, "Pardon me saying, but I don't see any provisions. No skin off my nose, but if you want an egg sandwich, our house is that green one there with the tall attic window."

"See, Pete, I said you were jake."

I returned the tarp to the waiting grave. Walking to his house,

457

Pete – apparently hungry for talk – told me he'd spent his life as a petroleum engineer in oil fields all over the world. He'd made decent money and raised his family, but knew something was missing. And somehow he ended up in DC teaching high school math. He stuck it out for two years, but it was awfully tough at his age. I said I could imagine, trying to pound math home, given kids' attention spans these days. No, the classes were fine, he said, sparsely attended, but the kids who showed really wanted it. It was all the rest that he couldn't hack, the homeroom, plus the cafeteria and hallway duty. It was a young man's game.

Then, life was such, it got beyond him to think of moving back where he came from. Besides, he liked his sleepy neighborhood, though he was sorry the Plunge meant the Nationals and all their traffic hadn't left. Hitting his front walk, I asked if he was all alone in the big house, and he said might as well be, that his wife wasn't much company anymore. I said, well, that happens in a marriage, but he said it wasn't like that.

We walked down the side of a tidy, green house with a beaming yellow door and neat hedges and lawn. A wooden table and chairs anchored one side of the back yard, a screened-in enclosure with a couple of chaise lounges anchored the other. A natural-cut big black poodle roused herself from under the table to greet us. I laughed, and he said he told me he liked dogs, just not ones that piss on war vets' graves. He introduced her as Lucy and told her to keep me company a moment.

Through the kitchen screen door I heard him talking low. He came out with soap, washcloth, shampoo, a towel, a plastic razor and a brush. He said he'd had his sense of smell pretty well burned away in an oilfield accident, but he imagined I was a little gamey, sleeping out like that. "You can take a whore's bath on the driveway there with the hose if you want. Whatever your day brings, that'll probably make it go down a little easier." Folks reach for the soap at first glance. He left to get some eggs going, and I took him up on his offer, stripping to the waist. Tricky not to soak my pants or shoes, but shaving was easy in the side mirror of his old, green Saab convertible.

The blue dress shirt I'd put on for the Transit Adjudication Bureau on Monday was done in, finally and inexorably, by sleeping out. As for my sweat-absorbing black tee shirt, it stank – no more, no less. So when Pete came out with a tray and a black polo shirt over his arm, I accepted his generosity. He tried to get me to take my two shirts with me. But, traveling light, not galumphing around with two dirty shirts in a bag, I insisted on a trade.

"Eat these before they get cold and, if you feel like it, tell me a bit of what brought you here. Like I said, I don't get much conversation these days. I've encountered a couple of people sleeping in Congressional Cemetery before, but never one who spoke of impromptu sojourns or cared about an epitaph. And certainly not one I invited to my … backyard. I hope you understand." And he nodded over his shoulder towards the house.

We sat at the table, Pete with coffee, me the same, plus, wow, fresh-squeezed OJ, which my wallet hadn't coughed up in, like, forever, three bulls-eye eggs nestled in their hollowed out toast of thick black bread, plus the toast squares and a quarter cantaloupe.

I said that after the game, this baseball fan just ended up in the cemetery, and that I'd actually had a pretty good night's sleep once I got that tarp working. Wanting more, he said something about all kinds of people making alternate arrangements since the Plunge. I reached for my second bulls-eye and, hell, some guy all set in life tossing everything to teach in the inner city at his age, I decided to trust him. Besides, I'd already hung a bunch of tawdry laundry on *Warpath*'s line. So I told him I'd been unwilling to use my credit card for a hotel and had pretty much gone to ground.

"Credit card, huh? I wouldn't imagine you're too intimidated by that ridiculous Minders' fairy tale. Like any system with that *sup-*

posed amount of data is scalable, or even readable. Whatever the Minders are, if anything, they can't be half as bad as the psychopath running the DC cops' Terror squad."

"No, it wasn't the Minders per se."

"So can I hope you're down here chipping away somehow at the splintering façade known as HeadFuck?"

"Only in the most indirect sense. Still, I did manage to publish a story I was down here researching. On a little site that's actually quite good called *Off the Warpath*."

"So this is you, Mr. Fremson. I thought I recognized you from a certain TV whole-vid I figured you didn't need to hear about." He smiled. "But I bet that orgy in that Senate office building was probably worse than you wrote it, right?"

"Slime oozing all over the carpet, Pete."

"Somebody on the *Symington Referendum* was whooping and hollering about taking down that general, plus you being in the vanguard against these useless security-theater searches. The DC searchers like to specialize in dogs going after African-Americans – young, old, male, female – long as you're black. Works fine to keep them beaten down."

"I saw it in action. I thought this asthmatic lady was gonna expire right there."

"Your letter to that Syriac site is bouncing all over. Though it does seem an odd statement. Disjointed, somehow, if what you're trying to do is spark protest about the searches. How's your head, by the way?"

"My head's better, thanks, but it's been tough. I gotta get home and write something coherent. Explain where I'm at and how I got there." I decided the cantaloupe didn't necessarily have to wait for dessert. "Hell, Pete, how *we* got here. I figure everything started going downhill when radio stations stopped telling you the songs they played."

"I peg it to when they outlawed light bulbs you could actually read by. We let 'em get away with that and boom! they ban whole-vid enabled micro-zaps. An East German writer, Christa Wolf – who knows something about it – says it comes down to a question of character, whether you fight the lie or not. That most of us just fight against ourselves as we, quote, 'lusted for slavery and pleasure. Only some knew it and some didn't.' "

"Which is worse, I wonder, the slavery or what passes for pleasure these days?"

"Still, you never know, Mitchell, about something simple like refusing a search. People have to be ready for it. But look what happened when Lutherans started invoking the Sermon on the Mount in a Leipzig church. It took years, but you get some folks praying in church, and you turn around and it's seventy-thousand marching, and then the Wall came down."

"As simple as that? The hunter is captured by the game?"

"It's like a run on the bank, the difference being it's the top guys who've lost confidence, not the depositors."

"My thieving-scum general spoke last night of infighting at the top. We'll see. Meanwhile, Pete, I gotta go."

"HeadFuck's gotten so weird, ineffectual like. But anybody new might be worse. So, eat and run, huh?"

"I wish it was five o'clock. Cause I didn't get to celebrate my article like any good reporter should, not at RFK Stadium's beer prices last night. After five, you and me'd be having a few and solving the world's problems – until the wrong drone flew overhead."

"I've been looking for a reason to break open that six of Natty Bo growing stale in my fridge."

"Don't tempt me, cause it doesn't end good for people when Turd-Touch starts working his magic. The eggs were delicious. Plus the ablutions – and, oh, the shirt!"

"Sure thing. But earn your breakfast first."

"Name it."

"Elizabeth would love it if you went to the screen door there and said hello. We don't get many visitors. Just a simple hello, the less said the better. And no matter what, keep the door between you or you'll scare her half to death."

"It'd be my pleasure. She's probably the first person I've met recently who won't immediately think of me in a certain pair of shorts."

"Elizabeth rolled my clay into something out of nothing and gave me forty-six of the best years anyone could give – and now three of the worst."

"My mom says old age isn't for the faint of heart."

"Not unless you're lucky. So if I'm friendly to a guy in a cemetery, you'll understand. You're not supposed to say this, but I get so bored and lonely. I tried getting Lucy to talk politics, but it didn't take, the old flea-bag."

She was waiting for us by the door, tall and slim in a white sleeve-less nightgown, her long gray hair a bit jarring through the screen. I was glad she was lovely her whole life before her face took on that certain cast. I said, "Good morning, Elizabeth. I'm so glad to meet you. Pete has been telling me how happy you've made each other all these years." She nodded gravely, smiled, then frowned, but didn't speak. Pete took me gently by the arm.

"Thanks, that was perfect. But anything more will just make her nervous wondering why she doesn't remember you."

Down on the driveway, I gave Lucy a good rub and, I couldn't help it, Pete a hug – a real one by two lonely men, not one of those scared-of-your-shadow excuses. I was halfway down the drive when he called me back to press thirty dollars on me. "Take it, damn it! Consider it a contribution to your civil-rights campaign. It's all I can offer to help since I have no reason to ride the Metro. Look, money's not an issue for me – I got out before the Plunge. Besides, what do I have to spend it on?" I took the twenty, balanced the ten on Lucy's head, and said thanks, my socks were sticking to my feet, and I'd let him buy me some if I encountered a store in DC that sold such exotic fare.

"It *is* a pathetic excuse for a city," he said. "I go over that bridge there, do all my shopping in Maryland." I turned at the end of his drive for a wave and saw him down on one knee, murmuring to Lucy. "Mitchell! I'll be following your progress. You don't have any kids, any *young* kids, do you?" I shook my head. "Good. And good luck." Nothing to say to that, I waved again. He cuffed Lucy to get her going and headed out of sight towards the screen door that framed his day.

Chapter Fifty-Three

Whacked out of Whack

Happy to be clean and rid of two shirts past their sell-date, I headed for the train to get to a computer to see if Everett had upped his threats. A guy my size bestowing a slick black shirt optimal for the sweating ahead – figure the odds. And Lurch falling out of the sky well off the beaten track at ThinkTanked, no point in not presenting myself all big and bold at downtown's nearest Deskless. That's right: Can't Touch Me!

Not wanting to panic anyone by writing on the train, I worried instead about Bodega Dude confronting Short Leg and wondered how poor Mac was making out. I got out within shouting distance of the National Mall and soon logged on to find Joe in a happy lather over *Warpath*'s site being attacked like never before, not to mention an eleven-hundred percent traffic boost. Before losing interest, he'd traced several of the attacks to "one of those loony end-times churches in Colorado." He'd been forced dark for about ten minutes, but otherwise his and his server's defenses held. After inquiring after my health, he added, "That's not much of a concern for me these days, not after my latest CT scan – it's *all* medicinal, son. Our Whitaker story is just the start of me checking out with a bang. Of the things I've got simmering, a couple might be right for you, your byline already so fraught."

No surprise, but H-DM was blowing steam out of both ears. Joe linked to its statement and also to the Germans' tangled response to Whitaker's e-mail to its man, Pantly. Buried in a bunch of artful words swallowing their own tail, they admitted to Chrysler, yes, talking to

Whitaker about potentially, down the road, *perhaps* "accessing his knowledge base so as to fortify our efforts to protect the Homeland's Heroes."

There you go, Joe, flick your Bic in whatever time you got left.

Joe ended, "So, many thanks for Whitaker's head on a stake. A check for $250 was mailed last night to your address a la *The Daily Chirp*. More of those big bucks where that came from, so remember: Think *Warpath* First!"

Payment the day of publication! I could get to like this guy. Along with far more than the usual amount of trash in my queue, came this with the subject line: "From his wife – a warning here."

Hello:
I feel I know you, I've heard your name so much around my house, said in hope the first week and then more and more angry. Of course yesterday, he liked to blow the roof off he was so mad you published that story on the Grinder and the General but did nothing about you know what. I tried to tell him people do what they can, and maybe you're not the right man for it, but you know how he is.
He's been fixed on you off and on for months now, so it just seems natural to think you two know each other. Though I guess you don't. All he says about picking you out that day is something about a hunch.
I don't know if you have any kids or not. Probably not, you even <u>thinking</u> of putting his stuff out under your own name. But I am writing you with a heads up. I saw the e-mail he sent you yesterday and I know how reckless that is. I saw it after it was sent – too late.
Anyway, he was out all night last night, ordinarily no big deal. No one's stopping him or his friends from drinking and driving the back roads. He's not able to sleep much, partly because he doesn't like dreaming. At least he drives <u>slower</u>. He parks and sleeps it off somewhere, then wets his head down, brushes his teeth and gets to work by the seven o'clock start. He refuses to carry the micro-zap I got him, but he always stops to call me driving in.
Except today he didn't. And then a friend called me that he didn't make it in to work. And we had a deal about his job.

465

No more no doctor's note absences. He had a string of them when he got back from his last Sands and instead of putting him on leave, him with his head all messed up from that blast concussion, fucking H-DM put him on probation.

God knows he tried to find another reporter with the guts to put his name on it to get the whole-vid out. He contacted five or six, but they're all too scared. I don't blame them, and I don't blame you, even if you did make him some kind of promise I'm not too clear on.

I love my husband and his little girl needs a father. It was rough when he got back, trying to be a daddy again. But they worked it out, and they're each other's whole lives now just about. That means he's not looking to check out. If he shows up in Queens, don't hurt him, but don't let him hurt you either. He's not doing his girl any good being in prison till she's grown. I can't believe that newspaper told everyone your address. Maybe if you could just go stay somewhere for a couple of days till I can track him down and shake some sense into him.

I know this is tough on everybody. Good luck to us all.

His Wife

Another woman telling me not to go home. And, yeah, Short Leg associated with the last one – tough shit. Cause I was tired of running, bone-tired. Sick of DC and sick of scuttling under the fridge every time someone turned on the light, I was sleeping in my own lonely bed that night. No way Everett would just blast me to kingdom come without first trying to force my hand getting his stupid whole-vid out. And maybe I would.

Ah, a posy from Turncoat Wife. At least there at Deskless, I didn't care if it harbored some super-dooper Trojan worm. She skipped any salutation.

Look, here's my damn address, which I can't believe I'm giving you. But your shitty micro-zap is out – trouble with the bill or, about as old as me, did it finally die? It's the third tower east of Third Avenue on 78rd Street, Apt. 47-J. (Across the street, the buildings only reach about thirty stories.)

466

Building security has scanned a photo of you I didn't throw out for some dumb reason, so you're pre-screened for them to call me. Great – another link to you. But otherwise the building won't even initiate contact.

I caught Carole on *Breakfast Raunch* yesterday morning. MoneyBags with the wandering eye insisted, not surprising after the splash the whole-vid of her leaving Bellevue made, miles of thigh disappearing into a red leather miniskirt and a midriff-baring top highlighting her big shooting scar. But yesterday, she was disappointingly demure in a white dress. Short and unavoidably tight, but up to her neck for some reason. The host actually complained that he didn't know if the "Network" – there's a laugh – got its money's worth.

You used to talk about those Chaminade snot-noses all you Mineola guys hated when you were in high school, how on-the-ball they seemed. So maybe it's her Catholic high school, cause Carole was pretty articulate, her sentences actually more than six words long.

And, amazingly, she blamed the cops for both of you getting shot. She said it was obvious you were holding a radio because she could hear it. Then she saw it in your hand and wondered what kind of a goof actually still used a transistor. So they cut her off with a whole-vid of her va-va-va-vooming down that corridor.

They tried to get to her off-camera, but the chick didn't budge. When they came back she said – and it's bouncing all over, that's why I can quote her – "I don't care what you're trying to get me to say or the rabbits you pull out of a hat to try to intimidate me off-the-air. I'm the only other civilian who was there, and Mitchell Fremson was just talking to the cops and showing them that all he had was a radio. It was playing loudly, some peculiar news show. Then I saw that short one, Officer Reisner, with his gun out, and I started rushing up thinking I could put a stop to a dangerous situation. But then Reisner 'discharged' – right – and – "

They broke suddenly for commercial, and no more Carole, though when they were hyping the spot for days they said she was the whole half-hour. Amazing thing was, I liked her. And you wouldn't believe how she's getting trashed today, something horrendous about a joint in a park as a teenager. So a deal's still a deal, Mitchell, if you want to talk, now that you know where I live. Cause I am not trekking out there to stand on your porch any more. I think the guys from the projects have started selling tickets. Besides, I'll probably be too busy looking for work.

Nicki.

Well, well, Nicki, 78th Street. Further south than I would've thought *and* with a 47th-floor monthly nut. More to the point, Carole proved a mensch and got kicked off the air as a result. Despite everything that had been painted on her generous tabula rasa, all I really knew was she volunteered to cheer orphans and old folks, was getting married for love not money, and hid none of her beacon under a bushel. And here she was standing up to the MoFos at least as much as I was and with a shit-load more to lose – her being younger the least of it.

And I suddenly thought of Lurch, unplugged the machine and ran three blocks. Not wanting to get my new shirt all sweaty yet, I dialed it back and stopped to look around, and realized I was about at the National Mall. So I joined the parade of tourists on its well worn paths and then graced a bench for some "Penn Etc." scribbling. No one (good) awaiting me at the Hovel, no need to rush home.

The words flowing OK, I might have sat longer but my pen ran dry. So I strolled down closer to the Potomac just to escape the throngs in pleated shorts. And only then did I see it, across the river on a rise on the Virginia bank, a colossal billboard of HeadFuck himself. His big bald head gleaming, he wore a vaguely martial jacket and pointed out at us resolutely. One word flashed red, then the next and the next: *Bold. Extolled. Impregnable!* a bromide that was getting harder and harder to laugh off.

Early afternoon, it was a hundred-and-one degrees I heard someone say. The day before almost balmy by comparison, it never ceased to amaze the difference a few degrees made. HeadFuck looming over the city like a noxious cloud was the last straw as far as me and DC were concerned. Yup, time to quit the throngs and make my way home, see what excitement awaited me there. Slogging east towards Greyhound and questing for two slices and a soda, I was glad of the water fountain, but baffled by its need for instructions: "Push Button. Wait for Water." Only in DC. I gave the White House a wide berth, vowing to see the famous new gun emplacements on the lawn some other time.

Cops, soldiers, dweebs with IDs, aloof ex-presidents of the French club, pairs of slyly smug, fecund women in their updated Mennonite dress – they all started to waver in the heat. I resorted to my own damn B.E.I.: Boundless, Exemplary, Indomitable! Still, I kept stumbling in the heat and finally had to quit my light-headed quest in favor of a twelve-buck "personal pan pizza," total intake of cardboard crap less than two regular slices. Criminy – get me to the bus on time!

Restored mostly by the clip joint's AC and gulp after gulp of water in its bathroom, I pressed on. Barbara ("His Wife" as she loyally called herself) had written me that morning telling me not to go home. Could I hope that Everett had finally shown himself, cha-grined about being too hungover to face an arm-chewing drill press, still boiling mad at me, but safely confined to Indiana? I decided to check at the Cyber-Bound a block back – Can't Freaking Touch Me!

Nothing from Barbara or Everett, but someone had sent a Milwaukee IndyMedia story about the search-refusals spreading. It focused on a concerted little Demo four woman had done at the local bus station with suitcases stuffed with brassieres. (Folks stoned the dike with whatever rock they found at their feet.) Man, I had to get "Penn Tale" out to add my bit to – shit-yeah, call it a Movement.

Then up popped the day's second from Barbara.

I write because if I scared you earlier today, that was for your own safety. Now I'm the one scared. Everett's H-DM buddy and I decided to go look for him around noon. Ev was afraid in the Sands plenty of times – he'd say it right out. He knows there's no good reason to make someone fearful. So it wasn't like him to not contact me on his ten-thirty break.

His buddy and me split up to look. I found his stupid little Datsun. He says he still drives it because it's the vehicle we went courting in, but I know he's just too cheap, long as it runs. I found it off the road, but not in a place where Ev would have slept it off last night. It wasn't even really hidden, cause it had taken out a path of late corn. And that's not something Everett would do, no matter how drunk he got, wasting money and work like that.

But here's the thing that's really scary. Inside was about fifteen empties of Hoosier Meth. The man loves his Genny Cream, right. But as much as he does, he hates Hoosier Meth more.

What I'm trying to say, no way he would 1. drive through that corn or 2. drink one, let alone fifteen of them H-Meths. Somebody has snatched him and is trying to set it up to look like he took off somewhere. Moved to Nevada to work in a silver mine or something.

H-DM loses that Grinder contract, that place is gonna be a ghost-town. This whole county would shut down. How many goons does an eight-billion-dollar contract buy? And my fool husband is threatening that. No, I'm not worried who's reading this now. They already have him, so let them know that I know. Let him go free, and we'll just slink away I promise. Or I'm making the loudest noise I can starting with this letter.

I sent our little girl away before I went out to look. And not to anyplace obvious. Nobody can find her. Let them come after me. I hope they do, because I will show those motherfuckers. Let them think cause I'm a woman I can't. Trying to make it seem like Ev is the guy to go off and kill himself somewhere. Like he'd do that after surviving three long Fomentings. One Sands was almost two years. He wasn't going to hurt himself. Not after night after night with a bulls-eye on his back going door-to-door in those Sands. Plus watching his best friend get burned up in a stupid Grinder rollover. Did he tell you that part?

Part of me wants to just grab my girl and run. But that's a small part. He loved her to death, and he wasn't checking out while she was still Daddy's little girl. They're going to paint him like all the other vets killing themselves cause they got the shakes and can't sleep, depressed and all that. Maybe when his daughter turned 15 and started running wild, but not now.

So, they got him and they killed him. Be with a man for twenty-three years, something like that happens – you <u>know</u>! You don't have to be told.

And you helped kill him, sitting on that thing that he sent you. So what are you going to do about it now, mister bigshot New York writer? What I want to know is are you coming out here to help bring some justice to my man? Justice to protect me and my child, to clear his name of suicide and get the bastards who did it. Well are you?

His Wife

Everett was playing in leagues bigger than he knew, and he'd screwed both of us from the moment he slipped that map in my jacket pocket. Sorry, Barbara, but Turd-Touch was clean on this one.

But of course I wasn't. Everett brought the big smelly bucket, but I provided the ladle.

I stormed blindly out of the computer joint. Jesus, get a pint of whiskey, get on the damn bus and sit and stew and be safe for however many wonderful hours it took. Hopefully Homeland Control would be up to its usual idiocy and prolong the ride. Buy a big-ass sandwich and a trashy novel and just sit, glad of the baby screaming his fool head off and the couple arguing in some foreign tongue. Racket trumping thought.

Screw Everett, the smug, macho –

And some skell, raggedy and nappy and nasty and dirty, loomed up from nowhere and slashed the meat of my palm right by the cut I got destroying my micro-zap.

It took a moment to register as the blood began to flow. In a charming, drawing-room accent the skell said, "Take this if you would, please. It has everything you need. Clean the wound with the swab – it'll sting a bit, I'm afraid – then apply the bandage. And don't worry, both contain military-spec coagulant and self-cauterizing agents. Besides, I only penetrated the stratum granulosum, maybe the stratum licidum at most. Just apply them both without delay, Bob's your uncle."

Floored by this performance, I half expected him to slap me on the butt and back onto the pitch. Instead, his rubber-gloved hand – the pristine gloves a far remove from everything else about him – thrust a neat little packet into my good hand. "Off you go, right as rain," he said, then dropped a bright, bloody scalpel on the sidewalk and leaped into the back seat of a spewer that drew up with its back passenger door open. It tore out as the people gaping at me turned and fled. And no, I couldn't make out the half-covered license plate.

Marked and in pain, worrying I'd offend – heck, the *Vic* fearful of MoFo attention – I ran around the corner and behind a big planter sprouting a flag. A thin trail of blood followed, not much. A professional talking of strata, then scooting away in a flashy vehicle, obviously he knew how to inflict a mere flesh wound. A garden-variety DC cop wouldn't have laid a glove on him.

I fumbled my little present open to find an antiseptic wipe, a large square bandage, some adhesive tape and a small, puissant looking scissors. Applying the wipe, I yelped, then tried to somehow flee a pain far worse than any alcohol or peroxide. But there was nowhere to go. I howled into my arm – hell, bang a drum, no one cared, not if the people running from me around the corner were any indication. No one rallied to help a guy knifed on the sidewalk in HeadFuck's DC. Then the bandage sent the pain off the charts. I bent over whimpering, but managed to get it taped down.

Marching blindly off, the pain lessened some a few blocks on. I stopped to catch my breath and caught sight of myself in a store mirror and almost laughed, the look on my face. I might've –

I ripped the damn bandage off. Christ, had I just dosed myself? Told to jab myself in the leg with a sharp-tipped umbrella, would I? No, no – you'll much prefer *this* goblet of claret, my Lord, not that one there. Yikes! Though impossible that quick, the wound looked like it had almost closed, any poison coursing its way to my vitals.

Miraculously (for DC), I encountered a drug store and bought some rubbing alcohol and band-aids. What came next, Cat Wrangler's kooky, look-at-me red duct tape? The alcohol barely registering, how in the world had a deep cut closed up like that? I almost dispensed with the band-aid, but then thought of riding a bus all evening if I didn't just morph into a swamp creature from my hand on up. I pocketed the slick little scissors, which looked like they cost at least ten bucks, nothing like them in the Hovel's plastic bag of a medicine cabinet. (Good for the nose hairs I'd just started to sprout.) Alright, to the Greyhound, avaunt, Goddamn it!

Christ, it probably was poison, otherwise what was the point? Did I dare get stuck on a bus in Beltway traffic? Or should I just go check into a DC hospital and wait for someone to air-bubble my IV? Probably get better care from a bus driver, anyway. Throw a dart at the gallery of my numerous potential assailants, but what *message* to take from a very peculiar attack? 'Please, your bandage if you will, sir.' Like having a doctor present to keep the detainee alive for further interrogation.

I walked and it felt good, despite the heat and everything else, to locomote upright on the earth. Pocketing a couple of band-aids, I donated the rubbing alcohol and the rest to the next homeless gathering. Glad of them, one guy confirmed the bus station dead ahead. *Alcohol*, right – a concept. Fall out on the damn bus one way or another, come what might. I crossed behind the box-on-stilts convention center and kept on sweating.

Heck, the place had potential. There was enough space in DC's poorer areas for all kinds of surprising things, car dealerships and broke-down parks, and there, for instance, another big, *grass* football field connected to a church a couple of blocks down from Union Station. You'd no more find that in Manhattan than a vineyard. And then, across a huge patch of fenced-in asphalt pretending to be a parking lot though not a car in sight, I saw the gray dog ready to gallop. No deli or anything nearby, they presumably had the crap I needed inside the bus station – all except booze, probably. Should've snagged a bottle blocks back when I had the chance. Well, just hope for some old man playing the harmonica, leading us all in train songs and passing some fine sippin' whiskey round the back of the bus.

Chapter Fifty-Four

Leave the Driving to Me

And lookey-there, a chance to join my very own Movement. DC dispensing with the usual four-man, full-employment deployment, one lonely cop was set up outside the bus station's single entrance, a scavenged, orange road construction barrel his table. Not that a flock of passengers was descending on him, but still. A wan, weak-chinned fellow, this cop, he didn't look any too happy beckoning over a substantial woman in tight red pants dropped off by an ancient Oldsmobile.

Damn. Washington's air starting to burn going down, I just wanted to collapse on a bus headed north. No pressing agenda up in Herald Square the week before, I'd stood idly by condemning the folks lining up to get home after a long day. But approaching the DC Greyhound, like them, I was hankering to get somewhere. Maybe the cop was only doing African-American females that quarter-hour, and the civ-lib lottery would let me skate without betraying my Movement. Otherwise, folks in *Milwaukee* telling MoFos to shove it, I needed to punt the prevarication and Goddamn stand up. Thrust my wrists for the cuffs or declare myself irredeemably half-assed.

The cop fumbled with her suitcases as I wandered up, and he and the lady both swore as a bag slid off the orange barrel. What if I missed the New York bus by thirty-seconds, the post-Plunge next not for another three hours? Was I even safe on DC's streets that long? Hell with it – I turned towards the door. Without looking up, the cop said, "No, no. Sir! Behind her. There's been an Alert. Behind her, now!" He pointed as he groped her bags. Fussing with a zipper, he mumbled something, and she snarled, "You want it open, you open it yourself, cop."

Nice. Then it hit: I had a pair of sharp little scissors *concealed* in my pocket. I regretted their loss, but looked to the trash basket a few yards off, not wanting the approaching trio of scruffy young Bulgarians, Oregonians (something), all with enormous packs, to get ahead of me. Let them profit from my *Just Say No* once I disposed of my lethal weapon. I stepped towards the trash.

"Sir, I'm not telling you again: behind her! There's been chatter!"

"Chatter – what the hell is chatter?"

"Chatter is you shut up and get behind her."

"But I'm just – "

"But nothing. Once you ... *present* on line, if you leave, that's an Indication. Which means a trip to lock-up. Now stand there or go downtown! Your choice, but believe me, I'm sick of this shit out here in this heat."

The woman turned with a look of exasperated solidarity. That's right, darling, what bus you catching? Such indignities visited upon us, you got any sippin' whiskey in one of those bags? Defeated by the zipper, he said, "You don't have any bad stuff in here, do you Miss?"

"What do you think?" And she grabbed her bag off the barrel, picked up her other two and stormed off. Shit, what about the e-mails in my pocket I'd forgotten worrying about the scissors? He looked after her working his mouth silently, then turned to me. Holding nothing to obediently place on his barrel, the realization dawned that I wasn't actually subject to a search.

"Cop, I don't have any bags, so there's nothing to search. Besides, you got no right to search me. *None.* I *refuse*! You got that? This boy says no! Like it says, I'm secure in my person that I got nothing on anyway. So, see ya!"

Thus my formal, stirring refusal. Rhetoric for the ages spouted in a sea of asphalt, none but the offending cop to hear. But I'd gotten it out, my meaning and thus my conscience clear. Milwaukee, Oakland, Indianapolis, et. al. – grasp my hand across the miles.

Him gaping, I said, "Look, nothing. See?" I held my hands up in a see-idiot-no-bags gesture.

"Wait a minute, what the fuck's that on your hand? Don't move." He was suddenly so agitated, I didn't. The three 'Bulgarians' plowed up, all about twenty and laughing and goofing and suddenly quiet when they saw something was going down. Thumbing his micro-zap, the cop barked, "I said, what happened to your hand? We got Regs on that."

I cut it shaving your mother's snatch popped into my mouth as my teeth clamped shut. "Why? Uh – "

He found what he wanted. "Alright, forget the hand-wound Regs. This is you, even in a different shirt." He held his micro-zap up so I could admire a fine portrait of myself in the blue dress shirt I'd worn all over DC. "Don't move!"

He got all tangled up putting his micro-zap away and reaching for what, a tazer? "Am I under arrest for changing my shirt, cop? Cause I've done nothing but get my hand cut by some weirdo. I'm the vic, not the perp, and I'm leaving."

I turned, and he shouted, "Don't move! That's an order from a sworn Homeland Protector."

Jesus, he'd turned bright red. And he brought up a big gun with a dull gleam and pointed it at my chest from ten feet away.

Fuck me. Should I run? No, rush him, maybe – more props than getting shot in the back. Getting blown away carrying no bag but obviously refusing a search would do the Movement more good than any six "Penn Tales" I might write, however stirring. Would being foreign lead the Bulgarians to spread the tale or stay mum?

"Not so funny now, is it, you big piece of shit." He waved his gun around with a little laugh.

Al and Elaine would just have to foist their scoop off on some other intrepid scribbler – probably already had. As for the SecDef whole-vid, that had been screwed from the start. Keep looking, Everett, you'll find that greater fool. Go ahead! Rush the MoFo, the ultimate refusal. Too damn much was definitely enough. Do it! Nobody would care. Fuck Nicki. Punch that button opening the elevator doors on an empty shaft and leave her with a lifetime of guilt. A month, anyway. Do it! I closed a step, and the cop put both hands on his gun. And a vision of Lois laughing at the top of her stairs flashed before me. She'd care. And I stood very still.

The cop ordered the Bulgarians with their bulging packs to get their asses into the bus station, go on, scram! The gun not wavering, he got his micro-zap back out. "Got him," he told it. "Who do you think – Fremson! At the Greyhound. Of course I'm sure it's him, though he tried to get sneaky, changing his shirt to escape. Get here quick. What – no! Some damn foreigners saw us. Besides, there's a camera right here. Nope, no way! Look, I already said, only if *he* makes it absolutely necessary. And no cash here. Yeah, OK."

Cash – great. "Cop, I repeat: unless I'm under arrest, I'm free to go. I've got nothing to search, they're illegal anyway, and I refuse." A Goddamn comedian was I. Careful, cause he sure looked freaked. "Since I've done nothing, I can't be under arrest. Now, I'm turning and walking that way, over *there*. If you'll just put your little – "

"Shut the fuck up! Get down, get down now!" And holding his gun far on the other side of his body, he darted around his barrel. "Get down. You're a known T-Symp who's already engendered a discharge within the last thirty days. If I feel threatened, you're the one responsible! Nobody's gonna question a Protector on the front lines of the C. P. Crisis."

He reached to push down on my sore shoulder, then slowly brought the gun up and pointed it at my head. I dropped, and was still lying there minutes later with his boot on my back when a heavy vehicle squealed to a stop, and I found myself nose to toe with a pair of enormous tasseled loafers, the fancy-pants cuffs breaking over them in a soft, rich wave.

"Right, Mr. Swyve, you take it from here, B.E.I. I'm going on break now. The department's gotten strict about taking them on time. You'll call me like you promised when the paperwork's gone through, right?"

Whoever snarled, "How many times have I told you never, ever to use my name? Huh, Umbert? It happens again, there's going to be trouble. Now, you'll get your money, though it would have been a lot easier – *cleaner* – if we were calling for the meat wagon right now. A front-lines Hero under constant threat guarding mass transit, nobody would have questioned a forced discharge with this scum. But I guess you didn't want that bonus we talked about."

Christ, that voice sounded familiar. A squeamish Umbert said, "I got him for you fair and square. Now, that's it."

"Fine. You'll get your money, but you're going to have to wait. There's been a glitch, and my firm isn't fronting it anymore. Not for just turning him over and dumping the disposal on me. You sit tight and wait till you hear from me. Got that? Now get out of here before some stinking bus rider shows up and sees him with a *Protector* – give me a fucking break."

The boot lifted, and the familiar voice said, "Alright, Fremson, get up slow."

I did and tried not to flinch. And I had to laugh that Lurch was driving the same absurd, no-payload Grinder pickup that he'd stormed ThinkTanked in the day before. Umbert had fled as far as the door to the bus station, but turned to watch.

"Go ahead and laugh, if that's how you're going out." He lunged, turned me quick and latched a fierce grip on my head from behind, his hands locking in front. I dug in my heels and flailed wildly but, pulling me by my head, he started marching us around the back of his vehicle to the passenger seat. I swung my elbows, but he was too far back for anything solid. I scratched at his hands, then tried to stomp his feet and claw his face. He yelled, "Don't! Or I'll snap your neck in half. And then we won't get the chance for a proper goodbye."

He had muscles on his knuckles he was so damn strong. I stopped my useless grappling and tried to think as Lurch shoved me around the back of his enormous vehicle. He ground my face into the side of it and then got the passenger door open, a coil of rope falling out at our feet.

I grabbed at the scissors in my pocket as he tried to shove me in, got them and stabbed him in the hand, lucky that he didn't flinch at the last second. Blow-back, baby! He swore and I stuck him again, much harder and deeper, it getting easier as I went. He flung his hand up and jumped back and tripped over the rope and went down. I kicked him twice hard in the ribs with the black work boot so scorned by Hart's Silver Fox gatekeeper and felt a very satisfying crunch both times. He made a noise like metal ripping and floundered around trying to get up. Another big vehicle pulled up behind us.

Let some bus riders watch as I killed the bastard. That's right – *him*, not me! Fucking-A, this vic wasn't taking it no more. One for our side to the many thousands on yours, MoFos! So what, I went to prison, I'd be a hero. Three hots and a cot, it had to be safer than out here. Like Orwell said of his time on the front lines in Spain, if everybody killed just one Fascist, they'd soon be extinct.

He tried to rise, but something inside staggered him. I drew back my leg and aimed for his temple. And a voice calm and unhurried enough to be telling me the three-o'clock bus to Hempstead leaves from Gate Six said, "Fremson, I wouldn't do that if I were you. A lot of cameras right here by the bus station."

Somebody screaming 'No!' would've whipped my leg faster. But a voice that languid, I had to turn and look. A big old bull cop was standing by a black spewer, a smallish gut over his wide belt, big head, big shoulders and a big gun in his hand, silver hair on top of a face that laughed when others turned away. Looking green and holding his hand to his chest where I'd kicked him, Lurch had risen to his knees. I brandished my weapon.

"Cummings, this faggot's mine!" he rasped. "Have a nice fucking day, cause this doesn't concern you."

Jesus – *Cummings*. Yeah, people feared him.

"The way it looks from here, you might be glad of a little police protection, Swyve. You brute, Fremson. Can't you play nice?"

"I'm warning you Cummings, back off." The rasp grew stronger.

"It's Commander Cummings. And *you're* warning me?"

Lurch finally rose, and Cummings said, "Swyve, you know what I think of you. Don't tempt me to have to protect a Homelander. Or are you so used to picking on defenseless small fry, you didn't hear the safety coming off?"

That'd give folks something to digest, a top DC MoFo shooting a top private MoFo as I looked on. All prompted (slightly) by my better-late-than-never search refusal. Lurch stopped, and Cummings motioned him back with his gun. Two big, ugly men facing off, one stooped with pain, blood dripping from his hand, the other happily astride his wicked world.

"So what'd you do, Cummings, have Homeland Control tickle you if this asshole's name was mentioned on any micro-zap in the District?"

"Piece of cake with the real-time access you private guys still don't have, mostly. But what I want to know is the name of that DC cop who ran into the bus station when I drove up. Some uniform thinks he can line his pockets without forking over my half? How much you paying him, Swyve, to call if bright boy here showed?"

"What cop? I didn't see anybody."

I piped up to prove I retained the power of speech. "I think his name is Umbert, something like that."

"Thanks, Fremson. I didn't even know Umbert got his gun back. Well, he's pulling solo midnight foot-patrols in Anacostia starting tomorrow. Now get this and get it good, Swyve. I am not some Homeland tool you can push around. This is *my* town – I don't care what you private bastards think. Look at you, dressed like you're selling women's shoes! No wonder you let this, this … *amateur* kick your ass. Driving around in a pimp-mobile. You expect to get any real work done in a ride that loud? My town, you got that?"

"Yeah, for how long? Once ASPIC gets that new contract, you're cut off at the knees, Cummings."

"Maybe you ASPIC whores aren't getting that contract."

So Lurch/Swyve worked for ASPIC. Well, well, well.

"Winds shift, Swyve. I thought we got things straight in that little sit-down we had last month, you, me and Miller. Your boss is not nearly as stupid as you like to think. Now it's time for you to leave. Bye-bye."

Lurch winced at his dripping hand. "You got a handkerchief, Cummings?"

"A hanky, no. I've got a kit in my vehicle, but it's too far."

I looked at it fifteen feet away and grinned. Stabbing him, I must have gone past those two top strata of skin. Lurch finally just held his hand up above his heart and used his florid tie to staunch the bleeding.

"Look, Cummings. This T-symp's been messing with the MTA up in New York, and you know how deep ASPIC is into them. Plus he's annoying the Army for fuck's sake, and now he's an *existential* threat to a new client of mine. It's time to solve this little problem once and for all."

Cummings laughed. "How you hold on to your job, Swyve, amazes me. You made $537,000 last year. Chump change to us dedicated public servants, but not bad. It ever occur to you if this big zero here just disappears, they'll make a martyr out of him for his miserable little Movement? Which, believe me, is getting strangled in its crib, I don't care what those pansies in the Indianapolis PD do."

"I thought Oakland was our biggest worry."

"Is Oakland still part of this country in any way that counts?

Anyway, far better to keep him alive and keep him scared. He's not some Null we can disappear. Leave him stumbling around, he'll trip hard soon enough."

"Dudes, I appreciate the heartfelt consideration two such high-powered MoFos are giving my future. But I got a bus to catch."

Shut-up, they both snarled, and Cummings said, "Since he exposed that moron, Whitaker – which isn't the worst thing in the world if it wakes somebody way senior to him the fuck up – he's off-limits. However long Whitaker stays a Calfer, this idiot is under my protection."

Wow, our story worked! Saving me from the likes of Lurch was a damn good return on any article. I couldn't wait to tell Lois.

"So, *Commander*, with your great Intel, have you heard that that slut up in New York who wormed her way into getting shot with him is planning a search-refusal? She's getting some douche bag at one of the New York TV stations to whole-vid her staging it big and loud. I'm telling you, Current P. Crisis or not, shit-wipe here can smash the piggy bank."

Wow – Carole! You go, girl.

"Beauty and the Beast, so what. I'm telling you, his case is stagnating with him playing tourist here. Did you even notice I gave his hand the new Raytheon branding? You still report to Miller, Swyve. So how about you climb back into that toy of yours and go waste some Homeland pencil-pusher's time. Go, I'm bored." He motioned with his gun.

"You're going down, Cummings. I know. I dot-link. And I'll be the first to dance on your grave. As for you, Fremson, enjoy it while you can, cause that ain't long."

About to smear blood on his fancy pants fishing for his keys, he tried with his other hand across his body, gave up, got his pants bloody and roared off.

Chapter Fifty-Five

Cummings' Tease

"Alright Fremson, let's go. We've created enough of a stir here. We'd go to Union Station, except with that cut I gave you, those ridiculous Regs on wounds to the hand'll foul you up. Why don't you have your own fucking car – oh, I forgot, you're a *writer*."

I stared at him as he motioned towards his spewer till he gave his bone-in-the-throat laugh. "What, dummy? If I wanted something to happen to you, you'd be with Swyve right now. You know, a handsome guy like me, you'd figure I'm a sweetheart. But I'm not, or haven't you heard. So get in the vehicle. Believe it or not, I got other shit to do today."

There were enough screens and gauges and pulsing lights and whiz-whats jammed in Cummings' spewer to fly the freaking Chinese moon mission. I pointed to one with the outline of a man as its screen saver, and he said, "That's a honey. Can download biometrics from nine different databases. You know, all this crap is fine as far as it goes. But I still learn a hell of a lot more the old-fashioned way – someone in a chair, just me and him."

As big as his spewer was outside, the seats were damn cramped, the steering wheel scraping Cummings' modest gut. I found the control to move the seat back, but it already was. He laughed and said he'd ordered the special "Big-Man Package" – yet another hollow marketing triumph. He added he was glad of the opportunity to talk man to man.

"Long as only one of us has a gun, it ain't man to man."

"You really are a disagreeable little shit. I hand you my gun, you're still mine. Could you even *point* to the safety in under ten seconds, by which time I've damaged you maybe six different ways. Don't think you didn't get damn lucky with Swyve, though I'll be laughing for a while, driving up and finding the likes of you ready to bash his brains in. That kind of violence isn't in your current profile, so welcome to my world."

"You can only push a good man so far, Cummings. You MoFos'll learn that someday."

"For somebody living in a couple of rented rooms filled with cardboard boxes of crap nobody cares about, you act like you're swinging a big one. Speaking of which, heard from your wife lately?"

"I don't have a wife. The MoFos – you or not, doesn't matter – put the final nail in that coffin."

"That was out of New York. But the tape I heard, she wasn't bad for her first time. You didn't catch on till the conversation was half over. We should sic her on her Wall Street boyfriend, the shit he's into."

"What'd you want to talk about, cop? It wasn't my private life."

"Your *what*? See, you don't know how to play nice. No wonder the only thing remotely like a friend you got is that alcoholic, Ralph."

He plucked any string he wanted, then wrapped it round my neck. "Nothing to say? Right. So, the first thing you gotta know, Fremson, is the rule in this town: you don't mess with Calfers. And if you don't know – here in DC, assume he is."

"Like you and Whitaker."

"Parnell? Unless you get your man in that chair, who knows deep down what anyone believes."

He blipped his siren, got a cab to move and rolled through a red light. I said, "And what about you? You into the heifer?"

"Get real, Mitchell. A high school grad doesn't rise from busting heads in Southeast to running half of one of the country's most … *lucrative* police departments by shoving my head up my ass. But go along to get along. A concept you might consider."

485

"So why do I care about any of this?"

He slammed on the brakes, and stared hard. "You think I have to fill out one single sheet of paper to drop you into any holding tank in DC? Then a word from me to turn your cellmates loose, by the time they're done, there's not enough of you left to scrape off the floor and mail to your parents in Mineola – in a regular envelope."

I stayed shut up.

"I'm a patient man, but I'm a little busy with these damn Nepalese coming to town tomorrow," he said, the vehicle rolling again. "Now, you care because Whitaker's an idiot, but he *was* a useful idiot. And it doesn't look good if a National Guard private and some buffoon – what's with those shorts, man? – take out a major defense company."

Feigning hard, "What in the world are you talking about?"

"The Grinder – leave it alone. And how the hell did you get Whitaker's e-mails, anyway? Fine, don't tell me. That's Whitaker's look-out. Though I am surprised Bettinger has lost it enough to fax you instructions. He was never the same after that blast concussion he got showing off over in We're-Fuckedistan 'mentoring' the T-scum who turned around and blew him up. Bottom line, taking down the Grinder sets a bad precedent, too many of you Homelanders getting way too many ideas as is. Look at your search-refusal bullshit spreading like ditch weed."

"You don't care about all them Boots, three-hundred a year, getting killed in unnecessary rollovers, not to mention all the wounded?"

"The Grinder's not that bad, you drive it right. Just have to know what you're doing, war or not. Gonna get some for the department. No payload, but the new ones with fake windows, traffic gets the hell out of their way."

"Three-hundred deaths a year – fuck 'em?"

"Fremson, nobody questions Pentagon spending. Not before HeadFuck and certainly not now. The number of foreign replacement Boots we got signing up, personnel is just another line item on a budget. There's always plenty more brown boys who want to learn English with a flag on their shoulder. But a little closer to home – "

"You mean something you actually care about."

He gave me a grin I definitely did not want to see again. "Swyve, amazingly enough, is a big-shot in ASPIC's DC office – you know about ASPIC, right? And they are getting way too damn greedy with search privatization. Someone who couldn't even keep you under his thumb confined to a hospital room is gonna give me orders? That little embarrassment, by the way, is another reason he wants you so bad."

"What, there's not enough T money to go around? In DC of all places?"

"Ain't never enough. Till you learn that, you'll never have more than that one window you got. Or are you satisfied with that, a man your age? Still, somehow you keep feeding yourself into a buzz saw and coming out the other side."

"I need to unplug it."

"Here's a start: you get any good shit on ASPIC, run with it – big. Not your usual ridiculous outlets."

He drove a block, pointed out some poor unfortunate scratching on the corner as "a Null ripe for it." Then, "I see you can keep your mouth shut, you get interested."

"Keep talking, Cummings. Hasn't cost me anything yet."

He slammed on the brakes again – oh spare me. "Do you have any idea who you're talking to or what these two hands have done the last year alone? How easy it'd be if not for the *possibilities* you represent."

"I'm not kissing your ass. I'm past that now. Aside from killing me, which I agree is strategically contraindicated, you can't really marginalize me at this point, so – "

"You aren't so fucking marginal anymore. Or haven't you heard? And just so you know, no file is ever truly closed. Maybe that's where you Homelanders get your myth about the Minders."

"You mean the Minders, as such, don't exist?"

"You'll never know, certainly not with the Blue – give me a break

– coming your way. But, as tight as we got our hands on the wheel, you think people like me were gonna hand steering over to some new outfit just cause HeadFuck is on top for a while? Something he created out of thin air? No sir, not after it took me thirty-seven years to get what I got. Me and a lot of others like me. Bold. Extolled. Impregnable! my ass."

"Oh come on, Commandant, B.E.I. is the only thing with the remotest whiff of humor he's done these whole three years."

"It's Commander. Like you didn't know."

"Sure, sure thing, copper. And please spare me the histrionics with the brakes."

"Do you even know if HeadFuck is still alive? When was the last time you saw him not in some controlled situation already behind a desk or a podium? Months ago, right? Remember the surgery on his throat, those 'polyps.' Your voice changes, OK. But that doesn't explain why this HeadFuck looks a little shorter than the first one. Or why when he's angry and yelling, this one looks like he's faking it. The first one, you knew it was real."

"Why the hell you telling me this, Cummings?"

"Maybe because I'm a patriot – just like you, Byline Boy. Or maybe I just think things have gone a little too far when hyenas like Swyve start acting like it's their turn at the water hole."

"So everyone turns to the dude in the nasty shorts to get their story out for $250 a pop."

"It'd be for a lot more than that, trust me. A lot more. But here's your bus. Listen, Fremson, like all bullies, Swyve's a coward. He won't dare cross me for a couple of days. Plus Washington's top Calfer spoke to Whitaker last night and reined him in. You should make it back to Queens OK. After that, turn the buzz saw around."

"It's bolted to the table."

"So pick up the table, asshole, a big guy like you. The ASPIC story should be easy enough, you get your hands on the right stuff. As to the story exposing HeadFuck – depending on how you do on ASPIC – contact is strictly me to you. And no, it won't be someone with a short leg. Now get out and try to keep your ass in one piece. Maybe make some money for a change."

✶✶✶✶✶✶✶✶✶✶✶✶✶✶✶

Man, an editorial tryout before he handed me the big score. Maybe he'd have it all typed up just awaiting my name on top. Taking HeadFuck down, or his simulacrum, that'd get me *Morning Dyspepsia* for sure, they got the balls. Just spend the money quick, I guess.

The guy behind the window in the shabby waiting room said the six-o'clock bus was sold out. I got a ticket for the eight o'clock and left to buy the kid's composition notebook that was all I could find and the treat of a four-dollar pen (speaking of spending). My whole arm felt weird, the gunk no doubt working its way up. Damn! I forgot to ask Cummings about him branding me, but it sounded like he wanted me healthy. Back in the waiting room, the shrill Chinese music halted word-production. Despite the danger of showing myself on the street, I found a spot on a wall to wedge between two bushes and scribble away.

Heck, if Carole was joining the team, she could use "Penn Tale's" support. Surely our louche strategy summit was in the offing. So I took to writing of Frankie and his gun, the heart of it I'd been shirking. Happy with the effort, I wandered back around 7:30 to find the bus late getting in and not leaving till at least nine. Hence a decent plate of squid in the world's most deserted Chinatown.

The bus driver sucked a cigarette down hard, then lit a new one off the first, the clock near ten. On the verge of escape, I silently egged him on, hoping his cluster of shiny gold pineapples by the door would keep me safe. Preoccupied with yelling into his micro-zap, he piloted the groaning old bus through DC's twists and turns with two fingers on the wheel. Darn ironic, to buy it in a bus crash.

But on we drove till a mammoth delay at that tunnel in Baltimore cost well over two hours. As we sat and inched and mostly sat, I got my window open to inquire of a young guy in a sleek Eurotrash convertible. He said Homeland Control was "testing a new T-enhancement at the other end." I asked why they were worried about something *leaving* the tunnel, and he said, "Are you questioning T, B.E.I.?"

"It's the wave of the future, dude – all aboard!"

He digested that, flipped me off and said, "That's obviously why you're hanging out the window of a *bus* begging for information." And he scooted into an opening in the far lane. By the time we finally crept through the tunnel, there was nothing to see.

I sat and scribbled and marveled that this baby seal to Statie's club had, these several days later, been about to kill a man, or at least try. Taking advantage of a couple of uninterrupted hours to finish finally! a draft of Penn/Bellevue (ASPIC to follow), I regretted buying no whiskey when I could and wished for the Entertainment System to hear the same old same old in a different town. A clock reading 2:39 as we wound through Philly, I jammed my work under my thigh and clipped my fancy new pen to my styling new shirt. Everything else I carried was out of sight.

PART TEN

Epilogue

Wedged hard up against it, something droning away nearby, I've either been gobbled by a dragon and ended up jammed between his ribs and fire-maker, or I'm sprawled across two seats of a bus back by the engine. I open my eyes: bus. Manhattan's towers visible through the murk, where had the night gone? Sleeping in my own bed come what may Thursday night was a prime reason to quit DC. Then I remember the pointless foul-up at the Baltimore tunnel, jamming the biggest road in the country. Just a reminder, folks, life can get lousy any way, any time the MoFos choose.

Christ, looping down and around into the Lincoln Tunnel, there he is again, HeadFuck looming up way too close on a giant billboard. Part of a new campaign, maybe, to compensate for him being so seldom out and about. A stylized portrait like in Virginia, all martial and resolute, but the B.E.I. is in static red letters ten-feet high, not Virginia's flashing neon. Whether his sterner glare here is anything more than the man's natural reaction to being so close to New York, I can't say.

Hey, *Lincoln* Tunnel, the skinflint bus company purchasing landing rights in midtown. Cool, less of a trek to Nick's, cause time to get our little meeting crossed off both our lists. And soon enough I'm on a stool gazing out a deli's big window pounding a four-buck bacon-egg sandwich and coffee ($9.79 in DC, powdered eggs and grinning lout to greet you at the door included). Outside, a cute punk couple out all night stop to kiss and rub it in.

Should I have taken one of those jobs over the years and *maybe* still be ensconced with Nicki? What, and miss all these thrills and spills, women in Milwaukee trying to smuggle bras through enemy lines? I mop egg and, despite her betrayal over the phone, dread seeing her. And, holy crap, what happened to my hand? The hot coffee cup dislodging one end of the band-aid, something peculiar peeks out from underneath. I yank it off to see the cut's morphed into an ugly, raised purplish scar that looks awfully permanent. Bright, garish and jagged, getting Raytheoned was just the ticket to drawing MoFo attention from from here on out. Statie'll cream his jeans for sure the first time he spots one of these.

Keeping my fist clenched – what the times demand – I go get divorced way up in 47-J. Nicki's building a tall, jagged tooth, I can't quite make out its exact color. The lobby guy dials up my picture on a large screen, one worth saving, yeah, from years ago, the sun *visibly* setting over my shoulder on the ferry. He mumbles, compares it and me to my even more ancient license photo and brings some suit out from in back to confer – a whole lot of rigmarole for simply ringing a tenant. I tell them only something crucial would have me there that time of morning, and wheedle enough that they finally deign to call Turncoat Wife to authorize access.

Nicki opens the door wearing a soignée, dark blue robe I've sure never seen. A present from MoneyBags? She turns and flips a switch to mechanically part the drapes and reveal the bit of western Queens not shrouded in murk. I drink my fill while she flops on a big, fancy leather couch, not a word from either of us. The Comb-Over Bridge (re-christened in honor of the former mayor's recent departure) looks odd curling the wrong way, seeing it here from Manhattan.

"Are you going to stand there with your back to me?"

And, yup, right where it should be is Stap's roof, the back yard so enormous I spy a tiny slice of weeds. I turn and take in the haute living room with its purple-glass coffee table and complicated, uncomfortable chairs. One wall is alternating tiger stripes of shiny yellow and matte black, while another sports a painting, I guess you have to call it, a big, abstract excrescence of the sort Nick and I used to snicker at in galleries. Her grandmother's sore-thumb oak armoire the only item I recognize, her place is all shivery and spare and a far, fancy cry from our once comfy crib.

Jesus, she's cut her hair, all that crowning glory reduced to a horrible, executrix-bob length just below her ears, and has she colored it too? I voice surprise, and she shoots back, "You're right, it's ugly as sin. You ever think, genius, that thanks to you and your little crusade I have damn good reason to kiss my old self good-bye. Maybe try to throw off the leeches of the press, especially the jerks with licensed whole-vids."

I'm saved from any weak, shrill reply by Otis running up to snaggle back and forth between my legs. We have a glorious reunion and – certain a small crane will have to hoist me from the depths of her weird chair – then he's on my lap, his machine going full blast.

"You watch sports now, or what's with the giganto TV?"

"I just use our crappy little old TV in the bedroom, because finding what I want with this one's three remotes is just too much. Still, a place like this requires something anchoring the wall opposite the couch, and those dusty paintings of ours didn't cut it."

I damn sure would've liked that swell painting of a canal that cost us like eighty-five bucks. "So the TV is for show – like this whole freaking place. And all our books are crammed in your bedroom?"

"The building doesn't let you move in with paper-based books."

"So you threw out the books *and* the paintings, including that expensive one of the canal that I paid like two-thirds for? You couldn't even call me? I mean, moving out, I figured all that stuff was safe with you."

She sniffs at that and says she paid for all the books, that I was always just going to the library. Before I can muster a claim to the moral high ground over the trashing of books (surely worse than trashing a job devoted to swelling HeadFuck's columns of Boots), a copy of yesterday's *Node* catches my eye. A giant block headline, "DISGRACED!" tops probably the only *relatively* unappealing photo of Carole extant. (She's leaping awkwardly to cover first base while twisting to grab a throw, a feat major league pitchers practice all Spring.) Distracted like everyone else, I point: "What she do?"

"Big, big scandal. Years before her fireman, her boyfriend was busted with a joint in his pocket after-hours in a park in Queens when she was an innocent slip of a girl of seventeen. Her under-age, they wrote her up too."

"And all along we thought she was like Jessica Rabbit: not bad, just drawn that way."

"She defended you as carrying nothing but that dumb radio of yours in Penn Station. Plus there's talk she's planning to refuse a search herself. So the knives come out. Speaking of which, you've never actually refused a search, have you, oh Great Mahatma?"

Sure, that counted. I'd told Officer Umbert to shove it *and* told him why. "Actually I have, yesterday to a cop at the bus station in Washington. But there was no one else around. It – "

"How convenient: no one else around. So what happened? I mean, how'd you end up here so bright and early the next morning? Which thrills me no end, by the way."

"A top cop intervened on my behalf – no joke! He sees the bigger picture."

"Like I believe any part of that. You know, Mr. Big Shot, I had it going pretty good up here for all of two months before you came flying over from *Queens* and crashed through that window there. I was going to be the chief copywriter on by far the biggest account in the history of the agency, and now I'm probably getting fired today. If Ernesto doesn't fire me, it's only because he thinks my notoriety, which I did *nothing* to invite, might attract some bottom-feeding clients when all this dies down."

Floundering for a reply – what, she never would've made it to Bayonne that one time without me? – I doubt she can get any angrier. But she does. "And all because of you and some little abstract civ-lib principle that nobody gives a shit about. Not anymore, Mitchell. Not after years of HeadFuck – Minders Turn Elsewhere!"

"The Minders don't exist. They're just the latest boogeyman to keep us in line."

"So you're Mr. Inside now, privy to the councils of the high and mighty? You with a big 'scoop' on a *general*, surprise, surprise, trying to line his – what the hell is that?" she demands, pointing. "That disgusting mark on your hand. What is that?"

"That? Oh, nothing."

"It sure as hell looks like something."

"They cut me and then they got some goop in it, so now I guess I'm carrying this around." I feel no need to tell her my attacker handed me the goop and instructed me on its use.

"It'll go nice with those shorts of yours that you refused to let me throw out years ago. Like you're not already enough of a target without some mark on you, you and this stupid, diehard 'Movement' of yours. The HeadMan has won, Mitchell, and anyone with any sense accepts that. We maybe could've challenged him his first month or two, but the leopard was too clever to show his spots right away."

The Headman – Jesus. "Maybe. Too bad the Disruption was so murky – how it spread and all – that it was hard for folks to support. Plus the governor of Maryland getting attacked."

"Well, we thought about supporting it, till the Goddamn Battle of 45th Street. After that, we turned tail like everyone else."

"Not everyone."

"We sure did, you and me both, Mahatma. But who cares, that was years ago. And as far I can tell, so what? If you have a decent job – hint, hint – and you mind your Ps & Qs, what's the big fucking difference? Nobody cares about the shit you worry about. Most of what the Minders go after is boring. What, you still want to have sex outdoors at your age? I was a secretary a couple of years ago, and look at where I've landed. Look at this Goddamn couch!" She's screaming.

"Nicki, it's awfully early for all this. Don't you care about your neighbors?"

"Those creeps? Even before you unleashed your big disaster, they'd rather choke than say hello." She gets loud again. "All my life I've wanted a one-hundred percent Carpathian leather couch. Never mind I'll still be paying for it I don't know how, it's gonna look damn silly in whatever hole I end up in back in Queens. Queens *again*, I can't fucking believe it! I'll be lucky to get another secretary job."

She sits there sobbing. Memories all I have left, I don't want them unmoored by uncertainty about her goosing me for info on the phone. Had she really turned on me to that degree? Nick at a weak moment, catch her by surprise to scotch the lie. "So keeping a grip on all this splendor here entitled you to rat me out on the phone Monday night on the train? What, you were spying for some MoFo who said he'd put in a good word with Ernesto? Huh, Nicki? Right?"

Her sobs grind to a sudden halt. "What the fuck are you talking about now? You think this is some kind of game? No. This morning is about me telling you what's what and you leaving."

"Nicki! We've been married a long time, and you've always been a lousy liar. It was obvious Monday night on the phone, all that butter-wouldn't-melt, 'Oh, I'm just so *fascinated* by what takes you to Washington' crap. And mentioning the Harrisburg 'right downtown' about six times, and then, for all the dunces listening in, saying that *Sy-ri-ac* – remember? – is easy enough to spell. Huh, Nicki? Before you lie to me, know that I've got proof."

"What proof!" I keep staring. Then, quietly, "Alright, look Mr. Reporter. I wasn't spying, not really. That schmuck – this was in a freaking F&F conference room, him, me and Ernesto late Monday afternoon – said they just wanted to be aware of your intentions so as to keep you safe given the controversy surrounding you. Or some shit."

"So safe they couldn't bother to keep some clown from shooting at me in Stap's backyard."

"Poopous wasn't even mad at you over that. He's *amused*. Anyway, they lie so much, and even when they're not it's couched in such bullshit, it's hard to know. What could I do?"

I put Otis down, haul myself up and to the window, and note with satisfaction the bleary outline of the 59th Street Bridge. I whirl on her. "You could quit your damn job. Decide maybe you don't want to be part of convincing black kids to kill and get killed. Maybe, this the only ride you get, Nicki, you might figure there's stuff to give a shit about beyond a couch."

"Like you, you self-righteous prick? Right, quit a job *post-Plunge* that pays like mine does. Or did, thanks to you. Now get out! Like you really had 'proof' about my call. *You're* the liar! Go! You sleazed your way to what you wanted. Fine, we're *divorced*, you hear that? Face-to-face, so it's official. Tell Stapapoopous to sign for the papers for you if you're off on one of your little self-involved, save-the-world missions."

There it was, the pronouncement. The axe. However expected and inevitable, still a dead fish in the chops. I fall into the stupid chair and Otis immediately leaps up. "Yeah, well, don't waste any money on a lawyer. I don't have any to fight over, and I don't want any of yours."

"Too late. I had to show Ernesto a letter from an attorney."

"Punt the lawyer and download a form. I'm telling you, I got no way to fight it."

"No kidding. Look, I've gotta go figure out what to wear to keep Ernesto from firing me today."

She looks pretty good sitting there in her gorgeous robe on her ridiculous couch. Pissed as she is, there'll probably be no hug and kiss to commemorate the good times. "You haven't exactly let any grass grow under your ass since we split, have you Nicki?"

"What the hell is that supposed to mean?"

"MoneyBags isn't your first, is he?"

"Wouldn't you like to know. But you want to hear something funny? I did everything Ernesto and that prick asked of me in that room at F&F. So I stupidly thought it was a one-time deal with you on the phone Monday night. But it's never enough. That bastard came back Wednesday afternoon and said I was such a natural, he needed just one more 'favor.' "

"Favor, huh?" What, take them out to Mineola to scare Mom and Pop into showing them my boyhood room?

"Ernesto was smart, he just walked me to the room and told me to go inside and do what the men said – men, cause there were two of them, the new one even more slippery and threatening than the first. Turns out there were a couple of things they wanted me to try to get MoneyBags to discuss at dinner that night."

Christ, did Cummings know about this, or is the over-grasping MoFo mind just always chasing the next score? "Yeah?"

"They said don't worry, they already knew where we were eating, they'd take care of recording it and everything. Just get him to talk about a few specific financial issues. It'd be easy cause they were putting something in his drink."

"And what issues were those?"

"All this technical shit. I had trouble enough memorizing it for that evening. The Chinese and different 'tranches' and U.S. debt and stuff. Plus were any of his clients shifting out of the dollar into that new currency all the South American countries got together on."

"He talked?"

"On and on, putty in my hands all night. The next morning,

Ernesto said they were really happy with me, and they had some-body else in mind."

"A regular pro, huh? Jesus, I should sit on the thing, feel the wonder of it."

"You're not sitting on anything, whatever you're talking about."

"You're willing to do an awful lot for a stupid couch."

She gets up and flings the door open and orders me out. Otis on in years, I pick him up for our likely last cuddle, and almost lose it, him purring and kneading his paws up towards my face, me rubbing his belly. I turn to my ex-wife and say "Well, see you later" and go to kiss her cheek. But she darts away and points at the door. "Out, now!" Nope, no hug, no kiss, a decade down the drain. No nothing, no mas.

✳✳✳✳✳✳✳✳✳✳✳✳✳✳✳

Having cut it short, not the wind-in-her-hair girl I'd married. A week ago I still loved her. God, to think how thrilled I was that she dropped into an e-mail that she missed me, a meaningless pearl before swine. More crushed than I'd counted on, I shoulder my way past too many damn fancy-pants, Upper-East-Side Despoilers who barely veer clear as I barge blindly on to Central Park. You have to present photo ID to walk through even the free part of the zoo, so I hump up a hill and around.

Down the steps at 5th and 59th to the train, I blunder into the newsstand and, holy mackerel, there in all her prim glory on the covers of both the *Chirp* and the *Node* is Chilean Cassandra in a sky-blue summer suit sitting serenely on one of those weird canes with an attached little round seat. The *Chirp* I buy has her sitting in the middle of Penn Station with about nine cops massed behind her looking miffed, all under the headline: "Aristocrat Says No!" At the bottom: "Chilean Diplo's Wife Snarls Penn Refusing Bag Search".

499

The two-page spread inside (which describes me as the "ethically and sartorially challenged, de facto founder of the No-Search Brigade") identifies my prickly friend as Magdalena Marquez Carrillo y Acosta. She was "acting suspicious" in Penn yesterday evening, drifting around carrying her cane-seat and a little valise filled with what turned out to be nothing but tangerines. She meandered in front of the LIRR search table long enough to be finally summoned forward for a search at 9:27 p.m., and then she loudly refused " 'based on centuries of American law.' " She also claimed diplomatic immunity for, though separated for decades from Chile's ex-foreign secretary, they've never formally divorced.

Then Magdalena unfolded her seat and sat – and sat – and such was her steely mien, the cops came no nearer. They ended up closing Penn Station, no trains in or out (absurd given the size of the place versus the size of her bag) and, in typical overkill, evacuating the office tower above for close to an hour. One heck of a gnarly, expensive stick in their spokes. Finally one of those guys in a Michelin Man suit waddled up, and she couldn't have been more gracious, offering tangerines all around. Being led away in handcuffs, she said her Demo made her feel decades younger, " 'when I protested the Disappeared in my country.' "

I'm but a cog in a big wheel gaining speed downhill. Fine by me. Carole and Magdalena make damn better figureheads than the mope staggered by the spotlight. Let me try to reign in ASPIC; that'd be a good job of work. Whitaker in *Warpath* saving my bacon yesterday afternoon, here's hoping "Penn/Bellevue/ASPIC" provides some long-term protection. Luckily, the first two-thirds were pretty well ready to type up, assuming my Stuffing-scrawls still littered my kitchen table.

Things moving fast, I need to google myself, find out what I missed boycotting the papers while in DC. Will I be allowed to sit and pound the keyboard addressing civ-lib 'abstractions' – screw you, Nicki – then go out and pound a few beers, wake up and repeat, all with the cops having found explosive residue on the pack they'd exploded? Damn, I should've read my copy of *It Can't Happen Here* when I had the chance, maybe get a clue.

✳✳✳✳✳✳✳✳✳✳✳✳✳✳✳

I come sweating up the walk, no cops or reporters visible, Mr. Staphilopoulos on the porch smoking a nail, his styling new sports shirt untucked.

"Hey, what's cooking, good looking? Somebody die and leave you a new shirt?"

"Ha-ha. I need such a shirt. A regular Penn Station around here since you been gone. Lawyers, newsies, cops. All kinds of people. Your *father* comes by – very nice man. Why you such a problem to him at his age? Anyway, everybody easier if I look like guy owns this big house."

So Turd-Touch has benefited Stap's wardrobe at least. "My father liked you too. Anyone else I want to know?"

"I get to her. But first I have to say sorry. No, first, you still this side of the dirt. That's good, cause no one knows what happened. Some man shoots my garage and, bingo, no more you. So nice to see you. It hot in Washington? Then maybe, who knows, big shot flies to London, have lunch with the King."

"Come on! I've been riding a Chinatown bus. So what'd I miss?"

"I don't like saying sorry, so I talk nonsense. But there were four of them, four big toughs. I try to stop them, but they push me hard up against that post there. I thought they break my hip. And – "

"Who did? Someone messed with an old guy like you? Did you call the cops?"

"Cops? They say *they* the cops. Who knows, they don't leave names. Besides, me and cops not friendly right now, they always taking all the parking spots on the block."

"I'm sorry about your hip – you OK? What'd they want?"

"They wanted you, what you think? But my hip, that's the thing. You get a broken hip my age, not so good. I got a little scared – also something I don't like saying. So I lie there on *my* porch, right there" he points "and don't stop them going up."

"Stap, Jesus, nobody expects you to, four men against one. They knew my rooms?"

"Must have, because later – I got behind my locked door when they go – your door was closed but unlocked. And it was locked the whole time you're gone, I make sure. *Lots* of exercise climbing stairs up and down. I couldn't tell if they took anything. Your computer's still there on the table."

The SecDef whole-vid under the sink! "I'll find out soon enough. I'm really sorry about your hip. You sure you're OK? And sorry to be so high maintenance – you know, like a Ferrari."

"You mean like that Plymouth going all rust in my backyard. The hip, it's OK, an excuse to get drunk that night, a tall bottle of your green beer. But drunk mostly cause I feel bad I let them push me around. Fifteen years ago, *they* be the one getting pushed. What's that nastiness on your hand?"

I turn my palm, and the scar glares up at us. "They branded me, Stap, like a cow. No big deal – privacy was a memory for me anyway."

"They scum. People are not going to take their shit anymore, you'll see. Oh, before I forget, some cop making all nicey-nice left this for you, him practically begging. Like an old man can't carry paper around in his pocket." He fishes out a crumpled envelope.

Just a business card inside, from an MTA Detective Tiggert, with a scrawled note on the back that I read out loud: *Please call at your convenience – there's reason to talk.* "They're scared, Stap, at least the cops who shot me. They're trying to play nice. That's cause Carole – you know, hubba-hubba – went on TV saying it was all their fault."

"She getting in bed with you, another mystery. Your regular mail is upstairs on your table. I figure best not leave downstairs for some curiosity-cat. You got at least three from lawyers – trouble-chasers. I read my lawyer friend their names off the envelopes, he says put all three in the toilet. "

"Yeah, well, I got ninety days to file notice of claim." I hold up the card. "I'll call this bastard Monday, see what he has to say. Can't afford a lawyer right now, so maybe just take notes and say as little as possible myself."

"That's what everybody thinks – smarter than cops. Then they start talking nice and offering coffee and cigarettes."

"I don't smoke cigarettes. So please tell me nobody got shot at the bodega down on the corner."

"You gone, no one here to ask. Tuesday, I went there to find out about all the cops there on Monday. The sandwiches you can't eat, especially the bread, even with those new guys they got running it about seven years ago. So that's when I got that beer of yours. Good, because I had it for my hip that night. Better than most American beer."

"Right, Ballantine, great. Next I'll get you riding the subway. But what the hell happened?"

"You saved him, that man who broke my garage window he still owes me. Cause the NYPDs already in the store know the train cops are after you. So they think the man in a suit, maybe he a train-cop detective. So they not shoot him. They standing there with guns out yelling at him to drop his gun. But he doesn't – *and* they still not shoot, you believe that? Then everybody's hero, the store guy, sneaks up and puts his mop handle over the man's neck and wrestles him down. So the cops jump on top."

"The counter guy did that, really?"

"Right. The counterman. The man by the cash – what you call it?"

"What? Cash Register."

"Register, right – he not move. But the other guy jumps him, and now he's a big hero. Illegal, from Egypt, but Commissioner Ted, that dick, says he take care of that. So you do something good for somebody."

Bodega Dude, right on! "Me? I didn't do anything."

"Sure you do. Bring man with gun in there, and now Egypt gets his papers. So now what you do?"

"What, next?" He nods. "I'm going upstairs. I got something to write."

"You mean like when you hang that general. What's the matter, *colonel* not good enough for you?"

"Aim high, Stap."

"Naked girls in the Senate – good, like Greek beach. My friend with the computer, the Turk, prints it out, and we all read it right here on the porch. Big arguments over your show-off English words. Army with orgy, like Greece in the old days. So, you go after HeadFuck next, that phony?"

"Nah. Not yet." I stand there smiling, deflecting an editorial conference.

"OK. You keep quiet till it comes up on the Turk's computer. How come you don't get in *The Daily Chirp* I can go buy? But you got your own ways."

"Thanks, Stap. I sure appreciate all your help and support. I mean – "

"Sit on my balls, mister. My hip's OK, so the bad thing is yesterday she turns me into your mailman."

She? Divorce papers? What did it matter, though Nicki could've mentioned it. "Yeah, what, somebody send me a chocolate cake?"

"Cake – you mean brick. The one hit me when another looker shows up looking for you, all whispering and nervous. And this one was *young*, too. Pinch her anywhere, no fat. That one calls herself your wife, she a looker too, especially in that yellow dress. You know her yellow dress?"

"I've seen it, Stap."

"She always getting stuck on my porch. I'll drive her home to Manhattan next time. But she's at least the same planet as you, your age and hers. But this one yesterday – twenty-six, tops!"

Should I thank the *Chirp* for printing my address? "Alright, I'll bite: she wants to bear me six sons. Who the hell is she?"

"Wait, big shot. You in a hurry? I was yelling at a cop parked all sloppy, taking *two* spots. So he plays with his siren. Like before: loud! Then he goes. So I sit here waiting for it to cool down – ha! – and up this little looker-mouse shows. She asks for you, and she not a newsie, I can tell. So instead of saying 'who?' I say you not seen head or tail."

"This was yesterday?"

"Yesterday, yeah, like I tell you. Now shut up. She was sneaking, watching the house, and she says she likes the way I handle that cop. Handle – that for broom. I just say what any American New Yorker say about parking right on a crowded street."

"More folks speaking up every day. But Stap, where's the mail she gave you – you're making me crazy."

"Good, all the people you make crazy, including Mexico upstairs. They even more mad at you, you should know, one more of them get taken. Anyway, come in."

He leads me inside and – a first – into his big dark apartment. "It was ten last night, and I tried to tell her I drive her to the train. It's OK, she can trust an old guy like me. Or get her a car service, call a Greek friend. The only one come down here now, another of your magic tricks. But she says no, she has a car around the corner."

He ushers me in to a surprisingly spotless kitchen, spotless cause, looking around, I realize it's not much used beyond the opening of jars. He reaches into his oven and takes out a manila envelope. "That's the safest place, no fire. Look. I put my own tape on right on top of hers. Nobody can say nothing!"

If it was from Elaine, the girl's motivated. Christ, could she possibly be in league with Cummings, him worrying about ASPIC encroaching on his turf and telling me an article on them is easy as pie? Come on, dummy, I presented myself at Al's office on Monday; the contact was me *to* him. My landlord stands there clutching it maddeningly.

"Stap, did she say her name?"

"You crazy? She just said she hated to leave it, but she was going to have to trust me. Me old enough to be her father's father, I had to stop myself yelling about trust, looker American girls think every day the sun rise for them. But she says, and what this mean? I try to figure, but it's worse than that vest-pocket president you told me about. I wrote it down to ask you. She says she has to leave the envelope 'before things go bump in the night.' "

"Right. So, Stap, please let me have it. I gotta get upstairs." I force myself not to grab it from him.

"Sure, sure. But what that mean, bump in the night?"

"Before something gets her – before a ghost materializes out of nowhere and goes boo!"

"*Boo*? She said bump."

"Stap, I'm gonna scream. It's just a phrase, like: staying left of the boom." He stares blankly. "You know. Or – or, the early bird catches the worm. It means before the MoFos get her, like the ones that are after me."

"Who are MoFos?"

"Stap, the motherfuckers!"

"They come through me first. I don't give a Goddamn anymore, me at my age. This the most fun I had since *before* the colonels. They not fun – not like the dumb Americans after you."

I tell myself to count to ten before taking the damn envelope from him. He finally forks it over, apparently expecting me to open it right there. I wave it at him, smile and shake my head.

"Good, do your job right," he says.

"I'm trying. A lot of people are helping me."

"OK, a surprise, OK? September's rent doesn't count."

"What do you mean, it's not the first yet, not even close."

"Hey, mister, listen to what people say to you. A little birdie paid

506

for you for September. So keep that in your pocket, you need it. What I got to spend it on? Maybe you buy a big ad about no cops going in your bag. Put it up next to the new sign HeadFuck's got on the BQE with those words nobody knows. Why he say he can't get pregnant?"

"What? Oh, Impregnable. That means, you know, unassailable." He gapes in turn. "Locked safe in a box. But Stap, no rent! Jeeze, I don't know what to say. You sure? I mean…." My protest sputters quickly.

He grunts, then gets animated again. "These MoFos you call them, like sharks driving slow around and around the block. God help you, you beep at them. It take at least *five* of them to get past me now. Like I said, I don't care." He pulls up his shirttail and shows me a big knife in a sheath on a second belt fastened cockeyed around his leathery, old-man's waist.

"Mr. Staphilopoulos! What are you, crazy? Put that away – I don't even want to see it. They'll shoot you. Jesus, Stap!"

"Yeah, yeah. Be a good boy and go write your stories and save the world. And let me take care of my porch. *My* porch!"

I give him a hug and browbeat him again into putting the knife away. All his talk of fun, I hope he realizes there's still a little more of it this side of the dirt.

✶✶✶✶✶✶✶✶✶✶✶✶✶✶✶

Up four flights and behind my papier mache door, the Hovel doesn't look horribly awry. Maybe the cartons of story files on the far side of the bed aren't stacked exactly as I'd left them – not that they wouldn't do me a solid stealing that old junk. As for my computer, anything truly important was printed out and in those boxes.

Bump, Elaine said. Unlike me, Al does have a young, very dependent child, Pete. (Had Pete intended to be quite so ghoulish asking me about any *young* children as I quit he and Lucy's driveway?) Do I dare a vague, pay-phone hello to check up on them tonight?

Probably not, about to brandish their leak. Weren't no help I could offer – except maybe write a story, I guess.

For of course the envelope is from them, not that they included a note. Two contracts, fourteen pages in all. A twelve-page "Executive Summary" of ASPIC's contract to privatize the MTA's search program and a two-page employment contract for that deputy MTA police commish, Walton Everidge.

And, yup, the phrase "$159-million per annum" leaps off the front page. Flipping through, there's additional appealing verbiage: "Dedicated T Professionals, the armaments ASPIC's operatives carry will be left to the Contractor's discretion." Plus, "Sworn Protectors, ASPIC's operatives retain full powers of arrest." I can hope there's something buried somewhere about consultants. Only a few women, it'd be cake, maybe, to identify the MTA board member's wife. As to Everidge, he'll pull down a cool $315,000 per, plus incentives for providing "operational oversight support" – i.e., being a figurehead. And, holy shit, they're contracting to do five million searches a year! That's like thirteen- or fourteen-thousand a day, my pen and paper indicate.

So, combine my existing verbiage, including that squeezed from my pen mid-Stuffing which I saw there still on the table, with these documents and get "Penn/Bellevue/ASPIC" the heck out. Probably will have to call ASPIC, the MTA, and the police union to insert their florid, rote responses. (And give them a twenty-minute deadline so they can't send the Man with No Nose crashing through my door before I hit send.) Quote Carole and Magdalena too, assuming I could reach them, to acknowledge their place at the Movement's helm, especially Carole regarding the Entertainment System. Can I go for a big score, or do I owe it to *Warpath* Joe for shouldering some of that Whitaker risk?

Hell, hole up here and write the whole megillah up as a novel. With Stap's astonishing September dispensation, I still had October's rent socked away. Screw reporting, it's a mug's game. Nobody'll believe the last two weeks, anyway, so just spin my web. *Two weeks,* yeah, going back to the Saturday night on the LIRR that started it all and then ratchet it right up to today. One month to write up one week and October to write the second, no problem. Come up with a catchy title, that's the tough part, and make a bundle long as I can unearth someone to make me a shiny cover. Offer the artist a case of tuna fish. Cause, with "the oddities that abound with me" – whatever Joe had said – I already have a hook. Get it out for the Christmas rush and go sit on a beach for a week with Lois.

There's a loud hammering at the door downstairs. Can't Freaking Touch Me! Not till I hit send on "Penn/etc." Now –

The SecDef whole-vid! Had Stap's four toughs missed it? Hundreds of uselessly dead Boots a year. Was that the zen-nugget secret of not giving two shits, Everett? That *not* giving them actually makes you care more because, nothing else left, all you got is the Cause? Is that what these last couple of weeks have been about? I hear Mr. Staphilopoulos yelling about a warrant, and his taxes and this and that. Keep the Goddamn knife sheathed, Stap! It ain't your Cause.

I grab at the low door hiding the pipes under the sink, then reach way high up on the front wall to find the micro-zip right where I taped it months ago. I jab at the computer. Please don't let them have turned it into a doorstop.

OK, Joe, get ready! I fumble to download it as I hear Stap yelling to signal me. "You think he's up there somewhere, OK, misters – you find him! You monkeys come in here pushing me in my own house! Fuck you, American shits think you own the world!"

I get the two ASPIC contracts and shove them in different files, deep in different boxes in my bedroom. The best I can do, the Hovel not offering many more hiding places, really, than a hospital room. Ah, Maureen, my lovely!

What if they've gotten to Joe, Calfers shutting him down cause of the Whitaker piece? Stanley seems pretty damn crafty. So send it to them both, suspenders and a belt, and tell 'em up top, and let them AP-UPI it. Fingers scramble as I hear tromping up and down the third floor, people yelling in Spanish.

Friday
Dudes:
They're ALMOST at the door! This whole-vid legit. At Aberdeen testing ground, late Spring/early Summer. Check site, SandsCasualties.org. for stats on non-combat Grinder deaths, hundreds a year. Them SecDef legs – you'll see – it'll bounce. Sneding to you both, suspenders and a belt. Use my name on top, may be all it's got left. MoFos on my stairs NOT a metaphor. No reply to queries likely at this end. Just run the fucker and then push search-refusals!!! Tiny acorn, mighty oak.
Repeat: no reply to queries likely.
Boots thank you, me too.
Mitch (byline, Mitchell)

And … and … there, sent, Joe's name first in the address box, so he'll get it a millisecond before Stanley – ha!

There's a whole big brouhaha downstairs, some gorilla yelling at someone to get the hell out from under the bed, someone else yelling to yank him out by the feet.

Damn! "Penn/Bellevue/ASPIC" not yet loosed upon the world, I might have to leave clearing the Barmy Bungler's name to others. Heck, even if I'd skipped that baseball game to write, I'd still have been waiting on Elaine's envelope. Besides, I'm glad to have seen the Roughnecks run rough-shod. I can think of that – along with Lois at the top of the stairs.

Will I ever see her again, my lovely, stern collaborator? And what of Maureen, the lustrous Crimson Colleen, stiffener of spines, fellow refuse and resister and lover of soup – assuming she wasn't deported, or worse?

More immediately, who to summon to help kick some MoFo ass?

Whoever was working their slow, inexorable way through all the rooms down below, ain't no singing telegram. Lois has all that unarmed combat training and might even show with some weapons. But who knows what revolutionary, street-fighting shit Maureen might know. Hell, get 'em both (though they won't like each other), and maybe Pete and Lucy the poodle too. Some MoFo messes with Pete, I bet Lucy goes ape. Mac might have a little extra tension to dispel, just a tad. Get Al up here. He's skinny, but he knows a lot. Plus Lincoln Center Bartleby and Wife, Dexter and Jennifer, just to prove it's possible to say no. And kung-fu Delores, she's got some anger in her after Tuesday night. Zeke the orderly to compare notes on the proper cracking of MoFo ribs, and Aretha Franklin for provisions. Zafar to teach them a little history and Shandre to plain stare 'em down. Bodega Dude, long as he brings his mop. Marko and Bethany to immortalize us all, and Joe to run their whole-vid, Barbara to swear and tear her hair and Everett – sure, he's alive, just DWI-delayed in Pennsylvania – to smite them righteously. H-DM's cookie monster, Wilson, to improve blast dispersal. Stan the Man too, in case Joe gets too medicinally fogged. A risen Fielding Ablegar to overawe them, Judge Fennerly to sentence them, Cat Wrangler to gouge their eyes out with her heels and Coney Island Enchantress to take their breath away. God, to think of the thrill just dancing with Emily way back that Sunday at Coney Island. Penn Station's National Guardsman to throw off their aim and get a medic quick. No, no, no. Get Magdalena, she's done the most for the Movement so far – plus she's got diplomatic immunity – and Carole to exonerate everyone on our side. Pop to hit 'em in the knees with a lead pipe, and Mom so they'll choke gobbling her carrot cake. Creep up the stairs behind them, Stap, you'll know what to do. Otis, claw their lips! Shit, just holler for the "fighting machine from the Third ID" and sit back and enjoy the show.

Jesus, they're stomping up the last stairs. Maybe it's only the

Minders with a Blue. Minders Come Hither! Just as long as it's not Lurch. I know damn well I'm not getting lucky with him again. No reply likely. Or....I ignore my advice to Stap and root out the carving knife Nicki insisted I take for some reason. There's a fierce bang on the door and someone wrenching the knob. Now where –

The End

Afterword

This tale was sparked by my wife and myself getting assaulted by the NYPD at Lincoln Center. Chapter Seven, "At the Behemoth's Beck and Call," is a slightly fanciful account of the whole ugly incident. (Slightly fanciful, as in, my wife – a lustrous brunette Mitchell might rhapsodize over, not a redhead like Jennifer – was roughed-up, but not groped by the police. I was injured, but my wrists remained intact.)

A bystander whose name I've never learned reported the cops' egregious action to the Civilian Complaint Review Board, which undertook a formal investigation: CCRB Case Number 200408189. We became aware of it months later when a hobbled, but nonetheless dogged CCRB investigator contacted us out of the blue.

My disorderly conduct charge was dismissed by a New York County criminal court judge by mail since the responding officer mangled some of the necessary jargon. And the trespassing charge (this in a City park) was tossed when I appeared in court to contest it. After researching and worrying over it myself for months, I was pro bono guided through the court appearance by a friendly civ-lib attorney referred by the National Lawyers Guild. David Milton, then with Moore & Goodman, LLP, is near the top of my owe-a-beer list.

Leading that list is a lion of the New York bar, my and my wife's attorney, Jeffrey A. Rothman, who represented us in the suit for damages we subsequently brought: United States District Court, Southern District of New York. 1:05-cv-07331-NRB. After years of tenacious effort, Jeff achieved a settlement with co-defendants Lincoln Center and the City of New York. In an article in the *New York Law Journal*, "Applying the Constitution to Private Actors," Christopher Dunn of the New York Civil Liberties Union cited the federal lawsuit Jeff so ably shepherded as bolstering free-speech case law. http://www.nyclu.org/oped/column-applying-constitution-private-actors-new-york-law-journal.

Following the assault at Lincoln Center, this tale was written from 2005 to 2010. The political unraveling of the unfortunate most recent few years serves as vindication rather than inspiration. A first draft or two already complete, I encountered *Democracy Incorporated: Managed Democracy and the Specter of Inverted Totalitarianism*, Sheldon S. Wolin's 2008 warning regarding, as Lois puts it, the country's no longer nascent, "sleight-of-hand, smiley-face, fascism-lite." Though speaking of current conditions, Wolin's thinking certainly helped flesh out my conception of HeadMan's America.

The story occupies its own time in the near future, two weeks in a specific August. The year is indicated here and there if you peer closely, maybe do a little arithmetic. To ease calculation, the timeline is occasionally fudged.

Some liberties are taken in this true tale. For instance, I've kept the Washington Nationals at Robert F. Kennedy Memorial Stadium, the old football mausoleum over by the river in Southeast, and certain car companies still own certain other car companies as the story has it.

But exception to the rampant fictive veracity is scant – now or in a future careening ever closer. The hush-hush, rush-rush cremation of many hundreds of human remains to make way for the New Jersey Devils hockey arena in Newark is true. I've interviewed people involved for an article I somehow never wrote (my bad, *New York*). The New York Public Library did require patrons to create a photo ID for the privilege of perusing – not removing – books in its Lion Library reading room. The damn things tipping so often, Humvee Egress Assistance Trainers were widely deployed by the U.S. Army. And Congressional Cemetery really is a members-only dog run. Dues as of this writing is $250 per annum ($200 in *Derail this Train Wreck*'s post-Plunge economy), and there's a waiting list.

Chapter Eleven, "Moo!" is straight shoe-leather reporting, aside from a bit of dialogue with the police officer at the end. Carrying my book-filled, East German Army knapsack, I did futilely parade myself before cops doing searches and did encounter a long line of uncomplaining New Yorkers up the stairs at the Herald Square subway station, plus an MTA officer recording the demographics of those searched at Penn Station. For many months a real sign at Penn Station curiously instructed us to call "MTA.PD." I called several times, only to reach the bum-number recording, since that's a few numbers shy. PATH train announcements did encourage riders to carry nothing at all – a step, perhaps, towards carrying little between the ears.

Acknowledgements

This journey of many steps would never have been completed without these folks generously prodding my feet: various Forbeses, Kurt Andersen, Caton Gates, Robert Dolan, Stephen M. Feldman, Jeff Keller, David Kiley, Philip Harris, David Milton, Peter J. Nickitas, Jeffrey Rothman, Anastasios Sarikas, Melissa Vu, Laurie Wen and especially Herself. I am also indebted to Fomite Press and Marc Estrin's able editing, plus Donna Bister's fine design.

Fomite

A fomite is a medium capable of transmitting infectious organisms from one individual to another.

"The activity of art is based on the capacity of people to be infected by the feelings of others." Tolstoy, *What Is Art?*

Writing a review on Amazon, Good Reads, Shelfari, Library Thing or other social media sites for readers will help the progress of independent publishing. To submit a review, go to the book page on any of the sites and follow the links for reviews. Books from independent presses rely on reader to reader communications.

Visit http://www.fomitepress.com/FOMITE/Our_Books.html for more information or to order any of our books.

As It Is On Earth
Peter M Wheelwright

Dons of Time
Greg Guma

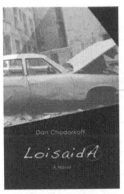

Loisaida
Dan Chodorkoff

My Father's Keeper
Andrew Potok

My God, What Have We Done
Susan V Weiss

Rafi's World
Fred Russell

Fomite

The Co-Conspirator's Tale
Ron Jacobs

Short Order Frame Up
Ron Jacobs

All the Sinners Saints
Ron Jacobs

Travers' Inferno
L. E. Smith

The Consequence of Gesture
L. E. Smith

Raven or Crow
Joshua Amses

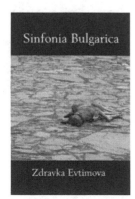

Sinfonia Bulgarica
Zdravka Evtimova

The Good Muslim
of Jackson Heights
Jaysinh Birjépatil

The Moment Before an Injury
Joshua Amses

Fomite

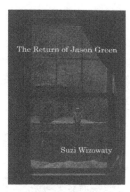

The Return of
Jason Green
Suzi Wizowaty

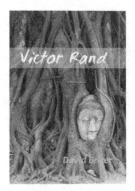

Victor Rand
David Brizeri

Zinsky the Obscure
Ilan Mochari

Body of Work
Andrei Guruianu

Carts and Other Stories
Zdravka Evtimova

Flight
Jay Boyer

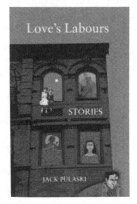

Love's Labours
Jack Pulaski

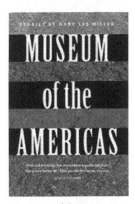

Museum of the Americas
Gary Lee Miller

Saturday Night at Magellan's
Charles Rafferty

Fomite

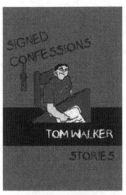

Signed Confessions
Tom Walker

Still Time
Michael Cocchiarale

Suite for Three Voices
Derek Furr

Unfinished Stories of Girls
Catherine Zobal Dent

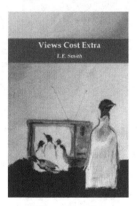

Views Cost Extra
L. E. Smith

Visiting Hours
Jennifer Anne Moses

When You Remeber
Deir Yassin
R. L. Green

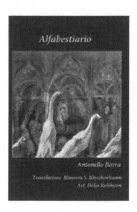

Alfabestiaro
Antonello Borra

Cycling in Plato's Cave
David Cavanagh

Fomite

AlphaBetaBestiario
Antonello Borra

Entanglements
Tony Magistrale

Everyone Lives Here
Sharon Webster

Four-Way Stop
Sherry Olson

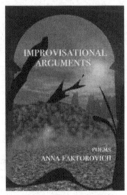

Improvisational
Arguments
Anna Faktorovitch

Loosestrife
Greg Delanty

Meanwell
Janice Miller Potter

Roadworthy Creature
Roadworth Craft
Kate Magill

The Derivation of
Cowboys & Indians
Joseph D. Reich

Fomite

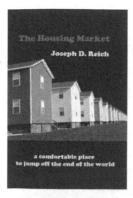

The Housing Market
Joseph D. Reich

The Empty Notebook
Interrogates Itself
Susan Thomas

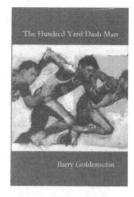

The Hundred Yard
Dash Man
Barry Goldensohn

The Listener Aspires
to the Condition of Music
Barry Goldensohn

The Way None
of This Happened
Mike Breiner

Screwed
Stephen Goldberg

Planet Kasper
Peter Schumann

My Murder
and Other Local News
David Schein

Picking Up the Bodies
James F. Connolly

Fomite

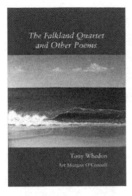

The Falkland Quartet
Tony Whedon

Drawing on Life
Mason Drukman

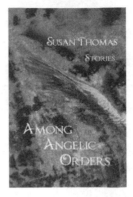

Among Angelic Orders
Susan Thoma

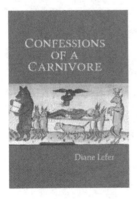

Confessions of a Carnivore
Diane Lefer

Principles of Navigation
Lynn Sloan

A Guide
to the Western Slopes
Roger Lebovitz

Planet Kasper
Volume Two
Peter Schumann

Free Fall/Caída libre
Tina Escaja

Made in the USA
Charleston, SC
17 April 2015